The PERFECT BRIDE *for* MR. DARCY

MARY LYDON SIMONSEN

sourcebooks
landmark

Published by Sourcebooks Landmark, an imprint of Sourcebooks, Inc.
P.O. Box 4410, Naperville, Illinois 60567-4410
(630) 961-3900
FAX: (630) 961-2168
www.sourcebooks.com

Library of Congress Cataloging-in-Publication Data

Simonsen, Mary Lydon.
  The perfect bride for Mr. Darcy / Mary Lydon Simonsen.
    p. cm.
  1. Darcy, Fitzwilliam (Fictitious character)—Fiction. 2. Bennet, Elizabeth (Fictitious character)—Fiction. 3. Austen, Jane, 1775–1817. Pride and prejudice—Fiction. 4. England—Fiction. I. Title.
  PS3619.I56287P465 2010
  813'.6—dc22

                          2010033281

Printed and bound in the United States of America.
VP 10 9 8 7 6 5 4 3 2 1

To Paul, the love of my life and my own Mr. Darcy,
and Deb Werksman, my editor at Sourcebooks,
for her guidance and patience

Chapter 1

Summer 1808

FITZWILLIAM DARCY PACED UP and down the side of the road. He had been within five miles of Netherfield Park, the country estate of his friend, Charles Bingley, when the carriage had veered violently to the right. After learning from his driver that the axle was bent, he had sent his footman in search of a horse, so that he might continue his journey.

A month earlier, Bingley had signed a lease on a handsome two-hundred-acre estate in Hertfordshire with a well-stocked lake and an uninterrupted view of the surrounding countryside. The manor house was the perfect size for Bingley and his small party. The rent on the house, which was owned by the Darlingtons, was reasonable, and above all, it had stables and pastures for Charles's horses.

Before Darcy gave his opinion on signing the lease, he had gone into the neighboring village of Meryton and had found a typical market town near enough to the London road so that it had some amenities, such as a circulating library, an assembly hall, and a variety of shops that would meet Bingley's simple needs, if not those of his sisters, Caroline and Louisa, who were to keep house for him. He also made inquiries as to the local society. With Sir James Darlington, a baronet, gone to take the waters in search of a cure for his gout and relief for his wife's arthritis, Sir William Lucas, who had been knighted the previous year, was the only person of rank within easy riding distance of Netherfield Park. Darcy knew that Bingley, who loved dancing almost as much as he loved horses, would sign the lease as soon as he heard that there was an assembly hall in Meryton.

By the time his footman had returned with a horse, a light rain had begun to fall, but Darcy would push on to Netherfield nonetheless and hope that the weather would improve or at least not get worse.

The weather got worse, and by the time Darcy made his entrance at Netherfield Park, his only interest was in being shown to his room, as he was chilled to the bone. Despite dripping all over the tile in the foyer and his apparent discomfort, Caroline Bingley was attempting to engage him in conversation, and her sister, Louisa Hurst, whose voice resembled a newly hatched chick, was asking if he wanted her to order some tea.

"Thank you, Mrs. Hurst, but I would prefer to go straight to my room, so that I might change out of these wet clothes." He looked down at his feet and an expanding puddle, and Louisa directed a servant to show Mr. Darcy to his room.

A short while later, Bingley came bounding in. Charles's enthusiasm for life was usually infectious, but Darcy was so tired from the ride that all he could think of was his bed. "Darcy, we were expecting you hours ago. Were you waylaid by highwaymen?"

Darcy merely shook his head. "If you were hoping for a bedtime story about how I eluded capture by brigands, I am sorry to disappoint you, but perhaps your governess is in residence?"

"Ah, good old Darcy, always in fine form no matter what the circumstances." As he watched his friend shed his wet garments, he explained that he had sent a servant to rummage through the house to look for clothes for him. "Unfortunately, Sir James Darlington was a rather rotund man and not a great tall fellow like you are, and you could not get into a pair of my breeches with a shoe horn. So let us hope that your carriage will be here early in the morning." Bingley exited the room, but then poked his head back in. "Oh, by the way, there is an assembly in the village tomorrow evening."

"Bingley! An assembly? We will speak of it in the morning," the exhausted traveler answered.

"No need, Darcy, I have already accepted an invitation on your behalf," and he quickly left the room.

❧

The next day, Darcy tried to find an excuse for not going to the assembly. But if he did not go, Caroline and Louisa would have a reason to stay behind, and then Darcy would have to play cards with them or listen to Mr. Hurst drone on about how difficult it was to find a shop that stocked brandy and French wines, and if you did, how damn expensive they were. The wars on the Continent were a great inconvenience to Bingley's brother-in-law.

"Come now, Darcy. It will do you of world a good. I am told there are many local beauties, and they most certainly will be in need of partners."

The matter was finally settled when Mr. Hurst, who had been sprawled out on the couch, sat up and let out a loud belch.

"If you insist, I shall go, but I warn you, Bingley, I am in no humor to dance."

"Darcy, I cannot force you to dance, but may I ask that you remove that scowl from your face? We do not want to frighten our neighbors."

In late morning, Darcy's manservant arrived at Netherfield Park. Mercer, who had been with Darcy for the past five years, was the most capable and ingenious man he had ever met. Upon hearing the sound of crunching gravel on the main drive to the house, he went to the window and laughed when he saw his servant at the reins of a farm wagon carrying all of his chests.

Darcy was not looking forward to attending the assembly. He was always uncomfortable in these country settings. Even in Lambton, the nearest village to Pemberley, or on the farms of his tenants, where he knew everyone by name, he did not know how to converse with people not of his class, especially if they were of the opposite sex. You could discuss breeding sheep with a farmer, but what did you talk about with the farmer's daughter? Fortunately, his young sister, Georgiana, had no such difficulties and was able to converse on any number of subjects, including, to his amusement, the need for road improvements between Lambton and Matlock with a local farmer.

Upon entering the assembly room, the party was introduced to Sir William Lucas and his daughter, Charlotte, a rather plain lady, but one who seemed to have a pleasant disposition. Following on Sir William's heels was the master of ceremonies, who asked if there was any lady to whom Darcy wished to be introduced, but he answered by saying that it was not his intention to dance. Within minutes, the hall was buzzing with news of the amiable Mr. Bingley's unpleasant friend, who refused to dance because he was above his company.

Darcy spotted Bingley dancing with a lovely creature with blond hair and blue eyes. This was all so familiar to Darcy. Wherever they went, Bingley's engaging ways quickly won over his new acquaintances. Within minutes, he would be besieged by gentlemen wishing to arrange introductions for their daughters, and he would always end up dancing at least two sets with the prettiest girl in the room.

"Come, Darcy. I must have you dance," Bingley said during a break in the music.

If Darcy gave any hint that he might be persuaded, he would have Bingley after him all night. So with great emphasis, he answered, "I certainly shall not. You know how I detest it, unless I am particularly acquainted with my partner."

Bingley continued to push and encouraged him to dance with the sister of the golden-haired Miss Bennet. "Miss Elizabeth Bennet is very pretty, and I daresay very agreeable."

After a quick glance, he said, "She is tolerable, but not handsome enough to tempt me," and told his friend that he was wasting his time. After Bingley left, he looked over his shoulder and realized that the young lady had heard what he had said.

"Blast it all," he thought. He had not meant to give offense. His intention had been to stop Bingley from further entreaties. He was sure he had offended, but since he would not be seeing her again, he made the decision to say nothing. Instead, he went into the cardroom, where he soon found himself playing against competent players, who lightened his purse by a pound or two.

After spending most of the evening in the cardroom, he returned to the assembly and watched as Miss Elizabeth made her way through the complicated steps of a quadrille. Now that he had an unobstructed view of the lady, he saw that she was quite pretty, especially when she smiled, and he also noticed how softly her long, dark curls fell upon her shoulders and the brightness of her eyes and the fullness of her mouth. Shortly after realizing how appealing Miss Elizabeth Bennet was, he told Bingley he was sending for the carriage.

A few weeks after the assembly, on a lazy summer's day, Charlotte and Elizabeth were walking along the wagon road between Lucas Lodge and Longbourn, discussing how their friend and sister seemed to have captured Mr. Bingley's heart. And they were not the only ones who had noticed. Ever since the dance, the town was humming with rumors of an engagement between the two, and some of the shopkeepers were busy circulating the news that Miss Bennet had been in their shops looking at bonnets and ribbons and other paraphernalia, which would obviously become a part of her trousseau. This greatly amused Lizzy because Jane and she often went into the shops to see what new goods had come in on the London coach, but now everything Jane did had a hidden meaning.

Another topic of conversation was Mr. Darcy of Pemberley. Because Lizzy was one of the prettiest girls in this corner of Hertfordshire, Mr. Darcy's remark that Lizzy was only "tolerable" had insulted every lady who was less attractive than she was. But Charlotte Lucas was of a different opinion.

"Lizzy, at the risk of challenging one of your reasons for disliking Mr. Darcy, I must say that I do not think his comments were directed at you."

"Really! Mr. Darcy's comments were not directed at me?" Lizzy said, laughing. "Charlotte, it will not do. He looked right at me, and please do not concern yourself. This matter is no longer of any interest to me. Any hurt I might have felt has long since passed because my father has assured me I am definitely more than tolerable."

Because Charlotte lacked the good looks possessed by many of the young women of her neighborhood, she often found herself without a dance partner. No matter how unenviable her situation, it afforded Charlotte an opportunity to observe the subtle beginnings of a new relationship: the covert smile, the accidental touch, the whispers, and the long gazes. Lovers rarely realized how obvious they were to others.

"You must hear me out, Lizzy. Mr. Darcy was directing his remarks to Mr. Bingley, and before you start laughing again, let me tell you what I think actually happened. Despite Mr. Darcy repeatedly telling Mr. Bingley that he did not intend to dance, he would not let the matter rest. That was the cause of the harshness of his reply. I was looking right at Mr. Darcy, and I can tell you that from where he stood, it was impossible for him to take your likeness, especially since he merely glanced at you over his shoulder. Contrary to what you think, Mr. Darcy admires you."

"Nonsense, Charlotte! Mr. Darcy spent most of the evening in the cardroom. If he had wanted to make amends, there was ample opportunity to ask me to dance, but he chose not to do so."

"But you did not see how he looked at you when he came

out of the cardroom. At first, I thought he was looking for Mr. Bingley or one of the sisters, but then he walked by his friend and kept looking until his eyes had settled on you. And the same thing happened the other night at Lucas Lodge. His eyes followed you everywhere you went, and when you challenged him about listening to your conversation, he admitted he had been doing that very thing."

"That is because we were speaking of dancing. Earlier, Mr. Darcy had been talking to your father about that same subject, in which he expressed the opinion that, 'Every savage can dance.' And I do not care what Mr. Darcy thinks of me. I shall be very glad when I hear he has returned to London or to his grand estate in Derbyshire."

"Lizzy, I do believe you are making a mistake. When a man of consequence such as Mr. Darcy admires you, you would do well to take notice."

Chapter 2

In light of all that followed, Darcy regretted that he had not left Hertfordshire shortly after the assembly. The dark-haired Elizabeth Bennet had succeeded in capturing his attention as no other woman ever had. With each subsequent meeting, his admiration grew, and he soon found her occupying most of his waking moments.

While attending a gathering at the home of Sir William Lucas, he had listened in on her conversations and had followed her movements like some lovesick puppy. When Elizabeth came to stay at Netherfield Park to care for her ailing sister, her proximity exposed an underlying sexual tension that he found disconcerting. But it was no longer just the physical that he found so alluring. A series of conversations had revealed a woman who possessed a natural intelligence and who was confident enough to challenge the opinions of those with whom she disagreed, including his own.

Humiliated by his behavior, he had returned to London. But Elizabeth had followed him there. In his dreams, her presence was so real that he had imagined that he could taste her lips, smell the scent of her hair, and feel the rhythm of her body as she moved beneath him. And although it had been his intention to send word to Bingley that his business affairs required that he remain in town, after less than two weeks, he was on the road to Hertfordshire to attend the ball Bingley was hosting at Netherfield Park.

It was during his absence that George Wickham had made his first appearance in Meryton, and in that short time, Wickham, a man without scruples, had managed to convince Elizabeth that Darcy was someone who could not be trusted and who did not keep his promises. But Darcy did not know that at the time and was caught unawares when Elizabeth had remarked during the Netherfield ball that Wickham had lost his friendship "in a manner for which he was likely to suffer from all his life." That remark, and the general consensus that Bingley would shortly make an offer of marriage to Miss Jane Bennet, spurred him to action.

The next morning, he wrote a letter to George Bingley, in which he informed Charles's eldest brother that there were expectations within the neighborhood that Charles would soon become engaged to Miss Jane Bennet, and he outlined his objections to the match. With all of his being, he believed that such a marriage would be a disaster. It was not just a matter of the lady's inferior position in society or the lack of propriety displayed by her family; Darcy believed the lady did not love his friend. But because it would be financially beneficial to her and her family, she would agree to an offer of marriage.

However, George Bingley's intervention was not required as Charles yielded on the matter the day after they had reached

London. He relied heavily on Darcy's superior knowledge of such affairs, and considering his sisters' emphatic opposition to the match, he had allowed himself to be convinced that any such union was doomed to failure.

The next day, Charles left London to attend a horse fair in Surrey. Although he valued his friendship with Darcy above all others, Charles resented his role in separating him from Miss Bennet, and because Darcy was a reminder of what he had lost, he decided he could do without his company for a while and sent word to his sisters that he would remain in the country.

With no communication between the two gentlemen, Darcy realized that Bingley was taking the forced separation from Miss Bennet much harder than he would have expected because it was Darcy's experience that his friend was often in love.

Upon learning of Charles's return from Surrey, Darcy immediately went to the Bingley townhouse. While waiting for his friend, he was sitting in the drawing room trying to figure out what it was that he found so annoying about Caroline Bingley. There were nine Bingleys, and he had met seven of them. But it was only Caroline who got under his skin. Not even her intellectually challenged sister, Louisa, came anywhere near to irritating him as much as Caroline did just by entering a room, and that is exactly what she had done thirty minutes earlier.

"Mr. Darcy, please join us for some refreshments," Caroline offered. "There is something about an autumn day in London that makes one want to drink coffee."

But before he agreed to join them, he wanted to know where Charles was and when he would be expected.

"Charles has decided to replace his entire wardrobe, and today he is visiting the boot maker. He has been gone two hours, so I do expect him momentarily." Actually, Caroline had no idea when her brother would return, but she would detain Mr. Darcy as long as possible. She was convinced she held some attraction for the gentleman as she often caught him staring at her, as he was doing now.

Caroline was correct. Darcy *was* thinking about her. He found her to be an attractive, intelligent woman. With her ability to draw, paint, sing, play the pianoforte, and speak French fluently, she truly met the definition of an accomplished woman. However, she was also catty, but so were most of the women in London. Just last evening at a card party, he had overheard two women lavish praise on a third lady, only to tear her to pieces as soon as she had left the room. He simply did not understand it. With the exception of political debate, it was something that men did not do.

"Mr. Darcy, we have quite lost you. May I inquire as to what is occupying your thoughts?" Caroline was hoping that his thoughts were of her.

"I was thinking that if your brother does not come home in the next ten minutes, I shall have to leave."

Caroline was not about to allow that to happen and said the first thing that came into her head.

"Did you know that Miss Jane Bennet is in town?"

"How could I possibly know that?" Darcy said with an edge in his voice. Although comfortable with his efforts to get Bingley to leave Hertfordshire, he certainly understood that Jane Bennet would have been disappointed. He would have preferred to think of her at home with her family.

"Apparently, she arrived in town three weeks ago. It seems that visiting Louisa and me was her first order of business. She sent us several notes, and her persistence was finally rewarded. I visited her yesterday at her uncle's home in Cheapside."

It was not a good visit. Caroline was disappointed to find that the Gardiners lived quite comfortably in a large house in Gracechurch Street, featuring Meissen porcelains, a Sevres tea service, and richly carved French furniture. She had not expected to find the Bennets had relations who were genteel and obviously well off.

"She probably thought of you as her friend," Darcy responded.

Louisa gave her sister a look to warn her that she had gone where she should not have.

"Of course, she is our friend," Caroline said quickly, trying to cover her gaffe. "It is just that I wished to spare her any embarrassment. Obviously, she cannot come here. It would not do for her and Charles to meet, and as soon as I had an opening in my schedule, I visited her. It was never our intention to hurt Miss Bennet, and Louisa and I were very grateful that you were with us on that day when we convinced our brother he should not see her again."

"Miss Bingley, I do not need to be reminded that I was a party to that discussion. I think of it almost every day. I just do not derive as much satisfaction from it as you do."

"Mr. Darcy," Louisa interjected, "Miss Bennet traveled to London with her sister, Miss Elizabeth, and she happily shared with Caroline that both had attended a ball as well as the theatre and were enjoying being in town." Louisa wanted to get the conversation away from the subject of tearing Charles away from the woman he loved, especially since she was having second thoughts about her own role in parting the two lovers. Despite Caroline's many criticisms regarding Jane Bennet, Louisa liked her. "I think we can safely say Miss Bennet is well on her way to getting over any hurt feelings she may have had because of our brother."

Caroline looked at her sister with alarm. Mr. Darcy had once made a remark about Eliza Bennet's fine eyes, and she had noticed how he sought her out at the Netherfield ball. She did not want to discuss anything to do with that particular lady.

"Mrs. Hurst, are you saying that Miss Elizabeth Bennet is in London?"

"No, sir," Louisa said, shaking her head. "She *was* in London. However, she has since gone to visit friends somewhere in Kent, and Miss Bennet alone remains in town."

"Has she gone to visit Mrs. Collins? I believe they have a close friendship."

"Yes, Mr. Darcy, that is the lady. I could not think of her name, but she is the one who married Lady Catherine's vicar. So Miss Elizabeth is definitely not in town."

Caroline was unhappy with Louisa for providing so much information about Eliza Bennet's whereabouts. The Collinses were near neighbors to Lady Catherine, and it was possible that if Mr. Darcy chose to visit his aunt in Kent, he might encounter her in the nearby village or, very likely, in church.

Any thought of Bingley immediately went out of his head. Ever since leaving Hertfordshire, Darcy had tried not to think about Elizabeth. He did not want to remember her dark eyes or hair, her beautiful smile, and infectious laugh. And her wit! What had she said at Netherfield about the efficacy of poetry in driving love away? He would never again read a romantic poem without thinking about her comment. For a time, he had been angry with her for her defense of Wickham and for believing his lies, but the anger had dissipated only to be replaced by an emptiness he had never before experienced.

Caroline, seeing the effect Louisa's news had had on Mr. Darcy, attempted to regain his attention. "I imagine Miss Elizabeth will thoroughly enjoy her stay at the parsonage. It is my understanding from Mr. Collins that the house is well situated and has a lovely garden. I am sure the attractions of the nearby village will be appealing to someone who is so content to live near Meryton."

Caroline mistakenly believed she was being gracious, or at least as gracious as she could be when discussing someone whom she considered to be a rival. But Darcy saw it for what it was: a reminder that Miss Elizabeth was merely the daughter of a gentleman farmer, and as such, beneath his notice.

Darcy finally declared he could wait no longer, and after handing his card to Mrs. Hurst, he asked that Bingley call on him. Although he was unable to see his friend, the visit was successful in one regard. It was no longer a mystery as to what he found so unappealing about Caroline. She was an attractive woman on the outside, but her beauty only masked a deep well of unkindness and the satisfaction she derived from belittling others.

Chapter 3

ON THE RIDE FROM London to Hunsford Lodge, Lizzy reflected on all that had happened in the few months since Mr. Bingley had come to Netherfield Park, and in her musings, she also recalled the many conversations Jane and she had shared as young ladies on the cusp of adulthood. While snuggling in their bed, they talked of the men who would come into their lives and win their hearts. Ironically, it was Jane who was the more practical of the two. She wanted a man with a kind disposition, who was handsome and charming, and who would be able to provide for her and their children. Her greatest hope was that she would marry for love, but considering her lack of fortune, she realized it was all a matter of luck.

Lizzy, on the other hand, wanted a man of understanding who would engage her intellectually. Before they married, her husband would appreciate that she held opinions on matters great and small, and that there was a wider world she wanted to explore, even if she could only do so by reading magazines and newspapers and visiting the circulating library. And there were so many exciting things to read about and to discuss. England, most especially London, was at the center of the world, as was evidenced in the shops with their Chinese silks, American tobacco, Indian teas, and Madeira wines, and great political and military events were taking place on the Continent and in America.

But in one thing Jane and she were in complete agreement: Both wanted to marry for love. In Jane's case, it had very nearly happened. Mr. Bingley was all Jane had ever wanted and more, and she had fallen deeply in love with him and he with her. So what had happened? She knew the answer to that question. Mr. Bingley's sisters and Mr. Darcy had happened, and together they had worked against the match from the very beginning. She was sure that Caroline and Louisa were sensitive about the Bingley fortune having been made in trade, and it was their intention to climb the social ladder and never look back. It was obvious Mr. Darcy held considerable sway over his friend, and in the end, he was able to convince Mr. Bingley that marriage with Miss Bennet was not in his best interest.

At the Netherfield ball, if she had spent less time thinking about Mr. Wickham, she would have anticipated what was shortly to happen. She would have seen how the inappropriate behavior of her mother and sisters was being viewed by Caroline, Louisa, and Mr. Darcy. And to make matters worse, there was Mr. Collins. Anyone who condemned the behavior of her mother and three younger sisters would come to the conclusion that even the extended Bennet family lacked refinement and common sense.

But all that was in the past, and nothing would be gained by thinking about it. Lizzy refocused her attention on her visit with Mr. and Mrs. Collins, and a smile came to her face. Charlotte was her dearest friend, and there would be so much to discuss, and as for Mr. Collins, she could safely rely on him to be an endless source of amusement.

When the chaise pulled up in front of Hunsford Lodge, Lizzy understood why Charlotte could be happy here—even with Mr. Collins. It was a pretty house with a lovely garden and a fine view of Rosings Park, and it was near enough to the road leading into the village that Charlotte could easily visit with her neighbors.

As expected, as soon as Lizzy had both feet on the ground, Mr. Collins began to point out every advantage of living at the parsonage, clearly with the intention of making Lizzy regret her refusal of his offer. No matter how unexceptional or insignificant the object, right down to the fender in front of the fireplace, each merited a comment from her cousin. After the tour of the house had concluded, Mr. Collins led Lizzy to his favorite vantage point from which he could see Rosings Park and, therefore, the comings and goings of his esteemed patroness, Lady Catherine de Bourgh.

After supper, Charlotte remarked to her husband that Elizabeth had had a long journey and might wish to retire. With the excuse of making sure that everything was as it should be in Lizzy's room, Charlotte went upstairs with her friend and closed the door.

"Finally, we are alone," Charlotte said, and she gave Lizzy a hug. "How good it is to have company from home. After Papa and Maria left, I was quite homesick, but now you are here and I am content."

"So tell me, Charlotte, is everything to your satisfaction?" Lizzy asked while sitting on the bed and unlacing her boots. "Do you take issue with any of Mr. Collins's claims that everything is perfect and beyond criticism? You said that Lady Catherine was a most attentive neighbor, but I could not decide if you were praising or censuring her."

"By attentive, I meant nosy," Charlotte said, rolling her eyes. "When I said that she shows an interest in all we do, it was the truth, for nothing is beneath her notice. She comes into the house and finds fault with everything and everyone, leaves instructions for the necessary corrections, and departs. But despite all this, I am quite content to be here and to be the mistress of my own home, and for all of Mr. Collins's faults, he is a kind man who sees to the needs of his parish."

"I am happy to hear it, truly, but what about your needs?"

"Easily met. Monday and Tuesday are reserved for visits to his parishioners or church business. On Wednesday, we dine at Rosings Park, so that Lady Catherine may criticize the sermon Mr. Collins has written. He spends as much time as possible on Thursday in the garden, an activity he enjoys, and one which I encourage. It seems that Lady Catherine has outlived most of her friends, so we usually dine at the manor house on Friday as well so that we might entertain Her Ladyship. On Saturday, we do all our shopping for the week in the village, and that night, we perform as man and wife. Sunday, he preaches, and then the cycle repeats. Very little changes from week to week, and because my marriage is lacking in romance, I can see you are unimpressed."

"Charlotte, I made no comment." Nor would she. The thought of Mr. Collins performing as a husband could result in the loss of her appetite.

"Lizzy, you do not need to say anything. Unlike you, I never was romantic. All I asked was a comfortable home, and I have that. But speaking of romance, Miss de Bourgh called this morning to say that they are to have visitors at Rosings, her cousins Colonel Fitzwilliam and Mr. Darcy. What a coincidence! You are here, and Mr. Darcy is coming to visit his aunt."

"Surely, Mr. Darcy is free to travel about the country without giving any consideration as to where I might be," Lizzy said, confused at Charlotte's continued insistence that the gentleman had some interest in her.

Charlotte just nodded, but she thought it unusual that Mr. Darcy was coming to Kent when he had just been to Rosings a few weeks earlier. There must be a special reason for him to return so quickly.

Chapter 4

COLONEL FITZWILLIAM REREAD THE latest post from Fitzwilliam Darcy. With only three days' notice, Darcy had asked that he join him at Bromley so that they might visit with their aunt, Lady Catherine de Bourgh. This was something the two cousins did about four times a year, more if they received an appeal from Anne de Bourgh to come to her rescue. Since they had already made the obligatory visit a month earlier, he did not understand why they were returning to Rosings Park, especially now, at the height of the shooting season.

Darcy was aware that it was his aunt's fondest wish that he marry Anne. However, neither party wanted any such thing. After having survived a nearly fatal illness as a young girl, which had permanently affected her health, Anne had decided she would never marry. She knew or had heard reports of women who were invalided by childbirth, or in the case of Darcy's mother, had died because of it. As a result, she wanted nothing to do with the marriage bed, which made Darcy's note so puzzling. His quick return to Rosings Park would be seen as his finally coming around to his aunt's point of view. It was all so confusing.

Unfortunately, Fitzwilliam had little say in the matter. As the younger son of Lord Fitzwilliam, his father had provided him with a paltry annuity. His elder brother, the current earl, had quite successfully squandered a good portion of the family's fortune in London's betting parlors and at its gaming tables and had nothing to spare for his little brother. If Lord Fitzwilliam died tomorrow and the colonel succeeded to the title, there would be little left, except the title. The manor house was mortgaged, there were liens on the contents of the house in town, and creditors were baying at the doors crying for repayment. Every time the colonel visited the ancestral estate, he noticed another family heirloom had gone missing, and the outlines left by paintings sold at auction were an embarrassment.

Darcy was sympathetic to Colonel Fitzwilliam's situation and had provided him with an allowance. In exchange for Darcy's generosity, the colonel agreed to just about anything his cousin asked as long as it did not interfere with his duties as an officer in His Majesty's Army. So to Rosings he would go.

If the colonel was confused before the journey, he was completely perplexed once he arrived in Kent. Before they had even paid their respects to their Aunt Catherine, Darcy insisted they stop at Hunsford Lodge, the parsonage of the Reverend Mr. and Mrs. Collins. On their last visit, Darcy, who had little appetite for sermonizing, had found his aunt's new vicar to be more tedious than the previous parson. But here he was paying a visit to the very man he had accused of inducing a coma-like state in his congregants. Furthermore, during the visit, Darcy had said almost nothing, leaving the colonel to bear the full weight of conversing with the Collinses. But things became much clearer when the lovely Miss Elizabeth Bennet joined the party.

On the journey to Kent, Darcy had spoken to Fitzwilliam of a charming, intelligent, and beautiful young woman, the daughter of a gentleman farmer, whom he had met while visiting with Charles Bingley at Netherfield Park. Although all of his compliments were buried in lengthy generalities involving life in the country and society in a market town, the conversation always returned to this unnamed young lady. But Fitzwilliam had no doubt that Miss Elizabeth Bennet was the gem Darcy had discovered in Hertfordshire.

Fitzwilliam found the whole scene to be amusing. As the scion of one of England's ancient Norman families, Darcy was well aware of his pedigree. He understood that any lady he chose as his wife would have to be from another Norman family or a daughter of the aristocracy, but even among those who met his criteria, no one had caught his fancy. If the woman was beautiful, she was not intelligent. If she was accomplished and well versed in current affairs, she was not attractive. The daughter of a baronet was rich and attractive, and possessed a truly pleasant personality, as well as a diamond-encrusted neck, but to Darcy she was "dimwitted." This is what made the scene before him so delicious. Darcy was smitten with the daughter of a no-name gentleman farmer from a country town. Of course, knowing his cousin as well as he did, nothing could come of it, but there was something very appealing in learning that Darcy had a vulnerable side that the colonel had never seen before. This visit might actually turn out to be a nice diversion.

Now in her late fifties, Lady Catherine de Bourgh found it difficult to stay awake after dinner. Fearing she might miss some juicy tidbit about what was going on in London or in the nearby village, she sat dozing, night after night, with her unsupported head bobbing between her ample bosom and the back of the chair. It was only after she had stopped snorting and had advanced to full-blown snoring that her lady's maid, the saintly Mrs. Pentup, was able to convince Her Ladyship that no one would object if she retired for the evening.

As soon as she was sure that her mother was truly gone, Anne de Bourgh let out a sigh of relief and removed the quilt from her lap. Mrs. Jenkinson, Anne's nurse, came over to her charge, patted her hand, and removed to an adjacent sitting room where she would be available but not intrusive.

Colonel Fitzwilliam, who had been waiting for his aunt to leave the room, started pacing the floor. After ten days of continued interaction with Lady Catherine and listening to her soliloquies on everything from tending a garden, which she never did, to commenting on great art, which she had never seen, to the great cities of Europe, which she had never visited, he was exhausted. And with Darcy in his room refusing to come down, it was impossible to play even a game of whist.

"Anne, play something on the pianoforte," her cousin pleaded. "Even if you play badly, at least we will have something to laugh at."

"Richard, as you know very well, the pianoforte is here exclusively for the use of our visitors as no one in the house has ever learned."

"But as your mother has stated on several occasions, if she had learned to play, she would have been a great proficient."

"And if my health had allowed for me to learn, as Mama has frequently stated, I would have performed delightfully. So much untapped talent in one house. It truly is a shame," Anne said with a chuckle. "But I thought Miss Elizabeth played quite well. Although she insisted she has little talent, I think she displayed a degree of competence that made listening to her quite pleasant. I am sure Will enjoyed her playing as he went over to the piano as soon as she had begun. What do you think?"

"What do I think? What I think is where in the deuce is Darcy? He said he had business letters to write, but he cannot still be at it. When I went to his room to plead with him to come to dinner so I would not have to bear the burden of your mother's undivided attention, he waved me off. Then he called me back to tell me to be ready to leave for London no later than noon tomorrow, implying that I was responsible for our delayed return to town. My bags have been packed and ready for the last three days. It is he who keeps putting it off. Mercer must be beside himself with all of the contradictory instructions he has been given. His behavior has been odd since our arrival. I have never seen him so unsettled."

It was not unusual for Will to be out of sorts when confined indoors, and confinement was the very definition of a visit to Rosings. He hated to be cooped up for any length of time, and idle chatter drove him to distraction. The dearth of truly good society had Darcy on edge, and his annoyance usually generated biting comments. "If I hear one more time about the condition of the roads between here and Bath, I shall pay for the repairs myself."

"Anne, I can wait no longer as I am committed to joining the Aldens in Hampshire. I shall have precious little time for shooting, as I must return to my regiment within a fortnight.

Blast it all! I am sure all the best coveys are already gone," Colonel Fitzwilliam said, pounding the mantle in frustration. "Having said that, for some reason, I do think Darcy means it this time. He only has so much patience for your mother, and if he is keeping to his room, then he has obviously used it all up."

Anne agreed that her cousin's behavior was unusual. To begin with, Darcy's visits never lasted more than a week. He felt obligated, as the son of Lady Catherine's only sister, to visit his aunt, and insisted that Colonel Fitzwilliam, as the son of her only brother, come with him. But ten days? Rarely had he stayed this long. Anne was pretty sure she knew why he had extended his visit, and she intended to ask him about it when they were alone.

As if on cue, Darcy entered the room, and it was immediately apparent his mood had not improved.

"There you are, Darcy. Will you play cards as Anne is thoroughly bored with my conversation?"

"No, I have come down to say good-bye to Anne."

"Then we truly are leaving in the morning?"

"Fitzwilliam, is it your habit to ask the same questions over and over again? It must be very tiresome for your staff."

Colonel Fitzwilliam rose. "Still the bear, Darcy?" and walking over to Anne, he kissed her on her cheek. "Be careful, Anne. Although I do not think he will attack, he is still dangerous, so be on your guard or you may find yourself suffering lacerations from his sharp tongue." Bowing from the waist, he added, "I bid you both a good night, and my dearest cousin, I shall see you sometime in December," and looking at Darcy, "if not before."

Once Fitzwilliam left the room, Anne got right after Darcy. "He is correct, you know. You *have* been a bear ever since you came back from the parsonage."

"Who said I went to the parsonage?" Darcy asked with some alarm in his voice.

"Didn't you? I assumed you went there once you had learned the reason why Miss Elizabeth did not dine at Rosings. You left in such a hurry. I could think of no other reason."

Darcy started to pace. "Yes, I was concerned. During my morning rides, I have become accustomed to meeting Miss Elizabeth on her walks in the park, but I did not see her this morning. When the Collinses said she was unwell, I thought I should go to the parsonage and inquire after her health."

"Very considerate of you. And how did you find her?" Anne's question was met with silence. "Did you talk to her? What was said?"

"She said she was well. She certainly looked well. I should have left it at that."

And then he said nothing. Anne was used to his taciturn nature. When things did not go his way, he often withdrew into himself. Trying to get him to talk when he was in such a mood was difficult, but not impossible.

"And what were the consequences of your remaining?"

"It was the damnedest thing," Darcy said, staring off into the distance and, once again, became quiet.

"Will, please tell me what happened. I can see something is wrong. Did she say something unkind?"

Darcy laughed to himself. Everything she said was unkind from her terse greeting to her accusation that he was acting in an ungentlemanlike manner. That had truly stung. He knew his faults. He could be sarcastic, impatient, aloof, but not a gentleman? No, he would not concede that. It was true he could have chosen his words more wisely, but he had not gone to the parsonage with the intention of asking Elizabeth for her hand in marriage. His purpose in calling was to ask after her health because he would be returning to London in the morning. But as soon as he had entered the room, he was overwhelmed by her beauty, especially her dark luminous eyes and a mouth begging to be kissed, all framed against the last rays of the afternoon sun. It was then that all of the barriers he had erected gave way, and he knew how ardently he loved her. And the words just poured out of him, so much so that he could not remember all that had been said, although he did recall mentioning her inferior position in society, expected opposition from his family, and his lack of success in attempting to overcome his feelings for her. But was it not important for her to know how he had struggled? Was there any greater proof of his love than the fact that he had honored her with his offer of marriage?

Darcy felt Anne's hand on his arm. She was asking what had happened at the parsonage, but all he could manage to say was simply, "I made her an offer of marriage."

Anne took a deep breath. That was not the answer she had expected. Darcy had no idea how much his expressions revealed about what was going on in his mind. Once he had learned from the Collinses that Elizabeth would not be coming to Rosings for tea, he had emotionally withdrawn from his company. After muttering some excuse no one could understand, he quickly departed, and Anne was pretty sure where he had gone. But a proposal? That she would not have guessed, but it brought a smile to her face.

Darcy motioned for her to sit down and then plopped into the chair vacated by Fitzwilliam. "There is no need to smile, Anne. There will be no announcement made. No congratulations given. Miss Elizabeth Bennet refused my offer."

"What?" Anne was stunned. The Darcys were one of the oldest families in the realm and belonged to a Norman aristocracy that held as much importance and prestige as many families with titles. And there were other factors. She knew from Darcy about the anxiety in the Bennet household because there were five daughters in need of husbands. From Mr. Collins, she understood the Bennet estate was entailed away from the female line to his benefit, and from her mother's interrogations, she knew Elizabeth lacked some of the accomplishments most families expected before approving a prospective bride.

"I do not understand. She will never receive a better offer." Anne's mind was racing trying to find an explanation for Elizabeth's actions. But everything she could think of was a reason for her to accept the offer, not to reject it: financial security for her and her family, her elevation in rank, a house in town, and becoming the mistress of the magnificent Pemberley estate. She finally said, "I did notice an attitude of independence, but to refuse your offer..."

"You need not trouble yourself. I have had all day to think about what transpired at the parsonage, and upon reflection, I now look upon Miss Elizabeth's response as a piece of good fortune. Considering her background, I am convinced a marriage between two people of such varying interests would have little chance of success, and both of us would have come to regret our choice of partner, and very quickly, I am sure."

"But what reasons did she give for her refusal?"

Darcy went over to the fireplace and started to stir the ashes with the poker. With his back to Anne, he answered, "She believes I separated Charles Bingley from her elder sister, Jane, and accused me of ruining forever her most beloved sister's chance of achieving true happiness. Eligible bachelors must be light on the ground in Hertfordshire for this event to be nothing short of a tragedy."

Ignoring the sarcasm, Anne asked if he did interfere.

"Yes, and I do not regret it at all. There were some very strong objections to the lady's family," and he turned to face his inquisitor. "Anne, if you could only see them in society! Good grief! Her mother shows no restraint whatsoever if she thinks her actions might secure a husband for one of her daughters. A younger sister has not a modicum of talent, but that does not prevent her from playing the pianoforte at every gathering. The two youngest sisters are out in society without proper preparation, and their behavior jeopardizes the very thing Mrs. Bennet seeks. Who will marry into such a family?"

"Apparently, you would, Will. These objections are valid, but if you were willing to overlook them, then why should Charles not do the same?"

"Are you serious? I could marry the innkeeper's daughter, and my place in society would not be jeopardized. Bingley's place is so tenuous that a marriage to the daughter of a farmer would end forever any hopes he had of making his mark in society. You do not know the history of the Bingley family. Their fortune was made because the grandfather invented an advanced process for the smelting of ore. Bingley's grandfather was a blacksmith, and his father never ventured farther south than York."

Darcy had met Charles Bingley while both were guests of a Leicestershire family who hosted one of the finest hunts in England. An expert horseman himself, Darcy had rarely seen anyone who could ride as well as Bingley, and their mutual respect for each other's riding skills had proved to be the basis of their friendship. Because of his affection for his friend, Darcy wanted Bingley to make his mark in society and took it upon himself to educate his friend as to what was expected of a man who, if Darcy had his way, would move in the top circles of England's elite.

"To a large degree, the gentleman Bingley has become is my creation."

"And you did an admirable job, Will, as Mr. Bingley is most certainly a gentleman," Anne said in a voice she hoped would be calming, as she had never seen her cousin so riled. "I have only met the gentleman on two occasions in town, but with Mr. Bingley's ample income and, if I remember correctly, the prospect of additional monies from a family trust, Jane Bennet's position in society would be of little importance to Charles. With so many aristocratic families deeply in debt, people like Charles Bingley can no longer be ignored no matter whom he has chosen as his wife."

Darcy had no response because he knew of at least a dozen individuals, including Lord Fitzwilliam, who relied on loans from families like the Bingleys to help them pay down their debts.

Anne understood Darcy's silence was a validation that what she had said about Bingley was correct. "Other than your concerns regarding the family, did you have any objections to the lady?"

"Absolutely! A most important objection. I do not think she loves Bingley. There certainly was nothing in her attitude or manner that indicated a deeper regard for him than for any other man with whom she had conversed. Her expressions showed interest, but to my mind, no real affection."

"I see. So it was you who interpreted Miss Bennet's actions

for Charles. And it was you who decided that Charles's rank in society was more important than securing the love of a woman whom he had found to be delightful. And it was you who convinced Charles to return to town and sever any relations with the young lady because you know what is best for your friend."

Darcy avoided Anne's gaze. His relationship with his cousin was closer than even that which he had with his sister. Following the death of their parents and because of the ten-year age difference, Darcy had emerged as a father figure to Georgiana. But that was not the case with Anne. He loved her as dearly as a sister and hated to disappoint her, but with Elizabeth's rebuke still fresh in his mind, he continued to defend his actions.

"I acted in the best interest of my friend, and for that, I make no apology, and I have nothing more to say on the matter. However, according to Miss Elizabeth that was not my most grievous sin. I fell short in her eyes because of a perceived transgression against George Wickham."

Darcy spat out Wickham's name as if it was a malignancy. Anne was aware that Wickham had attempted to arrange an elopement with Georgiana a year earlier. The very thought that Wickham might have succeeded caused a fire in his belly.

"In my letters, you will recall I mentioned Wickham had received a commission in a militia regiment encamped near Meryton," Darcy continued. "I believed he would not reveal his connection with my family for fear that the true story would become known. But I was wrong. Apparently, he convinced Miss Elizabeth that I am a villain and that I denied him the living promised to him by my father."

"Did you tell her the true story?"

"Certainly not. I would not risk exposing Georgiana."

"You must not hold Miss Elizabeth in very high regard if you are concerned she would repeat a story shared in confidence."

"Of course, you are right there," he responded, staring off into the distance. "Miss Elizabeth would recognize the importance of secrecy, so no additional harm might be done to Georgiana. I will give you that.".

"Then you should immediately acquaint Miss Elizabeth with the truth of the matter, so she might know of Wickham's villainy. Once she knows what actually happened, she will see you in a different light."

"I have done exactly that. The reason I did not come to supper was because I was writing a letter exposing Wickham for the liar and moral bankrupt that he is. I have written truthfully and fully of my role in Bingley's decision to quit Hertfordshire as well, and in the morning, I will put it all in a letter, which I will deliver to Miss Elizabeth when she walks in the grove. I know her favorite spot."

"Will, let me caution you. You should not give Elizabeth a letter that you wrote while you were still so angry. Wait until you get to London. Once you place the facts before her, they will speak to the justice of your argument. You do not wish to give offense when none is necessary."

"Give offense? Me? If you heard the things she said, you would not concern yourself with her feelings. And you are right; I am angry. Is she so gullible that she was willing to believe every word that came from the lips of someone whom she had not known a week earlier? Did she not think it inappropriate that a stranger should share such personal information? I was so taken aback by her accusations regarding Wickham that I could hardly remain composed enough to say something civil before leaving."

"That is exactly my point. Miss Elizabeth was so very angry with you because of your interference in her sister's affair that it was only natural that she would listen with prejudice to anything else you had to say. For your own sake, I suggest you not give her that letter. Remember, you might very well encounter her in society, and you may come to regret your actions."

"There you are wrong, Anne. Our paths will never cross again. It was only because Bingley asked me to go to Netherfield Park before signing the lease that I met her at all. I went to the blasted dance in Meryton because Bingley would give me no peace. Do you think I am in the habit of running about the country attending local dances? Other than the annual Lambton harvest dance, I avoid dances held in assembly halls, inns, or barns."

With that sarcastic statement, Anne knew there was nothing more to be said. He had been wounded by Elizabeth's rejection, and he was striking out against the source of that hurt.

"Anne, my character demands that I refute these accusations. After tomorrow, I shall never see her again, but she will know the truth before I leave Kent."

After Darcy returned to his room for the night, Anne thought about all that had happened between Will and Elizabeth and recognized that her cousin had got himself into a real mess. But Fitzwilliam Darcy was in love with Elizabeth Bennet, and Anne had seen real interest on Elizabeth's part during their evenings together at Rosings Park, so something had to be done. Before retiring, she had settled on a course of action. It was as complicated as any battle plan, and it would take luck and timing to make it work. But her cousin's happiness was at stake, and so she began to work out the details of her scheme.

Chapter 5

Mr. Darcy stood by the tall window of the second-floor library of Rosings Park. From this view, he could make out the cream stucco of Hunsford Lodge with its rust-colored roof and flower-lined walk. This was the only room in the manor house from which the parsonage could be seen, and Darcy was waiting for Elizabeth Bennet to return from her morning walk. As soon as he saw Elizabeth, he would know she had read the letter, and his reputation, at least with regards to Wickham, would be restored. How could it be otherwise? Her charges were not only wrong, but unjust.

Darcy paced back and forth in front of the window. Where was she? At the time Elizabeth had taken the letter from his hand, she had been walking in the lane reading a book. Was her interest in her book greater than the contents of his letter? Or was it Nature that beckoned her? Darcy knew of no other female who enjoyed the outdoors as much as she did, and her opinion was that it must be observed on foot. When he had asked if she knew how to ride, she had said that she did, but rode only when necessary and never for pleasure. Most likely, the horses she had ridden were ones that were chosen for their ability to pull a hay wagon. However, if she were to sit upon one of the fillies from the Pemberley stables, she would know the pure pleasure of riding a spirited animal and would come away with a very different opinion. He would have changed her mind.

On his morning rides, Darcy frequently saw Elizabeth walking with her bonnet in hand. When she caught sight of him, she had quickly returned the hat to its rightful place, but the evidence of outdoor exercise only highlighted the beauty of Elizabeth's dark eyes and her animated expression when she saw something on her walks that delighted her.

But his mind returned to the letter. If Elizabeth had started reading his missive as soon as he had presented it to her, she would by now have read the part where he exposed Wickham's immoral behavior. Darcy remembered the day when he had first seen Wickham in Meryton. His reaction was that there must be an unattached female in the neighborhood who was in possession of a large fortune. Why else would he be in a small market town, the usual attractions for a man of such low tastes being absent? There were no women of easy virtue to be had nor horse races to be run, and betting on a cockfight behind the village smithy would not have satiated his appetite for gambling. His disgust at seeing Wickham was further heightened when he saw Elizabeth talking to him. He was puzzled how someone with her keen intellect had not seen through his façade. But she did not know Wickham, and truth to tell, she did not know him either. He had revealed so little of himself in their conversations, and the tension that existed when they were together was such that it acted as a barrier to any greater intimacy between them.

But now that she had become acquainted with the truth, she would see him in a different light. She would know he had acted honorably, if unwisely, in seeing that Wickham received his full inheritance in one lump sum payment in order to be rid of him all the sooner. He had acted rashly there and should have known that any animal will return to the place where it has last eaten. What he did not anticipate was that his unctuous charm would play so well on the feelings of his sixteen-year-old sister. In hiding Wickham's true nature from Georgiana, he had set the stage for Wickham's attempted elopement.

Darcy did not wish to think of these things any longer. Once Elizabeth returned to Hunsford Lodge, he would be on the road to London. But where was she? She was now in possession of the letter long enough to have read through it several times. Was she chewing on each sentence as a dog would worry a bone? Or was she concentrating on the part that dealt with her beloved sister Jane?

Would Elizabeth's judgment have been so harsh if she had known of the criticism he had endured when he had befriended Charles Bingley? His aunt, Lady Catherine, had made it clear that Bingley was not welcomed at Rosings. To her, he was the thin end of the wedge, a threat to her world, and she would not have a "nobody" dining at her table. Bingley, who had barely established his own place in society, might very well have sunk under the weight of an unfortunate marriage.

Anticipating that his aunt might send someone to look for him, Darcy had pulled a chair over to the window in such a way that a servant might come into the room without seeing him. He knew that there were those who would expose him, his aunt's butler for one. Trent was a tired soul, and after having served

Her Ladyship for thirty years, he was entitled to his peace and quiet and would have disrupted Darcy's to achieve it.

Thoughts continued to swirl around in his mind. He now wondered if it had been wise to reveal in the letter that he had known of Miss Bennet being in London, but had deliberately kept that information from Bingley. Having been informed by Elizabeth that Miss Bennet cared deeply for his friend and that it was only her sense of modesty that had prevented a more open display of affection, he was uncomfortable with how forcefully he had pushed the matter to its conclusion.

Damnation! This might possibly have been avoided if Miss Bennet was as animated as her sister. If she had not sat there demurely with her hands folded in her lap, then surely it would not have been possible for Darcy to persuade his friend that the lady was not in love with him. It was difficult to imagine such a situation happening with Elizabeth. There was no guessing at her feelings. Her eyes revealed everything: the joy she experienced in dancing and being in the company of her friends, the annoyance she felt when asked to dance by Mr. Collins, and the puzzlement she showed when she danced with him at the Netherfield ball and tried to "take his likeness." He saw something else again in her eyes yesterday when she had refused him. He saw the hurt she felt for her sister and her indignation at his supposed ill treatment of Wickham. Her anger was real and deep, and the contents of his letter may have caused further injury.

What would her eyes show now? Upon reflection, could she find any good in him, or had he left her with the impression that he was an unfeeling, boorish man? At that moment, he saw a flash of yellow, the color of her bonnet. As he had imagined, she was not wearing it, but held it in one hand and his letter in the other. He stood up and drew nearer to the window. This would be the last opportunity he would have to look upon the woman he had hoped to take as his bride. He would drink his fill, and then move on.

Elizabeth stood outside the parsonage, but did not go in. Instead, she sat on a bench outside the front door holding his letter to her breast and looking up at the sky as if to hold back her tears. She sat quietly for several moments, but then her gaze followed the contours of the hill leading to Rosings and the line of the house up to the window where Mr. Darcy stood. What was she thinking? If only he was closer, he could have looked into her eyes. Her eyes would have revealed everything.

Chapter 6

THE MORNING AFTER MR. Darcy's proposal, Elizabeth was able to leave Hunsford Lodge only after satisfying the Collinses that she was well enough to go on her morning walk. She was eager to get out of the house and away from her friend's probing looks. Charlotte had seen Mr. Darcy leaving the parsonage the previous afternoon, but Lizzy had said nothing about his visit and had kept to her room after supper. She intended to share what had happened with Charlotte, but not now. She needed time alone to think.

To silence Mr. Collins and hasten her escape, Lizzy mentioned that she wished to begin the study of *Fordyce's Sermons*. Mr. Collins had made a gift of the book earlier in the week when he came upon her reading a novel, a book he considered inappropriate for an unmarried woman to be reading without the supervision and guidance of her father. He would have been appalled to learn that she had read *Tom Jones* and *Tristram Shandy* in the library at Longbourn without any supervision and at the recommendation of her father. Finally, after multiple assurances regarding her health, the weather, distances, etc., she was allowed to leave the parsonage and immediately went in search of a place where she could reflect upon the events of the previous day.

Rosings Park had beautiful vistas at every turn, but Lizzy's favorite was where woods and pastureland met. The contrast of the dark greens of the forest and the lush bright greens of the pastures made it a favorite stop, and at this slice of Eden, the de Bourghs had placed stone benches paralleling the path. It was the perfect place for reflection, but she was not to be alone this morning, as sitting on one of the benches was Mr. Darcy. It was too late to turn away because he had already seen her, so she pretended to be engrossed in her book so he might pretend not to have noticed her. But she soon realized his being in this particular spot was no accident. He quickly approached, and after asking her to do him the honor of reading his letter, he just as quickly departed.

After seeing Mr. Darcy well down the lane, Lizzy turned her full attention to his letter, and after finishing it, had to restrain herself from tearing it to shreds and scattering it to the winds. What pride and insolence! His purpose was clear: He wished to put behind him forever all memories of the scene at Hunsford Lodge. In this, they were in complete agreement. His words still echoed in her mind: how he had struggled to overcome his feelings for her, the inferiority of her connections, rejoicing in his success in separating Bingley from Jane, her pride, his shame. But before he could close the door on this chapter of his life, he demanded her attention one last time in order to justify his actions and refute her assertions.

For several minutes, Lizzy watched as a hundred black-faced sheep moved into the glade with three border collies nipping at their heels. The shepherd walked behind the flock, leaving the dogs to do their work. Was there such a view at Pemberley? Of course there was. The landed gentry and aristocracy all had the same things: great houses with portrait galleries and magnificent art, ballrooms and music rooms, gazebos and terraces, lower gardens, upper gardens, servants in livery behind every door. Yes, she could easily picture such a scene at Pemberley. And to think she might have been mistress of such an estate. Lizzy, who loved to laugh at the ridiculous, might have seen the humor in all of this if her emotions were not so raw.

Calmly, or so she believed, she began to reread Mr. Darcy's letter from his point of view. It was easy to understand why he had started his letter by saying that there would be no repetition of his proposal. He was a proud man who believed he had honored Lizzy by making her an offer of marriage. She had wounded him, and he had lashed out at its source.

Then there was Mr. Darcy's confession that he had willingly, knowingly, almost gleefully, separated Bingley from Jane. As a defense, he wrote that Bingley was often in love. That had given her pause. Often in love? Yes, she could see how that was possible. As a handsome and charming young man in possession of a large fortune, Bingley must have been sought out by many of the young ladies in London, and he could very well have imagined himself to be in love with some of them. In that regard, it was not unreasonable for Mr. Darcy to have believed that Jane was just another pretty face who had caught Bingley's eye. And did Jane's natural humility and modesty create the impression that there was little affection on her part as evidenced by Mr. Darcy's statement that "the most acute observer would draw the conclusion that her heart was not likely to be easily touched"?

The next part of the letter was particularly painful. Lizzy could hardly bring herself to reread Mr. Darcy's description of the behavior of her mother and sisters. But what did he write that was not true? Her mother, in her understandable concern to see her daughters well married, acted inappropriately in her search for the family's savior: the man who would rescue the Bennet sisters from the consequences of the entail. After Darcy had learned that there was a general belief that Bingley and Jane were to become engaged, he did everything he could to separate the couple. But was that not something a true friend would do?

And then there was the matter of Mr. Wickham. If Mr. Darcy was unable to judge the depth of Jane's regard for Mr. Bingley, then she had failed in discovering Wickham's true nature. In light of the events revealed in his letter, she knew in her heart that all he had written was true. She remembered, with embarrassment, how eager Wickham had been to expose the defects of Mr. Darcy's character, and didn't Jane warn her to be skeptical of Wickham's assertions, wondering how it was possible that Darcy's intimate friend could be so deceived as to his true nature? And was there any greater proof of Wickham's true character than his actions regarding sixteen-year-old Georgiana Darcy? It was impossible to believe that a brother would invent such a sordid tale and then share it with another.

Elizabeth removed her bonnet, hoping the breeze would clear her mind of all the horrible things she had said to Mr. Darcy regarding Wickham, including the accusation that he was responsible for Wickham's current state of poverty. As for Jane, it was true he had greatly injured her, but now she realized it was never his intention to cause Jane any pain. His actions were dictated by his concerns for his friend.

With the sun on her face, it was all becoming clearer—why Mr. Darcy had followed her movements at Lucas Lodge, his asking her to dance at Netherfield, his visits to the parsonage, his meeting her on her daily walks, and his words at Rosings while she played the pianoforte: "No one admitted to the privilege of hearing you can think anything wanting." And most of all, his declaration of love: "You must allow me to tell you how ardently I admire and love you."

Lizzy refolded the letter. At the ball at Netherfield, Mr. Darcy had asked that she not sketch his character as there was reason to fear "that the performance would reflect no credit on either of them." Oh, how true that statement was! She had refused to see any good in him because of the unkind remarks he had made at the assembly. As for his part, he had honored her with a proposal of marriage, but found it necessary to remind her of her inferior position in society and the failings of her family.

Her emotions were in turmoil. From the time she came into Kent, she had learned so much about him, and if she had not been so blinded by prejudice, she would have seen a very different Mr. Darcy from the gentleman she knew in Hertfordshire. His cousin, Colonel Fitzwilliam, held him in the highest regard and spoke of an amiable and conversant Mr. Darcy when amongst his friends. Despite his aunt's overbearing nature, he visited Rosings because Lady Catherine was his mother's sister, and as such, was deserving of his attention, and Lizzy suspected, by looks exchanged between them, that he had a good relationship with Anne de Bourgh when her mother was not about. But was there anything that showed him in a better light than his affection and concern for his sister and the fear that must have gripped him when he believed he had lost her to a man with no scruples?

Lizzy walked the lane, trying to sort through all the images flashing before her. If things had gone differently, could she have loved him? After reflecting on the whole of their history together, she realized that, over time, she could have. She would have chipped away at his hard shell and would have softened his look. If only they had been able to break through the barriers that separated them, his pride and her prejudice, yesterday would have ended very differently.

When Lizzy arrived at the parsonage, she sat down on a bench outside the front door of the house. She read the letter once again, but with understanding and not in anger. A wave of regret passed over her as she realized what had been lost. Clutching the letter to her breast, she felt the tears well up in her eyes, and through her tears she looked up towards the manor house and wondered if Mr. Darcy was still there. Considering the tone of his letter, that was unlikely. So there would be no more encounters in the park or visits to the parsonage. Her acquaintance with Mr. Darcy of Pemberley had come to its dramatic conclusion.

Chapter 7

LIZZY WAS IN HER room lying on the bed staring at the ceiling. After sharing with Charlotte the awful scene that had taken place in her parlor, her friend had tried to lift her spirits by suggesting that once Mr. Darcy had time to recover from the hurt of her rejection, he might renew his attentions. But when Lizzy acquainted Charlotte with the contents of his letter, she suggested that they go into the village and think of other things.

Lizzy kept Mr. Darcy's letter under her pillow, but no longer needed to look at it as she could now recite it from memory. "I write without any intention of paining you, or humbling myself, by dwelling on wishes, which, for the happiness of both, cannot be too soon forgotten."

Despite Mr. Darcy's hopes, Lizzy doubted that either of them would soon forget what had been said, and the angry words she spoke still echoed in her mind. "You could not have made me the offer of your hand in any possible way that would have tempted me to accept it." She groaned and turned on her side. If she expected Mr. Darcy to examine his actions, then she must do the same. This whole sorry affair was not about Jane or Wickham; it was about Elizabeth Bennet and her wounded pride. She had shut her eyes to all that might be good in him. When Jane said Mr. Bingley doubted the truth of Mr. Wickham's story, she refused to hear it. She would not listen to anything that challenged her assumptions. At the Netherfield ball, she chided Mr. Darcy for his lack of conversation, but when he suggested sharing their opinions on books, she refused. "No, I cannot talk of books in a ballroom. My head is always full of something else." *So go away and leave me alone, so I might think about George Wickham.*

Lizzy stood up, ran her hands over the creases in her dress, and returned her curls to their rightful place. Revisiting the scene time and again was doing her no good, so she decided to join Charlotte in the parlor. As she was going down the stairs, she heard the bell ring, and fearing for a moment that it might be Mr. Darcy with another letter, she went back upstairs. *Please, no more letters! One is quite enough.* However it was not Mr. Darcy, but Miss Anne de Bourgh, and she quickly returned to her room. A few minutes later, a servant knocked on the door to let her know that Miss de Bourgh was waiting for her downstairs. When Lizzy went into the parlor, she found her visitor was all alone.

"It is very good to see you again, Miss Elizabeth," she said, giving a slight bow, which Lizzy returned. "Mrs. Collins excused herself, as she needed to discuss the household accounts with her housekeeper, but she has ordered tea for us."

While Miss de Bourgh was removing her cloak, Lizzy noticed what fine features she had: thick, dark brown hair; beautiful, flawless skin; clear, blue eyes with long dark lashes; and the high cheekbones so favored by painters, but she also saw how she appeared to be as fragile as a porcelain doll.

"Miss Elizabeth, may we sit nearer to the fire? I am quite chilled from the ride."

Lizzy moved a chair closer to the fireplace and offered her guest one of Charlotte's heavier quilts. The day before, Charlotte had taken them out of the storage chest, guessing correctly that the warm temperatures could not last.

"I hope you do not object to my unannounced visit. Since my cousins, Mr. Darcy and Colonel Fitzwilliam, are now gone, the house is quite empty—and silent. And I miss conversation. I very much enjoyed listening to you when you joined us for supper. You have such a sparkling wit."

"I do not think your cousin, Mr. Darcy, would agree with that assessment."

"Oh, I can assure you that you are wrong. He found your conversation to be engaging, even challenging. You gave him pause for thought, and in several instances, got the better of him—something quite new to his experience."

Lizzy rose to help the servant with the tea, but she also needed time to reflect on what was happening. Charlotte had deliberately made herself scarce because Lizzy knew that Monday was the day when she went over the household accounts with Mrs. Elvin. Today was Thursday. For whatever reason, Miss de Bourgh wanted to speak to Lizzy in private.

"Shall we dispense with the formalities? If I may call you Elizabeth, you may call me Anne." Lizzy smiled and nodded her assent. "I understand you are shortly to return home, and I did not want to miss an opportunity to visit with you before you left."

Anne picked up the teacup and clasped her hands around

it for warmth. After taking a sip, which she needed because she was shivering, she continued.

"Colonel Fitzwilliam and Mr. Darcy, or Richard and Will, as I call them, are like brothers to me, and I shall miss them. We are very fond of each other and have been since we were children. Along with Richard's elder brother, Lord Fitzwilliam, we are all very close in age, and we spent hours together in the playroom at Rosings. It is quite large—large enough to have a theatre for plays and a stage for puppetry, and our seamstress made the most wonderful costumes, each one having lots of feathers. We were very keen on feathers. We wrote the plays ourselves, and according to my father, Lord de Bourgh, the boys always kept the funniest lines for themselves."

Lizzy smiled at the thought of Mr. Darcy and the colonel on the stage. What would their plays have been about? Pirates, of course. Boys always wanted to be pirates with eye patches, earrings, and swords. Or possibly knights in shining armor with Anne playing the damsel in distress.

"When Will was at Cambridge, Richard and I went to see him play cricket," Anne continued. "He is a superior batsman, and to this day, he will boast of the time when his *alma mater* defeated Eton in two contests within a period of three days," Anne said, smiling at the memory. "Did he ever mention it when he was in Hertfordshire?"

"No, he did not. Our only opportunity to speak was on the dance floor—not the best place to learn about your partner, and Mr. Darcy left Netherfield Park shortly thereafter."

"How unfortunate—for both of you. Perhaps there will be other opportunities."

Not if Mr. Darcy had any say in it, Lizzy thought.

"As I have said, he is very much like a brother to me, and when I find myself quite overpowered by my mother, I need only send a letter to Will, and he will come and rescue me. Before Mama leased our house in town, we spent many happy hours together during the season in London. I am not very strong, and I cannot dance more than one or two dances. But even though all the ladies were making such a fuss over him, Will was never far from my side.

"Because of my health and the distance, I do not often visit the Darcy estate, but I have very fond memories of long summer days in Derbyshire. But, of course, now that Will is the master of Pemberley, everything is changed from when we were children. He holds himself to a very high standard. It is he who must visit all of the tenants. It is he who must know how many lambs were born in the spring and how much grain was gathered at harvest time. His tenants hold him in the highest regard, as do the villagers. He can hardly walk down High Street without people rushing out of the shops to greet him, and if you allowed him, the vicar would go on and on, singing his praises about his generosity and kindness to those in need.

"And with all of these responsibilities, he tells me they are nothing compared to that of being his sister's guardian. He is quite devoted to her. Georgiana is eighteen now, and as you can imagine, is very eager to come into society. He has done everything he can to prepare her. It was almost laughable to see him with her at the milliner's shop. But she insists on hearing his opinion, as she is equally devoted to him."

Lizzy thought back to an evening at Netherfield Park when Caroline Bingley had asked Mr. Darcy if he admired her new bonnet. "Miss Bingley, as you well know, you will wear what is currently in fashion, and when it is out of fashion, you will stop wearing it. So if I said I liked your bonnet today, I might find come next spring that I must say that I do not like it. Wear what pleases you. I have no interest in such things." And, yet, Anne was saying Mr. Darcy went with his sister to the milliner's shop. Lizzy could just picture him, crossing and uncrossing his legs, and drumming his fingers on the top of his hat, when he was not pacing the floor. Lizzy wondered if he would have done the same for her if she had accepted him.

"There are so many people who look up to him that I think the weight of his responsibilities has taken some of the joy out of his life. With so much to do and at such great distances, I have noticed he has less patience and his speech can be brusque and, therefore, easily misunderstood." Leaning towards Lizzy, Anne added, with tears in her eyes, "He truly is the best of men, and it would pain me to think there was someone out there in the wider world who thought ill of him because they do not know him as I do."

Lizzy now understood the purpose of the visit. There was no doubt Mr. Darcy had shared with his cousin that he had made her an offer of marriage and her rejection of it. Her presence confirmed that he had related the details of the scene that had played out in this very parlor, and Anne was determined that before Lizzy returned to Hertfordshire, she would hear about the Mr. Darcy she knew and loved.

Lizzy could hardly look at Anne. There was such longing in her face, and she wanted to reassure her. But what could she say? She sat quietly staring into the fire, and it was several minutes before the words finally came. When they did, they came from her heart.

"Anne, I admit that when I first met Mr. Darcy he puzzled me exceedingly, and as you say, he can be brusque. But I have learned a great deal about him since those first days in Hertfordshire. I cannot speak for others, but I can assure you that I do not think ill of him."

Anne let out a sigh of relief. "I shall tell you, Elizabeth, that Mr. Darcy improves upon acquaintance, and when next you meet, you will find him to be a much more agreeable fellow."

"That is a most unlikely event. Mr. Darcy and I do not move in the same circles in town, and it is my understanding that it is Mr. Bingley's intention to quit Netherfield Park, which means I will not see him in the country either."

"Oh, I don't know. Life holds so many surprises," Anne said, standing up. Although she was clearly tired from the visit, she looked quite content while Lizzy looked much less so. "May I write to you, Elizabeth?"

"Of course, if I may write to you."

Taking Lizzy's hands in hers, she said, "I shall not say good-bye because I am quite confident we will meet again."

As soon as Anne's phaeton turned down the lane, Charlotte came rushing into the parlor. "Lizzy, what was that all about? When Miss de Bourgh asked if she could speak to you alone, I thought you had earned the ire of her mother, and she had come to warn you."

"No, nothing like that," Lizzy said, shaking her head. "When Miss de Bourgh learned I was to return home, she wanted to visit with me before I left Kent."

"But you were in there for more than half of an hour. What was discussed?"

"Little of importance, except how life does have its twists

and turns, and that certainly is true. However, one can predict the future with some degree of accuracy based on one's own knowledge of past events. And rare events do occur, but it is their lack of repetition that makes them rare." Was it really possible that she would see Mr. Darcy again?

"Lizzy, what on earth are you talking about?"

"I don't know. I honestly don't know."

Chapter 8

IF THE WEATHER HELD, the carriage would arrive at the coaching inn at Bromley in about an hour. Once there, Fitzwilliam and Darcy would part company, and Darcy would be left alone with his thoughts. He had left Rosings Park an hour after he was sure Elizabeth had read his letter. He had seen her sitting outside the parsonage holding his letter to her breast, and he sensed that it had distressed her. And that memory would be the very last one he would have of her, and as Anne had predicted, he regretted having written it.

"Darcy, you are contemplative this day," Colonel Fitzwilliam said.

"There are times when silence is beneficial."

Colonel Fitzwilliam and Darcy were exactly the same age, and the young Richard Fitzwilliam had spent many summers at the Pemberley estate. As young men, both had attended Cambridge, and from there, they experienced the Grand Tour of Europe's great cities. Without a care in the world, the duo drank champagne at the Chateau de Crecy in Picardy, joined costumed revelers at Carnavale in Venice, saw Rome and its catacombs by torchlight, and danced into the early hours of the morning in Paris. They were traveling to the south of France when a rider intercepted them with a message from Pemberley: Darcy's father was dead.

In that one instant, Fitzwilliam Darcy went from being someone with few responsibilities to a young man who was now the master of a great estate. The staff, the tenants, the villagers, all would look to him to make decisions that would affect their everyday lives. But the greatest responsibility was that he was now the guardian of his sister, who had just celebrated her thirteenth birthday. Until Georgiana married, everything she wanted to do required his approval, and his decisions would chart the course her life would take. These changes in his circumstances had an immediate and permanent impact. Darcy was much more serious, and although Fitzwilliam was used to long rides with Darcy saying very little, even for him, no conversation at all was not the norm.

"Darcy, it is quite obvious that something is troubling you, and I would like to think that you could speak of it to me."

"I *have* been preoccupied," Darcy confessed. "As you know, since that episode with Wickham and Georgiana, I am ill at ease when we are apart. Once I am back in town and see that all is well, everything will be as it was before," and Darcy turned his attention to the passing countryside.

"Does your preoccupation have anything to do with Miss Elizabeth Bennet?"

"What?" Darcy said, sitting up straight. "Why would you say that?"

"On the evening Miss Elizabeth was at Rosings for dinner,

I noticed how often you looked at her. She is a very attractive woman with an inquisitive mind and a sharp wit and is completely without airs. I was totally taken in by her. However, being the younger son of an earl, I cannot marry where I wish, so I do not form attachments for ladies with no fortune. On the other hand, you are rich, and you may marry whomever you please."

"Why are you speaking of marriage? You interpret my admiration for her technique in playing the pianoforte and a few glances in her direction as a prelude to a proposal. That is quite a stretch, Fitzwilliam."

"It will not do, Darcy. You were not admiring her technique; you were admiring her. And it was not a few glances. You could hardly take your eyes off her." When Darcy said nothing, Fitzwilliam continued. "Let us suppose for the sake of argument that you are in love with Miss Elizabeth and that you would like to marry the lady."

"If I asked you to stop before you made yourself ridiculous, would you?"

"No, because I think you want to hear me out. So let us examine what would happen if you chose to go down that path. Because of your position in society, you would be able to weather any storm that would ensue. You are rich and well connected, and as such, cannot be ignored no matter whom you marry. As for the matter of Elizabeth being the daughter of a gentleman farmer, theoretically, you are equal. She is the daughter of a gentleman, and you are the son of one. From my perspective, you lose nothing, but there is much to be gained."

"Richard, these are all fine arguments. But you obviously did not notice that Miss Elizabeth does not like me very much."

"That is because she does not know you as well as I do.

She needs to see the man who cares so deeply for his sister or who will travel to Rosings to surprise Anne. She does not know of your kindness to me in keeping me out of poverty or in rescuing my brother from embarrassment. My advice to you is to seek the first opportunity that offers for the purpose of courting her."

The carriage pulled into the courtyard at the inn, and while the colonel waited for his horse to be saddled, he said, "If all I have said does not persuade you, think of my brother and sister-in-law, Lord Fitzwilliam and Lady Eleanor. You have seen them together, when they are together. Both have impeccable pedigrees, but they cannot tolerate each other and all of this was easily predictable. Will, pursue Miss Elizabeth. She will challenge you."

Pursue Elizabeth. Simple advice. But what Richard did not know was that he had already attempted to pursue her and was rejected with a vehemence that had stunned him: "I felt that you were the last man in the world whom I could ever be prevailed on to marry." She would have accepted an offer from a dustman before she would have consented to marry him.

Thinking back to that afternoon, he wondered at his own behavior, which was the antithesis of how he usually acted. It was spontaneous, irrational, and, in the end, self-defeating. He had never intended to ask Elizabeth to marry him, which was obvious by the mode of his declaration. He was working it through in his mind. Unfortunately, that process was spoken aloud, and not realizing that Elizabeth might find his musings to be offensive, he did not even look at her while he was pointing out her defects. If he had, he would have said no more. In his mind, he could now recall the pursed lips, the raised shoulders, the flashing eyes. He had seen eyes like that before, at Pemberley, when a bull had chased him out of a pasture.

Well, what had been done could not be undone, so he would make his way to London. Once at home, his beloved sister would put him in a better humor.

Chapter 9

DARCY'S FIRST OPPORTUNITY TO visit with his sister was in the early afternoon when she had finished her lessons with her German tutor. It was not too long ago that she would have run across the room and thrown her arms around him, but within the last year, he had noticed that she walked in the measured steps of a lady *before* throwing her arms around him. These changes were inevitable, but he missed the complete lack of inhibition of her younger years.

Georgiana was a talker, and although the intrigues of young ladies who had not yet come out into society were of little interest to him, Darcy listened to her as if she were discussing the debates in Parliament.

"Will, must I continue with German? I hate it. I always feel as if I am spitting at someone. The only reason I have to study German is because the old king speaks it, and I very much doubt I shall ever have an occasion to address him in English or German. I have been declared to be proficient in Italian and French. May I please stop my German lessons?"

"Yes, when you return to seminary after Twelfth Night, you do not have to study German." He was entirely sympathetic on this point. He had never liked German lessons and did not do well at them despite his parents having employed a tutor from Saxony.

Georgiana had been expecting her brother to insist that she continue and was thinking of additional arguments when he had given in. This was not like Will. A lot of discussion was required before any decision was made regarding her education. Looking at her brother, she wondered if something had happened at Rosings Park. She knew that a visit with Aunt Catherine was unpleasant because her constant negativity wore on everyone, but Will was very good at paying only enough attention so that he could answer a question if asked. He never engaged, as that only served to prolong the pain. Putting her hand on her brother's arm, she said, "What is the matter, Will? You look so tired."

"I am tired. The journey from Kent took longer than usual because of the rain, but as I wrote in my letters, Aunt Catherine and Anne are well and send their love, as does Richard."

"Are you sure there is nothing wrong? You look sad."

"Georgiana, I need a good night's sleep, and then all will be well."

"But all is not well. I can see it in your eyes. You have had a sadness about you ever since Wickham…"

"You are mistaken," he said, interrupting her, "and we shall not speak of him or anything to do with that matter."

"But what if I wish to speak of it?"

"Georgiana, this is not subject to discussion," and he got up to pour a glass of Madeira.

"Will, that is unfair. You have determined in your own mind

what happened, and a good deal of it is wrong. And, yet, I cannot tell you the truth as you will not hear it. So I have to bear this burden of you thinking I would have eloped with Wickham, but I never would have. Never."

Will sunk back into the chair. Were the stars aligned against him? Is that why he was unable to say or do the right thing as far as the female of the species was concerned?

"I know it pains you, but you will have a different understanding if only you will listen."

Darcy shrugged his shoulders in resignation. "I will hear you, and then we will not speak of it again. Is that agreed?"

"Yes, of course, and you will be glad when I am done."

Just the mention of George Wickham's name infuriated him. Darcy knew little about Wickham's early background, except that, as a young child, he had been placed in the care of Pemberley's steward and his wife, who were childless and who loved their adopted son dearly. Darcy's father also grew fond of Wickham, who had a most pleasing manner, one that hid a deceitful and conniving character, and had agreed to support him at Cambridge. In an act of generosity, Darcy's father informed Wickham that once he had completed his studies, some money would become available so that he might purchase a living in the church, a commission in the army, or study the law. From that one conversation and because of old Darcy's interest in his welfare and education, Wickham had decided that he was the natural son of his uncle, George Ashton, who was known to have fathered several children and had scattered them about the country. Because of Ashton's association with the Darcy family, in Wickham's mind, he was entitled to much more than the purchase of a living.

After the elder Darcy had died, Wickham left Cambridge and came to Darcy to ask for the value of the living and had disregarded all of Darcy's arguments against such a scheme. At Wickham's insistence, he had provided him with a draft on a London bank for the full amount. Within six months, Wickham was back at Pemberley asking for additional sums, but was refused. An angry George Wickham had declared that he knew who his father was and would expose Ashton if his demands were not met. The conversation and his response were still lodged in his memory.

"I do not know who your father is, but I know who he is not. And he is not George Ashton. My father agreed to manage a sum of money on your behalf as long as you pursued your studies or a career. It is obvious that your intention is to do neither. You made a mistake by coming to me today with your demands. You will get nothing from me, and you are to leave Pemberley immediately."

In a rage, Wickham had told him, "You will come to regret your decision. I will see to it." And he had come very near to succeeding.

A year earlier, on the spur of the moment, Darcy had decided to visit his sister in Ramsgate. Instead of enjoying the sea air with her companion, Georgiana had been receiving, in her rooms, George Wickham. The scoundrel had followed his sister to Ramsgate and had convinced her that he was in love with her, so much so that they should marry immediately. Because Darcy had thought it improper to discuss the man's appetite for gaming and loose women and his spendthrift ways with a girl who knew nothing of how the world really worked, Georgiana had been unaware of Wickham's true nature. As far as Darcy was concerned, Wickham had ceased to exist when he had accepted a cash payment in lieu of a living.

Although Georgiana insisted she would never have married without his consent, Darcy believed he had prevented their elopement, and now she was asking that he listen to the details of Wickham's plan. And he signaled for his sister to begin.

"At my brother's insistence," Georgiana said, smiling weakly, "before being allowed to go to Ramsgate, I had to promise to study my German and practice my pieces on the pianoforte for at least two hours every morning. Mrs. Younge would sit with me in the parlor, but I thought it was unfair as there was nothing for her to do. So we agreed that during that time she could go to the shops or down to the pier and enjoy the sea air. Somehow, Mr. Wickham discovered I was in Ramsgate, and after learning that Mrs. Younge was my companion, befriended her. At this point, she was completely innocent."

"If you wish for me to listen to you," Darcy said, preventing his sister from continuing, "please do not refer to Mrs. Younge as being innocent. If she is to be believed, she talked to a man not of her acquaintance, and if for no other reason, she failed in her primary duty to protect you."

"I understand," his sister said. "But before I go on, I must step back. While you were at Cambridge and I remained at Pemberley, I would often go out onto the lawn and sketch with Mrs. Bridges. One day, Mr. Wickham came by and admired my sketch, and he asked for one of my chalks and drew a very funny picture of Mrs. Bridges. And we laughed because it was very funny. The next day, he brought me a sketch of himself, which was also funny. There was no third day because Mrs. Bridges insisted I remain in the classroom and draw, saying that

Mr. Wickham was neglecting his duties. Other than seeing him about the property, we had no further contact.

"And now to the heart of the story," and taking a deep breath, Georgiana plunged in. "One morning, Mrs. Younge encountered Mr. Wickham on her walk, and it was then he revealed that he had grown up at Pemberley and asked if he might call on me. She asked, and I agreed. Well, it was a very pleasant hour, and he suggested that I join him for a walk around the harbor the next day, which I did, and continued to do for another three days. I must confess I was flattered by the attention, especially when he bought me a jewelry box decorated with seashells. After that day, the weather turned against us, and he now called at the house, and much to my surprise, he professed his love for me. Not having been introduced to society, I did not realize that this was a common ploy used by men who were in search of women who would inherit a fortune.

"Finally, he asked if we might go for a carriage ride without Mrs. Younge. I agreed, but as soon as I did, I knew that I would not. I realized that I should have written to you to ask for your permission before I had ever agreed to receive him. It was my intention to do so, but it was not necessary. That morning, while Mrs. Younge was doing my hair, she repeated stories Wickham had told her about providing endless hours of amusement for me while we were at Pemberley, including walks in the garden and our reading poetry together, neither of which had ever happened. And I realized what a fool I had been, and without saying anything to Mrs. Younge, I waited for Wickham in the parlor for the purpose of telling him he must never come again. That is when you arrived, and you know the rest."

Yes, he did know the rest. He had missed his sister's

company and was looking forward to visiting her, and in order to surprise her, he had not written to inform her that he was coming to Ramsgate. When he went into the parlor, the first person he saw was not Georgiana, but Wickham, and he had no doubt why he was there. He grabbed him by his coat, pushed him down the stairs and into the foyer before throwing him into the street. Hearing the commotion, Mrs. Younge came to see what was happening and encountered her employer in full fury. He very quickly got the whole of the story, and giving her only enough time to gather her belongings, demanded she leave immediately.

Georgiana was correct. Despite tears and protests, he had refused to hear what she had to say. He sent her to her room and ordered the servants to pack up everything as they would be returning to London immediately. On several occasions, she had tried to tell him the truth of what had happened, but he could not bear to hear Wickham's name.

"I know what I did was wrong, and now that you know the whole of it, you will understand that I would never, ever marry without your consent. What I did was foolish and immature, but I love you, and I would not hurt you for all the world. I was never at risk of becoming Wickham's wife."

Darcy opened his arms to his sister, and she came running to him. He kissed her on the top of her head and told her, "I was not angry with you, but with myself. It was I who had personally interviewed Mrs. Younge and had decided she was an appropriate companion for you. But that is in the past."

Gesturing for his sister to sit down, he said, "Your future is quickly upon us. In the spring, you will come out into society. It is well known that you are to inherit a great deal of money.

There are men who will say anything if they think it will give them access to your fortune. Allow me to give you an example. You are acquainted with Abigail Curzon," and Georgiana nodded. "Would you describe her as a 'jewel plucked out of the night sky'?" Georgiana tried not to laugh because poor Abigail was one of those unfortunate people who had inherited the very worst traits from both of her parents, and Georgiana shook her head "no."

"Exactly. She is an intelligent and thoughtful young lady, but she is not handsome, except to Lord Corman's spendthrift son, who paid her that compliment within my hearing."

"Will, did Mr. Corman actually say 'plucked'?" Miss Curzon was often described as having a "swan neck," and in her case, it was true. She had the longest neck of anyone Georgiana had ever seen.

"Yes, he said 'plucked.' And I understand why that word came to mind." And both of them started to laugh.

"Oh Will, I can see your spirits have lifted. I am truly sorry for the hurt I caused you, but I am much wiser now. I understand that there are people who will lie and deceive for their own gain. I shall be on my guard against such ruses."

"Georgiana, you know you are the dearest part of my life. You and I, we are a pair. Anything that injures you hurts me. So come and give me a kiss, and we shall say good night."

Later that evening, while in his study drinking his nightly glass of brandy, Darcy wondered at his inability to take the true measure of a woman. He did not have this problem with men. He knew Wickham to be a liar, and possibly a thief, from when they were mere boys. And then there was Charles Bingley, an awkward young man, who had very few social graces but who was a stellar fellow. He had recognized his attributes from the very beginning of their acquaintance.

But women? They were something else entirely. He had seriously misjudged Mrs. Younge. His housekeeper, Mrs. Reynolds, had cautioned him that she might be too young, but then he thought of Mrs. Jenkinson. As devoted as she was to Anne, she was old enough to be her mother. Darcy believed the ten-year age difference between Georgiana and Mrs. Younge would make her presence not only tolerable but enjoyable. But it had all gone so badly.

And Jane Bennet. There was another one. He had truly believed she liked Bingley very much, but he did not see any depth of regard in her looks. But Elizabeth insisted she was very much in love with him, and it was only her modesty that prevented an open display of affection.

And had he fallen any shorter of the mark than when judging Miss Elizabeth Bennet? He knew her to be a fighter from their time together at Netherfield Park. She challenged almost everything he said with a biting wit and sometimes just biting. How could he have believed that the same woman who had made such sharp remarks while dancing with him at the Netherfield ball would put aside all prejudices because he was honoring her with his proposal?

Darcy stared into the fire and remembered the evening at Rosings when Elizabeth was sitting at the pianoforte. They had a pleasant, almost playful, exchange in which she accused him of trying to frighten her, and he teased her in return, but concluded by praising her playing. If Aunt Catherine had not interrupted the conversation, he would have said more. But before she resumed her playing, Elizabeth had looked at him with a puzzled expression that he had interpreted as her wanting to know him better so that she might understand him better.

He would have to put these thoughts from his mind for the time being as he had promised Georgiana that they would spend the holidays with the Smythes before returning to London for her last term at seminary. After that, he would be free to make the journey to Pemberley, and the view of the Peaks with their ever-changing landscapes would restore his spirits. Because of the lingering memory of Elizabeth sitting outside the parsonage clutching his letter to her bosom, he refused to be devoid of all hope, and if there was a solution to be found, it would be found at Pemberley.

Chapter 10

Shortly after Lizzy and Jane returned to Longbourn from their travels, Lizzy was finally able to unburden herself as to what had transpired at the parsonage. Jane's response was to be expected. Because of his place in society, she was greatly surprised by Mr. Darcy's offer of marriage and equally dismayed by the mode of his declaration. However, it was merely in the blink of an eye before she went from chastising the gentleman for assuming so much to feeling sorry for him.

Jane was even more surprised when Lizzy acquainted her with all of the facts concerning Mr. Wickham and Miss Darcy. She now believed the very worst about him, and she would shortly have proof of it.

The Bennet family had very good relations with their servants, but it was Mrs. Hill whom they loved and trusted. Because of her many years of service to the family, there were very few topics that were not freely discussed in front of her, and Mrs. Hill understood that any confidences shared with her would remain within the confines of Longbourn. However, Mrs.

Hill often shared news of what was going on in the village and the surrounding farms because every piece of gossip was quickly circulated amongst the servants of the farmers and shopkeepers.

"I was talking to the Smart girls," Mrs. Hill began. "All four of them was hired by Miss Bingley when she come to Netherfield, and while the Bingleys were there, they hardly shared a thing of what was going on abovestairs, afraid they was of being sacked. But now that the lot of them are gone, they could hardly wait to get all of it out. But I doubt that you two would be wanting to hear such tattling."

"Oh, how wrong you are, Mrs. Hill. We want to hear every juicy morsel, and nothing should be left out," Lizzy said, laughing. Although Jane had resigned herself to the fact that Mr. Bingley and she would not see each other again, Lizzy understood her sister would want to hear everything she could about him.

"First of all, Martha said Mr. Bingley was as nice as could be, and the only thing that could put him in a sour mood was two rainy days in a row so he couldn't go out riding. What Martha said about the others was that Miss Bingley was never happy with their work and was always complaining, that Mrs. Hurst went along with anything her sister said, and that Mr. Hurst couldn't be kept from the port wine no matter what his wife said to him. The only juicy piece of gossip was that Miss Bingley was flirting with Mr. Darcy all the time, but he wasn't paying her no mind. She heard that from Jeremy Stockard, who was hired on as a footman. He could hardly believe that people were willing to pay him good money to stand by a door with a powdered wig on his head, so the ladies wouldn't have to open it themselves. But that's what Miss Bingley wanted, so he lined his pockets and kept his mouth shut.

"I says to Martha, 'Well, there's not much news there. It's just as you'd expect,' and she said that was true but there was a surprise, and that was Mr. Darcy. Now, I know you don't like Mr. Darcy, Miss Lizzy, but it seems that he was a good friend to Mr. Bingley, and when Mr. Bingley decided to have the ball, well, there was no way it could happen without some help. So Mr. Darcy sent a letter to wherever he lives in Derbyshire, and the cook, butler, and a wagonload of servants come down to get everything ready for the big night. And all of Mr. Darcy's servants went on and on about how good it was to work for him and Miss Darcy. Well, I never would have believed it from what I heard about him from the time at the assembly when he snubbed Miss Lizzy."

Jane looked at Lizzy out of the corner of her eye. It seemed as if evidence was building that her sister had seriously misjudged Mr. Darcy.

"But that's nothing compared to what's being said about Mr. Wickham," Mrs. Hill said in a conspiratorial whisper. "Sally Smart, who works for the Drapers, says Mrs. Draper has been crying on and off for days because Mr. Wickham didn't pay any of his bills. What Sally said was that Mr. Draper had ordered some expensive heavy fabric and a brass clasp from London for a cloak that Mr. Wickham wanted made special. He told them he'd pay them when he got paid, but he never did, and Mrs. Draper is afraid he never will. And once word got out that Mr. Draper hadn't been paid, others from the shops said they were owed money too. But they hadn't said nothing before with Mr. Wickham being an officer and a gentleman and all. But Mr. Corbin said, gentleman or no, he's writing to Colonel Forster. He wants his money."

There was more news, equally bad, about Wickham taking liberties with some of the local girls, as well as extensive gaming debts and displays of bad temper and drunkenness. If only half of the rumors were true, Wickham was as vile as Mr. Darcy had described him.

Both sisters were truly distressed by Mrs. Hill's news, but Lizzy was heartsick. She could hardly bear to think about how she had taken sides in Wickham's favor and at the expense of Mr. Darcy. Now, she completely understood the look of disgust on his face before he left the parsonage and the necessity of his writing that awful letter.

"Lizzy, I can see what you are thinking. But it was not only in the matter of Mr. Wickham on which your dislike of Mr. Darcy was based. You had other provocations."

"Yes, I did. However, in the light of all that I now know, it can be argued that I am a terrible judge of character."

Jane was beside her sister in a moment. "You are too harsh. The Wickhams of the world succeed because they excel at deception. He succeeded in fooling everyone, Lizzy."

"Except Mr. Darcy. Apparently, he never succeeded in fooling Mr. Darcy."

Chapter 11

Darcy and Georgiana celebrated Christmas with Lord and Lady Smythe at their country estate in Sussex. Their daughter, Agnes, and Georgiana attended seminary together and had become the closest of friends. The Smythes were having a ball to celebrate their daughter's eighteenth birthday, but the dance had another purpose: to serve as a practice ball, as both Agnes and Georgiana would come into society when the London season began in earnest in May. Darcy watched the event with mixed emotions. His sister had emerged as a beautiful butterfly from the cocoon he had kept her in these past five years. After admiring how gracefully she danced with the young swells and how easily she mingled with all the guests, he realized that he would soon have to set this butterfly free.

After the holidays, brother and sister returned to London in preparation for Georgiana resuming her studies for her final term. From that point on, everything she needed to know would be learned as young people had always learned them, by trial and error, and she would know heartache and joy, success and failure, and the peaks and valleys of being in love.

Georgiana was excited about their return to town as her brother had hired a Madame Delaine who would assist her in acquiring all the clothes and accoutrements necessary for her debut. That decision had been made after his last visit with his sister to the milliner. Seeing his growing impatience, the owner had suggested he employ Madame, who would relieve him of all such duties. Shortly thereafter, the pair began making the rounds of London's finest shops.

For the past year, a departure had been made in Georgiana's education. After demonstrating a mastery of those subjects expected of a daughter of one of England's great families, her brother had agreed to find another outlet that might possibly satisfy his sister's seemingly insatiable curiosity about nearly everything, and she had been enrolled in Mrs. Margaret Bryan's Academy, where she was instructed in mathematics, philosophy, and the natural sciences. Because the academy was located at Hyde Park Corner, Georgiana received her instruction in the morning and divided her afternoons between her German tutor and dancing and music masters.

Each evening, Georgiana came into her brother's study to tell him about her lessons, more or less to get that subject out of the way so that she might discuss the much more important things in her life, such as fabrics, bonnets, the latest styles, etc. Darcy looked forward to their evenings together and their evolving relationship. He was feeling more like a brother and less like a guardian.

"Will, have you ever been in love?"

Darcy was no longer surprised by Georgiana's questions, as

they were becoming a regular feature of their after-dinner conversations. When he first heard the question, he immediately thought of Elizabeth Bennet, but quickly put her out of his mind and replaced the dark-haired, dark-eyed Elizabeth with the first woman who had ever touched his heart, the beautiful Christina Caxton.

Seven years earlier, after having finished their studies at Cambridge, Darcy and Richard Fitzwilliam had traveled to the Continent during the Peace of Amiens, a two-year interval in the wars between England and France, to begin their tour of the great cities of Europe. With letters of introduction in hand, they had traveled from one exciting destination to another, and one of their stops was at the Chateau de Crecy in Champagne where Christina had been living following the sudden death a year earlier of her husband, a British wine broker, who had foolishly walked behind a horse.

The chemistry between Christina and Darcy was immediate and sparks flew. Five years Darcy's senior, Christina was the perfect lover for a young man of twenty-one, who was more than willing to be educated. A pattern quickly emerged where Christina would visit a friend and suggest that an invitation be extended to Darcy and Fitzwilliam, and the affair would resume. Richard found that creating diversions so that Christina and his cousin could be together provided him with his own opportunities for romance. But it had all came to an abrupt end on the road to Pau, a spa in the south of France, when Darcy had received news of his father's death.

"Will, you are smiling. You *have* been in love," Georgiana said, before practically jumping out of her chair and joining her brother on the sofa. "Please, Will. Tell me all about her. Please."

"Ah, if you insist, I shall tell you. She was like a goddess. Eyes like emeralds, teeth like pearls, skin of the purest ivory, all surrounded by a halo of gold, a walking, talking jewel case."

Georgiana looked at her brother and frowned. "You are teasing me."

Actually, that description was very close to accurate. He remembered with great fondness the last time he had seen her—every inch of her. She was standing in front of him like Botticelli's Venus telling him it was time for him to leave while it was still dark. He had convinced her to return to bed, and they had made love again and fell into a deep sleep with his body conforming to hers. When he left that morning, he had no idea that was the last time he would ever see her.

"Why do you say that I am teasing you? Cannot my first love be as beautiful as Helen of Troy or at least as handsome as some of the women in the novels you read?"

When Will found himself at the age of twenty-two to be the guardian of a thirteen-year-old girl, he had immediately sought the advice of Georgiana's namesake, the Duchess of Devonshire, a friend of his late mother's. One of Her Grace's recommendations was to allow Georgiana free rein in the Pemberley library. As a result, she had read everything from Aristotle to the godless Voltaire and the revolutionary Thomas Paine, but she had also read *The Mysteries of Udolpho* and other gothic novels. He had to bite his tongue when he had found her reading *The Insider*, a gossip magazine he despised, especially since he had been included in its pages. The writer had hinted that Darcy would shortly make an offer of marriage to Letitia Montford. Although Letitia was intelligent and accomplished, with a pleasant disposition, she lacked the one thing he greatly prized in a lady: a sparkling wit. The only person who had met his ideal was Elizabeth Bennet.

"Was there really someone as beautiful as Helen of Troy in your life? I mean were you really in love with such a creature?"

"Yes, I was in love with such a creature, but so was every other young man who crossed her path. She was kind enough not to tell us we were all making fools of ourselves. When the armistice between France and England fell apart, the widowed Mrs. Caxton was detained as an enemy alien. I later learned that she had decided to remain in France and married a Frenchman. That, my dear, is the end of the story."

"How disappointing! It would have been much more interesting if you and she had been desperately in love, and it was only because of Napoleon's armies that you were unable to be together. You would have searched for her everywhere, but of course, you could not find her because of the war. And when you learned of her marriage, it broke your heart, and you never recovered from the loss of your one true love."

"Good grief, Georgiana!" and he changed his tone of voice, letting her know that this conversation had come to an end.

Georgiana knew she could press her brother only so far, or he would retreat into silence. She went over and kissed him on the cheek and said "good night," but before letting her go, her brother counseled her, "Georgiana, love is as complex an emotion as exists. There are many reasons why love does not prosper. I was once told by an intelligent lady that 'one bad sonnet' was sufficient to drive love away. So the waters are perilous, and you would do well to know that, because unlike your novels, not every story has a happy ending."

The next evening, when Georgiana joined her brother at the dining table, he was preoccupied with a letter he had received in the afternoon post. Because his brow was furrowed, Georgiana assumed it was a business letter and that he was not happy with its contents, but that was not the case. The letter was from Anne.

"Anne wants to come to London and possibly continue on to Pemberley."

"Will, that is such good news. Why do you look displeased?"

"It is not that I am displeased. It is that Anne never comes to London before late May. The air is too dirty, and with her weak lungs, it puts her health in jeopardy. And as for Pemberley, she has not been there in two years because the journey is so arduous."

"But I think it is wonderful she wants to come. You know we have had a very mild winter and, thus far, a beautiful spring, and you said she looked very well when you were in Kent. But I wonder why Aunt Catherine is allowing her to come."

"Apparently, Lady Hargrove is visiting, and since Anne is not required for our aunt's entertainment, she has agreed to her coming to London. However, she has not thought this through, and I am sure she will reconsider."

"I do not think she should reconsider. Think of her life, Will, in that big house with only Mrs. Jenkinson for company. I was so very glad to hear that she has befriended Mrs. Collins because otherwise she would have no one near to her own age. And as for her health, who is in a better position to determine if she is well enough to come to town? She is, what, twenty-four years old and quite capable of making these decisions."

"But what is this business about Pemberley? I, more than anyone, would love to welcome her to our home, a place with such fond memories for both of us, but it is an impossibly long journey for her."

"But you should let her decide if she is well enough to continue."

"It is not that simple, Georgiana. According to her schedule, we would have to leave for Derbyshire a week earlier than planned. You will still be at your studies, and remember, Bingley and his sisters are to join us. They would all have to change their plans."

Georgiana gave her brother a half smile, which was something she did when she knew she had got the better of him.

"You have already agreed that I have accomplished all my goals at seminary, and as for Miss Bingley, she would drop everything, change every plan, cancel every appointment in order to be with you."

"Oh, you have become a wicked girl."

"You have not said I am wrong. You are just annoyed because I am right. With Anne at Pemberley, maybe it would allow us to have some time together without your being continuously annoyed by Caroline Bingley."

"Georgiana, please do not be unkind. Mr. Bingley is as fond of his sisters as I am of you. I admit I am often cross with Miss Bingley. There is a smallness about her that I have such trouble overlooking. I wish it were not so."

"The reason for Miss Bingley's pettiness is that she is insecure with regard to her position in society. It takes three generations to make a gentleman. Whether or not Mr. Bingley's grandfather was the first generation is subject to dispute. If that is the case, then Mr. Bingley is only the second generation, and, therefore, not a gentleman, which means Caroline is neither the sister nor the daughter of a gentleman."

"Who told you this?"

"I heard Lady Mitchell say that to Lady Arminster about Mr. Bingley. But that is Lady Mitchell's opinion. It is not mine, and it certainly is not yours or you would not be his friend."

"May I ask where you are acquiring all of this wisdom?"

"From you, brother. I listen to all you say even when you do not know I am listening. Although I am not out in society, it does not mean I do not pay attention to what is being said all around me, and I am happy to report that there are very few men who come anywhere near to you in the depth of your knowledge and its practical application."

Darcy laughed and smiled at his sister. What a charming young woman she had become. And he thought how fortunate was the gentleman who would win her affection and her hand in marriage.

"I was once accused of being of a taciturn nature. According to you, I am guilty of verbosity."

"No, Will, that is not the case at all. Although you can go on at length when you speak of certain subjects, such as cricket."

"Ah, but cricket is a subject that merits a detailed description. But as to the other matter, I shall write to Anne and make arrangements for her to come to London, and I shall speak to Bingley. You will correspond with Mrs. Reynolds to inform her of our early arrival." After giving his sister additional instructions as to what should be included in her letter to Pemberley's housekeeper, Darcy admitted that the change in their schedules would be beneficial for both of them. "We have been in town too long, and a visit to White Peak will rejuvenate us and prepare us for the upcoming season."

After supper, both Georgiana and Darcy read quietly in the study while listening to the rain hitting the windows. Hopefully, it would clear the air of the accumulated coal dust that drifted over the city in menacing clouds all during the winter. He still was not convinced that Anne should come to London, but as Georgiana had said, who knew better than Anne if she was capable of making the journey.

"I was hoping to finish Miss Edgeworth's *Leonora* this evening, but I am too tired," Georgiana said, stifling a yawn, and she went to her brother and kissed him good night. Before leaving the room, she asked him, "Is the lady who said you were of a taciturn nature the same one who spoke to you of a sonnet driving love away?"

"Why do you say it was a lady who said I was taciturn?"

"What man would care? It is the ladies who are in need of good conversation."

Darcy nodded but said nothing else.

"I hope I shall have a chance to meet her. Shall I have a chance to meet her?"

Darcy waved to his sister indicating that she should retire, but he answered her question after she had left the room. "I hope that someday you will have a chance to meet her, but that remains to be seen."

Chapter 12

"Lizzy, you have another letter from Miss de Bourgh. She has become quite a faithful correspondent."

"I like her very much, but I am sure she has many correspondents. I know I would if I lived in that big house and with such a mother! She writes a good deal about Charlotte, and, of course, Mr. Collins. But let us read this latest missive and hear what Miss de Bourgh has to say."

Dear Elizabeth,

Knowing of your love for walking in the grove near the gazebo, I am happy to tell you that the first flowers of spring are now in full bloom. There are crocuses and red and yellow tulips, and some of the flowering trees are budding. It will be only a matter of days before they will burst into color. There are robins hopping about everywhere on the lawn, and Mr. Greene is already complaining of the rabbits eating his shoots. I am of the opinion that there are few gardens in the south of

England that are as lovely as Rosings, especially at this time of year.

There is another garden of equal beauty, but it is in Derbyshire at Pemberley, the Darcy estate. So when I read your letter that you are taking my advice and journeying to the Peak, I thought I should write immediately to insist upon your visiting Pemberley's gardens as they were designed by Humphry Repton and executed under the direction of Mr. Darcy's father. They will take your breath away as the many beautiful peaks and valleys can be seen in the distance, and each garden is situated perfectly for some of the best views in the whole of the county.

All that is required is that you apply to the housekeeper, Mrs. Reynolds, who is a wonderful woman, who dearly loves to conduct visitors through the manor house, and Mr. Ferguson, the head gardener, provides the same service in the gardens. If you do not go, you will be depriving both of the opportunity to show off their knowledge of the history of the estate.

"Oh, Lizzy, you must go," Jane said, interrupting her sister. "How could you not? If you had accepted Mr. Darcy, you would have been the mistress of Pemberley."

"I most certainly shall not go," Lizzy said emphatically. "What if Mr. Darcy is in residence? What would he think of me touring his estate?"

"But I should think it would be an easy thing to find out if the Darcys are at home. I am sure when they go to Pemberley they must go right through Lambton, and the villagers will know because they will have seen the carriages and wagons go by. Ask the innkeeper if the Darcys are in residence, and if they are not there, why on earth would you not go?"

"If you are so interested in Pemberley, then you should go with Aunt and Uncle Gardiner."

"I do not have the love of the outdoors that you do, and I have promised Aunt that I shall look after the children. Lizzy, do you regret your refusal of his offer? Is that why you are so reluctant to visit?"

"I try not to think about it at all. I am not happy with my performance in Kent, so I choose not to dwell on it as it serves no purpose."

Lizzy reread Anne's letter. She loved touring gardens and had seen some of Repton's work at Woburn Abbey, and she had heard that Derbyshire had some of the most dramatic landscapes in the whole of England. As she had never been to the Peak, it would be wonderful to see such scenery.

"All right. If the Darcys are not in residence and if Aunt and Uncle agree, I would very much like to see Pemberley. Just from an aesthetic point of view, of course." And both sisters laughed.

Chapter 13

WITH A STEADY RAIN playing tattoos on the top of the carriage, Charles Bingley was organizing his thoughts as he rode to the Strand for the purpose of calling on his brother. With George being the eldest and Charles the youngest of nine children, Charles had come to regard his brother as a father figure, but today it was his intention to change that. He was no longer a boy, and as such, he should be allowed to make his own decisions. And the first decision he had made was his intention of renewing his addresses to Miss Jane Bennet.

"Charles, come in," his brother said, clearly pleased to see him. "It is hard to believe that we live in the same city, we see each other so infrequently, but then you are often in the country, aren't you?"

"I hope you do not mind, George, that I have called here at the office, but with all of the children, it would have been difficult to have a discussion."

"No need to apologize. Seven children and grandchildren clinging to the legs of their favorite uncle is not conducive to conversation. I hope that there is nothing wrong. There was some urgency in the tone of your note."

"No, it is not urgent. I mean, it is urgent, but not in a bad way," Charles said, stumbling over his words. "I probably should say that it is important rather than urgent."

George's secretary brought in a tray and a pot of coffee. There was a coffeehouse next door, as the older brother had developed a taste for the brew and now preferred it to tea. After pouring the coffee, the secretary left, and George asked his brother to get to the point—whether it be urgent or merely important.

"Caroline, Louisa, Hurst, and I have been invited to go to Pemberley with Darcy and his sister, and we have accepted. It is my intention to stop in Hertfordshire on the return trip to London for the purpose of calling on Miss Jane Bennet. I know you do not approve of the lady. However…"

"Why do you say I do not approve?" George said, interrupting. "I have never met her."

"But it was you who summoned me to London for that very reason."

"I did not summon you. I asked you to return to discuss recent events. You could have said 'no,' and when you did not visit, I assumed that you had come to your own conclusion."

"But Caroline said…"

"Said what? We discussed nothing. After Caroline wrote to me regarding Miss Bennet, I asked that you come to London." Leaning back in his chair, he continued. "Charles, you must understand that in addition to being your brother, I have a fiduciary responsibility with regards to the management of our father's estate. You have inherited a considerable amount of money, and I wanted to learn more about the lady, especially in light of your sisters' objections and Mr. Darcy's concerns."

"That is why I have come—to discuss the matter. I mean, I wish to bring you up to date—to keep you informed." Charles took a deep breath. "With regards to Caroline and Louisa's concerns, in the past, they have accused me of falling in love too often and of not being resolute. Of this, I was guilty. However, it has been such a long time since I last saw Miss Bennet. I have been out in society and have met many charming young ladies, but I have no interest in them. My feelings for Miss Bennet remain unchanged.

"As for Darcy, he had objections to Miss Bennet's family. It is true that the youngest sisters are all out in society and are three silly girls. But what, according to Darcy, is their older sister's defect? He was unable to gauge the depth of Miss Bennet's affections because of a lack of animation on her part. George, Darcy cannot have it both ways. He cannot criticize the young Bennets for being all emotion and then turn around and criticize Miss Bennet for not being emotional enough.

"I had allowed myself to be convinced that Miss Bennet held no affection for me, but in my heart, I know that is wrong. I sat with her. I danced with her. I talked with her. And I know that she cares deeply for me, but unlike her younger sisters, she thinks it is inappropriate to make a public display of her affection."

George Bingley sat quietly listening to Charles speak with a degree of emotion that he had never before witnessed in his youngest brother. His words were coming from his heart, and it produced a natural eloquence.

"Charles, as you know, the Darcys are in the very top tier of society, and because of his affection for you, Mr. Darcy wants you to marry well. That is his primary concern."

"But I do not give a fig about high society, George. I do not care that I shall never be invited to join Brook's or White's or to dance at Almack's. I shall tell you in all honesty that I would not want to be a Darcy as it would require me to limit my circle of friends. And if the truth be known, Darcy finds most of the social aristocracy to be total bores and often complete fools. You only need to spend one half hour with his cousin, Lord Fitzwilliam, to understand why."

"Darcy meant well, and it was at my request that he looked out for you."

"What do you mean, looked out for me? When? I don't understand."

"What I am about to tell you must remain in confidence and must not be repeated even to Mr. Darcy," George said, turning around as if the gentleman could be found lurking in a corner. "When Mr. Darcy returned from the Continent upon receiving news of his father's death, he learned that the estate was in difficulty as a result of expansion of the existing manor house and gardens. It was a liquidity problem, which is a common disease of the aristocracy. Mr. Darcy came to me for assistance. I told him what needed to be done. He did it, and the problem was resolved. I was impressed by his calm demeanor, business acumen, and high moral standards. In our conversations, I mentioned that I had a much younger brother who had recently come of age. When I spoke of your love of horses, he mentioned that the Quigleys were hosting a hunt at their Leicester estate, and he offered to secure an invitation for you."

"If I understand you correctly, without my knowledge, you set Darcy up as what—a chaperone, a guardian?"

"Neither, Charles. The friendship that evolved was genuine. As I have said before, you are a rich young man and a handsome one at that. There are so many members of the aristocracy who are stretched to the absolute limits of their credit. They come to me for help every day of the week, but when I tell them what must be done, they leave. So in order to secure additional funds, they are marrying their sons and daughters off to those of us who have no pedigree but who have plenty of hard cash. Mr. Darcy would know who these people are. My only request to him was that he alert me if such a situation developed."

"But, George, Miss Bennet is not a fortune hunter. She is an angel. I was never so happy as when I was with her and never so unhappy since I have been deprived of her company."

"Please do not misunderstand me, Charles. The example given in no way applied to Miss Bennet. Mr. Darcy's concerns were her lack of connections and the difficulty she would have making her way in society. As to matters of the heart, I can assure you I am totally sympathetic. I was fortunate enough to marry for love. Although Hannah is the daughter of my tailor, I have never had a moment of regret. On the other hand, Louisa married for prestige and look what it got her. Well then," George said, standing up, "the matter is settled. If you love Miss Bennet as ardently as you say you do, then you should marry her. So I say, go to it."

As George walked his brother to the door, he remarked, "Charles, I can provide you with guidance, but in the end, the decisions are yours, as are the consequences. I only ask that you not judge Mr. Darcy too harshly. He thinks of you as his brother, and in that capacity, believed he was acting in your best interest."

Charles left George's office with a spring in his step. During their visit, the rain had stopped, and the sun had come out. It was a good omen. After his visit to Pemberley, he would continue to seek Darcy's advice but with the understanding that any discussion was between equals. His only concern was for Miss Bennet. Knowing the financial situation of the family, Charles was hoping that in all these months no one else had made her an offer of marriage and that he had not lost her forever.

Chapter 14

WHENEVER ANNE CAME TO town, Darcy always met her carriage at the inn at Bromley because as soon as Georgiana was with Anne, he would hardly be able to get a word in edgewise. So he greatly valued the uninterrupted time they shared traveling the London road. While waiting for the carriage from Rosings Park to arrive, Darcy had been going over their last meeting in his mind. Following Elizabeth Bennet's rejection of his proposal and her accusations regarding Wickham, Anne had cautioned him that it would be imprudent to write a letter to Elizabeth while he was still smarting from the events that had taken place at the parsonage. But his character had been called into question, and he was determined to rebut her accusations. In the time it took for him to walk to the manor house, he was already regretting the tone of the letter, especially that part where he had written of "the total want of propriety so frequently betrayed by your mother, your three younger sisters, and occasionally even by your father." In his haste to defend himself with regards to Bingley, he had made

Elizabeth's case for his showing "a selfish disdain for the feelings of others." Anne was wiser than he.

Darcy saw through the window that Anne's carriage, with the de Bourgh coat of arms emblazoned on its doors, had arrived. Assisted by Tetley, one of the many servants at Rosings, who would do anything for their mistress, and the ever-faithful Mrs. Jenkinson, Anne stepped out of the carriage and onto the dusty courtyard of the inn. The diminutive figure searched among the faces for her cousin, and a smile signaled when she had found him.

Because so much time passed between visits, Darcy was always taken aback by how frail his cousin was. That had not always been the case. She had been in robust health until she was nearly fourteen when she had become so ill that everyone believed that she would die. The realization by Lord and Lady de Bourgh that they had come very close to losing their only child resulted in the hiring of Anne's nurse and constant companion, Mrs. Jenkinson, a sensible woman who understood Anne's needs better than anyone. But the young Anne, who had raced Richard and Will through the gardens of Pemberley, was no more as the illness had taken its toll on her lungs. After her recovery, she sought to reassure her loved ones that the restrictions on her activities really did not matter because it was no longer proper for a "woman of her age" to be found chasing after boys.

After sharing a board of bread and cheese washed down with a pint of ale, the travelers set out for London. After exchanging news of their families, and with Anne cautioning her cousin that she would not tolerate repeated questions regarding her health, the two fell into an easy conversation while her nurse slept.

"Poor Mrs. Jenkinson," Anne said with a slight laugh. "She can never stay awake when we travel. The rocking of the carriage causes her to fall asleep almost immediately, just like a babe in a cradle."

"She is a wonderful woman. Each of you complements the other."

Anne could hardly imagine her life without her companion. Because of her loving attention, life was bearable at Rosings. Although she knew her mother loved her, Lady Catherine's overbearing personality was so oppressive that Anne used her illness as an excuse not to engage. As a result, she rarely spoke, and because of her mother's penchant for dominating every conversation, she was left alone with her thoughts while her mother pontificated. It was only in the quiet hours after her mother had retired that Anne, Mrs. Jenkinson, and the head housekeeper would talk in her sitting room.

"Will, you have been a poor correspondent since you left Kent." When Darcy furrowed his brow, Anne continued. "Oh, you are generous enough in sharing news about Georgiana, but as to matters that affect you, you leave me nothing but crumbs."

"If you are referring to the situation regarding Miss Elizabeth Bennet, I shall own to it immediately. You were right, and I was wrong. I should never have written that letter."

"And your feelings for the lady?"

"Unchanged. But there is nothing new there. I assume she is at Longbourn with her family."

"I know that she is at Longbourn because I correspond with her."

Darcy gave Anne a wary look. "And pray tell, what is discussed in your letters?"

"Oh, do not look so concerned. I speak of you only in the most general of terms. Since I lead such a sheltered existence and my circle of friends is limited, I write about Mrs. Collins and the friendship that has grown up between us. And then there is Mr. Collins, whose fawning and cooing over my mother provides comic relief. On Elizabeth's side, she always inquires after Richard. She is concerned that Britain will be drawn into the wars on the Iberian Peninsula, and that he will be in the fight."

"Do you think Elizabeth has feelings for Richard?"

"She likes him very much. But both are wise enough not to encourage the other, as his poverty is only exceeded by hers. And in my opinion, there was no spark on Elizabeth's part. But why are we speaking of Richard? You say your feelings are unchanged, so what have you done in these four months to advance your cause?"

"I do have a plan, which is very sketchy at the moment, involving Charles Bingley. As I wrote to you, until recently, Bingley has kept his distance from me. He resented my interference in his affairs regarding Miss Bennet, thus my invitation for him to join us at Pemberley. Once there, I will admit to an error in judgment and will encourage Bingley to approach Miss Bennet for permission to renew his attentions."

"Oh, I see what you are planning. Following this discussion, Mr. Bingley will proceed to Hertfordshire, where he will win anew the lady's affections, and by virtue of your friendship with Mr. Bingley, you will find yourself in Elizabeth's company once again. I think it is a splendid plan with one exception. It separates you from the object of your affection for several more weeks."

"Yes, but I have obligations. I have recently become a venturer with George Bingley, Charles's eldest brother. Along with other investors, I am involved in a scheme that will transform the Derwent Valley into a model for industrial development in England. A flannel manufactory is being built as we speak, and George insists on input from all the venturers. While I am in Derbyshire, he wants me to seek out other possible investors. I cannot complain as the man seems to spin gold out of straw, but I am a gentleman, not a man of business, and all of this is new to me."

"But your plans to arrive at Pemberley in three weeks' time remain unchanged?"

"Yes, you were very specific as to that date, although you have yet to tell me why we must be in Derbyshire exactly at that time."

"Do you think you are the only one who has obligations?"

"No, of course not, but schedules had to be rearranged and…" Darcy went quiet. He could see he was at risk of hurting Anne's feelings if he pressed the issue. But, good God, what obligations could she possibly have? By her own admission, she had a limited circle of friends, and her health placed restrictions on her activities. But he decided there was nothing to be gained by asking more questions. "I was more than happy to accommodate your request, and we will be there exactly at the time you have chosen."

"Perfect."

Chapter 15

JANE WAS WAITING FOR Lizzy at the top of the stairs and hurried her sister into their room. "What did Papa say? Is Lydia to go to Brighton?"

Earlier in the afternoon, Jane and Lizzy had returned from Meryton only to find the house in an uproar. Mrs. Bennet and Lydia were laughing, Kitty was crying, and Mary was pounding on the pianoforte in an attempt to be heard above all the noise. It was then that they had learned of Mrs. Forster's offer to have Lydia accompany her when her husband's militia regiment removed to Brighton. Lizzy immediately sought out her father in a vain attempt to have him forbid the excursion.

"Yes, Jane, Lydia is to go to Brighton. Papa would not be dissuaded. He said Lydia would never be content until she had exposed herself in some public place and that Brighton afforded her that opportunity and at such little expense to the family."

"Oh, Lizzy. Please tell me he said that in jest. Even Papa, who turns a blind eye to the foolishness of his three younger children, must recognize Lydia's behavior barely warrants her being out in society under the supervision of her parents and older sisters, no less being free to move in society in Brighton where the streets are full of officers."

Lizzy repeated all that she could remember of their conversation. "I reminded him that it was his responsibility to check her more exuberant spirits, not Colonel Forster's, but he insisted she is under the protection of the colonel, who is a sensible man."

"But Mrs. Forster is not a sensible woman. She is very young, and although newly married, I am sorry to say that at the ball I noticed she continued to flirt with the young officers who are under her husband's command."

"Such strong words, Jane! How unlike you. But I agree. I saw the same thing and was embarrassed for both of them. But Papa insists that Lydia's poverty will protect her as she has no fortune to be an object of prey to anyone."

"We shall go and talk to him immediately. If he hears our combined voices in pointing out the danger of such a plan, he will reconsider."

Lizzy shook her head. "It will do no good. He sees Lydia going to Brighton as a way for her to learn of her own insignificance."

"How so?"

"To his mind, she will be of less importance even as a common flirt as the officers will find women better worth their notice."

"And if he is wrong?"

"We are doomed."

At that moment, Mrs. Hill knocked on the door, so that she might replace the candles. She could see both sisters were in distress because of Lydia's news.

"Miss Lizzy and Miss Jane, I know you two are unhappy about Miss Lydia going off with Mrs. Forster when the regiment leaves Meryton, but it might not be as bad as you think."

Both looked at Mrs. Hill with hopeful expressions. Whenever something happened at Longbourn, Mrs. Hill was always the first to know of it.

"Mrs. Forster has a bun in the oven."

Jane and Lizzy exchanged glances before Jane asked, "How do you know that?"

"Because Sally Smart's aunt did the Forsters' laundry. You can tell a lot about a family from their laundry, especially the women. What I'm saying is Miss Lydia might not be going out as much as she thinks if Mrs. Forster gets the sickness. I don't think she'd take kindly to Miss Lydia being out dancing while she's eating pieces of dry bread to keep her dinner down. And if that don't cheer you up, remember April showers bring May flowers, and it rains all the time in Brighton.

"And if I may say one more thing, Miss Lizzy, you sitting here worrying about Miss Lydia won't change a thing. Remember what the reverend said, 'Parents have to instill the right principles in their children, but then it's up to the children to live up to those principles.' So, Miss Lizzy, you go to Derbyshire and not worry about a thing. It's out of your hands."

After Mrs. Hill left, Jane asked Lizzy what she thought.

"Well, they've certainly been married long enough for Mrs. Forster to be with child, and if she is as selfish as our sister, then she will insist on Lydia staying with her, which should, at a minimum, decrease her outings and limit her opportunities to get into trouble."

"I imagine it is the best we can hope for," Jane said, but

knowing Lydia, she was not entirely reassured. However, it might allow Lizzy to put Lydia out of her mind and think about her upcoming holiday with the Gardiners.

Chapter 16

When the carriage pulled up in front of the London town-house, Darcy could see his sister peeking out from the upstairs window. In the time it took for Anne to alight from the carriage, Georgiana had come through the front door. Without saying a word to her brother, she escorted her cousin into the house.

"Oh, I am so glad you have come," Georgiana said, taking hold of Anne's hand. "It has been such a long time since we have visited, and I have such good news. I will shortly finish at Mrs. Bryan's Academy, and thanks to you, I will be released early. After that, we will all go to Pemberley, and after that, I will come out into society."

"Georgiana, allow Anne to take off her coat and then show her to the parlor while I arrange for tea to be served," her brother instructed.

After giving Georgiana sufficient time to bring Anne up to date on the most urgent of matters, such as the new bonnet she had ordered just that morning, Darcy came into the room followed by a servant bringing in a tray of cucumber sandwiches.

"Is your mother in good health?" Georgiana asked about her Aunt Catherine.

"Very much so. She is enjoying her visit with my father's sister, Lady Hargrove. They are a quite a pair, very much alike."

"Oh, dear!" Georgiana said.

Anne started to laugh, but her brother was anything but amused, giving her a withering look.

"Will, it is all right. Everyone knows what my mother is like. There is no need to walk on eggs amongst us three."

After that remark, Georgiana quickly asked if Anne remembered her father as she had no memory of him.

"Oh, yes, dear Papa. I was sixteen when he died. Even though I did not see as much of him as I would have liked, since he preferred town while Mama wished to remain in the country, I have nothing but fond memories of him."

"Are the de Bourghs more interesting than the Darcys?"

After Darcy rolled his eyes at her comment, Georgiana shifted her position so that she was not directly in her brother's sight line.

"Yes, they are. They made their money quite dishonestly by smuggling goods in from the Continent. That was the foundation of their wealth."

"Oh, how exciting! Is that why Rosings has turrets? To defend against rival bands of smugglers?"

"Georgiana, defend against smugglers? Smugglers do not launch assaults. When challenged, they run away," her brother said, amazed at the ideas that came into his sister's head.

"No," Anne said, laughing, "the turrets are there because Rosings was built shortly after the Civil War. There was great concern that another such war might erupt, and because of that, defensive elements were included in Rosings's design. But the de Bourghs are not the original occupants. The family's name was Belifort, I believe, but their line died out. Because the de Bourghs remained loyal to Charles II, after his restoration, he transferred Rosings to my family. And I am sorry to disappoint, but it was never necessary for any de Bourgh to man the ramparts. And although Pemberley lacks turrets and arrow slits, it is truly lovely."

"Oh, I know that, and although I dearly love Pemberley, it does not stir the imagination as Rosings does. You cannot imagine anything bad ever happening there."

"Georgiana, would you please favor us with a tune?" Darcy asked. He was uncomfortable with the direction of the conversation, believing that Georgiana was being overly romantic—again.

After supper, the three played cards, and Georgiana told Anne of all the fine things that Madame Delaine and she had purchased in preparation for her debut. As far as Georgiana was concerned, that day could not come soon enough. Her brother was of a different mind.

The following morning, after Georgiana left for the academy, Darcy apologized for his sister's overactive imagination.

"Oh, you should not apologize. She is like a breath of fresh air."

"I am convinced she is writing a novel in her room after she retires each evening."

"What is the harm in that?"

"None—as long as she knows it will never be published. I do not approve of the gothic novels she reads, and I do not understand why the fathers or husbands of these authoresses allow their publication. It is unseemly."

"She is quite changed from our last visit at Rosings. At that time, I found her to be cautious in her conversations and reserved in her manners. That is obviously no longer the case."

"I agree there has been a change in the last month. I believe the alteration is a result of our discussion of that sordid affair involving Wickham. She has convinced me that she would never have married him. Even at her young age, she was able to see through his façade. That conversation seems to have had the effect of clearing the air, and the exuberant Georgiana that lay hidden has emerged. But that is behind us, and it pains me to mention it. So let us talk of your visit.

"You must tell me what you want to do while you are in town, and we will do it. Georgiana has visited Vauxhall and has said that the gardens are 'a riot of color.' The Royal Conservatory has an exhibition, and Mrs. Colbert has asked that she be allowed to call. On the other hand, if you do not wish to do any of those things, we shall stay at home, play cards, drink sherry, and if Georgiana has anything to say about it, play charades."

"We have three weeks, Will. I hope in that time I shall be able to do all you have suggested and possibly more."

Darcy went over and took Anne's hand in his and said, "I am so glad you are here. You are so very dear to me."

"And you are very dear to me, and I want you to be happy. If it is within my power to assist you in that regard, I will always do so."

"If you are referring to Elizabeth Bennet, I created the situation, and if it is to be set right, I alone must do it."

"We shall see," Anne said to herself.

Chapter 17

WHILE LIZZY PACKED HER trunk for her visit with Aunt and Uncle Gardiner to Derbyshire, her sister was watching her closely. Having never been to the Peak District or Matlock or Chatsworth, Jane would have expected Lizzy to be talking nonstop about all the wonderful things she would see in her travels. Instead, her thoughts were obviously elsewhere as she kept folding and refolding every piece of clothing in her trunk.

"We have had another letter from Lydia, but this one is quite different. She is not as enraptured about Brighton as she was in her earlier letters when she wrote of meeting officers at the library and of her new gown and parasol. Apparently, Mrs. Hill was correct about Mrs. Forster, and because of her condition, she is sick for most of the day, thus limiting her excursions. Lydia is chafing at having to stay indoors, even though she writes about visiting the shops, a concert, and a number of dances. But as you and I know very well, Lydia requires constant entertainment."

"I shall be very glad when she has come home. If we are

fortunate, she will return to Longbourn without embarrassing herself or her family," and then Lizzy returned to her packing.

"Lizzy, what is the matter? Why are you not excited about your holiday? You seem unsettled."

Lizzy abandoned her packing and sat down on the window seat next to her sister.

"I *am* excited about our visit to Derbyshire, but I have to admit I have been unsettled ever since my return from Kent. I have had a letter from Charlotte in which she reiterates that she is content to be the wife of Mr. Collins. However, I ask myself, how is it possible for her to be satisfied with her situation when she is married to a man of such meager intellect and who is often ridiculous? But Charlotte says she is content, and I must believe her."

"Are you afraid that you will be forced into a similar situation?" Jane asked. "I know I am. I do so want to marry for love and not just for the protection marriage provides women like us who have no fortune."

"Jane, unlike me, you need not worry," Lizzy said emphatically. "You turn heads wherever you go, and this summer, you will visit Aunt Susan and will be introduced to a whole new crop of gentlemen. You know she is determined to see you well married."

"I think, if asked, Aunt Susan would include you in the invitation. I would be glad to write to her on your behalf."

"As you are well aware, Aunt Susan does not like me as I am guilty of having my own opinions and expressing them. Lady Catherine said something similar about me," and Lizzy imitated the high-pitched voice of Her Ladyship. "'You have very decided opinions for one so young.' She did not like me either."

"Lizzy, you made the mistake of thinking Aunt Susan and Lady Catherine actually wanted your opinion. What they desired was one-sentence responses, so that they could take over the argument. But you will not perform as they wish. If you are to remain in their good graces, you should do as I do. You must say, 'Yes, no, and thank you.' That is all that is required, and you will be assured of being asked to visit again."

"In other words, I should pretend ignorance of all that is going on about me and limit my conversation to the weather and other mundane topics. And I must not read the books or newspapers in Papa's study or visit the circulating library. It will not do, Jane. I have never had any patience for the things society dictates that a young woman must know or do. My French is painful to the ear. Instead of walking in the meadows, I should have practiced more on the pianoforte, and I would have been better served if I had remained at home, as you did, painting tables and making sketches of the dogs instead of playing with them. Unlike Miss Georgiana Darcy, I shall never be considered an accomplished lady."

"And yet, Mr. Darcy proposed marriage. It seems he did not care if you painted tables or made sketches, and words of love sound just as beautiful in English as they do in French. I think he was attracted to you because you were different from the other ladies he meets when he is in London. I daresay he had grown tired of deference."

"Well, I certainly never deferred to him," Lizzy said, laughing. "I do not think he said anything that I did not challenge, possibly accounting for the quizzical expression he wore whenever he was in my company. But I fear I have painted too unflattering a portrait of Mr. Darcy. He is a man of parts, and I fear I have judged him too harshly. If I can but forget that awful afternoon when he proposed and that dreadful letter, there were times when he was quite pleasant."

Lizzy thought back to the conversations she had had with Mr. Darcy and Colonel Fitzwilliam in the great room at Rosings Park. While discussing events on the Continent, Lizzy had learned that both men had gone on the Grand Tour after finishing at Cambridge. Before being interrupted by Lady Catherine, Colonel Fitzwilliam was on the verge of sharing a story about Mr. Darcy from the time when they were in Venice for Carnavale. She would have loved to have known what costume Mr. Darcy had chosen for the masked revels—something with a black cape, she imagined, that would conceal everything but his eyes.

"It must seem unreal to you," Jane said, "Mr. Darcy of Pemberley asking you to be his wife."

"Oh, I can assure you that it is *very* real. Jane, can you imagine the storm that would have ensued if I had actually accepted Mr. Darcy? Looking at it from that point of view, I believe that he is in my debt. I have saved him from the rantings of his aunt and the ridicule of his friends," she said with a laugh in her voice. "But seriously, I have the greatest fear that I will encounter him at Pemberley. He would rightly ask what I was doing there and what would I say? I would be mortified."

"But being the gentleman that he is, Mr. Darcy would offer to show you about the estate, and after you had left, he would wonder if you had reconsidered his offer and if he might renew his attentions to you. And this time, he would receive a very different answer."

"Yes, I can picture Mr. Darcy down on one knee making a second offer of marriage to me," Lizzy responded, shaking her head at the absurdity of her sister's idea. "Oh, Jane, those things only happen in novels. But should such an event occur, you will be the first to know."

To Jane, the reason why Lizzy was so unsettled was obvious. She had rejected an offer of marriage from a man of elevated rank and with very high connections, and Jane recognized that she was part of the reason why her sister had refused Mr. Darcy. Although Lizzy had not said anything about it, she understood her sister's temperament well enough to know that she did not become angry without sufficient cause.

It was true that Lizzy's dislike of Mr. Darcy was based on his unkind words and haughty behavior at the assembly, but that would not have been enough for her to reject out of hand a proposal from a man of such consequence. And as sympathetic as Lizzy was to Mr. Wickham being denied a promised living, Lizzy had not known Mr. Wickham well enough to become so angry as to be dismissive of Mr. Darcy's offer. The intensity of Lizzy's rejection could come only as the result of someone she loved being hurt, and that someone was Jane.

In all these months since Mr. Bingley had left Hertfordshire, Jane had gone over and over every moment she had spent in his company. She recalled their first dance and how he had looked at her. Even while he was dancing with the other ladies, his eyes kept seeking her out, and he would smile or wave. When he asked her for a second dance, she felt something stir within her. In her twenty-two years, she had had her share of flirtations, but this was something very different, and she knew it from that very first evening.

Right up to the Netherfield ball, everything had been going splendidly. That evening, Mr. Bingley had abandoned all pretense of being interested in any other lady, and during supper, he had told her that he anticipated great changes in his life in the very near future. But within the week, he was gone.

Jane now understood that Caroline, Louisa, and Mr. Darcy had worked in concert to ensure that Mr. Bingley made no offer of marriage to a woman who had no fortune, no connections, but who did have a family who was guilty of the most inappropriate behavior. Despite this realization, Jane did not blame any of them. Caroline and Mrs. Hurst believed they were acting in the best interest of their brother, while Mr. Darcy was looking out for the welfare of his friend. She could bear that. But the thought that Mr. Bingley was insincere in what he had said to her was too painful to contemplate. She finally concluded it was simply a matter of the depth of his affection not matching hers. As she had once said to Lizzy, "Women fancy admiration means more than it does."

However that was not the case with Mr. Darcy. He was so in love with Lizzy that he had set aside the very same objections he had raised with regard to Mr. Bingley. His feelings were so overwhelming that the impropriety of her mother and sisters receded into the background. Poor Mr. Darcy! How he must have suffered at her sister's rejection, but a love so strong would not just go away. But what could be done to reunite the two? If only it were possible for Lizzy to meet Mr. Darcy during her time in Derbyshire, but as her sister had said, such things only happened in novels. But one could hope.

Chapter 18

As Mrs. Hill had predicted, Mrs. Forster was soon experiencing not only morning sickness but also afternoon sickness and evening sickness, and it was not sitting well with Lydia. She was tired of holding her friend's hand, soothing her brow, and fetching her broth. Even the weather was conspiring against her as it rained nearly every day. She wanted to go out to the shops and to go dancing and to forget about the ailing Mrs. Forster, but Colonel Forster was making that difficult because he kept thanking Lydia for being such a faithful friend to his wife.

Faithful friend or not, after a week of reading to Mrs. Forster, Lydia had had enough, and the complaints began. Lydia griped to Mrs. Forster, and Mrs. Forster grumbled to the colonel.

"I invited Lydia to come to Brighton because she was my most particular friend, but it seems my condition has proved to be an inconvenience to her. She goes on and on about the weather as if I had some control over how many rainy days we have had since our arrival. Yesterday, when the rain stopped, she grabbed her cloak, and without so much as a by your leave, was out the door and off to the shops. She had given me warning that she would do just that, but even so, I thought it very rude when she actually did it."

It was at times like this that Colonel Forster wondered why he had given up the benefits of bachelorhood to marry a woman who was half his age and in need of constant entertainment.

"Harriet, my dear, I have been told by Mrs. Miller, who knows a lot about these things, that the discomfort you are currently experiencing will pass. In the meantime, why should Miss Lydia not go out to these evening events, which you cannot enjoy at this particular time, especially since you retire so early?"

"I think Lydia should go home. If she does not wish to provide some comfort to her friend, why should she stay here?"

"I cannot agree to that," Colonel Forster said emphatically. "It was you who insisted that Miss Lydia come for at least six weeks, and it is not even a full month yet. We must keep to our original agreement, but I will speak to our guest and see if a compromise can be reached."

There *was* a compromise. Lydia promised Harriet that she would spend each afternoon with her; in return, Lydia would be allowed to go to the evening entertainments. As a result, once again, Mrs. Forster and her particular friend became as close as sisters. Each day, some amusement was arranged for Lydia and Harriet. One afternoon, the regiment's piper came and played tunes; the next day, the two ladies laughed and giggled while they and their friends played at charades; and on the third day, two officers came to join them in a game of casino. One was a Lieutenant Edgar Fuller, and the other, Lieutenant George Wickham.

The request to attend Mrs. Forster's card parties had not

come as a complete surprise to Wickham. Two weeks earlier, Lieutenant Fuller and he had encountered the colonel's wife coming out of a stationery store on King's Road accompanied by Lydia Bennet, who Wickham knew to be a hopeless flirt. While in Meryton, he had paid her scant attention because of her age and her inability to hold a thought in her head for more than one minute. He much preferred her older sister, Elizabeth, who was not only very pretty but who also displayed a gift for repartee that he enjoyed. Verbal fencing was often a prelude to sex.

When his engagement with Mary King came to nothing because her family had whisked her off to Liverpool, Wickham attempted to resurrect his friendship with Miss Elizabeth, but his reception had been cool at best. When he learned that she had visited with Mr. Darcy in Kent, he understood the reason for her indifference. Darcy had obviously shared the story of his attempted elopement with Georgiana Darcy, and with that, any hope of an affair with the dark-eyed beauty evaporated.

When Captain Wilcox came into the officers' mess to tell Wickham and Fuller of their new assignment, he found them slumped in their chairs discussing how their poverty had forced them into a profession they both despised.

"I have a change of duty for you two," Captain Wilcox said. "Oh, don't look alarmed. It seems Colonel Forster's wife is bored and is in need of entertainment. Apparently, you became acquainted with the lady while the militia was encamped in Meryton. You must have put on a good show because you were asked for by name. All you two reprobates have to do is play cards with Mrs. Forster and her guests. It also serves the purpose of keeping both of you away from the gaming tables. It is no secret that each of you has debts of honor to settle. This will put you out of range of the other officers for a few days. They will not dare approach you while you are amusing the colonel's missus."

The captain started to leave but then returned. "A word of caution, Wickham. You're a handsome bugger, and I've seen you at work. You are to use your talents with the ladies only insofar as to flatter and flirt. You are to have no contact with any guest of the colonel outside of the colonel's residence. Keep your cock in your breeches. Is that clear enough for you?"

"Perfectly clear," Wickham said, smiling.

After the captain had left, Fuller let out his anger. "We should have told him to bugger off. The colonel knobs his wife, and we're supposed to amuse her?"

"Don't be an imbecile, Fuller. All that is required is that we play cards with Mrs. Forster and her friends. In return, we dine at their expense, drink Madeira, sit by a warm fire, and ingratiate ourselves with the colonel. Mrs. Forster is pleasant to look at, and if her guests are equally attractive, then it will be an improvement over the ugly mugs we have to look at around here."

Wickham was willing to do anything that would free him from the endless maneuvers and parades he had endured since arriving in Brighton. And although Lydia Bennet was wholly incapable of offering Wickham the intellectual stimulation he enjoyed, the lady had other attractions to offer, and he might be the very one who could convince her to share them.

Chapter 19

As the travelers set out for Derbyshire, Lizzy was determined to ban all thoughts of Mr. Darcy from her mind. It was not in her nature to brood, and she had been doing too much of it since her return from Kent. As the trio traveled north, they visited the university town of Oxford, Warwick Castle, Coventry Cathedral, Blenheim, and Kenilworth. By the time they arrived at Lambton, Lizzy had grown tired of anything that could be described as "great." Once they had settled into their rooms at the inn, Lizzy confessed to her aunt and uncle that she was weary of visiting the manor houses of England's aristocracy. After spending the previous day touring Kenilworth Castle and its grounds, Mr. Gardiner had come to the same conclusion. It was not the manor houses of these vast estates that beckoned him, but their stocked lakes and coursing streams. He wanted to dip a fishing rod into some body of water, any body of water, and be free of another day spent riding in the carriage.

"After visiting so many houses with their fine carpets and

satin curtains and great paintings and enormous fireplaces, I am looking forward to rocks and mountains and listening to rushing streams. I eagerly await our excursion to the Peak," Lizzy continued.

"But surely you are interested in seeing Pemberley, a place you have heard so much about, and it is not more than five miles from Lambton." When Aunt Gardiner received no response, she added, "George Wickham passed most of his youth there."

The last name she wanted to hear was George Wickham. What sort of man would seduce any sixteen-year-old, but most especially the daughter of a man who had provided him with an education and a living and whom he had declared to be "the best of men?" She could hardly bear to think of what he had cost her.

"But Uncle has said that it is not in our direct route and have we not seen every style of house, Tudor, Elizabethan, Jacobean, and Georgian, and they all have beautiful china and fine furnishings and portraits of five generations of Lord and Lady We Are So Very Rich?"

"If it were merely a fine house richly furnished, I should not care about it myself; but the grounds are delightful. They have some of the finest woods in the country."

"And some of the finest trout streams, too," her uncle added enthusiastically. "The Darcy estate is mentioned in Walton's *The Compleat Angler*."

Lizzy knew she was being unfair. Her uncle had been so patient, and despite his lack of interest in the furnishings and collections of these great estates, he had followed his wife and niece about as they toured the manor houses and gardens. In return, all he asked was for one day of fishing. And then there was Aunt Gardiner, who had grown up very near to Lambton. It was only natural she would want to spend time in a village that had been such a large part of her childhood. The mere mention of the Pemberley estate had brought on a stream of reminiscences.

"Every year, during harvest time, the church bells would ring, summoning the farmers to their fields. At the start of the harvest, the local council would appoint one of the most respected men in the village and name him as Lord of the Harvest, a great honor. When the harvest was complete, the horse bringing in the last cartload of grain would be festooned with garlands and ribbons and bells, and as a child, I would run alongside of it.

"There was a tradition that Mr. Darcy and Lady Anne would host a harvest feast. Each table had a goose stuffed with apples, and as I recall, other fruits and vegetables and breads were served with a mild ale. While the guests ate, Mr. Darcy and Lady Anne as well as their son, the current lord of the manor, would walk among the guests and inquire after their families. When the dinner ended, the musicians would strike up a tune, and the dancing would begin. My mother would take my brothers and me back to the house, but we would lie awake listening to the music and laughter coming from the feast long after we had been put to bed."

After seeing how much pleasure her aunt's memories brought her, Lizzy gave up the idea of avoiding Pemberley.

"If the family is not at home, I shall gladly go to see Pemberley." And after having agreed to the excursion, Lizzy went to her trunk and took out a letter from Miss Anne de Bourgh. "Lady Catherine's daughter, Anne, is a favorite of the Darcy family as she is their cousin. I had the pleasure of visiting with her when I was in Kent. When I wrote to her that we might be traveling very near to Pemberley, she told me that I should apply to the housekeeper, Mrs. Reynolds, and to mention her name to ensure admittance. She said the estate is closed on Sundays and Mondays, but is open every other day of the week."

"Well, we have arrived at exactly the right time," Aunt Gardiner said. "The day after tomorrow is Monday, and we will make inquiries as to the best trout streams in Derbyshire and visit the Peak," she said, looking fondly at her husband, "and on Wednesday, we will make arrangements to tour Pemberley."

"*After* inquiring if the family is at home," Lizzy insisted.

"Elizabeth, you are overly concerned about the family being in residence. The Darcys have had visitors touring their house for generations. We could very well be viewing their art collection and at the same time have one of the Darcys walk right by us. It would be as if we were invisible to them; they are so used to it."

When informed by the chambermaid that the family was not at home, Lizzy finally agreed to tour Pemberley. Much to her aunt and uncle's surprise, Lizzy went from not wanting to visit Pemberley at all to eagerly anticipating the event. Mr. Gardiner, not being of a suspicious nature, attributed his niece's change of mind to the whimsical ways of women, but Mrs. Gardiner was beginning to suspect something else entirely.

Chapter 20

DARCY WAS WAITING FOR his sister to come to the breakfast room. He was still annoyed with her for the comment she had made to Anne regarding Aunt Catherine. He understood his aunt could be trying at the best of times, but he also knew she had played an important role in his mother's life—something Georgiana did not understand.

When Aunt Catherine was eleven years old, her mother had died, and her father, Lord Fitzwilliam, had remarried a year later. Darcy's mother, Anne, and her brother, Edward, were born of that union. As in many families of the aristocracy, the children were left to the care of a nurse until they were old enough to begin lessons with a governess. That arrangement worked well for the parents, but it often left the children living lonely lives in a far corner of a country house. Catherine, having already experienced the isolation of an attic nursery and classroom, did not want the same for Anne and Edward. Already possessing an assertive personality, she assumed the role of surrogate mother to the two children, and many of the decisions affecting their lives were made by their much older sister.

When Catherine came of age, a marriage was arranged to Lord Lewis de Bourgh, a baron, who was in possession of a great estate and a pile of unpaid bills. After their marriage, Lord de Bourgh used his wife's dowry to pay down his debt, but when Catherine took over management of the house, money was no longer a problem. She was so efficient a manager, and one who kept watch over every penny spent at Rosings, that her husband removed himself to London. It was only his beloved daughter, Anne, who could coax him back into Kent.

Darcy remembered Anne's comments about her parents. "Papa was a weak man with a pleasing personality who loved me dearly but who could never live within his means. Because of my father's failings, it fell to my mother to manage the estate, provide for the servants, and assume those duties that should have been performed by the lord of the manor."

The great irony was that the same woman who had provided much needed affection to his mother and uncle seemed incapable of doing the same for her own daughter, except in a crisis, as when Anne had nearly died. It was almost as if Anne had been evenly divided between the mother and father, one providing love while the other saw to her physical well-being.

"Good morning, Will," Georgiana said, interrupting his thoughts.

When his sister came to the table, he began immediately. "Georgiana, please sit down. I need to discuss something with you."

Before her brother could begin, she said, "You wish to talk to me about my comment regarding Aunt Catherine. You believe it was a thoughtless remark made at our aunt's expense. But you are wrong. It was premeditated. I wanted to make Anne laugh, and she did. Anne and I have discussed Aunt Catherine on many occasions, and her comments are much more cutting than anything I could ever say.

"I know you are also concerned that I shall be indiscreet when I come out. But I can assure you I shall measure every word before saying anything when in society. You need not worry that I shall embarrass you. I understand the difference between what may be said among family and what must never be discussed outside of our home." Giving him a peck on the cheek, she said, "I am not very hungry this morning, and the carriage is already here. No need to keep Mr. Oldham waiting unless there is something else you wish to discuss with me."

"No, off you go. You anticipated my concerns."

Darcy heard Georgiana say "good morning" to Anne on her way out, and then Anne came into the breakfast room smiling.

"You heard the whole thing, didn't you?"

"Yes, I did. I think you made your point, and the desired result was achieved with such an economy of words," and she started laughing.

"You may laugh, Anne, but no matter how overbearing your mother may be, she deserves our respect."

"I think you are overly concerned. Georgiana obviously knows what constitutes private and public discourse. Speaking of discourse, our cousin is to make a speech in the House of Lords on Tuesday, and I am to hear him from the Visitor's Gallery. He is speaking on British maritime supremacy with particular attention being paid to the Americans and the expansion of their merchant fleet. Will you attend?"

"Can you guarantee he will be sober?"

"Will, that is unkind. He is still Lord Fitzwilliam and our cousin."

"Anne, the last time I saw him, he was outside White's being supported by two of his friends while waiting for a hackney. If this excessive drinking does not stop, Richard will have a very good chance of becoming Lord Fitzwilliam. His daughters cannot inherit, and Eleanor will not have him in her bed for a king's ransom, so there will be no heir."

Anne knew well of Antony's excesses, and it made her sad to think her cousin was well down the road to an early grave.

"I was aware Eleanor will no longer perform the duties of a wife. Apparently, she has taken a certain Mr. Dillon as her lover."

Darcy nearly spat out his coffee. "Good God, Anne! Wherever did you hear that? Never mind. I do not want to know. What a topic of conversation for an unmarried woman!"

"Don't be silly. I may be a maiden, but I am neither blind nor deaf, and I *can* read. Besides, it was Antony himself who told me about Mr. Dillon."

Every day Darcy was witness to the great changes happening in society, and was there any greater proof of these convulsions than his sweet, angelic cousin discussing Lady Fitzwilliam being bedded by an importer of fabric from the East Indies?

Of late, so many things seemed upended, and he knew exactly when it had begun: on the road to Netherfield Park. First, the axle on the carriage had broken, and when forced to proceed on horseback, he had been caught out in the open in a rainstorm. His misfortunes multiplied from the time of that blasted assembly. He alienated Bingley, hurt Miss Bennet, insulted Miss Elizabeth not once but several times, and after following Elizabeth into Kent like a love-struck adolescent, his offer of marriage had been resoundingly rejected. He returned to London believing he would find some comfort in his own home. Instead, he found his sister dancing rings around him and his cousin discussing an extramarital affair with her male relation.

"Is there anything else our cousin shared with you?" he said, throwing his napkin on the table. "You know it was he who told *The Insider* that I would be making an offer of marriage to Miss Montford just as I had decided that I was not going to marry her. And do you know why he is doing this? Because he is being paid by *The Insider*."

Anne understood her cousin's anger, but it had little to do with Miss Montford. What had him so irate was an item that had appeared in several gossip sheets reporting that Will had been seen going into Mrs. Conway's salon in the evening, but not emerging until dawn. The only news there was that Will believed his relationship with the intelligent and gifted widow of a Whig politician was a secret. Antony, who was unembarrassed by his liaisons, thought nothing of sharing similar information with others, even about the man who had repeatedly come to his rescue.

"That was very wrong of Antony, especially since I am sure it raised Miss Montford's hopes of an offer, but on the other hand, Mrs. Conway can certainly take care of her herself."

Will was thunderstruck. "How the devil...?" but then he stopped. "Anne, I have a meeting this morning with George Bingley, and I shall see you this afternoon." And he went straight out the door, not even waiting for Mercer to hand him his hat.

When Darcy returned that afternoon, he presented his

cousin with a bouquet of flowers that he had bought from a flower stall. This was something he frequently did for Anne whenever she was in town because it distressed him to know that his cousin would never have a suitor. It had been her choice, but it saddened him nonetheless.

"You always were the sweetest boy, and that has not changed with the years. So come and sit by me, and let us speak of our visit to Pemberley. I cannot begin to tell you how excited I am to be going. After two long years, I shall be able to walk in the gardens where I can see all the way to the Peak. I am also looking forward to going into the village. Do you often go into Lambton when you are in residence?"

"I would not say often. But when Georgiana and I return to Pemberley for any appreciable amount of time, we do go into the village. My sister is quite the social butterfly. She visits all the shops, compliments the merchants, praises their wives, and pats their children on their heads. She knows everyone's name, and once she learns a baby has been born, she brings the mother a basket and writes the baby's name in her little book."

"Just like your mother."

"Yes, but there is more pleasure in her kindnesses and less of the obligation."

"Does Mrs. Culver still manage the inn at Lambton? She was such a nice lady."

"No, her sons have taken over the management. I am laughing because I have heard many words to describe Mrs. Culver, but 'nice' was not one of them. It is hard to be nice when you have travelers descending upon you at all hours."

"I remember her fondly. When we went there for tea, she always gave us sweets. Do you not remember?"

"Of course she gave us sweets. My father was the lord of the manor, and you were the granddaughter of an earl."

"Will, you are spoiling my memories."

Darcy sighed, another slipup, but added, "I stand corrected. Mrs. Culver meets the very definition of 'nice' in every respect."

"My goodness. How sensitive we have become. It is just that I loved going there for tea. Do you think we could go into the village and have tea at the inn? I would like to do so as soon as possible after we arrive at Pemberley. I am that keen on revisiting places of my youth."

"Whatever you wish will be done. I am at your service."

Chapter 21

FULLER AND WICKHAM WERE sitting in the officers' mess, and Fuller was smiling because, for once in his life, Fortune had shined on him. Not only was he winning at cards, but Wickham and he were still making frequent appearances at the Forsters' house. All they needed to do in order to stay in the colonel's good graces was to continue to kiss his wife's arse.

"Wickham, I can hardly believe we have not had to report for parade for three weeks, all because Colonel Forster's wife is pregnant and bored. Did I tell you Mrs. Forster slipped a crown into my hand yesterday?"

Wickham said nothing because she had been pressing a sovereign a day into his palm for more than a week.

"With the way she flirts, I can't imagine what she would be like if she wasn't expecting. She's already an irritant to the colonel, but I predict she will become a major annoyance." Fuller stood up and asked Wickham if he would like to go for a pint.

"I already have plans."

"Do these plans involve Miss Lydia Bennet?"

"They do. While Mrs. Forster is soaking her feet and whining to her husband about her condition, Lydia and I will be meeting in our continuing effort to get to know each other better."

"How well do you know her?"

"Not completely. But we are getting there. Slow but steady."

With Brighton crowded with the various militias and regular army regiments, along with their families and the types of people who had always followed armies throughout the ages, it was easy enough for Lydia to separate herself from her friends and meet Wickham at an arranged spot near the pier. He found her to be silly, uninformed, and undisciplined, but in every other way, quite agreeable.

"You know if Colonel Forster finds out, he'll have you up on charges."

"To hell he will," Wickham said, sitting upright in his chair. "I've had enough of the militia. The only reason I am still here is because you and I have made ourselves indispensable to the ladies. For three weeks, we have fawned and cooed and amused. While the regiment practices marching and maneuvers, we are having cake and punch. As soon as I find out that our services are no longer required, I will be long gone."

"Alone?"

"Not if I can help it."

Wickham remembered the first time he had kissed her. She had pushed off on him, giving him the usual line that she wasn't that type of girl, but when he had asked her, "Then why are we meeting in secret under a pier?" she had pulled him back and said no more.

With each meeting, she became slightly more liberal with

her favors, and all that was required was for him to speak of marriage. But she had her limit, and she had reached it. As a result, she had become a tease, and he was tiring of it. But there was one reason he continued to meet her.

As a matter of self-preservation, wherever Wickham went, he kept his eyes and ears open. If a merchant started grumbling, he would visit the shop and make just enough payment to keep the owner happy, thus creating the illusion that it was his intention to satisfy his debts. He used the same skills in avoiding angry fathers and brothers of girls he had bedded, and because he was always aware of what was going on around him, he knew that Charles Bingley had fallen in love with Jane Bennet. The romance was of little interest to him. What mattered was that Bingley was a friend of Fitzwilliam Darcy.

It was now in his power to seduce the sister of the woman Bingley wanted to marry. He had begun to make plans in which he would convince Lydia to agree to an elopement, and he would spirit her off to London. Once there, he would persuade her to resign her virginal status, and after that, he would abandon her. Wickham smiled at the thought of Darcy realizing that his old enemy had snuck into his camp and had succeeded in wounding one of his party.

The plan was in place. He was just waiting for the right time to execute it. For the time being, it was necessary to continue courting a sixteen-year-old tease, but there were worse ways to spend an evening.

Chapter 22

It had been a week since Jane had stood by the gate waving good-bye to Lizzy and the Gardiners as their carriage disappeared into the distance. When she had turned around, the four young Gardiners were waiting for their cousin Jane to play with them, but after a week, she was tired because the children required her constant attention.

As they did each evening after dinner, everyone adjourned to the front parlor. While Jane played with the children on the floor, everyone else was otherwise engaged. Mama was doing needlework, Papa was reading the newspaper, Kitty was drawing, and Mary was playing on the pianoforte. Looking around at this scene of domestic felicity, it dawned on Jane that the care of the children had fallen entirely to her. She was being treated in exactly the same way a governess would be. But she was *not* a governess, and she intended to make that fact known.

"Mary, stop playing the piano and start playing with your cousins," she said, rising from the floor. "The same thing for you, Kitty. And both of you will prepare the children for bed, and since you are so proud of your voice, Mary, you may sing to them. And tomorrow, Kitty, you may take the children outside. They love to run, and since you demonstrated your lightness of foot at the Netherfield ball when you chased after all those young officers, you may run with them. I am now going to my room where I shall spend the rest of the evening reading. Alone!"

Everyone, including the children, went quiet. No one had ever heard Jane raise her voice before nor could anyone remember her storming out of a room. Jane was reliably calm, which was an absolute necessity because of their mother's nerves, and had always shouldered more than her share of the responsibilities. She could be depended upon to do the right thing without complaint. What had happened to cause such an emotional outburst?

From the time she had come back from London following Mr. Bingley's return to town, her emotions had been in a state of flux. The initial sadness had been replaced by acceptance and resignation, but then things had started to change. How dare Caroline Bingley and Louisa Hurst pretend they were her friends, and who was Mr. Darcy that he should decide who Mr. Bingley would or would not marry?

When she had finished reproaching that trio, she looked to her own family. Jane and Elizabeth were well regarded in their neighborhood, but conversations regarding the Bennet family usually began with how well the two eldest Bennet sisters performed in public and ended with a discussion of what had gone wrong with the youngest three. And no one could speak of those younger girls without including the inappropriate behavior of their mother. Jane and Lizzy knew this, and there was no doubt in her mind that her father was well aware that three of his children were frequently a topic of conversation in the village.

Behavior that had once earned Kitty and Lydia a disapproving glance from the ladies in town had turned to full-blown criticism and finger wagging when the militia arrived in Meryton. Jane had first overheard it from the town gossip, Mrs. Draper. "Those younger Bennet sisters are always chasing after officers. I saw Lydia drag Kitty across the street for that very purpose." And as soon as Mrs. Draper voiced her opinion, everyone else felt free to do so. On more than one occasion, when Jane and Lizzy walked in the village, the gossiping hens would stop talking. They were all kindness while they were visiting, but as soon as the sisters were out of earshot, the whispers began again.

But the main culprit was outside her bedroom door asking if he could come in. She was shocked at how angry she was at her father. He, better than anyone else, knew of his wife's shortcomings but did nothing to correct them. Instead of providing guidance for his three younger children, he looked upon Mary, Kitty, and Lydia's behavior as theatre. And the combination of the mother and her daughters, and the friend, and the sisters had cost her dearly.

When Jane finally opened the door, she saw the look of concern on her father's face. Because it would provide the easiest explanation for her display of temper, he would attribute her outburst to "female troubles" and look no further. But not this time. Father and daughter sat side by side in the window seat in silence. If Papa was waiting for her to tell him why she was so angry, he would have a long wait. She was tired of him sitting back, watching instead of doing, but then he surprised her.

"Jane, I am sorry for making you so unhappy. I know you

place a good deal of the blame for Mr. Bingley quitting the county on me, and rightly so. As you know, your mother and I are from different ends of the spectrum. She shows too much emotion, and I show too little. But for these past twenty-four years, my mild temperament has served me well, and as a result, I have chosen to overlook the silliness of your sisters because it was convenient to do so. And now I know my lack of oversight has injured you.

"I cannot alter the past," he continued, "but the future is very much in my hands. As soon as Lydia returns from Brighton, you will see changes aplenty at Longbourn. I promise you that. There is little else I can do except to ask for your forgiveness."

Jane kissed her father but said nothing. She feared she might end up telling him what she was really thinking, but then decided that they could not part in silence.

"Papa, all is not lost. I have received a letter from Aunt Susan inviting me to visit with her for the summer, and in that letter she has told me that Mr. Dalton Nesbitt, whom I had met at her Christmas party last year, has asked if he may write to me. By yesterday's post, I informed her that he may. The gentleman is a solicitor and a pleasant man. In addition to his salary, he receives an annuity, which is sufficient to provide a handsome living, and he is worthy of my consideration. I just wanted you to know."

There was nothing for him to say. His reliance on producing a son, who would negate the entail, and his lack of foresight once it was obvious Mrs. Bennet was incapable of conceiving another child, had jeopardized his children's future. The result was before him. Jane would be forced to marry a man for the financial protection he could provide. With profound sadness, he acknowledged the information and returned to his library.

In her prolonged musings following Mr. Bingley's departure, Jane had found fault for her heartache with just about everybody, except Charles Bingley. But that was no longer the case. It was true he had never said he loved her, but it was implicit in all of his actions. During their walks at Longbourn, he had told her he was to inherit a goodly sum of money, which, under the stipulations of his father's will, had to be spent on a country manor that would represent all that was good in the Bingley family. But the money was still in the bank because he had no interest in building a house. He wanted to go to dances and visit different parts of the country, so that he might ride across their landscapes. However, since coming into Hertfordshire, he was of a very different mind. He had looked straight into her eyes when he had said that.

It was true her mother and sisters' behavior at the ball had been improper, but what about his behavior? There was no doubt in her mind that they were in the midst of a courtship when he had been convinced by his sisters and Mr. Darcy that any marriage with Miss Jane Bennet was impossible because of her family, the notorious Bennets of Longbourn Manor. She knew better than anyone of her lack of connections and her paltry fortune. All of this she understood, but what she did not understand was the total lack of communication on Mr. Bingley's part. He believed himself to be a gentleman, and yet he had left her checking the post for a letter explaining his absence for a fortnight before even she had to admit he was gone forever.

From the time she had come out into society, she understood her chances of marrying for love were not good. Considering her current situation, if Mr. Nesbitt proposed, she would accept him. He was a plain man, but of good temperament, and all things considered, she believed she would not receive a better offer. And because she would be forced into such a marriage, she would have been much happier if she had never met Mr. Bingley because now she knew what love was, and she would feel its absence when she married.

Chapter 23

WHILE JANE WAS CONTEMPLATING a future without Mr. Bingley, Charles was rehearsing his proposal of marriage in front of a mirror. He went so far as to get down on bended knee, only to be embarrassed when his man had come into the room. He pretended to have dropped something, and Rayburn got on the floor to help him find an object that his master could not identify by name.

Ever since his discussion with George, things had looked a good deal sunnier. Darcy and he had reconciled, and although his friend's approval on certain matters was desirable, it was no longer a necessity. Darcy did not yet know of this change in their relationship, but Bingley was confident he would understand as he had already seen a change in him since his return from Kent. According to Charles's plan, after a week at Pemberley, he would leave his sisters behind and ride to Longbourn to ask Jane Bennet to marry him. His love for the lady was so profound and so deep and their separation so painful that he could hardly keep his mind focused on the next few weeks. But the days would pass, and his journey to Hertfordshire would be very different from the sad one he had experienced on his return to London. This time, the end of the road was Longbourn, leading straight to his beloved and the endless possibilities of their future together.

✦

While Bingley was practicing his proposal to Jane Bennet, Caroline was in the room across the hall thinking of her visit to Pemberley. Her fear that Mr. Darcy would encounter Miss Bennet while in Kent had been unfounded. Upon his return to London, he had immediately called on Bingley, and during dinner, nothing had been said of that particular lady. Much to her relief, what Caroline had witnessed in Hertfordshire was merely a flirtation, and now that he had not seen Elizabeth for several weeks, her brief spell over him was broken.

Caroline too had noticed a change in Mr. Darcy. When he had asked Bingley if they could change their departure date, she was expecting him to say he needed to postpone the journey, but instead he had asked for it to be moved up. He apologized to her in particular for any inconvenience the change in schedule might cause her, but she had immediately reassured him that it was indeed a change, but a most delightful one. As an afterthought, he had said the request came as a result of a promise he had made to his cousin, Miss Anne de Bourgh. At first, that statement had alarmed Caroline because she knew it was Lady Catherine's intention to see Mr. Darcy and her daughter married. But from the way he had spoken about Miss de Bourgh, it was clear there was real affection, but of the familial type, and not romantic at all.

There was also the possibility Mr. Darcy was using his cousin as an excuse so they could be together sooner. The day after his request was granted, he had sent another note thanking her for being so accommodating and mentioning how eager he was to begin their journey as he found Pemberley to have restorative powers. Was he implying that he needed to repair their relationship, which had been strained during their time together at Netherfield Park? She could now see there was a very real possibility for a union between their two families. Charles would marry Miss Darcy, she would marry Mr. Darcy, and together they would start a dynasty.

⁂

Georgiana was positive something was about to happen. She just had no idea what it was. Ever since her brother had left for Kent to visit Anne, there had been something in the air. His reasons for his sudden departure did not pass muster, and when he had come back from his visit to Rosings, he was much altered. So something had happened in Kent. Was it possible that was where he had encountered the lady who had told him that one bad sonnet was sufficient to drive love away? And she went in search of Anne.

Anne loved talking to her young cousin. Georgiana looked at every day as an adventure. When she got into Mr. Oldham's carriage each morning, she was always hoping something amazing would happen, and on occasion, it did. She had witnessed the apprehension of a thief, a runaway horse, and a manned balloon flying over the city, and now she was sitting opposite to her asking about a mystery lady whom she had taken to calling Miss Sonnet.

"I do not think the time your brother spent in Kent was

long enough for him to have fallen in love. He was only there for ten days."

"Ten days! That is more than sufficient time for someone to fall in love," the young romantic quickly responded.

"Yes, that is true, and I can imagine someone of a less cautious nature falling in love in such a short time, but your brother, Georgiana?"

For several minutes, Georgiana sat quietly mulling over what Anne had said. It was true her brother was rarely spontaneous; in fact, she had never seen it. So she had to agree with Anne that it was unlikely that Will could meet a lady and fall in love with her in such a short period of time. But suddenly, she jumped up and said that she knew what had happened.

"When Will was in Hertfordshire with Mr. Bingley, he was supposed to stay there for at least a month, but one day, I came home to find him in his study, highly agitated, pacing back and forth. I asked him why he had returned so soon, and he said he had important business meetings to attend. You know he is a venturer with Mr. George Bingley, who is very nice but very dull. But he only went to one meeting, and then he went straight back to Netherfield Park. So Miss Sonnet must be from Hertfordshire, and something happened to separate them. And then he discovered she was in Kent and immediately set out to be with her again. And the *denouement* to their love story will take place at Pemberley."

"Pemberley?" Anne asked. Georgiana's reconstruction of what she believed to have been her brother's path to love had winded its way through Hertfordshire to Kent, but nothing had been said about Pemberley. Where had she got that idea?

"I am quite sure something is going to happen at Pemberley.

There is a force driving all of us to Derbyshire, which is why you are here."

Anne decided not to encourage any further investigation. Working with so little, Georgiana's vivid imagination had brought her very close to the truth.

"Your brother thinks you are writing a novel when you retire at night."

"Oh, I am, but it is entirely different from this scenario, as its setting is Pompeii. But as to the matter we are discussing, one of my tutors had the most clever way of teaching geography. He had a map mounted on wooden blocks, which he had cut into small irregular shapes, and we had to fit the pieces together to make a map of Europe. That is exactly what this is like. I just don't have all of the pieces yet."

Chapter 24

THE DARCY TOWNHOUSE WAS buzzing in preparation for their departure to Pemberley. Servants were busy making sure that everything that would be needed at the manor house was downstairs, so that it might be loaded onto the wagons that would precede the travelers.

Darcy had seen how his sister's eagerness to get on the road could barely be contained. Although Pemberley did not have secret passageways and dark corridors or skeletons in its closets to stir her imagination, Georgiana had stated that she was ready to be in the place where she was most comfortable, and in that, they were in complete agreement.

Bingley was also eagerly awaiting the day of departure. Until recently, Miss Bennet's name had not been mentioned by Charles in Darcy's presence, but now he was making casual references to their time in Hertfordshire and the pleasure he had derived from that lady's company. Darcy suspected that his friend was either in correspondence with Jane Bennet or that he planned to visit her on his way back to London. In either case, Bingley would have his blessing since Darcy now knew from Elizabeth that her sister was in love with his friend. Once the couple was reunited, his own plan to win Elizabeth could go forward.

His hopes for success were based on meager evidence: Elizabeth clinging to his letter outside the parsonage and Anne's visit with her in which Elizabeth had stated that she bore him no ill will. If that were the case, then she truly was capable of forgiveness. In the weeks since he had left Kent, he had sufficient time to reflect, and he cringed when he thought about his boorish performance at the assembly, which had set the tone for all that followed. But now that she knew the truth about Wickham, surely she would see him in a better light. It might possibly cause her to reevaluate her own performance and her refusal to see any good in him at all.

Caroline Bingley was especially keen for this day to come. Because Mr. Darcy obviously had a purpose in mind in inviting her to the Darcy ancestral estate, she was hoping he would ride in the Bingley carriage, but she had learned that Mr. Darcy and her brother would accompany the carriages on horseback. Perhaps their traveling together would have been too obvious, and as Mrs. Darcy, she would have to accept that her husband would never wear his heart on his sleeve. Because of concern for Miss de Bourgh's health, the party would stay for two nights with friends of the Darcys in Derby. After a night's rest, Mr. Darcy would continue on to Pemberley to prepare for his guests' arrival. She wondered what surprises were in store for her.

When Darcy went to the breakfast room, he found that his cousin had already been up and about for an hour. Anne was every bit as excited as her eighteen-year-old cousin, and her happiness was clearly in evidence in the glow of her face.

"Well, Anne, I see the servants are already bringing down your trunks."

"I am not embarrassed to admit how much I am looking forward to going to Pemberley."

"I hope you will not be disappointed. I find that memories, especially from one's childhood, very often do not live up to the realities."

"But, Will, I am not going to Pemberley just for the memories, but to make new ones. Besides, you tell me that the maze has been kept up, and I am in such fine fettle that I might very well chase you through it as I did so many years ago."

"You are more likely to encounter Georgiana, Mrs. Hurst, or Charles Bingley in the maze. The last time they were at Pemberley, the three of them spent hours in there, but then part of that was due to Mrs. Hurst, who seems to lack any sense of direction. Georgiana finally had to tie little ribbons to the end of each row, so that she would know which way to turn. Otherwise, we would have had to have gone in search of her by torchlight."

"She is a simple creature, is she not?"

"The Bingleys are a family of opposites. George Bingley is a genius, and Louisa is most definitely not. She told me that one of the things she liked most about Mr. Hurst when she had first met him was that his brother served in the Exchequer. When I asked her how that benefited her, she said she had no idea. She just liked the sound of it. And now she is married to a man whose greatest pleasures in life are cards, port, and sleep. And then there are Charles and Caroline. He is as engaging a fellow as you are likely to meet, while his sister often looks as if she has just sucked on a lemon."

"You do know that Miss Bingley is *very* interested in you."

"It would be impossible not to know, although I have never given her any encouragement. In fact, I have to check myself to make sure I am not being rude to her, and there are many times when I have failed." Looking at Anne, he continued. "Having said that, you are probably wondering why I invited her to Pemberley. You see, there are two sets of Bingleys. Charles, Louisa, and Caroline are separated from the six older Bingleys by six years. It seems that the older siblings bundled them together for convenience, and although they are as different as three people can possibly be, they are inseparable. But I look to Georgiana to keep them entertained. She too is aware of Miss Bingley's interest."

It was at that moment that Georgiana made her appearance, already wearing her traveling coat, hat, and gloves. "Why are you sitting there? Adventure awaits."

On the advice of the innkeeper, Mr. Gardiner had arranged for an open carriage to take them to Pemberley. "Mr. Culver said we shall pass through some very fine woods on the way to the manor house with stone bridges, rushing streams, and a waterfall. Once we pass the waterfall, the formal gardens will come into view, and as soon as we reach the top of the rise, Pemberley will be before us."

Elizabeth was aware that her aunt was watching her. She knew her behavior had been odd ever since the possibility of visiting Pemberley had been discussed, so she was trying to give the appearance of calm. But beneath her placid exterior, she could feel the rapid beating of her heart.

When the coachman pulled the carriage to the side of the road so that they might enjoy the waterfall, she wanted to get out and run ahead so that she might finally glimpse Pemberley. When the driver turned into a topiary garden and pointed out a mother goose and her five goslings and a hedge with only the tail of a fox showing, she oohed and aahed. But if he made one more stop, she was going to climb into the driver's seat and turn the horses in the direction of the manor house.

Finally, she could make out the faint outline of a building in the distance, and as the carriage came over a gentle rise, before her was Pemberley with the sun reflecting off the yellow gold of its stucco. It was so beautiful she almost wanted to cry. Mr. Darcy had wanted to bring her here as his wife, and of this elegant home, she might have been mistress. But to all of this, she had said "no."

When the carriage stopped in front of the portico, Mrs. Reynolds came out and introduced herself, and the three guests did the same. As soon as they entered the foyer, the housekeeper began her tour.

"As far as great country houses go, Pemberley is not very old. The grandfather of my present master, Mr. Fitzwilliam Darcy, tore down a smaller structure that had been on this property for nearly one hundred years, and construction of this house began around 1730. Mr. Darcy's father made improvements to Pemberley by adding the two wings and the terrace and greatly expanded the gardens. The interiors were done by Robert Adam, and the gardens and terrace were designed by Humphry Repton."

"I am surprised there are not more people touring this elegant estate," Mrs. Gardiner remarked.

"Oh, we have many visitors, but we are only open to the public on Mondays."

"But today is Wednesday, Mrs. Reynolds."

"Yes, but you were expected. Miss de Bourgh wrote to me to say that Mr. and Mrs. Gardiner of London would be arriving with a young lady. Are you a friend of Miss de Bourgh's?" Mrs. Reynolds asked Lizzy.

"I had the pleasure of making her acquaintance on a visit to Kent," Lizzy answered, looking at her aunt from the corner of her eye.

"Do you know my master will be arriving tomorrow with a large party, and Miss de Bourgh is with them?"

Lizzy shook her head "no."

"Since you and Miss de Bourgh are acquainted, will you be visiting while she is at Pemberley, miss?"

"No, I am sorry. That is not possible," Elizabeth quickly answered. "Mr. and Mrs. Gardiner and I are to leave tomorrow morning for Matlock, but Miss de Bourgh and I have visited recently so I shall leave her to her company."

Now, both her aunt and uncle were looking at her. It was true they were to go to the spa at Matlock, but nothing had been said about leaving tomorrow. And why was Elizabeth deliberately avoiding someone whom she claimed as an acquaintance? It was time for aunt and niece to talk.

Mrs. Reynolds quickly returned to her favorite topic. "I have been with the Darcy family since I was a girl. I started here as a parlor maid when Lady Anne Darcy was a new bride. She was as gentle a soul as ever drew breath, and Mr. Darcy was a loving husband and father. And their children are just like them. Miss Georgiana is as lovely a young lady as you are likely to meet, and my master is kindness itself. You will never hear a harsh word said against him. His servants, tenants, and all the villagers hold him in the highest regard."

While the housekeeper pointed out a Rembrandt here and a Greek antiquity there, Elizabeth took in the manor house as a whole. Pemberley was all she had imagined and more. There was a simple elegance in all that she saw. There were no larger-than-life paintings of a pack of hounds bringing down a stag as there had been at Rosings or the great battle scenes at Blenheim, and dusty tapestries were nowhere in sight. No, here there was a lightness that carried you from room to room and finally out onto the terrace for a view of the gardens and the valley beyond. She would not have a changed a thing.

"I will now turn you over to our head gardener, Mr. Ferguson, who will lead you on a tour of the gardens. It is such a lovely time of year here at Pemberley. It is my favorite season as the buds on the fruit trees are just beginning to open, and they are filling the estate with their perfume."

Once she met the ancient Mr. Ferguson, Lizzy understood why Anne had said he would be eager to share his knowledge of Pemberley. He might possibly have been alive when Mr. Darcy's grandfather had scraped the original house off the property. The gardener's eyesight and hearing were poor and his gait slow, but the colors and the scents of the flowers were so familiar to him that he could describe every bloom even if they were now nothing more than splashes of color to his tired eyes.

While her aunt and uncle walked to the far end of the garden so they might view Pemberley from a distance, Lizzy walked the paths between the individual gardens. It was all so beautiful, and she felt a calmness she had not experienced since that day at the parsonage when the master of Pemberley had told her he was in love with her. Whoever the future Mrs. Darcy was, she would be mistress to one of the loveliest estates in the country, and she wished her well.

❦

Darcy was looking forward to a bath. It had been a long morning, and the dust of the road was clinging to him. But there was nothing like a ride on a good mount to banish unwanted thoughts. For the first time in days, he had not reflected on his plans regarding Elizabeth Bennet, and now that he had stabled his horse, he must continue to keep his mind free of her image. First things first. He had guests to entertain on the morrow.

He immediately went in search of Mrs. Reynolds, who would not be expecting him until the next day. There was a time when his sudden arrival would have been welcomed by his housekeeper, but he had noticed that as she aged, she no longer enjoyed surprises. She wanted everything to be just so, and so he tried to give her as much notice as possible, whenever possible.

Mrs. Reynolds was sitting in her office going over the household accounts when he poked his head into the room. She immediately jumped up and greeted him with a big smile. She had seen him grow up from a sweet child into a considerate man, and nothing impressed her more than the care he had taken with his sister following their father's death.

"I apologize for not getting word to you that I would be arriving a day early, Mrs. Reynolds. I left my sister and the rest of our party in Derby, and I thought I should come ahead so that I might meet with Mr. Aiken and get some of the estate business behind us. In that way, I shall have more time for my guests."

"Oh, sir, it is no bother. You know how I love surprises. Earlier today, I gave friends of Miss de Bourgh's a tour of the house."

"Friends of Miss de Bourgh? Do you know their names?"

"Yes, Mr. and Mrs. Gardiner of London and guest."

"I do not recognize the name."

"It was not more than an hour ago that I took them into the gardens. Shall I go see if they are still out there?"

"No, do not trouble yourself. You may return to your books."

He wondered why Anne had said nothing to him about her friends visiting Pemberley. If she had only mentioned it to him, he would have arranged with Mrs. Reynolds to have a light meal served out on the terrace.

Looking down at his filthy boots, he debated whether or not he should introduce himself to the Gardiners in such a condition. Looking out of the library window, he saw that their carriage was still in the drive, but that the driver was nowhere to be seen. If he moved quickly, he would have time to go upstairs to wash his face and comb his hair.

From his bedroom window he could see a couple at the far end of the garden, and walking in the lower gardens, he could just make out the figure of a woman, possibly their daughter, who was walking backwards along the gravel path. There was something familiar about her; maybe he did know her after all. But he could not put any face to the name of Gardiner. Well, it was a puzzle that was easily solved, and after looking in the mirror to make sure that he had got all of the dirt off his face and neck, he went downstairs and headed for the gardens.

Chapter 25

ALL WAS QUIET AT Longbourn. Many changes had come about since Jane's outburst. Kitty had stopped whining about the absence of Lydia and the militia, and to everyone's relief, Mary had stopped singing because of Johnny, the youngest of the Gardiner children. While Mary was croaking out a lullaby, the youngster had put his hands over his cousin's mouth and had asked her not to sing. Everyone in the family now owed a debt of gratitude to the four-year-old boy.

For Jane, the greatest benefit was that her mother had stopped asking when Mr. Bingley was likely to return to Hertfordshire. In as firm a voice as she could command without being disrespectful, Jane had answered the question with one word. "Never!"

That evening, after they had retired, Mrs. Bennet complained to her husband about the new Jane. "I do not understand her at all. She has changed, but to my mind, not for the better. She is very short with me these days, and I cannot think why."

"Mrs. Bennet, you truly cannot think why Jane is unhappy?

Allow me to enlighten you. When Mr. Bingley dined at Longbourn, you itemized our daughter's assets as if she was being put up for sale in the village marketplace. At the ball at Netherfield, you announced to everyone within hearing that Jane would shortly become engaged to Mr. Bingley even though he had not made her an offer of marriage. But the mangling of Bingley and Jane's relationship rests with all of us, myself included. Out of laziness or a desire to be left alone with my books, I allowed my two youngest daughters to go out into society without proper preparation. Although she has no talent, I permitted Mary to sing in every venue, and now Jane has paid the price for you saying too much and me saying too little. But I can assure you, Mrs. Bennet, that is a thing of the past. Where correction is needed, I will not hesitate." And then he blew out the candle.

While her father and mother lay in their bed discussing their eldest daughter, Jane had been sitting at her writing desk trying to think of something to write to Mr. Nesbitt. How did one respond to a letter that said nothing? In December, when they had talked at her Aunt Susan's holiday party, the gentle-man spoke at length of his occupation as a solicitor and the importance of putting as little in writing as possible, as it could be used as evidence. Apparently, this rule applied to personal correspondence as well. On that same occasion, he had asked if she knew that an oral contract was as binding as a written one, thus accounting for the lawsuits originated by the aggrieved party of a breach of a promise of marriage. The inappropriate-ness of discussing broken engagements with someone he was considering courting was lost on Mr. Nesbitt.

That letter was bad enough, but the second one was much

worse as he had enclosed a lock of hair. Jane was offended that Mr. Nesbitt was so presumptuous as to make such a personal gesture so soon after they had begun corresponding. But that was not the worst of it. Although she could not account for all the gray in the sample, when she opened the folded paper, she had assumed that it contained her suitor's hair. But then she had learned from the letter that it was his widowed mother's hair. Was this his way of saying that Mrs. Nesbitt would be living with them after they had married? That was something Mr. Collins would do, and she shuddered at the thought of the two men having anything in common.

But write she must, and so she put pen to paper and began, "Dear Lizzy."

Chapter 26

WHILE WALKING AROUND THE gardens, Elizabeth was very glad her aunt had insisted that they tour Pemberley. She loved everything about the manor house: its magnificent wrought-iron staircase, the marble fireplaces with their classical themes, the rooms filled with elegantly carved French furniture, the ballroom with its French windows opening onto a Repton terrace, and the sweeping view of the valley from the first-floor gallery.

When the party went into the music room, Lizzy admired the brand-new pianoforte with its inlays of ivory and precious woods that Mr. Darcy had presented to his sister on the occasion of her eighteenth birthday. When Aunt Gardiner informed Mrs. Reynolds that Lizzy was proficient on the instrument, she had allowed her to play a tune because, after all, she was a friend of Miss de Bourgh's.

After they had finished the tour of the gardens, Mr. Ferguson returned to his work, but Lizzy was free to wander about the estate. In the lower gardens, there was a maze that had been designed for Lady Anne Darcy, and it was she who had been responsible for the animal topiary that popped up in the most unexpected places. Even though it had been ten years since her passing, Mr. Ferguson spoke affectionately of his mistress and shared with the visitors that unlike her neighbor, the Duchess of Devonshire, Lady Anne did not like moving from one country estate to another after the London season had ended. She often said she would rather be at Pemberley with her husband and children than anywhere else in England.

As explained on the tour, the gardens had been laid out by Humphry Repton, who had introduced the concept of themed gardens, but it was the elder Mr. Darcy who oversaw the preparations for the Chinese garden with its miniature temple and cascading waters at its heart. As much as Lizzy admired the quiet solitude afforded by such a refuge, if she had to choose only one place in which to spend an afternoon, it would be in the estate's wide expanses of lush lawn with its ancient chestnut and oak trees paralleling the different paths leading to the lake.

It was a glorious day, and Lizzy took off her bonnet, and with the sun on her face, she thrust her arms outwards and up towards the heavens and spun around in the pure joy of the moment. That was what she was doing when she heard someone walking down the garden path.

Mr. Darcy had been watching Miss Elizabeth Bennet for several minutes. At first he thought he was seeing a mirage, but mirages did not spin and laugh. He started towards her several times but stopped each time. Although he had been hoping for just such a meeting, now that she was before him, he had no idea how to proceed. Still without a clue as to what he would say, he walked down the gravel path towards her, and when she turned and faced him, she went from being a beautiful and animated creature to one who stood as still as any of the sculptures in the garden.

"Mr. Darcy, what are you doing here?" she asked with her voice cracking.

"Miss Elizabeth," he said, bowing, "this is my home," and he looked back at the manor as if to confirm he was in fact at Pemberley.

"Of course it is your home. What I meant to say is, why are you here today? My aunt, uncle, and I were told that the family was away. We would never have intruded on your privacy if we had known that you were to be here."

How had this happened? She had been assured by the chambermaid, the innkeeper, the carriage driver, and the housekeeper that the family was not at home. If that was the case, then why was Mr. Darcy standing in front of her?

"Please do not trouble yourself. I came ahead because I had business with my steward."

But Lizzy *was* troubled. She could not recall a time in her entire life where she had been more embarrassed. What must he be thinking? He had just witnessed the same woman who had insulted him doing pirouettes in his garden. By way of explanation, she informed Mr. Darcy that she had been in correspondence with Miss de Bourgh regarding her holiday, and it was Anne who had suggested that the Gardiners and she visit the Peak rather than go farther north to the Lake District.

"Miss de Bourgh was quite insistent that we visit Pemberley, but she must not have known you would be coming to Pemberley at this particular time. She certainly did not know when your house was open to visitors."

Mr. Darcy smiled and then started to laugh. Lizzy had never seen him laugh, and she thought what an incredibly handsome man he was when he did not have a furrowed brow. But those were thoughts for another time. For now, she could only wonder why he was laughing.

"You are mistaken, Miss Elizabeth. My cousin knew exactly when I would be coming, and I daresay she knew exactly when you would be arriving in Lambton."

At that moment, Aunt and Uncle Gardiner joined Lizzy. She introduced her relations to Mr. Darcy and emphasized that the Gardiners lived in Gracechurch Street because, if she had accepted his proposal, these good people would have been lost to her because of their want of connections.

"I am familiar with that area as my business associate, Mr. George Bingley, has his office in Cheapside within the sounds of the bells of St. Mary-le-Bow. But let us not speak of London while we are in Derbyshire. I consider that to be a sacrilege."

"We have visited many gardens on our holiday, Mr. Darcy, but I can say that there are few that are the equal of Pemberley," Aunt Gardiner responded.

"You will get no argument from me on that point, Mrs. Gardiner, as I am excessively fond of them myself." Looking down at his soiled clothes, he continued, "As you can see from my attire, I have just arrived by horseback, and if you will give me sufficient time to remove the uppermost layer of dirt, I would be very pleased to show you some of my favorite areas of the garden. But while you are waiting, may I order tea for you?"

"That will not be necessary as we dined at the inn at Lambton before coming to Pemberley, but we would be honored if you would lead us on a tour," Mrs. Gardiner answered. "Shall we wait for you in the Chinese garden?"

When Mr. Darcy was out of sight, Mrs. Gardiner suggested to her husband that he continue on and that Lizzy and she would shortly follow.

Turning to her niece, she asked, "What are we to make of Mr. Darcy? We hear such conflicting accounts. His housekeeper, who has known him since he was child, sings his praises, but from what you tell me, he offended many when he was in Meryton and grievously injured Mr. Wickham."

"Perhaps we might have been deceived with regard to Mr. Wickham."

"That is not likely, unless new information has become available that has altered your opinion of the gentleman."

"It is as you say, Aunt. Since we last spoke of Mr. Wickham, I have learned that the injured party was not Wickham, but Mr. Darcy. Wickham gives the appearance of being all goodness, but I can now say with absolute certainty that he is not a gentleman. I am not at liberty to share what I know as it was told to me in confidence by Mr. Darcy."

"This is very serious indeed. May I ask where you were when Mr. Darcy shared this information?"

"It was when I was in Kent. Mr. Darcy's aunt is Lady Catherine de Bourgh, and Mr. Collins is Lady Catherine's pastor. While I was visiting Charlotte at Hunsford Lodge, Mr. Darcy and his cousin, Colonel Fitzwilliam, came for a visit with their aunt and cousin and called on Charlotte at the parsonage."

Lizzy's discomfort with the next part of her story was evident by the change in her voice. "In the past, I have spoken to you of Mr. Darcy's behavior while he was in Hertfordshire. Because he showed such disdain for his company, I felt justified in my dislike. When Wickham took me into his confidence for the purpose of impugning Mr. Darcy's character, I was quite willing to believe the very worst about him. As a result, Mr. Darcy and I had a heated exchange, and being ignorant of Wickham's wickedness, I defended him. Needless to say, Mr. Darcy was greatly offended because he knew him to be a scoundrel. When we parted company, we were both angry, and I have not seen him again until today."

"Well, that explains your reluctance to come to Pemberley, but why did you not tell us all of this?"

"I was embarrassed because I had misjudged both men, thinking well of Wickham and ill of Mr. Darcy, and being wrong in both cases."

"Elizabeth, I can offer no explanation for Mr. Darcy's rude behavior in Hertfordshire," Mrs. Gardiner said, "but these great men are known to be mercurial in temperament. However, I believe we can safely say he has put aside any ill feelings as he has been all politeness, and I believe his desire for us to see Pemberley is sincere."

Before Lizzy could further confide in her aunt, she heard the crunch of the gravel as Mr. Darcy returned to his visitors. When they joined Mr. Gardiner in the Chinese garden, he was dipping his hand in a pool containing dozens of brilliantly colored carp.

"This garden was a particular favorite of my mother. There was many an afternoon when she would bring my sister and me here, and we would feed the koi, as they are known in Japan. She would sit on the stones by the pool and dip her hand into the water, just as you are doing, Mr. Gardiner."

Standing up, Mr. Gardiner responded, "As much as I enjoy

the beauty of these fish, I cannot help but picture others of its species at the end of a fishing line."

"Please forgive my husband, Mr. Darcy," Mrs. Gardiner said, laughing. "On our holiday, he has not had one opportunity to engage in his favorite sport, and that comment reveals his frustration."

"Then you must not leave Lambton before you have gone fishing on the estate. Sportsmen come from quite a distance to fish in Pemberley's streams, and how would you explain to your fellow anglers that you had an opportunity to test your skills in fishing sites mentioned in Mr. Walton's *The Compleat Angler*, which I am sure you are acquainted with?"

"Yes, indeed, sir. I revere it along with my Book of Common Prayer because when I hold a rod in my hand, I am often praying."

Everyone was laughing when Lizzy interrupted to say that they had already made plans to go on to Matlock in the morning. "Perhaps another time, Mr. Darcy."

Mr. Gardiner could hardly believe his ears. "Lizzy, dear, we are speaking of one of the finest fishing spots in England. Surely, we can delay our departure for Matlock for a few days."

"Miss Elizabeth, I would ask that you stay," Mr. Darcy said. "Tomorrow, Miss Anne de Bourgh is coming to Pemberley, and I know how much she would enjoy seeing you again, as she speaks of you with great affection. Also in our party are Mr. Bingley, his sisters, and Mr. Hurst. Recently, your family has been a favorite topic of conversation for Mr. Bingley as he has very fond memories of his time in Hertfordshire. And there is another in the party to whom I would wish to introduce you, and that is my sister, Georgiana."

Feeling that escape was no longer possible and being

curious about his sister, Lizzy agreed. "I would be honored to meet Miss Darcy."

"I should warn you that my sister is suffering from an acute case of overactive imagination, but I have been assured by knowledgeable people that this is an affliction that passes with age."

"You are a wise man, Mr. Darcy," said Mrs. Gardiner. "I believe you will look back at this time with great affection."

Darcy smiled at the comment and then continued. "My party is coming from Derby and is expected by mid-afternoon, so I would like to extend an invitation for you to dine at Pemberley in the evening." And after all three had agreed, Mr. Darcy said, "Now that we have settled the matter, shall we tour the gardens?"

They had been walking for about ten minutes when Mrs. Gardiner said that she and her husband were going to start walking back toward the manor as she was not a great walker. But she encouraged her niece and Mr. Darcy to continue on, which they did, until they had reached a gazebo located on the highest point on the property. From this height, the entire valley lay before them. Gentle slopes gave way to rolling hills before yielding to the wild beauty of the Peak. It was the most beautiful scene Lizzy had ever beheld.

Mr. Darcy's thoughts were not of peaks and valleys but of the lady before him. He could sense the heartache he had felt since leaving Kent begin to ease. He believed that the tension of their first meeting since his proposal had passed, and they could now move forward. To where he did not know.

Lizzy was enjoying the prospect, but she was also thinking of Mr. Darcy. She had said so many awful things to him, and yet, he was being so nice to her. Although she knew there would not be a second offer of marriage, she hoped they could part as friends. When she turned around, she realized that he had not been looking at the view, but at her.

"Miss Elizabeth, you do realize that it is no accident that you are here at this particular time."

"I do not understand, sir."

"This is the work of my cousin, Anne. It seems that once she learned of your intention to come to Derbyshire she put a plan in motion, and it has been brilliantly executed. I did not understand why she was so adamant that we leave London for Pemberley by a certain date, especially since it required Bingley and me to rearrange our schedules and for my sister to finish her studies early. But her purpose has been revealed, and as she had hoped, you and I are here together."

Lizzy now understood why Anne was so insistent on knowing every detail of the proposed route the Gardiners and she would travel on their journey to the Peak, and why she was most particularly interested in the date when they would arrive at the inn at Lambton. Lizzy felt the heat rise in her face. No matter how well intentioned, Anne had placed her cousin in an awkward position. Lizzy did not think it was possible to feel more humiliated than when Mr. Darcy had come upon her earlier, but now she knew that it was indeed possible.

"Mr. Darcy, you have been very gracious, but you are under no obligation to invite us to dine with you at Pemberley. In light of what we now know of Miss de Bourgh's scheme, it would be best if I continued on to Matlock."

"Best for whom? Certainly not for Anne nor Charles Bingley and most definitely not for me. I have been presented with an opportunity to make amends for the inexcusable things I said to you at the parsonage, and I mean to make the most of it."

"It would be best if nothing more was said about that particular day," Lizzy responded, embarrassed at the memory of it. "Considering what I know now, it is I who should ask for your forgiveness for the unkind things I said to you."

"I cannot agree to that plan, Miss Elizabeth. Although I regret much of what was said, there are other things that I would leave unchanged."

Unsure of what to say, she turned away from Mr. Darcy. Could he truly forgive her for her blind prejudices, and could she remove from her memory the hurtful things he had said or written because of his wounded pride? After thinking on the matter for a few minutes, she decided that she could forget what had happened in Kent because a good memory at such a time was unpardonable.

When she turned back towards him, she was smiling, and then he extended his arm. While walking back towards the house, Lizzy commented that she was in agreement with her aunt. "In all of our travels, we have not seen a more beautiful estate than Pemberley."

"But there is so much that you have not seen, including great expanses of the Peak that can only be reached on horseback."

"On horseback, Mr. Darcy?"

"Yes, Miss Elizabeth, on horseback."

Chapter 27

As SOON AS THE Gardiners and Lizzy departed, Darcy returned to the manor house to bathe. While Mercer dumped bucket after bucket of warm water over his head, he tried to analyze what had just happened. When Elizabeth first saw him in the gardens, her first inclination was to flee. Why? Was it because she was embarrassed? Or was she still angry with him for his remarkable performance at Hunsford Lodge? What was the last thing he had said to her? Oh, yes. "I perfectly comprehend your feelings and only have to be ashamed at what mine have been." Good grief! What an arrogant bastard he could be.

Darcy tried to recall what had happened in the minutes after he had rejoined the Gardiner party in the garden. Miss Elizabeth and he had walked to the gazebo, and he could see her face light up at the panorama before her, which had given him the courage to speak of their confrontation at the parsonage. He perfectly understood why she would want to forget that awful scene. Surely, he was equally clear that he was ashamed of what had been said, but that his feelings for her remained unchanged. After he had said that, she smiled, and that meant what? It must be a good sign, or she would not have accepted his invitation to dine at Pemberley. But she had been forced into that decision by her aunt and uncle. On the other hand, would she have accepted his extended arm if she was still angry with him? But it would have been rude not to. Damn it! What did it all mean? Would she be receptive to another offer or not?

"Mercer, have you ever been in love?" Darcy asked while soaking in his bath.

"Yes, sir, many times." When Darcy looked up in amusement, Mercer reminded his master that he had driven a mail coach for many years before going into service.

"I had forgotten. So you had a lady friend at all of the coaching inns."

"No, sir. Not at all of them."

"And none of them ran you to ground?" Darcy asked, laughing.

"No, sir, because I had enough lady friends to know that I didn't understand women and that was not likely to change. So I have been a bachelor for all of my forty-seven years."

"Then you are as perplexed as I am. Does anyone truly understand females? The more I am in their company the less I know. Their behavior is the opposite of everything in the natural order and flies in the face of logic."

"Sir, if you have any hope of understanding them, I'd suggest that you not put logic and ladies in the same sentence."

Darcy finished his bath and went and sat in a chair near the fire and motioned for Mercer to sit down. As much as he loved Pemberley, he found it a lonely place when his sister was not with him. It would not be lonely if Elizabeth had accepted him. She would be here by his side.

Mercer understood that a good manservant was there mostly to listen, but he also knew there were times when the well-being of the master required some intervention.

"I seen that you had guests today, sir. I was unpacking your clothes when they come into the garden. I was watching the young lady with the dark hair and very entertaining she was. She took off her bonnet and threw it in the air and then started spinning 'round in circles. She put me in mind of that pretty young friend of the reverend's wife who came to Rosings for dinner."

"You have a good eye, Mercer. The lady was Miss Elizabeth Bennet, the very same lady who dined at Rosings. She and her aunt and uncle were touring the Peak District, and Miss de Bourgh suggested that they come to Pemberley."

How much did Mercer know? He had been surrounded by servants his whole life, and he knew it was almost impossible to keep anything secret from them. The lives of those abovestairs were dissected on a daily basis by those belowstairs, and so it had been through the ages. But in Mercer's case, he was more like an able lieutenant than a valet, and he kept close watch on his master. No, Mercer definitely knew something.

"Will the lady be coming to Pemberley when Mr. Bingley and his sisters arrive?"

"Oh, damn. I have been preoccupied with other matters, and I put them out of my mind. Miss Bingley will arrive tomorrow afternoon, and Miss Elizabeth will be joining us for dinner."

"Is that a problem, sir?"

"Yes, Mercer. It is one lady too many."

On the best of occasions, he found Caroline to be insincere and manipulative, and that was when she liked you. She did not like Elizabeth Bennet.

"Well, sir, might I suggest that if Miss Elizabeth is still here the day after tomorrow, you should invite her to go riding in the Peak."

"I hinted at such a thing today, but the lady does not care to ride." That would have to change if she became his wife. No, he would hope that it would change if she became Mrs. Darcy.

"I guess that must be something common to the ladies, sir, because, as I remember, Miss Bingley doesn't ride at all. She's afraid of horses."

Darcy smiled. That was true. Caroline had a fear of horses and had since her childhood. That was not the case with Elizabeth. It was just that her preference was to walk. "Perhaps it will be possible to change Miss Elizabeth's mind," Darcy said, smiling.

Chapter 28

JANE AND MARY WERE sitting on the sofa in the front parlor opposite to Mr. Dalton Nesbitt. He had written to Jane to tell her he had business in Meryton with her Uncle Philips and asked if he might call. Jane had not seen him since her Aunt Susan's holiday party five months earlier. He was not a bad-looking man, although she did not remember him as being quite so tall, and she had pictured him with light brown hair, not red. It must have been the light from the fire. But then, she was not trying to commit his features to memory. Other than his extensive knowledge of the law, he had made almost no impression on her at all.

Shortly after Mrs. Hill served the tea, Mr. Nesbitt presented Jane with a small packet wrapped in tissue paper. She cautiously opened it, and when she saw a piece of note paper decorated with dried flowers, she was so relieved that it was not another lock of his mother's hair that she was almost giddy in her thanks. And she went on and on to the point where Mary squeezed her hand to let her know she had said enough.

This whole situation brought to mind Mr. Collins's proposal to Lizzy. When he had asked to speak to her alone, everyone had gone out onto the porch, and since the window was open, every word could be heard. Lizzy made several attempts to get Mr. Collins to cease and desist, but he would not. Finally, she walked right up to him to the point where she was less than two feet away. Mary nearly fainted, thinking that Lizzy was going to kiss him. In words, which she pronounced as if each one was its own sentence, she said, "In no way could I make you happy. My temperament is unsuitable for the wife of a clergyman. Good day, Mr. Collins." She said it with such emphasis that Mr. Collins had backed out of the room and right into the arms of Mrs. Bennet.

After tea, Mr. Nesbitt asked if she would like to walk to the village. With Mary serving as chaperone, her visitor told her of his plans, and they were ambitious. He would not be satisfied with being a solicitor. His goal was to become a barrister and possibly a magistrate. In addition to his business plan, he had a financial one too, which was his way of letting her know that he was capable of providing for her. It was so detailed that by the time they had reached the village, Jane was not sure if he was courting her or selling shares.

On the return trip, he asked her many questions about her likes and dislikes, and he could hardly believe how much she had in common—with his mother. They liked the same flowers and both read Cowper, and their favorite tree was the horse chestnut. But when he learned that her preference in teas was for Bohea black tea rather than Hyson green tea, Mr. Nesbitt knew she was the right woman for him, because was not that also his mother's preference. He was so excited by this discovery that it was all Jane could do not to laugh. The situation was simultaneously serious and ridiculous.

There was no doubt that Mr. Nesbitt was pleased with how things were progressing, Jane less so, but she had to face reality and evaluate her situation with her head and not her heart. Mr. Nesbitt was thoughtful and made a good living, and he had planned his future with exacting detail. But the thing that worked most in his favor was that he had hinted that if they were to become engaged, it would be a lengthy one as he was determined to become a barrister. That would give her the best of both worlds. She would have a suitor, so her mother would leave her in peace, but she would not have to do other things required of a wife. When the nuptials finally did take place, she believed that the possibility existed that they would be happy together—all three of them.

There was no fool like an old fool, and Colonel Forster was feeling very old and very foolish. At his young wife's request, he had invited Miss Lydia Bennet to Brighton to keep her company while he dealt with the logistics of relocating a militia regiment from a quiet village in Hertfordshire to the Channel coast, where they would serve as part of a first line of defense in case of a French invasion. While in Meryton, he had only spoken to Miss Bennet and Miss Elizabeth, and based upon his conversations with them, he had assumed that Miss Lydia, having been brought up in the same household, would behave in the same manner as her older sisters.

His error quickly became apparent. Instead of Lydia Bennet solving his problem, she had doubled it. Because of frequent quarrels between the two females, it had become necessary for the colonel to have his aide arrange a series of amusements. Captain Wilcox had set up a schedule by which some talented member of the regiment came to the Forster home at least twice a week to entertain Harriet and her friends.

These diversions were successful at first, but then Harriet, Lydia, and friends eventually grew tired of the musicians and singers and asked the colonel to arrange for some of his younger officers to come to the house to play cards on Tuesday and Friday afternoons. In order to avoid a return to his wife's constant whining, the colonel once again turned the matter over to Captain Wilcox, relying on his aide to invite officers with impeccable reputations to come to his home to entertain the ladies. Two of those suggested were Lieutenants Fuller and Wickham. Fuller, he knew, was the youngest son of a respected member of the staff of the Archbishop of Lincoln. As for Wickham, according to Wilcox, he was the natural son of a man from a prominent Derbyshire family. Although he had never been publicly acknowledged, the father had provided an annuity and saw to his education, not out of obligation, but affection. Or so he had been told.

The trouble began when Harriet, who was feeling much better now that the worst of the sickness had passed, no longer needed to retire so early. Realizing that it would soon be impossible to conceal her pregnancy, Harriet wanted to go to the theatre and concerts and other amusements that would shortly be denied her. One evening, Harriet had returned home without Lydia, saying that they had become separated when a large number of people had left the concert hall at the same time. Harriet was more annoyed than concerned that her sixteen-year-old companion had not come home with her. The colonel was putting on his jacket to go in search of her when a remarkably undisturbed Lydia came through the front door. He would have thought that someone of such an age would have been upset that she had been left on her own in an unfamiliar town. A similar incident occurred when Lydia went to the theatre with his adjunct and wife. In the crush of people leaving the venue, Lydia again became separated from her party. One time was an accident, twice was a coincidence, but a third time was a plan. And on that third occasion, Colonel Forster was ready, and one of his sergeants had followed her. He immediately reported to the colonel that there was no doubt a rendezvous had taken place, and although he could not identify the officer, he had his suspicions.

When Lydia came home, the colonel was waiting for her. He demanded that Harriet go to bed; he would deal with her friend alone. Lydia denied doing anything wrong. In tears, she explained it was only because Brighton had so many diversions that she had become distracted and had found herself separated from her party, but she would pay more attention and it would not happen again.

"No, it will not happen again, Miss Lydia, because you are going home. I will write to your father in the morning advising him of your return, and the necessary arrangements will be made." When Lydia started to protest, he cut her off. "You were followed, my dear, so there is no point in denying you had an assignation with an officer. We will know shortly who you met, and if he is one of my officers, I will see him flogged on the parade ground. You are not to leave this house nor have any contact with anyone outside of this house under any circumstance. It is entirely up to you, Miss Lydia. You can go quietly, and your father will deal with you once you are at home, or you can make a fuss, and everyone will know what you have got up to and your reputation will be tarnished. I suggest the former."

Lydia immediately calculated that she only had two, three days, at most to act. As soon as her father received the colonel's letter, he would be on the road to Brighton. She needed to contact Wickham to warn him that they had been discovered, and in her note, she demanded that he live up to his promise to marry her.

Once I am your wife, nothing will be denied you. Above all things, you must act quickly or we will be separated forever. Send your reply by Teddy. He can be trusted.
With love from your future wife,
Lydia

At first light, Lydia went to the kitchen where Teddy, the son of Mrs. Forster's laundress, was sleeping in a corner on a pile of army blankets. She pressed a coin and note into his hand and told him exactly where he needed to go. But Teddy could not find Wickham, and instead he delivered the note to his friend, Lieutenant Fuller. Just as assembly was sounding, Fuller was prying Wickham out of the arms of a prostitute, and because he had so much experience in such matters, Wickham had prepared for just such a contingency. He quickly moved to the home of a certain lady of the night and told Fuller it was his intention to bring Lydia with him to London.

"Why are you bothering with that girl? She will only slow you down."

"Because, Fuller, I have invested a lot of time in Miss Lydia, and I intend to get paid."

He also had a score to settle, and although he could not strike directly at Darcy, he could injure his friend, Mr. Bingley, and it might even make Miss Elizabeth regret that she had snubbed him in Meryton. All the anger Wickham had felt towards Darcy had been reignited when he had seen him in Hertfordshire. While every officer in the regiment was dancing at the Netherfield ball, he was in a public house drinking cheap ale. It was reminiscent of his childhood at Pemberley: the privileged Darcys abovestairs and everyone else below. He remembered the day the elder Darcy had called him into his study to tell him that because he was such a bright young man, he had decided to pay his way at Cambridge. In addition, he would support a living if Wickham chose the army, the church, or the law. From years of watching his parents and the other servants bow and scrape in gratitude at any bone the Darcys threw them, he knew exactly what to say. He believed his temperament would be most suited to the church. This had the desired effect, and it was then that Mr. Darcy, in all his munificence, told Wickham that if he did well at university, there was the possibility of an annuity of £200 per year. He feigned gratitude, but what he really wanted to do was grab the old goat by his collar. A lousy £200! He was supposed to be grateful for £200 when he knew that his son already received an allowance of £5,000 which amount would double on his twenty-first birthday. It would have been a bitter pill to swallow even if he had not known that George Ashton, Mr. Darcy's brother-in-law, was his father, but in light of his connection to the Darcy family, £200 was a paltry sum that would barely cover his tab at the local public house.

"This is madness, Wickham," Fuller insisted. "Once her absence is discovered, you will be looked for everywhere. Captain Wilcox will be in a fury, and when he finds you, he will call you out. And as for Miss Lydia, you have done enough damage, and I will not provide any further assistance."

"No need. It's already been taken care of. That little bastard she used as a messenger has threatened to expose me if I do not pay a ridiculous amount of money. He will have his payment, but only after he has brought Lydia to me." Then Wickham placed one penny on the table. "And there is his reward. Nobody threatens me."

Chapter 29

WHEN THE CARRIAGE CARRYING Anne, Georgiana, and the still sleeping Mrs. Jenkinson pulled into the courtyard at Hulston Hall, Sir Geoffrey Hulston was there to greet them. Darcy had known Geoffrey since his schooldays at Eton when they were in the same house together and Darcy had been the new boy to his friend's old boy, and they had been at Cambridge together as well. The Hulstons were first-rate people living in a third-rate house. Because repairs had been neglected by the two previous generations, the Hulstons found themselves picking and choosing which part of the manor house should be repaired first. It was only because of the extra money their property was generating as a result of the wars with France that any repairs could be made at all. But delayed maintenance was not on Darcy's mind when he had written to the Hulstons. His purpose was to secure one night's lodging for himself, as he would be leaving in the morning for Pemberley, and two nights for his party.

The house was nearly one hundred fifty years old and sprouted more chimneys than a street of terrace houses in

London, and pigeons, nesting in every nook, descended at the least provocation. When Georgiana stepped out of the carriage, she looked around at a scene that was custom made to feed a fertile imagination, and to her mind, the best things about Hulston Hall were the thick, leaded-glass windows that blurred the images behind them, giving the illusion of ghostly apparitions moving through the house.

"Oh, my! Sir Geoffrey, your house is…"

"In need of repair, Miss Georgiana. I am well aware that it is nothing to Pemberley."

"No, sir, I was going to say it was perfect."

Mr. Hulston burst into laughter, and after he shared Georgiana's remark with his wife, she had a good laugh, too. But to her brother, this was another example of what happened when a young mind was exposed to the gothic novels that were so popular in town. As soon as a new title appeared at Hatchard's Booksellers, Mr. Pickering would send a runner to the townhouse to let Miss Darcy know of its arrival. Every place they visited that was old, vine-covered, or in need of repair became a possible setting for a novel, and Darcy knew that before Georgiana departed Hulston Hall, she would have the outline of a story rattling around in her head.

The Darcy party had not been inside the house for more than fifteen minutes when Bingley, on horseback, and the carriage carrying Caroline, Louisa, and Hurst arrived in the courtyard. Looking through the window, Caroline could hardly believe the Darcys would know anyone who lived in this gothic nightmare. Anne saw the look of horror on Caroline's face as she scanned the courtyard with its multitude of pigeons being chased by a half dozen hounds. It was only when she saw Mr. Darcy that her demeanor had changed. No longer was Hulston Hall a dungeon, but a palace, where she was being greeted by Prince Fitzwilliam Darcy. Darcy had seen the same thing, and wearing an expression that would have been appropriate at a funeral, he had greeted Charles, Caroline, and the Hursts.

Anne had never met the Hulstons, and she was thoroughly charmed by them. Being the parents of four youngsters, while residing in a house with a leaking roof and falling brickwork, they believed that the only way to get through life's rough spots was to laugh whenever possible. For Anne, whose whole world had narrowed to Rosings Park, the laughter, confusion, and energy of this close family was a source of wonder and amusement, but the Hulstons were not the only ones providing entertainment.

Because of the age of the manor, the rooms were small, dark, and boxy. Even with every flat surface having a candle on it, everyone was cast in shadows. From the far end of a smoky dining hall, Caroline had barely been able to make out Mr. Darcy. Even so, she was certain he had glanced her way on and off throughout dinner. She had squinted so much that Georgiana asked if there was something wrong with her eyes and remarked on how tired she looked.

The following day, after Will had left for Pemberley, Anne witnessed the unfortunate sight of Caroline attempting to befriend the girl she hoped would someday be her sister-in-law. But her behavior was so forced and unnatural that it was the same as watching an actor deliver a poor performance. You just wanted it to stop. Fortunately, for Georgiana, it did. Without Mr. Darcy there to observe her efforts, Caroline realized that engaging his sister required too much effort for too little gain and went to her room until summoned for supper. Citing fatigue, she asked to be excused from the evening's entertainments, and Louisa and she took their leave.

Once Georgiana and she had retired for the night, Anne thought she should speak to her young cousin about Miss Bingley, because if she did not, Will would.

"Georgiana, I know Miss Bingley can be trying, and she is not the nicest person. However, she is the sister of your brother's dearest friend and worthy of your kindness. You must realize that until Will marries, you are the mistress of Pemberley. All the duties required of a hostess now fall to you, and you are obligated to see that all of your guests enjoy their visit regardless of your personal opinion of them. With adulthood comes responsibility."

"I do understand that things have changed now that I am an adult, but what about Caroline and her abominable behavior to the Hulstons? Her disdain for her hosts was so apparent, I was glad that the room was dimly lit so they might not see it."

"I agree with everything you say about Miss Bingley, but you must be better than she is. Do not descend, but rise above so ill-mannered a person. And because I require your assistance in a personal matter, I need for you to be nice to Miss Bingley."

For a moment, Georgiana feared that Anne was going to say she was unable to continue their journey. She did look tired, but not as much as one would have expected for someone with such weak lungs. In fact, Anne had mentioned that the farther she got from London the less she was coughing, so what assistance did Anne require?

"Tomorrow morning, as we continue on to Pemberley, I would ask that you travel with Miss Bingley and the Hursts."

"Why? We had such an enjoyable time together, and you

will have no one to talk to because Mrs. Jenkinson sleeps all the time. How have I offended?"

"My dear, you have not offended. It is that I do not intend to go directly to Pemberley, but instead to the inn at Lambton with Mrs. Jenkinson."

"Oh, Anne! I don't know about this. I really don't. I have been testing Will's patience quite a lot of late, and if I agree to this plan, I shall be guaranteed a rebuke."

"I am going to ask you to test your brother's patience one more time. I have arranged to meet a friend at the inn, and I want to visit in private."

Georgiana found this to be very odd. Who could Anne possibly be meeting? It could not be a man because it was Anne's intention never to marry. As far as she knew, Anne had no acquaintance in Derbyshire, except the Darcys, and then it came to her.

"Does this have anything to do with Miss Sonnet?"

"I am meeting a friend," Anne answered, amazed at Georgiana's ability to connect seemingly unrelated parts and merge them into a logical whole.

"Is your friend Miss Sonnet?" Georgiana repeated, giving every indication that she would keep asking questions until she got the answer she was seeking.

"I am not one hundred percent certain, but it is my hope that Miss Sonnet will be at the inn."

Georgiana was so excited that she hopped on the bed and nearly catapulted Anne out of it.

"Is Will in love? I think he must be. He looks so forlorn, and what causes greater pain than being separated from the one you love? Please tell me about her?"

"That I cannot do," Anne said, holding unto the bedpost. "Until I have actually been in contact with Miss Sonnet, I am very reluctant to say anything."

"What if you do see Miss Sonnet? Will she be invited to Pemberley, so that I may meet her?"

"Georgiana, this requires patience—yours and mine. If all goes as planned, you will meet the lady, and if it does not, your brother will be none the wiser. It is best this way. I intend to leave early in the morning, and it will be left to you to answer our friends' questions. All that need be said is that I have gone ahead to visit with a friend. Please do not encourage speculation, and say nothing that will make Miss Bingley suspicious."

"Anne, I assure you I shall do nothing to interfere with the success of your bringing Miss Sonnet to Pemberley, and I shall worry about my brother later."

After dinner at the inn, Mrs. Gardiner and Lizzy left Mr. Gardiner to prepare for his day of fishing with Mr. Darcy. Even though it was still two days off, his wife was unable to get him to talk of anything other than his upcoming excursion, and so she was abandoning him for more erudite company.

It was a beautiful evening and the air was filled with the scent of the blossoming fruit trees, and many of the merchants had filled their flower boxes with some of the earliest blooms. After they had been walking for a while, Aunt Gardiner finally broke the silence.

"Elizabeth, I do not usually pry into the personal affairs of my nieces; however, your performance this afternoon at Pemberley was so singular, I have to admit my curiosity has got the better of me. May I ask exactly how well you know Mr. Darcy?"

Since leaving Pemberley, Lizzy had been trying to decide how much she should tell her aunt. She had no concerns that she would repeat anything told her in confidence. It was the embarrassment of being so wrong on so many counts that caused her to hesitate.

"When I was in Kent, Mr. Darcy made me an offer of marriage."

Mrs. Gardiner, who had been walking arm in arm with Lizzy, stopped suddenly, pulling Lizzy back with her.

"Am I to understand you refused Mr. Darcy?" Having spent her childhood within view of the Pemberley estate with all of its grandeur, Mrs. Gardiner thought it impossible that anyone would walk away from an opportunity to become associated with such a great estate and its family.

Lizzy knew there was no way to make her aunt understand her decision unless she acquainted her with the whole of the story, and during the course of the next half hour, she explained the reasons for her decision.

After hearing Lizzy out, Aunt Gardiner said, "Although your speech at the parsonage was intemperate, surely Mr. Darcy understands your reasons for refusing him. In Mr. Wickham's case, you were deceived by a practiced liar and fraud, and in the other, you acted in response to the hurt Jane experienced as a result of his interference. If he was still angry with you because of your defense of Mr. Wickham, there was no evidence of it today. And I am both amused and touched by Miss de Bourgh's scheme to bring you two together, but it is for nothing if you do not love Mr. Darcy."

"I do not know what I feel for Mr. Darcy. I have not allowed myself to think about it because a man such as he would not make an offer of marriage a second time, so no purpose is served by dwelling on it. And there are so many other considerations. If I had accepted his proposal, would my family have been lost to me? Or would Mr. Darcy have accepted some family members, such as Uncle Gardiner and you, but not others, including Mama, Lydia, and Kitty? And what of his connections? Would he have been permanently banned from Rosings and shunned by London society?"

"My dear, you take too much upon yourself. If Lady Catherine de Bourgh refuses to see her nephew because of his choice of wife, that is entirely her decision, and she must live with the consequences. Seeing how you already have the friendship of Lady Catherine's daughter should most certainly work in your favor.

"As far as your dear mother is concerned, Mr. Darcy would not be the first to find himself with a difficult mother-in-law, including your Uncle Gardiner, and from personal experience, I can tell you there are many ways to get around it. Either I went to visit my mother or my mother visited when Mr. Gardiner was away on business, and over the years, especially since the birth of our children, they have grown closer.

"As to whether Mr. Darcy will make a second offer of marriage, for a man of his position, it was an extraordinary thing to make the first offer, and given any encouragement, he might very well make a second. So it is a good thing we are to visit Pemberley tomorrow as you will have ample opportunity to observe him in a place where he is most comfortable, and since Mr. Bingley is also there, you may do some good on Jane's behalf. I assume Mr. Darcy withdrew his objections to the match when you made him aware of your sister's feelings for Mr. Bingley.

This presents an opportunity for you to issue an invitation to Mr. Bingley to visit Longbourn. Such a visit might be enough to reignite the embers of their love."

"Yes, you are right," Lizzy answered. "I could do that. Oh, how happy Jane will be if Mr. Bingley does visit. But that will not sit well with Miss Bingley, and I shall see her tomorrow evening." Then Lizzy smiled. "I wonder if Miss Bingley knows that I have been invited to dine at Pemberley?"

Chapter 30

DURING BREAKFAST, LIZZY WAS buttering her bread in the great hall at the inn when she looked up to see Mrs. Jenkinson. What on earth was she doing at an inn in Derbyshire? Lizzy immediately went to her, but when she gently touched her arm to get her attention, Anne de Bourgh's companion nearly jumped out of her skin.

"Mrs. Jenkinson, I am sorry to have startled you. Are you a guest at the inn?"

"Oh, Miss Bennet, you are the very person I was looking for. Miss de Bourgh is in the carriage, but she did not want to come in until she knew you were here. She would like to visit, but it really would be best if you met somewhere where it was not quite so crowded."

"Of course. We shall visit in our rooms."

Ordinarily, Lizzy would have been surprised to encounter Anne de Bourgh at an inn in Derbyshire so far from Kent, but in consideration of what had happened the day before at Pemberley, she was not surprised at all.

While Anne and Lizzy waited for the servant to bring the tea, they did little more than exchange pleasantries, but as soon as the door closed, Anne took Lizzy's hand and said, "Elizabeth, are you angry with me?"

Lizzy shook her head no, and while holding Anne's hand, she wondered how someone so frail could be so determined as to execute such a complicated plan and at such a distance.

"Of course, I am not angry. However, I was greatly surprised to meet Mr. Darcy at Pemberley and embarrassed as well. When he came upon me, I was spinning around in circles. He must have thought I had lost my mind, but even so, he was brave enough to talk with someone who had lost her wits."

"And this first meeting? Did it go well?"

"Very well, I think. He was quite gracious, and he invited my aunt and uncle and me to dine at Pemberley this evening."

Anne clasped her hands together and smiled. "As I had hoped." Then in a more serious tone, she continued, "I have never done anything like this before."

"General Wellington could make good use of your natural talents for maneuvering in his campaigns."

"You must understand that everything I did was on behalf of Will and Georgiana, or I would not have been so brave. I just wanted Will to find a woman who would love him, not for his position or his wealth, but for who he is. When he told me that you had refused his offer of marriage, I was stunned, thinking all the advantage was on your side. How wrong I was! You have touched his heart as no one else has, and I wanted you two to be together again so that he might touch yours."

Anne rose, explaining she had to leave. "Georgiana has gone ahead to Pemberley. When Will finds out that we have separated, he may be very upset with his sister, or he might order his horse to be saddled and come straight here. But I shall see you this evening, and by that time, all ruffled feathers will have been smoothed and we may begin anew."

Darcy had sent one of the footmen to stand outside on the portico so that he might be immediately notified of his cousin's arrival, and if his cousin was not overly fatigued, he wanted to have a word with her about a certain person he had encountered in the gardens yesterday. But when the carriage arrived, Anne was nowhere to be seen.

"Miss Bingley, Mrs. Hurst, Mr. Hurst, welcome to Pemberley," Mr. Darcy said, but in a distracted manner that showed his concern for his missing cousin. "Jackson, show our guests to their rooms. After you have settled in, we will visit in the music room," and turning his attention to Georgiana, he continued, "I need to have a word with my sister—now."

Darcy led Georgiana by the elbow to the office where the business records of Pemberley were kept.

"Where is Anne?"

"Will, do not be angry. It was not my idea. Anne is fine, but she insisted Mrs. Jenkinson and she depart from our planned route, so that she might visit with a friend at the inn at Lambton."

Georgiana was waiting for the explosion. When Will had closed the door to the office, his face was all storm and thunder, and she had expected it to start pouring at any moment. But, instead of the deluge, Will started laughing.

"Our cousin has been very busy," he said, shaking his head in amusement.

"Then you are not angry?" and her brother shook his head "no." "Will, does this have anything to do with Miss Sonnet?"

"Miss Sonnet? Who in God's name is Miss Sonnet?"

"The lady who told you that love could be driven away with one bad sonnet."

"Georgiana, I am very glad your mind is put to use for purposes of doing good, because if it were not, you would be a power to be reckoned with."

Georgiana waited for his answer.

"Yes," he said, sighing. "Miss Sonnet is Miss Elizabeth Bennet of Longbourn Manor in Hertfordshire."

"I knew it! Did you know her only in Hertfordshire?"

"No, I was with her during my visit…"

"…to Kent. I was right again. When you came back from Aunt Catherine's, you looked like a tragic figure from one of Shakespeare's plays."

"Georgiana, I really must insist on some moderation in your speech. A coach with all of its passengers going over a cliff is a tragedy. Unrequited love is not."

"Unrequited love?"

"Yes. At the moment, it is unrequited, but it is my hope to change that."

"She does not love you? Then she must be a fool. I do not think I like her."

"Well, you will be able to make up your own mind this evening as Miss Elizabeth will be joining us, and I shall tell you that Anne likes her very much. It was she who arranged for Miss Sonnet to be at Pemberley at exactly the same time as I was."

"Oh, how very clever of her," Georgiana said, returning to her former good humor.

"But, my dear sister, please remember we have other guests, and I am relying on you to perform your duties as hostess."

"Of course. I shall be on my very best behavior, but I cannot guarantee the same for Miss Bingley."

Chapter 31

As soon as Anne crossed the threshold of Pemberley, she was met by her cousin, who had been pacing in the foyer. Although she had insisted she was too tired to talk, Will would not make way until he had Anne's assurance he could visit with her before joining the others in the dining room. After the agreed-upon fifteen minutes had passed, Will was occupying a chair across from Anne and Mrs. Jenkinson in his mother's sitting room. Only those guests who knew Lady Anne well were allowed to use her apartment, which, of course, included Anne, a favorite niece, who had been devoted to her aunt.

"Will, you cannot always have your own way," Anne said as soon as Mrs. Jenkinson left the room. "You demand an audience, and I must oblige you or you will be cross with me."

"Have my own way? I cannot remember the last time I had my own way. I have been repeatedly outflanked by my female relations. And since it was you who had arranged for Miss Elizabeth Bennet and me to be at Pemberley at exactly the same time, I look to you in order to know how to proceed."

"What do you want to know?" Anne was not really annoyed. In fact, she was relieved that her cousin was not angry considering how he had been manipulated.

"What do I want to know? I want to know everything!"

"Then you will be disappointed as I have little to say. I was not with Elizabeth for more than ten minutes for fear your anger would fall upon Georgiana."

"I am not angry with either of you. I am, however, a little disconcerted that you embarked on such an elaborate scheme after I had told you I already had a plan in place."

"Your plan was terrible. I have saved you weeks of anxiety about Elizabeth. You must own to it, Will. My plan was better than yours."

Darcy had to admit his cousin's efforts had shortened the timeline considerably. "Let us not quarrel, my dear cousin. Will you kindly share with me what Elizabeth *did* say?"

"Apparently, when you came upon her in the garden she was spinning in circles, and she was concerned you might think she had lost her mind."

Will laughed. "Not at all. I am well aware of the lady's great love of Nature. I knew exactly what she was doing."

"The only other thing she had to say was that she found you to be very gracious and was looking forward to dining at Pemberley this evening."

"But was there nothing to be discerned in her demeanor?"

"Of course, there was a noticeable difference to me. The last time I saw her was immediately after she had rejected your proposal, and so, naturally, she was ill at ease when discussing you. However, I detected no such uneasiness in our short time together. I do not think you have anything to worry about, and you will be able to decide for yourself in a matter of hours."

Things were not going as Caroline had planned. First, Miss Darcy asked if she could ride in their carriage, which limited what she could say to Louisa, and Caroline did not trust her. When asked why Miss de Bourgh had set off on her own, all she would say was that her cousin had business in Lambton. A twenty-five-year-old spinster, a virtual recluse, who lived in Kent, had business in Lambton? It was all very suspicious.

But as soon as the carriage had pulled up in front of Pemberley, Mr. Darcy was out the door welcoming them to his home. His enthusiasm over her arrival was palpable, and she thought this might be the visit when their courtship would begin; that is, until Mr. Darcy realized that Anne was not in the carriage. After that, he had all but pushed his guests up the stairs to their rooms, so that he might speak to his sister. What had Anne and Georgiana got up to that had caused such a reaction? She did not like any of this.

However, her mood again shifted when the Hursts and she came downstairs. Waiting for them in the foyer was Miss Darcy and Mr. Darcy, and he had escorted her into the dining room where Charles was already seated. Both of their hosts seemed to be in excellent spirits, so it would seem that whatever had prompted the scene in the foyer was of no lasting consequence.

After they were seated, Miss Bingley immediately praised Pemberley. "It is even more beautiful than I remembered. I have often told my brother that when he builds his manor house it should be in the style of Pemberley."

"But closer to London, if I recall correctly, Miss Bingley."

"I think I have changed my mind about that, Mr. Darcy. As long as one has a house in town, then the country house should be far removed, so that one may forget all the tumult of the city. And who would not want to spend as much of the summer as possible at such a beautiful estate? Your taste is exquisite."

Georgiana stifled a groan. If this was an example of what would be discussed during Miss Bingley's visit, the days would drag on and on and on. She anticipated spending a good deal of time on horseback.

"Caroline, I don't think Darcy had anything to do with the design of Pemberley," Charles said. And turning to his friend, he added, "Darcy, didn't you tell me that your grandfather designed the manor house, and your father worked with Repton on the gardens?"

"Yes, that is correct. There is nothing new on my watch. The only thing I have done is to see to the repair of the roof. The servants had grown tired of moving buckets around during a heavy rain."

"My brother was being quite ungenerous with his comment, Mr. Darcy," Caroline said, glaring at Charles. "Seeing to the proper maintenance of an estate is no small matter. One only has to look at Hulston Hall." She shuddered at the memory.

"But, Caroline, the Hulstons are very nice people and excellent hosts," Bingley said.

"The one has nothing to do with the other, Charles. Nice people can live in hovels. It is simply a matter of setting priorities. For example, one might have to choose between repairing falling brickwork or the purchase of a pack of hounds."

If Anne had not been the daughter of Lady Catherine

de Bourgh, she would have been amazed at Caroline's tone deafness. Just as her mother was oblivious to how her words insulted and injured, so it was with Caroline. If she had been less self-absorbed, she would have noticed that Georgiana was offended by her reference to the Hulstons, and Will was doing a slow burn.

"Will, I must correct you regarding Pemberley," Anne said. "There is something new here, your gift to Georgiana of that beautiful pianoforte. And, Miss Bingley, I understand that you are an accomplished musician. We would be delighted if you would favor us with a display this evening as we are to have additional visitors. I believe you are acquainted with them. Am I correct, Will?"

"Yes, I was just about to bring the subject up. Mr. and Mrs. Gardiner of London are visiting the Peak, and with them is their niece, Miss Elizabeth Bennet. They are staying at the inn at Lambton, and they have agreed to dine with us this evening."

The result was as expected. Louisa looked confused, Caroline's jaw dropped, and Bingley just about jumped out of his chair.

"Darcy, are you saying that Miss Elizabeth Bennet is but five miles from here?"

"Yes, she was here yesterday touring the house."

"Well, I shall visit immediately," Charles said enthusiastically.

"Bingley, she will be at Pemberley in a matter of hours. It is not necessary," Darcy insisted.

"I am sure they will not come before 8:00, and that is five hours from now. I was hoping to ride before supper anyway, and since Montcalm is in need of exercise, I shall ride to Lambton as soon as our meal is finished."

"You are too hasty," Darcy cautioned his friend. "Miss Elizabeth and the Gardiners are here on holiday. Do you really think they are sitting in their rooms on such a beautiful day?"

"But, Will, I think Mr. Bingley may proceed with some hope of success," Anne remarked. "Surely, the Gardiners and Miss Elizabeth will want to return early to the inn to prepare for their engagement with us."

"I should like to go too," Georgiana said, adding to the confusion. "I am the only one who has not met Miss Bennet and the Gardiners."

"There you have it, Darcy," Charles said. "Your sister and I shall go to Lambton."

"Charles, what are you thinking?" his sister asked. "If Miss Darcy joins you, how can you exercise Montcalm? You will have to go in a phaeton."

"I am afraid that is not possible as the phaeton is being repaired," Darcy interjected. Caroline was smirking at her brother when he continued, "But I can order the carriage, and I shall go with you. But it will have to be a short visit as we must allow our guests time to prepare for this evening."

"Perhaps Miss Bingley and Mrs. Hurst would like to join us," Georgiana said. Anne shook her head at her cousin, but Georgiana ignored her. "We now have a milliner in the village from Bristol, and they may wish to visit her shop."

Caroline stared at Georgiana. A milliner from Bristol? What next? Picking out calico at the draper's shop? Besides, she would not go one step out of her way to meet Miss Elizabeth Bennet, and since Mr. Darcy had been opposed to the idea of going to the inn, she could stay at Pemberley free of any concerns regarding Mr. Darcy and Eliza Bennet meeting again.

"That is very kind of you, Miss Darcy. But I think Louisa and I will remain with Mr. Hurst and Miss de Bourgh."

"Then it is settled," Darcy said, silently thanking Charles.

After the two gentlemen and Miss Darcy departed, Caroline quickly went to work, and the knives came out. "When we were in Hertfordshire, Louisa and I were told that Miss Elizabeth was considered to be a beauty. She looks well enough, but a beauty? And all of her dresses were out of fashion, and the colors she chose, especially yellow, did not complement her complexion in the least.

"And, Louisa, do you remember when she visited her sister at Netherfield Park? Miss Bennet had fallen ill, and her sister insisted on nursing her and remained for days. She greatly irritated Mr. Darcy. They came very close to having words on a number of occasions. I believe you knew her in Kent, Miss de Bourgh. What was your impression of the lady?"

"I did notice that at least two of her dresses had yellow in them as well as a bonnet, and she seemed to be fond of roses. But now that you mention it, Miss Bingley, I do recall Mr. Darcy and she did disagree on one matter."

"Yes," Caroline said eagerly.

"They were discussing the different bathing resorts, and if I recall correctly, they were unable to agree on whether Weymouth was better than Lyme. By the end of the evening, no agreement had been reached."

"Perhaps, Miss de Bourgh, we should take advantage of our hosts' absence and return to our rooms to rest," Caroline suggested. If that was the best Miss de Bourgh could do, then she might as well be sleeping.

Anne agreed, and once she reached her room, she shared her exchange with Mrs. Jenkinson, and they had a good laugh at Caroline's expense.

Although Darcy had ordered the carriage, Charles insisted on riding horseback. It had been months since he had had an opportunity to ride one of his favorite horses, a splendid hunter he had personally trained. And totally out of character for the chatty Georgiana, she was quiet on the ride to Lambton, and it provided her brother with an opportunity to think about Elizabeth, who was once again inhabiting his dreams. At Hulston Hall, Elizabeth had come to him clothed in a gossamer night shift that left nothing to the imagination, and she had allowed him to undress her. Once she had joined him in bed, she slid beneath him in an effortless motion, and he was just about to enter her when the damn cock had started crowing. "I'll have that bird for breakfast," he had shouted, bringing a startled Mercer running into the room. Darcy smiled at the memory, but at the time, he had found little humor in his situation.

When they arrived at the inn, he was almost hoping Elizabeth would not be there. His preference would have been to meet her again at Pemberley where he was always at his best. The gardens, the views, the clean air, and the scents of spring were a tonic for him and never failed to restore his spirits. But while he was in Lambton, he was the lord of the manor, and as such, he must visit and greet and acknowledge and listen, but with privilege came responsibility, and he always did his duty.

Bingley rode on ahead, and when Georgiana and he got out of the carriage, Charles had already made inquiries and learned that the party had just returned from an excursion arranged by the inn.

"Darcy, they are definitely in their rooms, so I have sent word that we are here."

Georgiana rested her hand on her brother's arm. "I am finally to meet Miss Sonnet. I might possibly be more nervous than you."

Good grief! Was it that obvious?

When they went into the anteroom, the first person Darcy saw was Elizabeth with her hair hanging loosely about her bare shoulders, and he quickly crossed the room, took her in his arms, and began kissing her and was lifting her onto the table when, alas, reality returned. He had heard Bingley telling Elizabeth how wonderful it was to see her again and had mentioned the exact date on which they were last together. When Bingley finally stopped talking, he asked Elizabeth if he might introduce his sister.

"Miss Elizabeth, I am very glad to make your acquaintance as I have heard so much about you," Georgiana said. "Well, actually, I did not even know of your existence until today. But you are exactly as I imagined you to be," and looking at her brother said, "Oh, don't mind me."

"I am pleased to meet you, Miss Darcy," Lizzy said, smiling at the engaging young woman before her. "Your brother speaks of you with great affection and marvels at your talent on the pianoforte. I hope this evening you will favor us with a performance."

"Oh, gladly, as I truly enjoy playing, but I cannot sing a note. My brother tells me you have a very fine voice."

"Well, I am very flattered by his praise because Mr. Darcy is my harshest critic," and when she turned to gauge his response, she found him looking at her in such a way that made her want to touch his face.

"I might say the same about you, Miss Elizabeth. I believe I fell particularly short of the mark at an assembly in Meryton."

"It is as you say. But none of us is perfect, Mr. Darcy, and you definitely improve upon further acquaintance." She would have said more, but Charles Bingley was craving her attention.

"Miss Elizabeth, may I inquire after your family? Are your parents well? And all your sisters? And Miss Bennet? Of course, Miss Bennet is one of your sisters, so I have already asked that question."

"All is well at Longbourn, Mr. Bingley. Just today, I received a letter from Jane, and she tells me that everyone is in good health."

"A letter from Miss Bennet. Very good. Just as I had hoped."

Before Bingley could further trip on his tongue, Darcy interrupted to say they needed to return to Pemberley. After greeting the Culvers, the owners of the inn, and chatting with the villagers who had gathered around him, Georgiana and he were finally allowed to leave. On the ride home, Darcy went over in his mind all that had transpired and felt reassured. The damage he had done in Kent was not irreparable. It was possible he had been given a second chance.

Chapter 32

ELIZABETH JOINED HER AUNT and uncle in the front room and spun around so that they might comment on her dress and hair.

"Truly lovely, my dear," her uncle said. "But I shall leave you ladies to compliment each other, and I shall have the carriage brought 'round."

"If I had known I was to see Mr. Bingley and Mr. Darcy on our visit, I would have brought another dress. They have seen this frock a number of times and look at the creases," Elizabeth said, pulling the fabric away from her body to examine just how bad the wrinkles were. "I am sure all of the ladies will be wearing the finest silk, while I wear muslin."

"There is nothing wrong with muslin," Aunt Gardiner said, "and surely they would not expect you to pack your finest dresses to go on a tour of the countryside. Besides, a dress is only good for a first impression. It is the person in the dress that matters, and if your reception is half as warm at Pemberley as it was this morning, then you have nothing to be concerned about."

"Yes, it has been a pleasant day. I liked Miss Darcy very

much, and it was wonderful to see Mr. Bingley again. I have hopes there, Aunt. As soon as he learned that we were at the inn, he came immediately, and you must have noticed how he twice asked after Jane. I am confident that Jane and he will have a courtship after all."

"And what about you, Elizabeth?"

"I shall wait for events to unfold," she said, without any of the confidence she felt on behalf of her sister.

"I understand your caution, but I believe Mr. Darcy's interest in you could not be mistaken."

"Nevertheless, I shall remain on guard because I saw how hurt Jane was when she realized Mr. Bingley had left Netherfield Park with no intention of returning. And there is the matter of Mr. Bingley's sister. I do not know how much progress can be made as I am sure Miss Bingley will be listening and watching everything I say or do."

"I think you are underestimating Miss de Bourgh. She has already proven herself to be an expert in masterminding and executing a plan. I cannot imagine she went to all the trouble of having Mr. Darcy and you meet, only to give way to Miss Bingley. And I suspect you have made a friend of Miss Darcy."

"It should be an interesting evening. I almost feel sorry for Miss Bingley. She wants Mr. Darcy so very badly, but everything she does diminishes her chances of that happening because he finds her so annoying."

"If that is the case, you may have a secret ally: Miss Caroline Bingley."

※

"Well, what do you think, Mercer? Am I presentable?" Usually,

Darcy allowed his man to lay out his clothing, but tonight he had picked out each piece himself because he wanted to look his very best for Miss Elizabeth.

"If I may comment, sir."

"Of course, Mercer. Speak freely. Have I chosen unwisely?"

"Oh no, sir. You have chosen to great effect. However, your expression is that of a man going to the scaffold, not supper."

"Hah! It is easy enough for you to say that it is just a supper, but you do not have to face a room full of women, each of whom believes she should have some say in my future. I was so looking forward to dining with Miss Elizabeth, but now that the time is near, all I can see are the problems created by having Miss Elizabeth, Anne, and my sister in the same room as Miss Bingley and her sister. It is as if I invited two warring parties to fight it out in Pemberley's dining room. I do not think it will go well."

"I believe Jackson anticipated the situation, sir, and I think you will be pleased by the seating arrangement. The warring parties, as you call them, have been separated to minimize damage."

"That is all well and good during the meal, but does Jackson have a plan for after supper?" Looking in the mirror one last time and after straightening his waistcoat, he told Mercer, "Well, what will be, will be. Onward into battle."

※

Before going down to supper, Darcy asked Bingley to join him in the study. It was his intention to apologize for his interference in his affairs with regard to Miss Bennet. He felt confident of his forgiveness, not only because Bingley was not one to hold grudges but also because there had been such a change in his friend. He was exuding a confidence that Darcy could only attribute to one thing: He had already made up his mind to call on Miss Bennet.

Charles was waiting in the study and had poured a brandy for both of them. He already knew the reason why Darcy had asked for this meeting. His friend had changed his mind regarding Miss Bennet because, if any reservations had remained, he would never have revealed that Miss Elizabeth was staying at the inn. It was evident that Darcy now approved of the match, and an unfortunate episode in their friendship could be put behind them. Charles was confident there would be a time in the not-too-distant future when Mr. Darcy would be welcoming Mr. and Mrs. Charles Bingley to Pemberley.

Taking the brandy from Charles's hand, Darcy got right after it. "You know me well enough to know I do not beat around the bush. The reason I have asked you here is to apologize for my interference in your affairs with regard to Miss Bennet. I completely misjudged the depth of her affection, and it was presumptuous of me to assume that I knew more than you did as to matters of the heart. I did not understand how quickly one could fall in love, and I regarded it almost as an affliction that one would eventually recover from. However, I now recognize that it is a force that reaches into every fiber of your body, and that it is something not to be resisted but embraced."

"Well said, Darcy. But are you talking about me or you?"

"The matter at hand is your love for Miss Bennet."

"Darcy, I understand you were acting in my best interest, but you arrived at your decision based upon how you would have acted. But I am not a Darcy. I do not have Norman blood running in my veins, and my ancestors were not earls. I am a simple man with simple tastes. I want no more than to be surrounded by family and friends and to have horses to ride about my property on a fine day. And who knows what the future holds? I have just learned that my brother, George, is on the king's birthday list for a knighthood, so the Bingleys are rising.

"In the early days of our friendship," Charles continued, "I looked to you as an older and wiser brother, but in the intervening years, I have grown up. I now trust my own judgment and am confident that I am capable of making wise decisions. Not that I won't need your counsel from time to time, but it must be a contributing factor, not the deciding one. So if it is my forgiveness you are seeking, you are forgiven."

"I readily agree to your conditions," Darcy said and hoped that Bingley would feel the same way when he had finished. "However, there is one other matter I must acquaint you with. A few weeks after our departure from Hertfordshire, Miss Bennet visited her aunt and uncle, whom you met this morning, in London. I knew she was in town but said nothing. I now know from Miss Elizabeth that her sister thought you knew she was staying with the Gardiners, but chose not to call. As a result, she was deeply hurt. Fortunately, Miss Elizabeth was able to reassure her sister that you were completely unaware of her presence. At the earliest opportunity, it is my intention to apologize to Miss Bennet. And now you know it all."

Bingley started to pace about the room, saying nothing, and as the silence lengthened into several minutes, Darcy was less sure that his friend would forgive him now that he knew the full extent of his interference.

"I should be angry with you, Darcy, but I am angrier with myself. I should not have taken your advice regarding Miss Bennet nor given in to the pressure from my sisters. However,

I cannot change the past, and since you are sorry for what happened in Hertfordshire and London, how can I not forgive you?" Charles stood next to Darcy and clapped him on the back, a gesture the older Darcy often did to his friend. It was the first time Charles had ever done it to him.

"Now, that we have cleared the air, in a gesture of friendship, I shall do you a favor. I know how much my sisters, especially Caroline, annoy you. Don't pretend that they do not. If it was ever a secret, it came into the light of day at Hulston Hall. Caroline's behavior towards our hosts put a permanent scowl on your face. So this evening, I will suggest that tomorrow we all go for a ride in the Peak District, knowing full well that neither of my sisters nor my bloated brother-in-law will get on a horse. Caroline will be unhappy, but she will be unhappy with me and not you. Of course, you must invite the Gardiners and Miss Elizabeth to go riding. I would be very surprised if Miss Elizabeth's aunt and uncle accepted the invitation, which will leave Georgiana, Miss Elizabeth, and you. While you are showing Miss Elizabeth the wilds of the Peak, I shall offer to drive the ladies to the various lookouts that require no exertion whatsoever."

"You are making it sound as if you are deliberately throwing me into the path of Miss Elizabeth, or am I mistaken?"

"Darcy, it will not do," Charles said, laughing. "You are finally able to understand my love for Miss Bennet because *you* are in love. I had guessed as much when I saw how you looked at Miss Elizabeth at the inn this morning, but when you confessed that love fills every fiber of your body, only a man in love could utter such words."

"It seems that I am easily seen through these days. Apparently, love lays bare your soul. It is quite a humbling experience."

"Yes, but there is nothing like it on earth."

Darcy's heart was keeping time with the gait of the horses as Elizabeth's carriage came up the hill. He was still unaccustomed to the physical change that came over him whenever he was in her company. It wasn't only his heart racing, but the feeling of being caught up in something beyond his control, and it quite overwhelmed him.

When the Gardiners and Elizabeth were introduced, everyone was in the music room listening to Mrs. Hurst play one of her pieces on the pianoforte. She lacked the precision of her sister, but her playing was heartfelt, and it led Darcy to believe that if she ever broke free of her younger sister, Mrs. Hurst would be quite a different person.

Anne immediately went to Elizabeth and greeted her warmly, which did not go unnoticed by Caroline Bingley. Just how well did these two ladies know each other? It had been her impression that they had only recently been introduced during Elizabeth's visit to Kent. If that was the case, why was Miss de Bourgh greeting her as if they were sisters? Caroline suspected a conspiracy, and the evidence was building.

"Miss Elizabeth, it has been too long," Caroline said, making no pretense at sincerity. "I believe it was last autumn at the ball at Netherfield when we last saw you and your family. If I recall correctly, we returned to London shortly thereafter."

"Was it only last autumn, Miss Bingley? How the months do pass when one is engaged in enjoyable pursuits in the midst of a loving family."

Georgiana was already so in tune to Miss Bingley that she

could tell by her inflection just how cutting any particular remark was. She knew nothing of the ball at Netherfield, but she had no doubt it was the first arrow out of Miss Bingley's quiver.

"Miss Elizabeth, you must come and sit by me and tell me everything you have done since arriving in Lambton," Georgiana said.

"Gladly. This morning, we went to a well dressing," Elizabeth said enthusiastically. "The workers were still creating their design when we left, but when it is done, it will be of four children dancing around a maypole. It was wonderful. There is nothing like it in Hertfordshire, so we found it to be very interesting."

Georgiana explained to Miss Bingley and the Hursts that a well dressing was a design made up entirely of flowers and other things taken from Nature, such as moss and leaves and pieces of wood.

"Oh, Will, we must tell our friends about the one we saw last year. It was the largest I had ever seen. It was a replica of a local ruin and very like."

By the time she had finished her description of various well dressings, Caroline could hardly believe that such a thing had merited fifteen minutes of discussion. Miss Darcy had barely uttered the final word on the subject when Miss Bingley said, "Miss Elizabeth, I understand you were touring the gardens of Pemberley when Mr. Darcy arrived. What a happy event. Did it require much alteration to your plans?"

"There was no alteration on our part, Miss Bingley. Our plans have been in place for several weeks. I came to Pemberley at the recommendation of Miss de Bourgh, and if any alteration was made, it was made by your party, not mine."

That was the second arrow out of Caroline Bingley's quiver,

Georgiana thought. But from that exchange, she decided Miss Elizabeth was quite capable of taking care of herself, and her brother was of the same opinion. The parties had engaged, but Elizabeth had got the better of Miss Bingley. And it looked as if it was going to be an interesting evening.

Chapter 33

As the current mistress of Pemberley, Georgiana had met with Jackson to discuss the seating arrangements for that night's supper and had requested only one change. She wanted Miss Elizabeth to sit on the same side of the table as Caroline Bingley. In that way, when her brother spoke to Elizabeth, Caroline would be unable to hear her responses, and if things went as Georgiana hoped they would, her role as mistress of Pemberley would be short-lived, as her brother would soon be marrying Elizabeth Bennet.

As soon as Caroline entered the dining room, she saw how it would be. Caroline was seated to Miss Darcy's right, next to her brother-in-law, and diagonally across from Miss de Bourgh. With Mr. Gardiner sitting opposite to her, she was completely boxed in. While at the other end of the table sat Mr. Darcy, and to his left, Eliza Bennet. She was sure Miss de Bourgh was responsible for the seating arrangement. It had been just the previous day when Caroline had declared Mr. Darcy's cousin to be a fool, but now she knew that she was anything but. Once Caroline learned that it was Miss de Bourgh who had suggested Elizabeth's visit to Pemberley, she remembered what Mr. Darcy had said when he came to the Bingley townhouse: "I would ask that the date for our departure be moved up at the request of my cousin, Miss Anne de Bourgh." That whole stupid conversation about yellow frocks, favorite flowers, and Elizabeth's disagreement with Mr. Darcy concerning bathing resorts, was part of an act to disguise her efforts on Miss Elizabeth's behalf.

Caroline had no doubt Miss Elizabeth and Miss de Bourgh were in collusion, and that the plot had been hatched when the two women became fast friends during Elizabeth's visit to Kent. It was only after Mr. Darcy's return from his visit with Lady Catherine that Caroline was told Miss de Bourgh was to accompany them to Derbyshire, a place she had not visited for two years because of her supposed ill health. But the success of their plan was thwarted when she had agreed to the sudden change in their departure date.

Caroline did not understand why Mr. Darcy's cousin would encourage such a match. There was nothing to recommend Miss Elizabeth. She was considered to be a beauty only because she lived in a backwater village and moved in a society of the meanest sort. If she attended the grand balls in London, she would not have merited so much as a passing glance from anyone in polished society. And her clothes! How many times had she seen that yellow frock when they were in Hertfordshire? And her complexion! At least her sister had the good sense to protect her skin from the sun, but apparently Miss Elizabeth thought that being brown complemented "her fine eyes," when all it did was make her look as if she worked out of doors.

In addition to the more obvious drawbacks to such a match, there was the matter of her inferior birth and lack of connections. The daughter of a gentleman farmer to be the mistress of Pemberley. Impossible! Or did Miss Elizabeth think her association with Mr. and Mrs. Gardiner would provide her with an introduction into London society? Equally ridiculous. The Gardiners could have the finest china and crystal in all of London, but what did it matter if the only people to dine at their London home were shopkeepers and merchants?

Mr. Darcy was completely innocent in all of this and would have been offended if he knew what the two women had got up to. She was sure he would be outraged if he had discovered that his sister had been drawn into their intrigue by appealing to her love of drama, which was so evident at Hulston Hall when Georgiana had gone up into the attic in search of ghosts. Her brother would not have approved of that either, but Anne had found it to be a lark.

"Miss Bingley, I think you and my wife may have something in common," Mr. Gardiner said after a prolonged silence by his dining partner. "Mrs. Gardiner's grandfather was born in Edinburgh, and I understand from your brother you too have some Scots blood in you. Have you ever visited Scotland?"

"No, I have not, and it is my intention to keep it that way. My grandfather moved to Durham when he was still a young man, and the Bingley connection to Scotland is so remote, I am surprised my brother mentioned it at all."

"I know the Scots have a reputation for being a bit rough at the edges," Mr. Gardiner said with a laugh, "but we all owe a debt of gratitude to some Scotsman. They are men of science and industry and medicine. If London is ever to be lit by gas, it will be because of Mr. William Murdoch. Have you not seen the public lighting at Pall Mall?"

"Of course, I have. But as you say, Mr. Gardiner, the Scots are men of science and industry and are not gentlemen."

Fearing that his attempt to engage the lady in conversation had only served to annoy her, he thought it best to change the subject. "I understand your oldest brother is to be knighted, Miss Bingley."

"Yes, I hope this will be the first of many honors for George."

"May I add my congratulations to your brother being so honored," Anne said, "but before we leave the topic of Scotsmen, since we are at Pemberley, we might add Robert Adam's name to the list of sons of Scotland to whom we are indebted, as he designed all the public rooms here in the manor house. Mr. Darcy would know more about that than I do because he had actually met the man when he was a child."

"Miss de Bourgh, the statement regarding Scotsmen not being gentlemen was not meant to be universally applied," Caroline said. "There are always exceptions, and I cannot think of one more thing to say about Scotland or its inhabitants."

Mr. Darcy had heard nothing of their discussion because he had been otherwise engaged in a conversation with Miss Elizabeth and Mrs. Hurst. Without embarrassment, Mrs. Hurst had shared the story of how she had got lost in the maze during her visit to Pemberley the previous summer. "I probably should not tell that story as it makes me look foolish, but I did so enjoy it."

Instead of being ridiculed for her inability to navigate the maze, Elizabeth complimented her on her desire to find humor in an awkward situation.

"I am glad you think so, Miss Elizabeth. Caroline was quite upset with me, especially when I got lost a second time. But Mr. Darcy assured me that it was a complicated design, and he did not know of anyone who had not got lost at one time or another. It is just one of the many pleasures to be found at Pemberley."

Darcy smiled at the compliment. Mrs. Hurst's relaxed attitude and pleasant conversation served to confirm what Darcy had already suspected. Mrs. Hurst was a follower, and unfortunately the leader was her sister, who seemed to find little joy in anything except carving up perceived rivals.

"Miss Elizabeth, Mrs. Hurst has expressed her opinion of Pemberley, but I was wondering if you had any comment to add."

"I do not think I do, Mr. Darcy. I am ill equipped to describe your own Garden of Eden. I have never been to a manor house that was so happily situated with its incredible views of the Peak and the gardens and the lake. You once said to me that your thoughts are clearest when you are at Pemberley, and I can well believe it. Who could think anything but happy thoughts when in the midst of such beauty?"

"I agree wholeheartedly with that statement, but such beauty should be shared. Would you agree, Miss Elizabeth?"

"Yes, I would agree."

Darcy smiled at her answer. He took it to mean that she would be receptive to another offer of marriage. Could it be interpreted in any other way?

After the pudding was served, Jackson asked his master if he intended for the gentlemen to withdraw to the study. Darcy decided that leaving the women alone for even a short period of time was not a good idea, and he told Jackson they would all adjourn to the music room and asked that coffee be served immediately.

Caroline was relieved when supper finally ended. Now, they would go into the music room where she would outshine everyone else. There was no doubt she was the most talented musician, and that included Miss Darcy, and her skills would be further enhanced because she would be playing on a pianoforte that was as fine an instrument as she had ever seen. But once she was mistress of Pemberley, she would have the piano moved to the other end of the room to allow for more intimate entertainments.

"Miss Bingley, perhaps you will favor us with a tune?" Mr. Darcy asked almost as soon as they had entered the room.

"Will, if I may make a suggestion?" Georgiana said. "Miss Bingley is such an accomplished musician that if she plays first we shall all pale in comparison. Perhaps, Miss Elizabeth could entertain us with a ballad, and Mrs. Hurst might accompany her."

Anne and Georgiana had anticipated that Miss Bingley would sit as close to Will as possible and would remain there until forced to move. If she was asked to perform later in the evening, she would have to get up, allowing Will and Elizabeth more time to engage in conversation.

Darcy was convinced his sister's request had nothing to do with musical proficiency, but he acceded without trying to puzzle it out. After the two ladies had completed their first piece, Caroline made no comment on the performance, but used the break to compliment Mr. Darcy on the design of the music room.

"Your cousin shared with us that Robert Adam was the designer of the public rooms at Pemberley. I cannot think of anyone else who brings such a light touch to his work. It is the perfect design for this room—so peaceful, so serene."

"Will, you could not hear our conversation, but we were

discussing our debt to Scotsmen and Mr. Adam's name was mentioned," Georgiana explained.

"Absolutely, we owe them a debt. Watt's steam engine is being used at a coal mine in the Derwent Valley not twenty miles from here. The man's a genius. Granted, Scotland can be a rough country. I can speak to that personally as our cousin married into the Hamilton family, and last year Georgie and I went to her wedding near Stirling. That was quite an experience. We ventured out on our own for a few hours, dipping our toe into the Highlands, so to speak, but it was worth it as we were surrounded by incredibly beautiful scenery."

"Mr. Darcy," Caroline said, "I mentioned earlier to Mr. Gardiner that my grandfather was born in Scotland. I think it would be a very easy thing to convince me to go there for a visit."

Georgiana just looked away, but Mr. Gardiner was now completely confused. At supper, he had the distinct impression that when he had mentioned the Bingley connection to Scotland, it was not appreciated by Miss Bingley. He must have been wrong and made no comment. Instead he said, "When I think of Scotland, I think of salmon, Mr. Darcy."

"I have not forgotten, Mr. Gardiner. I have arranged for Wilkins, the man who is responsible for stocking the ponds, to take you and Mr. Hurst to the finest fishing spot on the property. If you do not catch anything tomorrow with Wilkins as your guide, you will have no one to blame, sir, but yourself."

"Mr. Darcy, it is my intention to fill my creel to overflowing."

Mr. Hurst just grunted. He was not sure why he was being included in this fishing adventure as he had not been fishing since leaving Oxford. He must have said something to Darcy at Hulston Hall when he was in his cups.

As soon as Louisa and Elizabeth rejoined the party, Charles kept his promise to Darcy and suggested that everyone visit the Peak the following day on horseback.

"Charles, do not be so tiresome," Caroline said. "You know I do not ride nor does Louisa."

"Yes, of course, I know that, but others do. So I was thinking that, for those who do not ride, I shall take them into the District by carriage on well-traveled roads."

"Just because you race curricles, does not qualify you to drive a carriage," Caroline said, continuing her protest.

"Good grief, Caroline! Must everything be so complicated? Mercer is an old hand at driving a team of horses, and he will be beside me. You may choose to remain at Pemberley, but I believe Miss de Bourgh, Mrs. Gardiner, and Louisa would like to do this."

Even though the last thing Darcy wanted was for Miss Bingley to go riding, he still had responsibilities as host, and as such, courtesy demanded he extend the invitation to all of his company.

"Miss Bingley, Mrs. Hurst, before you decide whether or not to venture out with your brother, you should know we have a horse named Sugar, who is as gentle an animal as was ever born. Even the most timid riders are comfortable when seated upon her."

"Thank you, Mr. Darcy, but neither Louisa nor I have ridden since we were children and…," Caroline said, fumbling for an excuse.

"May I add, Miss Bingley," Darcy continued, "that this particular mare was not named Sugar because of her color, but because of her disposition, and since we will be riding a narrow trail, we will be going at a snail's pace?"

"Sir, I wish I could reward your persistence, but I do not

choose to ride." She had no intention of getting on any horse no matter what color, no matter how sweet her disposition, not even for Mr. Darcy.

Darcy had now fulfilled his duties, and he turned to Miss Elizabeth to make her the same offer after her aunt had declined.

"Since my Aunt Gardiner does not ride, Mr. Darcy, I think it only proper to accept Mr. Bingley's invitation to ride with him in the carriage. In any event, I am not a very good rider, and I would only delay the party." Unlike Caroline, Lizzy had no fear of horses. It was just that she had never mastered riding sidesaddle.

"Miss Elizabeth, it would be impossible to delay the party," Charles insisted. "You will be going clippity clop, clippity clop, and no faster. The trail will not allow it, which is why I shall not be going. I cannot stand riding at that pace. No matter how splendid the views, I have no patience for it."

Lizzy was about to repeat her decision to remain with her aunt, when she looked at Anne and Georgiana. Their looks said it all. What was she thinking? This was her opportunity to spend some time with Will free of Miss Bingley's interference. Anne decided that the situation called for a dramatic intervention.

"If Miss Elizabeth does not choose to ride, then I shall be very brave and ride Sugar."

Now all eyes were on Anne, who had not been on a horse in ten years because of her fear that she would have a coughing fit that would cause her great embarrassment.

Lizzy understood what Anne was doing, and was so moved by her efforts, that she took her hand in hers and said, "Mr. Darcy, I would very much enjoy riding to the Peak tomorrow, and since only one person can ride Sugar, I am afraid I must usurp your position, Miss de Bourgh."

Georgiana let out an audible sigh, which was the final proof Caroline needed to confirm that she too was a part of the cabal. If that was the way it was going to be, she would fight fire with fire.

"Miss Elizabeth, I understand that the militia has removed from Meryton to Brighton. It must be a great loss to the neighborhood and your family."

The only surprise in Caroline's comment was that it took her so long to make it.

"Fortunately, we were prepared for such an event, Miss Bingley. Knowing how these regiments are constantly on the move, we made the most of their limited time with us. But shortly before leaving for Derbyshire, I learned that an acting troupe will be visiting the village, along with the usual accompanying entertainers. That news lifted our spirits considerably."

"Oh, an acting troupe!" Georgiana exclaimed. "Every year, at midsummer, a troupe comes into Lambton, and how I do love the jesters because they make all the children squeal with delight. Did such a thing occur during your childhood, Mrs. Gardiner? I understand your earliest years were spent in Lambton."

"Yes, indeed. And I can remember all of the village children running out to greet them as soon as they heard the sound of the horns announcing their arrival. I must confess to following the men around who walked on stilts. Along with the other children, my brother and I would tease them in the hopes that they would fall. How awful we were."

"One year, when I was in Bath," Anne said, "there was a procession of entertainers, and the ones I could not take my eyes off of were the jugglers. How ever did they keep all of those objects in the air at the same time?"

"And you, Miss Elizabeth? Do you have preference among the entertainers?" Mr. Darcy asked.

"Oh, if I had to choose only one, I would have to pick the acrobats. It always amazed me how they could twist and turn themselves into so many different positions and so quickly. One minute this way, and the next, quite another, and just when you thought there was no other way they could further contort their bodies, they somehow managed it."

The room went quiet, but Mr. Gardiner, who did not understand the true meaning behind the exchange, broke the silence by asking Mr. Darcy for his preference.

"Oh, I think it must be the man who stabs himself with a knife. Of course, as adults, we all know that it is done with a collapsible knife, but it all seemed quite real while I was watching it. But enough about traveling shows. Miss Bingley, will you please honor us with one of your pieces, and since we all have a busy schedule tomorrow, I think it would be the perfect end to the evening."

Once Caroline returned to her room, she could barely contain her anger. She pulled off her earrings and threw them onto the dressing table. Louisa reminded her sister that the Darcy maid was in the room and that "pitchers have ears."

"You are dismissed," Caroline said to the maid. "I will ring when you are needed."

The young woman was barely out of the room when Caroline resumed her tantrum. "Do you see what is happening, Louisa? Miss de Bourgh is determined to have that no-account Meryton nobody marry her cousin. The whole thing was planned while Miss Elizabeth was in Kent."

"Caroline, I know you are so much smarter than I am, but Miss de Bourgh had never met Miss Elizabeth before she went to visit Mrs. Collins. Why would Miss de Bourgh be so eager for her cousin to marry someone she had only just met?"

"Obviously, this is a form of entertainment for her. What else is there to do in that big house with only her mother for company? But it will not work. You saw how disappointed Mr. Darcy was when I told him I would not ride tomorrow, and you and I have discussed how Mr. Darcy could hardly disguise his dislike of Miss Elizabeth when they were together in Hertfordshire. I will allow that he is doing a better job of concealing his true feelings at present, but that is to be expected since she is his guest. Even so, there is an undercurrent of resentment on his part that she is here at all."

When Caroline was in such a mood, Louisa knew it was best to say as little as possible, but the truth was, Louisa did not agree with anything Caroline had said. The supposed plot sounded preposterous, and as for Mr. Darcy's dislike of Miss Elizabeth, that was not what she had seen at all.

For her part, the evening had stirred memories that were both sweet and painful as she recalled the early days of her courtship with Mr. Hurst. They had passed notes in secret and had exchanged looks and talked in generalities only they understood, and it had been such an exciting time in her life. And because it had happened to her, she recognized it in others. She was less sure of the depth of Miss Elizabeth's regard for Mr. Darcy, but as for the master of Pemberley, he had totally failed in his attempt to hide his love for the nobody from Meryton.

Chapter 34

ON THE CARRIAGE RIDE back to the inn, Lizzy would have preferred silence to conversation so she might go over in her mind the events of the evening. She wanted to preserve forever the memory of having dined on the finest china in an elegant dining room of the softest green with candlelight reflecting off a crystal chandelier that had been custom made for Lady Anne Darcy in Venice. That experience alone would have been a golden memory, but to know that Mr. Fitzwilliam Darcy wanted her to be the mistress of Pemberley, the most beautiful home she had ever been in, quite overwhelmed her. Her awe at her surroundings brought on a rare experience for Lizzy: a loss for words.

"That certainly was an interesting evening," Mr. Gardiner began as the driver started down the gravel drive.

"How so, my dear?" his wife asked, yawning, a little surprised that her husband was taking the lead in the conversation. He usually had very little to say about social gatherings.

"Well, let me begin with the Hursts. I would not say they

dislike each other. It is more on the order of a total lack of interest, which is not difficult to understand on Mrs. Hurst's part. Once he realized we were not to play cards, Mr. Hurst had no interest in anything other than the wine. If it had not been for the occasional grunt or belch, I would have thought he had fallen asleep.

"In contrast to Mr. Hurst, I found Miss de Bourgh to be delightful, and she gave no indication that she lived shut off from the world in an ivory tower in Kent. She was well informed as to politics and literature and the adventures or misadventures, as she called them, of the Prince of Wales. As for the young Miss Darcy, I was more than a little impressed with her finesse in conversing with Miss Bingley, who seemed to be out of sorts during the meal. Despite her mood, it did not prevent Miss Bingley from expressing her opinion on just about everything, and the interesting thing was, her opinion changed from room to room. She did not like Scotland in the dining room but wanted to visit the country while in the music room, nor did she like the color yellow until Miss Darcy pointed out that the drawing room was yellow, and then she liked it.

"I felt that I had done my duty with so difficult a companion, so when we went into the music room, I sat where I would not bear the responsibility of carrying the conversation. But I could still hear her. She was unhappy with her sister's selection of a ballad, the lowest form of song to her mind, and one that anyone with a modicum of talent could play or sing. Oh, sorry, Lizzy. I thought you performed beautifully."

"Please do not apologize, Uncle. It is no secret that Miss Bingley does not like me. She believes I promoted a union between her brother and Jane, which I did, and considering the social chasm separating the Bingley and Bennet families, she was offended because I had presumed too much."

"Well, that is good for a laugh," Mr. Gardiner said. "Mr. Bingley's father began life as a blacksmith, but grew wealthy as a result of a smelting process he and his father had invented. Mr. Bingley was telling me, with great amusement I might add, that he remembered his father's fingers being permanently blackened because he was always at the forge doing experiments. He also said venturers would come from London to see demonstrations of the process, and Old Grandpa would deliberately chew and spit tobacco so that they would keep their distance. Bingley's father sired a brood of nine, and after he had made his fortune, he packed the whole lot of them off to be educated, girls and boys alike, which is why Miss Bingley is so knowledgeable, although it does not explain Mrs. Hurst.

"The eldest son, George, went to Oxford, and apparently is a financial genius. He took a modest fortune and turned it into an empire, which is what pays for the house in town and the clothes and the horses. Well, it obviously pays for everything for the three youngest Bingleys and possibly the other five as well. Mr. Bingley added that his father never traveled farther south than York, was unchurched, and unlike his daughter, had no social pretensions whatsoever."

By that time, they had arrived at the inn, and both Gardiners immediately retired and left Lizzy alone with her thoughts. As soon as she was under the covers, her mind returned to Mr. Darcy, and she went over every minute, every word, every gesture they had shared. The previous day, her aunt had asked if she loved Mr. Darcy, and she had answered that she did not know. That was no longer the case. When he had said that the beauty of Pemberley needed to be shared, he had looked right into her eyes, and it was then that she knew the answer. Yes, she was in love, and now that she had surrendered to her true feelings, she realized that she was truly and deeply in love with Mr. Darcy. And with that realization came wisdom. She better understood why he had fought against his own feelings. It was a humbling experience to trust one's heart to another, but by shedding his reserve, he had revealed the caring and loving man beneath.

And with all she had seen and heard and tasted, it was how she felt when Mr. Darcy took her by the hand and had escorted her to the music room that she wanted to commit to memory. In those few short minutes, she felt the physical side of being in love, and she had wanted him to take her in his arms and to kiss her. And that was what was on her mind while singing the ballad. Had he noticed that the verses were out of order? If he had, did he realize it was the effect he had on her that was the cause of her error? Elizabeth fell asleep wondering if tomorrow during their ride to the Peak there would be some time, even a few seconds would suffice, when she would feel his touch once again.

While Elizabeth was thinking of embraces and kisses, Darcy was trying very hard to put them out of his mind. During the time Lizzy was confusing verses, he was picturing the two of them making love in different rooms in the house. To avoid complete embarrassment, he had wisely decided to wear trousers instead of breeches, but this could not go on much longer or he would explode. There was a time in the distant past when he would have been able to exercise the *droit de seigneur*. As lord of the manor, he would have demanded that the Bingleys leave Pemberley immediately and that the Gardiners return to London without their niece, but with Anne and Georgie. And then they would make love until hunger finally drove them to seek nourishment.

This was reminiscent of his time with Christina Caxton when they had made love across the breadth of France. At the time, he was a young man of twenty-one, and it was a delight he had never before experienced. But since assuming guardianship of his sister, he had exercised an abundance of caution in everything he did, but he was a man and not a monk. So he had discreetly sought companionship and relief with the widowed Mrs. Conway, until his idiot cousin, Lord Fitzwilliam, had revealed to *The Insider* that he had remained with the lady until dawn. The irony was he had stayed so late so that he might share with her that he had fallen in love, and as a result, their time together had come to an end. He thought so highly of his friend that he did not want her to learn of it from anyone else. As always, she was gracious and asked about Elizabeth. As the daughter of a coal exporter from Bristol, she was surprised but pleased when she learned that the lady he hoped to make his wife was the daughter of a gentleman farmer.

If Fortune shined on him, at some time during the ride into the Peak, he would have a few minutes to talk to Elizabeth. He was not going to propose marriage until they could be alone, but he did intend to seek assurances that she would be receptive to an offer. With only Georgie and Belling, the groom, accompanying them, surely he would be able to have a private word with her. It must happen tomorrow, as she had informed him that the following day she would be leaving Derbyshire to return to Longbourn. It was his last chance to touch her heart.

If Darcy had been the soul of discretion, Bingley had decided to throw caution to the wind. Since he might not have an opportunity to visit with Elizabeth on the morrow, he had to act tonight.

"Miss Elizabeth, you mentioned your sister, Miss Bennet, is in good health," Bingley said as soon as she had finished her song.

"I know of no complaint, sir."

"The last time I saw her was at the ball at Netherfield, and she was in good health at that time."

"Mr. Bingley, please forgive me for being forward, but if you have something you wish for me to communicate to my sister, please speak freely."

"Do I have something to communicate? I have volumes to communicate. And I would begin with an apology for leaving Hertfordshire so abruptly without a note or letter. Oh God, here's Caroline! Quickly, if I return to Netherfield Park, would I be welcomed at Longbourn?"

Caroline was too close to make any comment, so Lizzy did what she could to assure Mr. Bingley that his attentions would be warmly received.

"Although I make no claim to be a musical historian, I believe that ballad originated in the West Country. But thank you for your compliments. Such kind words are always welcome, especially from old friends."

Those words were encouragement enough. In a matter of days, Charles would be in a position to begin to repair the damage he had done, and he could only hope that Miss Bennet would be willing to forgive him. It was his intention to leave Pemberley in advance of his sisters. One of Darcy's men would see them to Leicester, where he would arrange to have one of George's men meet them at the coaching inn.

Seeing that Charles was talking to Miss Elizabeth, Caroline had intended to inject herself into the conversation when Miss de Bourgh asked if she had heard anything new about the scandal involving Mrs. Clarke. The mistress of the Duke of York had been accused of soliciting bribes from the military in exchange for commissions from the Duke. If Caroline had a weakness, it was her love of gossip. Before leaving London, she had purchased a pamphlet detailing Lord Wardle's complaint against the couple, and in Caroline's eagerness to share the latest "dirt," Anne had successfully diverted her attention. But even if Caroline had known of the purpose behind her question, she would not have cared. Since tomorrow was to be Miss Elizabeth's last day in Lambton, Caroline only had one more day to keep her rival at bay, and then Mr. Darcy was all hers.

Chapter 35

MRS. GARDINER AND LIZZY were waiting outside the inn when the Darcy carriage, with Mercer at the reins, arrived promptly at 9:00 to take the two ladies to Pemberley. After stopping at the manor house, so that Mrs. Gardiner might join the other guests, Mercer went right to the stables where Mr. Darcy, his sister, and Belling were waiting for Lizzy.

Dressed in a riding outfit that Miss Darcy had given to her the previous evening, Lizzy was as ready as she was ever going to be. Apparently, the Darcys intended to leave as soon as possible, as Sugar, a dappled gray, was already saddled and waiting for her. Belling, a strapping lad of sixteen, gave her some advice as how best to handle the mare.

"Now, miss, Sugar needs only the lightest touch with the whip to get her moving in the right direction. I've never known her to go off the trail, and she's used to following Miss Darcy's horse, so no worries."

With Mr. Darcy assisting, Lizzy stepped up on a wooden box to get on Sugar. She hated riding sidesaddle. The weight distribution was all wrong, and she always felt as if she was going to fall off the horse. This time was no different.

"Miss Elizabeth, you need to flex your ankles and keep your heels below the toe," Darcy instructed her. "You are holding the reins too loosely; they have to be held evenly. Correct posture is essential, so you need to square your shoulders and hips and keep your spine in line with Sugar's." After checking her alignment, he handed her a whip.

"Will, let's have Miss Elizabeth ride about the yard for a few minutes," his sister suggested. "She has not been on a horse in a long time."

Belling led Sugar about the yard on a tether, and Lizzy felt comfortable enough to take the reins. She thought she had done well, but Mr. Darcy was of a different mind.

"Sugar needs very little direction, but she does need some. You are still holding the reins too loosely, and you have to cue her with your left leg."

"Mr. Darcy, I was completely honest when I told you that I did not ride well, and riding once around your yard is not likely to make me an expert, no matter how masterful the instruction. As you know, my preference is to walk."

"Of course I know your preference is to walk. You arrived at Netherfield ankle deep in mud because of your love of walking, but surely it is possible for one to both ride and walk."

This was the Mr. Darcy she remembered from Hertfordshire. Do it my way because I know best. "I know you did not approve of my walking to Netherfield, especially since it had rained that morning. However, I came to see how my sister was faring, not to pay a social call."

"I can assure you that my statement was not meant as a

criticism. I thought it showed a deep affection for your sister, but you must own to it that you would have been better served if you had ridden."

"But that would have meant taking one of the horses off the farm, which I did not want to do."

Georgiana came over and told her brother that Miss Elizabeth's skills were sufficient to ride a well-traveled trail and whispered to him, "Your tone does not serve your purpose." She walked over to Lizzy to tell her that Belling would take the lead and she would follow him. Miss Darcy would be immediately behind her, and her brother would bring up the rear. And off they went, clippity clop, just as Mr. Bingley had said.

There were few places on the trail where two horses could ride in tandem, but when they had reached such a spot, Georgiana spurred her horse to come up next to Lizzy.

"Once we get to the top, we shall have a little something to eat. Mrs. Bradshaw packed some bread and cheese, I believe. On our way back, we will go by a different trail that leads directly to a perfect spot for a picnic. Mercer will bring our friends there, and we shall all have a nice time." Turning back to see if her brother could hear her, she added, "Do not mind my brother. He excels at everything that interests him, but he was not interested in learning German nor ice-skating. We all have our strengths and weaknesses."

Lizzy smiled at this news. Most winters a small pond near Longbourn froze, and the children would go sledding or ice-skating. Unlike Mr. Darcy, Lizzy skated very well.

Their first stop was at an overlook, where Mr. Darcy explained that humans had inhabited the valley for thousands of years, leaving behind their primitive tools and evidence of fire. Fire had been used to burn vegetation in order to spur the growth of the grasses that would eventually provide forage for Pemberley's sheep and cattle centuries later. After allowing only a ten-minute respite, Mr. Darcy hurried the ladies back to their mounts, and they were again on the trail.

It was another thirty minutes before Belling came to a stop and dismounted. They had finally reached the overlook that provided a panoramic view of the Peak. Darcy had wanted to share this view with Elizabeth from the time he had seen her venturing off a well-traveled path at Rosings to go exploring on her own, not knowing where the trail might lead her.

Darcy was impatient for her to dismount, so he lifted her off the horse without waiting for Belling. Taking her by the hand, he led her to the edge of a precipice, and from this prospect, Lizzy looked out at the grandeur of the Peak. There was no one word that could possibly describe what lay before her. A marvel, magnificent, breathtaking, majestic did not do it justice.

"Now, do you understand why I insisted that you ride? Do you see why you could not walk?"

She merely nodded and watched as a passing cloud transformed the landscape, its shadow concealing and revealing the colors of the hills and dales below.

"As a boy, I climbed these hills and rode across these valleys. While on foot, I came upon limestone caves and huge stones with evidence of mound graves and remnants of circular structures, and Georgie and I often came here to search for minerals, which we would bring back to show the Duchess of Devonshire, our neighbor and an amateur mineralogist. I was with Belling's grandfather when I found my first axehead," and turning around, he called for Georgie and Belling, who had been laying out a blanket so that they could have a light repast, to come and enjoy the view. But what Belling saw was entirely different from what his master and the ladies were seeing.

"Sir, I think we got a storm moving our way," and as if on cue, the wind picked up and a swirl of clouds emerged over the distant peaks. After mumbling "Damnation!" under his breath, Darcy immediately began giving orders.

"Miss Elizabeth, Georgiana, you need to return to Pemberley immediately. Georgie, go by the south trail; that is the quickest way." And after Darcy had helped Lizzy onto her horse, he said, "Sugar likes to move at her own pace, so you will need to be a little firmer with the whip to get her to follow Georgie. Remember, hold the reins evenly and squeeze the saddle with your legs if you feel as if you might fall off. Now, off you go," and he slapped Sugar's haunch.

"Belling, never mind about the food. Pack up everything else," and with that Darcy started to gather up the plates and linen. The ladies should be fine, he thought, but with the storm moving in so quickly, he anticipated that Belling and he were going to be drenched by the time they reached Pemberley.

Apparently, Sugar did not like bad weather. Instead of using the whip, Lizzy had to rein her in, or she would have plowed right into the back of Georgiana's horse. Except for riding through a bracing wind, the two ladies reached the stables without so much as a drop falling on them. Darcy and Belling were not as fortunate. They were in the open when the storm burst upon them. Fortunately, the groom had packed a coat for his master, but poor Belling was soaked through. Darcy rode into the stables, and immediately ordered the groom to change his clothes.

"Will, I think you are bad luck," his sister said, laughing as her brother shook out his coat. "This is exactly what happened to us the last time we rode up to that promontory."

"If I were not a gentleman, Georgiana, I might say you were the source of our bad luck."

"If you will excuse me, Miss Elizabeth," Georgiana said, continuing to laugh, "I shall see to my horse."

"Georgie has always preferred to groom her own horses," her brother explained. "When she was young, she would come down here early in the morning and brush their coats and plait their manes, and on occasion, muck stalls. She would have much preferred to have been a boy."

"I certainly can understand that. She would not have to ride sidesaddle."

Darcy made a face, and so she continued. "We must not quarrel, Mr. Darcy. I hope we shall always be friends."

Without truly being conscious of what he was doing, he placed his hands on Elizabeth's waist and turned her so that she was facing him. "Don't you understand that I don't want to be your friend," and he ran his fingers along her cheek. Believing that he was going to kiss her, she closed her eyes and waited. But, instead…

"What the devil?"

"Excuse me!" Lizzy said, opening her eyes.

Coming toward them at full gait was Colonel Fitzwilliam. When he had dismounted, he said, "Hope I am not intruding, Darcy. Miss Elizabeth," he said, bowing, "I had no idea you were here. How good it is to see you again."

"Colonel, it is a pleasure. I am quite surprised to see you so far from Kent."

"That makes two of us," Darcy grumbled.

Chapter 36

As soon as Georgiana saw her cousin, she went running to him and practically jumped into his arms. Although Darcy shared her guardianship with Colonel Fitzwilliam, her brother took his role so seriously that there wasn't anything for Richard to do, and so he was the lovable cousin, who was a lot more fun than the strict brother.

"Richard, what are you doing here?" Georgiana asked.

"Once I had learned that you and Will were at Pemberley and that Anne had joined you, I felt left out. So here I am. And now I find the lovely Miss Elizabeth Bennet is also a guest. There is no comparison to be made between you lovely ladies and that of a regiment of redcoats, who are in ill humor because of too many parades."

"Colonel Fitzwilliam, I am actually staying at the inn at Lambton with my aunt and uncle who are now at the manor house. We were just waiting for a break in the rain so that we might join them."

"We have other guests as well, Richard," Georgiana added. "Mr. Bingley, Miss Bingley, and Mr. and Mrs. Hurst."

Richard looked at Darcy, and he could not help but smile at the thought of Miss Elizabeth, whom Darcy wanted, and Miss Bingley, who wanted Darcy, being together at Pemberley at the same time.

"Such a fun group. I am sorry I did not get here sooner."

"Georgiana, Mercer is coming with the umbrellas. The rain has lightened considerably, so I would ask that you go up to the house and see to our guests as soon as you have changed. Miss Elizabeth, my sister will see that you get a pair of dry boots."

"Very well, Mr. Darcy, I shall do exactly that as I am familiar with your opinion regarding muddy footwear." The two ladies made their way to the manor house with Mercer assisting them over any puddles.

Darcy smiled at the memory of Elizabeth's arrival at Netherfield on that misty morning. If he had to fix a time when he had fallen in love with her, it would have been that day.

"Sorry to intrude, old boy," Richard said, interrupting Darcy's thoughts. "I had no idea Miss Elizabeth was in Derbyshire. She said nothing of it when she was at Rosings."

"Nor did I know of her plans. Our shy cousin from Kent arranged for Elizabeth and me to be here at Pemberley at exactly the same time. I would have been impressed if you, with all of your military experience, had pulled off such a scheme, but to have Anne accomplish such a feat, it is nothing short of remarkable. I might add there is no need to apologize. These past few days have been a farce, so I welcome you to the play."

"Is Caroline Bingley also one of the players?"

"Richard, she has become my cross to bear, and I truly am at a loss as to why she is interested in me at all," Darcy said in a voice reflecting his bewilderment. "I give her no encouragement.

I use the same tone of voice that I would use to say 'please pass the salt,' but she acts as if my words have wings. I was well aware that she did not like Elizabeth, but her dislike is so intense that she finds it impossible to conceal it, either that, or she has no wish to."

"And how does Miss Elizabeth fare in all this?"

"She refuses to be brought low, and Caroline has been on the receiving end of her biting comments, something I too am familiar with. But I shall share my travails with you at another time. Please tell me what the devil you are doing here."

"I am here because of Anne. Apparently, she never told Aunt Catherine she was going to continue on to Pemberley. Once Lady Hargrove departed, our aunt wrote to her insisting she return home, but Anne wrote back saying she intended to stay in the country indefinitely."

"Why did Aunt Catherine not use the post?"

"Apparently, she wrote to you, but her letters went unanswered."

"I have had no letters from Aunt Catherine since Anne arrived in London."

"Perhaps Anne intercepted them knowing what was in them. In any event, our dear aunt sent for me. Apparently, she is under the impression that I am free to leave my regiment whenever she summons me. No matter. When I arrived at Rosings, she was in a fury at Anne's defiance, and I bore the brunt of it."

"Well, I shall speak to Anne, but I am not going to order her to return to Rosings. My God, she is nearly twenty-five years old, and if her health permits, she should be allowed to visit her cousins for however long she wishes. But I do not understand why you did not use a post rider. Are you telling me you were so intimidated by our aunt that you rode from Kent to Derbyshire to deliver this message to me?"

"Actually, the part about Anne was the good news. The bad news is that my brother is coming to pay you a visit."

Darcy started to laugh. "Surely, you are joking." When Richard shook his head, Darcy's whole demeanor changed. "He is wasting his time because I have told him I shall not give him any more money. I have already refused him twice, so he knows I am in earnest."

"It's not about money. That young hothead, Jeremiah Lynton, has called him out."

"Good grief! Jeremiah Lynton? I did not know he was married."

"He is not. This time it is not about bedding someone's wife. Apparently, Antony and Lynton were playing cards at White's, and my brother was getting the better of the young man to the tune of half his yearly allowance. He is known to be a sore loser, but Antony decided to tweak his nose about his losses anyway. One thing led to another, and Lynton challenged him to a duel. Lynton's father sent word that if Antony would make himself scarce for two or three weeks, the storm would pass."

"When is he coming?"

"Tonight. He is at the inn at Lambton. We came together in his coach." Seeing his cousin's distressed look, he added, "There is some good news. He is sober."

With Lord Fitzwilliam at Pemberley, Darcy could see any chance of his having a private conversation with Elizabeth slipping away. In the morning, she would return to Longbourn, and he could only hope his efforts to win her had been successful. But in the meantime, he had to deal with Lord Fitzwilliam, and that would take up most of his time and all of his patience.

Chapter 37

WHEN DARCY WENT INTO the dining hall, he found his cousin holding court as the guests at the inn were in awe of an earl being in their midst. After Darcy separated Lord Fitzwilliam from his admirers, he got right to the point. "I am under no obligation to have you at Pemberley. If you drink to excess or offend my guests in any way, you will be asked to leave, and you will have to deal with the young Lynton as best you can."

"Don't be angry, Darcy. This matter with Lynton is a mere inconvenience and will quickly pass. Things have been going quite well for me of late. In the last week, I have won more than £6,000, £4,000 from Lynton alone."

"I have no comment to make on how you come by your money, but I hope you will use it to pay down your debts."

"I already have. That horrid man from Coutts Bank was at White's and insisted on repayment of an overdue note right then and there, which was unfortunate because I had intended to use some of that money to recover our grandmother's portrait."

"Recover it from whom?"

"Christie's, of course. But do not worry. It will not be sold at a public auction. Mr. Garrett has been making discreet inquiries and has told me that there is a lot of interest in it. Grandmother Fitzwilliam was just adorable, with her doe-like eyes, and, after all, she was painted by Joshua Reynolds. Apparently, the *nouveau riche* do not mind decorating their walls with other people's ancestors."

After that comment, Darcy made no further attempt to engage in conversation. He had no respect for a man who would sell off his family's legacy.

By the time Darcy returned with his cousin, everyone was in the music room listening to Georgiana and Mrs. Hurst playing a duet. Upon Lord Fitzwilliam's entry, everyone stood up and curtsied or bowed, acknowledging his position as a peer of the realm. Because he had left London in such a hurry, he was not dressed in traveling clothes but, instead, in an elegant jacket, silk waistcoat and neckcloth, and Italian leather boots. Although wrinkled, he cut a dashing figure.

After the introductions were made, Lord Fitzwilliam said to his cousin, "Darcy, what a clever man you are. So many beautiful women at Pemberley all at one time. However did you manage it?" and he went and sat on the sofa between Mrs. Gardiner and Miss Bingley, and turning to Caroline, he said, "I have had such a long journey. Please tell me again who you are."

"I am Miss Caroline Bingley, and I am visiting from London with my brother, Charles, and my sister and brother-in-law, Mr. and Mrs. Hurst."

"Bingley? I know that name. Are you George Bingley's sister?"

"Yes, Milord. Do you know him?"

"I once sought him out with regard to a financial matter, but we could not come to terms because he had more rules than my mother, the Dowager Countess, which, believe me, is saying a lot. But I am sure that is the reason why he was sitting behind the desk, and I was sitting in front of it. Did I hear your brother's name is to appear on the king's birthday honors list?"

"Yes, Milord, you are correct."

"What an interesting turn of events we have here. A Bingley is to be knighted and will be addressed as Sir George, but here you have Mr. Darcy from an ancient family who has no such honors, and very likely it will remain so," Lord Fitzwilliam said, chuckling. "You see, Darcy disagrees with the king's conservative policies, so His Majesty will not bestow a knighthood on him, and although my cousin agrees with the Whig inclinations of the Prince of Wales, he agrees with him on nothing else, including the size of his allowance. So when His Royal Highness becomes king, he will not bestow a knighthood on Darcy either, and that is his reward for standing on principle, Miss Bingley. Let that be a warning to you."

While Caroline giggled, Anne coughed to draw Lord Fitzwilliam's attention. Recognizing it as a warning that cousin Darcy was not amused, he turned his attention to Miss Bingley.

"Excuse me, Miss Bingley, I am easily diverted. We were discussing how your family has ascended. If the gossip mill is accurate, you purchased the lease on the Barleigh townhouse in Mayfair and got the contents for a song. Apparently, Lord Barleigh needed ready cash to settle his debts. Did I get it right?"

"We do live in the Barleigh townhouse, Milord, but as to the other matters you mentioned, all the details were worked out between George and the Barleigh family. The particulars are unknown to me."

"Once again, we find George Bingley in the mix," Lord Fitzwilliam said, patting Caroline's hand. "He is like the London fog—everywhere—and unavoidable. That is a good-sized town-house, Miss Bingley, so from that, I can deduce that your brother has been more generous with his beautiful sister than he was with me."

Darcy was on his feet, fearing this line of conversation would lead to Antony's request for a loan. "I have asked Jackson to set up card tables in the blue room, and we are ready to go in. We shall all be playing a friendly game of whist," he said, looking directly at Lord Fitzwilliam.

In deference to his rank, Lord Fitzwilliam was the first to sit down, and Anne and Georgiana immediately sat down at the same table.

"Oh, I see how it is. My female relations have boxed me in. Anne, please tell me you are not going to scold me. It would bring back terrible memories of your mother."

Placing her hand on Antony's, she said, "I have missed you, my dear cousin. I want to hear all about your lovely daughters."

"Ah, my daughters," and looking at Charles Bingley, who made up the fourth, said, "If I am to be given credit for anything in this world, it will be because of Amelia and Sophia. At this moment, they are in the capable hands of my mother because their mother has been otherwise engaged of late."

"Milord, may I ask you to please deal the cards," Anne said, fearing her cousin might launch into a discussion of his wife and her lover.

While Anne was seeing to Lord Fitzwilliam, Richard was entertaining Caroline Bingley. It was the least he could do considering that it was he and his brother who had disrupted

Darcy's plans for the evening. The colonel found Miss Bingley to be a beautiful, intelligent lady. It really was too bad he knew her true nature, or it would have been very tempting when one considered the size of the dowry she would bring to a marriage. He would have to give it more thought.

As the evening progressed, Lord Fitzwilliam, who was on his best behavior since Anne's warning, changed tables, and his new partner was Louisa Hurst.

"Milord, I read the speech you delivered in the House of Lords regarding the cost of the war."

"I am so pleased, Mrs. Hurst. That means at least two people are acquainted with its contents," and addressing Mr. Gardiner, he explained, "I questioned the wisdom of deliberately antagonizing our American cousins by having our frigates in their territorial waters. We do not want, nor can we afford, a war with the Americans as well as with the French."

"My brother-in-law is Edward Hurst of the Exchequer, Milord," Louisa continued, "that is why I read your speeches, although I must confess that I do not understand them, Milord."

"Then you are in good company, Mrs. Hurst, as most members of the House of Lords can make the same claim, and you need not address me as Milord after every pause in a sentence. It will be sufficient if you sprinkle a few of them here and there."

Mrs. Hurst smiled. She was always happy when she was able to engage in conversation without fear of being humiliated because she was uninformed or did not understand the subject or said something silly. Unlike her sister, she was quite pleased with how this holiday was going.

When the partners changed for the final time, Elizabeth and Darcy moved to Lord Fitzwilliam's table.

"Darcy, please introduce me again to this beautiful creature."

"Miss Elizabeth Bennet of Longbourn Manor in Hertfordshire."

"Do I know your family?" Lord Fitzwilliam asked Elizabeth.

"No, Milord. My father is a gentleman whose farm is about five miles from Watford on the London road."

"Please allow me to say that whatever your father's farm produces, it can be nothing in comparison to his fair daughter."

Darcy groaned and made no attempt to hide it. He loathed this type of exchange, and although Lord Fitzwilliam had heard the groan, he proceeded nonetheless.

"You may have been born in Hertfordshire, Miss Elizabeth, but I suspect your ancestors lived nearer to the coast. With your beautiful dark eyes, I believe you must have some Spanish blood in you, possibly as a result of the Armada."

"There is nothing in family lore that speaks of Spanish ancestry, and the Armada broke up on the coast of Ireland, not England."

Lord Fitzwilliam started to laugh. "My goodness. A woman who speaks her mind. You would not do well in London society, Miss Elizabeth, where no one ever tells the truth."

"But to pretend I do not know something, Milord, when I do would benefit neither of us. I would have to feign ignorance, and you would be deceived."

"Good Lord, Darcy!" Fitzwilliam said, sitting back in his chair. "What a jewel we have here. A beautiful, intelligent, and witty woman, completely without guile. Where were you a dozen years ago, my dear?"

"Apparently, she was sprouting from the soil of Hertfordshire," Darcy said, pushing his chair back from the table.

As much as Darcy wanted to be in Elizabeth's company, he

was at the end of his patience with his cousin. Lizzy had noticed his souring mood and had suggested they play only one more round, as she had an early departure.

Darcy looked at her with longing and regret as this was a most unsatisfactory ending to their time together in Derbyshire.

⁂

While waiting for the carriage, Georgiana and Anne engaged Mr. and Mrs. Gardiner in conversation in the hopes that Will could have a few words with Elizabeth. Despite Anne's best efforts, events beyond her control had sabotaged her plan to bring Elizabeth and Will together.

"Mr. Darcy, may I thank you for your hospitality. I shall remember with great fondness our visit to Pemberley and the Peak. I only wish we had had more time."

"Can it not be arranged? I understand that your uncle must return to London, but would it not be possible for Mrs. Gardiner and you to remain?"

"That is a very tempting offer, Mr. Darcy. However, Jane has been with the four Gardiner children for weeks now, and it would be unfair to her to lengthen our holiday. Besides, my father has also written asking that I hurry home."

Darcy moved to Elizabeth's side, and using Georgiana and Anne to block the Gardiners' view, he took her hand and said, "Elizabeth, may I visit with you in the morning?"

"We are to be on the road by 9:00," she said, squeezing his hand gently.

"Then, I shall call at 8:00. I would also like you to know that Bingley has decided to reopen Netherfield Park, and it is my intention to visit."

Lizzy smiled and told him she was looking forward to seeing him in the morning and in Hertfordshire, and it was only when the carriage arrived that Darcy reluctantly let go of her hand.

Chapter 38

JANE AND KITTY WERE staring at Mr. Nesbitt's latest gift because they were not quite sure what it was they were looking at. It appeared to be a golden-brown stone with a bee in the middle of it.

"It is amber, a fossilized resin," Mary said, easily identifying the exhibit. "When it was still in its liquid form, it trapped the bee."

"But why is he sending an insect to Jane?" Kitty asked. This token of Mr. Nesbitt's regard followed a tin of ginger that he had sent earlier in the week. Apparently, "Ginger" was his mother's pet name for him.

"Is it not obvious? It is a B as in Bennet."

"Ah, very good, Mary. I had not thought of that," Jane said.

"That is because you do not understand Mr. Nesbitt," Mary said in a harsh voice that caught her sister off guard. "He has been excessively attentive to you, Jane. But he is not very handsome nor does he say all those sweet things young men are supposed to say when courting a lady, so you show no enthusiasm for him."

"Mary, calm yourself. We did not know what the object was. That is all."

"No, I will not calm myself because you are just like Lizzy with Mr. Collins. She did not appreciate him either, and he has made Charlotte a fine husband. And you will never love Mr. Nesbitt because you do not recognize his value. But I do. Of course, he would never look at me because I am so very plain, but if he did, I would let him know how fortunate I was to have such a fine man as a suitor."

"Oh, Mary, you are being ridiculous," Kitty said. "Mr. Nesbitt invites ridicule because of the gifts he sends. Is Jane supposed to whisper 'Ginger' in his ear or to discuss insects stuck in a piece of sap?"

"Resin! It is resin, not sap! There is a difference."

"Mary, what has brought on this outburst?"

"Your lack of understanding has brought it on. Oh, you think you are able to recognize the value of a man. But if Mr. Bingley, your bright shining star, was so wonderful, why did he quit Netherfield without leaving you so much as a note? And you and Lizzy and Kitty thought so highly of Mr. Wickham, and now everyone in Meryton knows he is not a gentleman, but a seducer."

"What are you talking about?" Kitty asked anxiously.

"Betsy Egger thought she was pregnant by Mr. Wickham, but then she found out she was not. But it was too late because she had already told her brother, and he is going to go to Brighton to find Mr. Wickham and beat him to within an inch of his life," and Mary turned on her heels and left the room.

Jane now understood the reason for the harshness of Mary's words. She was in love with Mr. Nesbitt. It was always Mary who sat with the pair during his visits, and it was Mary who showed an interest in all Mr. Nesbitt had to say. But she would have to talk to her sister later because now she wanted to know why Kitty had blanched when she had heard the news about Mr. Wickham, and she immediately went to her room.

"Kitty, what are you doing?"

"I received a letter from Lydia that I have not answered."

"What did the letter say?"

"The usual."

Jane crossed the room and faced her sister. "Kitty, I want to know if Lydia has seen George Wickham."

"It would be possible as they are both in Brighton."

"Let me rephrase the question. Do you know if Lydia has had any direct contact with George Wickham?"

"Oh, Jane! It was supposed to be a secret. Lydia wrote that she had had a falling-out with the Forsters, and they were sending her home. But, instead of coming back to Longbourn, she was going to elope with Mr. Wickham."

"Good God!"

Jane nearly fell down the stairs in her efforts to get to her father as quickly as possible and entered his study without knocking. With his chair facing the window, Jane could see that her father was holding a letter.

"Jane, a post rider has just come with a letter from Colonel Forster." In a state of total disbelief, he continued, "Apparently, Lydia has gone to Gretna Green with Mr. Wickham."

It took three days for Jane's letter to reach Elizabeth at the inn. While Lizzy was riding Sugar in the Peak District, her father had been on the road to London in hopes of finding his youngest daughter. Colonel Forster had come to Longbourn to inform the family that the couple had transferred to a hackney coach at Clapham, which meant they were going to London and not Gretna Green, where such marriages took place.

Because of the lateness of the hour, Lizzy did not read Jane's letter until the morning. Once she acquainted her aunt and uncle with its alarming contents, Mr. Gardiner left to arrange for the carriage to be brought 'round immediately, and Mrs. Gardiner began packing everything as quickly as possible. Lizzy was writing a note to Mr. Darcy explaining that a family emergency had required their hasty departure when the servant announced him. When he first saw her, he thought she was ill because she was so pale, but then he saw her tear-stained cheeks and he went to her.

"What is the matter? Are you ill? Shall I send for a glass of wine?" Darcy asked. A few short hours ago, he had seen her smiling and happy, and he believed that all barriers to their coming together had been removed. But now something was very wrong. To his mind, the only news that could cause such unhappiness would be news of a death in the family.

"There is nothing the matter with me. I am just distressed by some dreadful news from Longbourn," and Lizzy burst into tears. Taking her hand in his, he asked her to tell him what was causing her such anguish.

Lizzy did not want to say Wickham's name because she knew the effect that it had had on Mr. Darcy in Kent, and this time would be no different. When she acquainted him with the particulars of the supposed elopement, he rose from his chair and stepped back as soon as he fully understood what Lydia had done.

"It is absolutely certain?"

"They left Brighton together on Sunday night and were traced almost to London."

"What has been done to recover her?"

Lizzy shared all that she knew, but with each detail, Mr. Darcy seemed to withdraw further into himself. By the time she had finished, she knew he had already distanced himself from her in his mind, and after expressing his wishes that there might be a happier conclusion than there was at present reason to hope, he was gone. And with him went all of her hopes. There would be no visit by Mr. Darcy to Longbourn nor would he return to Netherfield Park with Mr. Bingley. His objections, so vigorously expressed at the parsonage regarding a union between them, had been validated, and by not making a second offer of marriage, he had escaped being bound to such a family. She had not the smallest hope of a different conclusion, and when her uncle returned to tell Lizzy and his wife that the carriage awaited, she felt as if she had fallen into a pool of despair and that there was no friendly hand to lift her out of it.

Chapter 39

Lord Fitzwilliam poked his head into the breakfast room and asked, "What are you all doing in here?"

"We are having breakfast, Antony," Anne answered, gesturing for her cousin to join them. "Would you like Jackson to prepare a plate for you?"

"Just ham and a piece of bread will do. I rarely eat at this hour. By the way, what hour is it?"

"It is 9:00."

"Good grief! What are you all doing out of bed? And where are my relations?"

"Will, Georgiana, Richard, and Mr. Bingley are riding on this beautiful morning. Mrs. Hurst, Miss Bingley, and I do not ride, and Mr. Hurst is under the weather."

"Where is that lovely creature with the black eyes? I didn't run her off, did I?" Lord Fitzwilliam asked while taking the chair next to Mrs. Hurst.

"Miss Elizabeth Bennet and Mr. and Mrs. Gardiner have

returned to Hertfordshire, and their departure had nothing to do with you," Anne reassured him.

"Well, that is a relief. It is too bad she has departed as I am very partial to dark-eyed women. I think my wife has brown eyes. I shall have to look next time I see her."

"Antony, Lady Fitzwilliam has beautiful blue eyes, just like your daughters," and with a puzzled expression she asked, "Do you know that your hair is standing straight up?"

"It always does," he said, running his fingers through his blonde mane. "My man has invented some concoction that gets it to lie down. Hopefully, he will arrive today with my baggage." Turning to Mrs. Hurst, he said, "You see, my brother, Colonel Fitzwilliam, inherited the good looks and the hair, and I got everything else."

When Louisa started giggling, Lord Fitzwilliam knew he had found his audience.

"I know it sounds unfair, but Richard had to get something since he did not get any of the money."

Louisa tried not to laugh, but the earl *was* funny. It had been such a long while since a man, including her husband, had paid her any notice. But her sister was looking at her from across the table, and she was anything but amused because today was to be her day.

This morning, Caroline had awoke with a smile on her face because, at long last, she would have an opportunity to spend time with Mr. Darcy. She anticipated long walks by the lake and private conversations about their future, and she took great pains with her toilette. Unlike her dark-haired rival, who could barely keep her curls in place, Caroline had long silky blond hair, which she wore with one long curl falling over her shoulder so that everyone could truly appreciate how beautiful her hair was. Unlike Miss Elizabeth's two lumps of coal, she had crystal blue eyes, and before going downstairs, she had taken one last look in the mirror and liked what she saw. The equestrians came in shortly thereafter.

"What a morning!" Charles said. "Absolutely perfect for riding, and Miss Darcy is one of the few women who can give me a run for my money."

"Thank you, Mr. Bingley. I learned from my brother, who would not allow me to use my sex as an excuse, and because of that, I had to work very hard," and turning to her cousin, she asked, "Will you ride with us tomorrow, Lord Fitzwilliam? I know you are a fine horseman."

"Past tense, my dear. I *was* a fine horseman. These days the only riding I do is in a carriage," he said with real regret because there was nothing like a fine mount to make you feel as if you could conquer the world. However, when you were never completely sober, the last place you wanted to be was on a spirited animal, unforgiving of error. But there had been a time when he had ridden like the wind, and even his brother and cousin could not catch him. "What have you done with Darcy? Hopefully, you have not left him lying at the bottom of some chasm in his nice riding clothes."

"My brother had business in Lambton, Milord, but he will be with us for dinner."

"Well, I am not waiting for dinner," Richard said, patting his stomach. "I am starving and Bingley has done nothing but talk of food since we got in sight of Pemberley."

Lord Fitzwilliam pushed his plate away from him untouched. The thought of eating before noon disgusted him. "Richard, you may have my chair. Mrs. Hurst and I were about to go into the gardens when you arrived, so if you will excuse us," and Antony stood up and extended his arm to Louisa.

Louisa and Lord Fitzwilliam's departure was as surprising as the sight of a nun strolling through St. James's Park with the Prince of Wales would have been, and no one was more surprised than Louisa Hurst. After finding a seat on the bench nearest to the maze, Lord Fitzwilliam told her, "Since I am an earl, I may say things that other people cannot, and you must listen. You are a delightful young woman, but I am afraid, my dear, your sister quite overpowers you, and you defer to her in everything. Last night, you told me you are rarely separated. May I suggest that you go away for a month or two, so that she might have an opportunity to miss you and thus recognize your value?"

It was true that Louisa deferred to Caroline. Because of her sister's strong personality, she usually found it best to agree with her, even when she really disagreed, as was the case with Jane and Charles. After so many years of bending to Caroline's will, was change really possible?

"Is there someone you may visit?"

"I have a sister in Ireland, Milord."

"My dear, it is not necessary to leave the country. Is there no one nearer?"

"My sister Diana lives near the Welsh border."

"But not in Wales, I hope. The Celtic race was pushed into the corners, Scotland, Wales, Cornwall, and in the case of the Irish, onto their own island. People who live in corners are always odd and should be avoided."

"She lives in Herefordshire, sir."

"Herefordshire will do. As for your husband, ordinarily, I am not a believer in reforming others as change comes from within. However, Mr. Hurst is a young man and of an age when reform is possible. So what can you do to help him? I suspect your husband is a younger son, so you might begin by approaching whoever provides his allowance. Bad habits require money. Or you may dilute the port as Jackson is doing on Mr. Darcy's orders for me. A bucket of cold water is also known to work. Temporarily. But it did get my attention."

Lord Fitzwilliam stood up and taking Louisa by the hand suggested that they attempt to navigate the maze.

"Milord, I get lost every time."

"So do I. But it is a beautiful morning, and we have all day. Although I doubt Darcy would send a search party to find me, I am sure he would send one out for you."

Chapter 40

WHEN ELIZABETH HAD SAID the name "Wickham," it had the same effect on Darcy as a punch to the gut. He had no doubt his intended target was not Lydia but him. Whether he had figured out that Bingley was in love with Jane Bennet or that he had feelings for Elizabeth, Wickham had decided to strike at Darcy through a Bennet sister. The urgency of finding Lydia was such that he had left the woman he loved to be comforted by others, but knowing the bastard had no intention of marrying a young girl with no fortune, he believed he had no choice. Once Wickham had his way with Lydia, he would leave her and never look back.

After seeing the Gardiners' carriage depart, he sent a rider to Pemberley with a note instructing Mercer to come to the inn immediately and to be prepared to set out for London. By the time his manservant arrived, he had written a letter to George Bingley explaining what had happened and relating everything that was known concerning the couple's whereabouts. Because George's investments were so extensive, he had men in London and throughout the country looking after the interests of the Bingley family. If Wickham and Lydia were in London, George Bingley would find them.

In order not to arouse suspicion among his guests, Darcy had to delay his own departure until the following day. He would use his time to acquaint Richard, Georgiana, and Anne with the drama unfolding in London, and he would need their help to entertain their guests and to keep speculation as to the reasons for his departure to a minimum. The fewer people who knew of these events the better, and he most particularly did not want Caroline Bingley to know. He would deny her the pleasure of finding out that the Bennets had once again fallen short, and, in this case, tragically so. Darcy regretted the necessity of this action as Anne had told him the previous evening that the steady drip of venom from Caroline's tongue had worn her down, and she was beginning to feel the fatigue that plagued her when she was with her mother. After speaking with Richard and asking him to keep his brother under control, Darcy returned to his guests, only to find Caroline venting her intense dislike of Elizabeth Bennet.

"I must confess I never could see any beauty in her. Her face is too thin, her complexion has no brilliancy, and as for her fine eyes, I never could perceive anything extraordinary in them. They have a sharp, shrewish look, which I do not like at all," and turning to Mr. Darcy, she said, "I remember, when we first knew her in Hertfordshire, how amazed we all were to find that she was a reputed beauty, and I particularly recollect you saying, 'She a beauty! I should as soon call her mother a wit.'"

"I did make that comment regarding Mrs. Bennet," Darcy responded, "and it was a demonstration of how ill-mannered I can be when I am out of sorts. As for Miss Elizabeth, for these many months, I have considered her to be one of the handsomest women of my acquaintance."

This brusque response to one of his guests put Georgiana on alert. She had earlier noticed Jackson speaking to Anne and her departure shortly thereafter, and five minutes after Anne's return, Richard had left the room. Had something gone wrong when Will went to Lambton to say good-bye to Elizabeth? That didn't seem likely because it was as clear as day that Elizabeth and her brother were in love. But something must have happened at the inn because it was obvious he wanted to be gone—but why and to where?

After supper, they all adjourned to the drawing room, but before going in, Charles warned his sister, "Lord Fitzwilliam is known to have a razor tongue. Say nothing that will make him turn it on you."

But because little had gone Caroline's way since her arrival in Derbyshire, her patience had worn thin. When Anne, now with Mrs. Jenkinson sitting beside her, asked to be excused from playing cards because she was overly tired, Caroline asked her, "Exactly what is your complaint, Miss de Bourgh?"

Mrs. Jenkinson gave Caroline a look that could have melted stone, and Louisa let out a quiet gasp and then whispered, "Caroline, you should not have asked such a question."

"It is quite all right, Mrs. Hurst. Why should Miss Bingley not inquire? When I was about fourteen, I became very ill, and although I recovered, my lungs were impaired. I no longer have the capacity to breathe deeply, and I find that I fatigue easily."

Darcy, who had been pacing the room, came over to talk to Anne. "What are you discussing?"

"My illness as a child. Miss Bingley was inquiring after my health."

"Surely, there are subjects other than Anne's illness to talk about. We very nearly lost her, and I do not like to speak of it," and he walked away. Fortunately, for Caroline, Darcy had not heard her comment, but, unfortunately, Lord Fitzwilliam had.

"Miss Bingley, when we are in London, I should like to introduce you to Lord David Upton. He sits on the backbench in the House of Lords and dissects everyone's speeches, chopping them into little bits, and throwing them back at the speaker with vicious retorts. I think you two would get along famously, and he is a bachelor in need of a rich wife."

As soon as the last of their guests retired, Georgiana immediately went to her brother. "Will, what is the matter? I know something is wrong."

"I shall be leaving for London in the morning," and he explained the events prompting his departure. "I am relying on you to see to our guests. You will have your hands full with Miss Bingley, who seems to have annoyed Antony. Keep them apart whenever possible. Mercer will see you safely back to London, and I shall arrange for Madame Delaine to come to the townhouse to prepare you for your debut. Nothing will affect that, Georgiana. No matter what. I shall be there."

"I do not care about that anymore. Will, what is going to happen?"

"I don't know. It's an ugly business, and no matter the outcome, I am sorry to say Lydia Bennet will pay for her lack of judgment for the rest of her life." He started to stand up, but then sat down. "There is another matter. I wish for you to write to Mr. Stone, our solicitor. Have him contact Christie's and put a hold on anything that Antony is trying to sell. Tell him I shall settle with him as soon as possible."

"But what about Miss Elizabeth and you?" Georgiana asked with tears in her eyes.

"One thing at a time, Georgiana. All my thoughts must now be directed to the recovery of Lydia Bennet. I can think of nothing else."

Chapter 41

A DEAD CALM SETTLED over Longbourn. Everything that there was to say about Lydia's elopement had been said, and since any resolution was out of the hands of its inhabitants, silence now prevailed. It was very different from the bedlam that had been loosed once Mr. Bennet had shared with his family the contents of Colonel Forster's letter. Mrs. Bennet let out a shrill cry that got the dogs barking, Kitty cried, Mary preached, the Gardiner children fretted, and the servants ran around in circles, not knowing what to do. Without a word of comment to anyone, Mr. Bennet had returned to his study, and Jane had heard the sound of a key being turned in its lock. Without instructions from the head of the family, Jane assumed control and brought some semblance of order out of the chaos.

Now that there was nothing to do but wait for news from London, Jane made good on a promise she had made to herself. After reading to the children her favorite fairy tale about a princess who went into a deep sleep and could only be awakened by her true love, she went to talk to Mary. As usual, her sister was in her room reading, but she put her book aside when she saw Jane. The two had barely had time to speak about anything that didn't concern Lydia, Mama, or the Gardiner children.

"Mary, I know you think that I am not sensible of Mr. Nesbitt's many attributes, but I truly am. He is very kind and attentive, and works hard at his profession, which is why I have continued to encourage him."

"But you do not love him, Jane."

"No, I do not. But I do hold him in high regard."

"But, Jane, do you think it is right to contemplate marriage with a man whom you do not love nor have any prospect of loving?"

"Yes, of course. I suspect there are more marriages made due to financial considerations than to love. When one does not have a fortune, one cannot marry where one wishes. I did so want to marry for love, but it has eluded me. Now I must face the reality of marrying for security and to ease the burden on our family because once Papa dies, our future will largely be in the hands of Mr. Collins. We can only hope he will permit us to continue to live at Longbourn, but even if he does allow it, we must have additional protection."

There had always been an expectation in the family that because Jane was so beautiful she would be the one who would make the most advantageous marriage, and in doing so, she would be able to introduce her sisters to men who would make good husbands for them. Once Mr. Bingley had stepped into the picture, everyone's hopes had risen, and when he had returned to London, they had just as quickly fallen. Mr. Nesbitt was not perfect, but if the union was viewed exclusively from a financial point of view, it would be a good match.

Standing behind Mary, Jane pulled the hairpins out of her sister's hair and began brushing her long brown tresses. If only Mary spent a little more time on her appearance, she would be attractive. It was not that she was so very plain; it was just that she was the plainest of the Bennet sisters and suffered in comparison. Jane asked her for more information on amber, and Mary, who was knowledgeable on more subjects than anyone else in the family, explained how the bee had come to be in Mr. Nesbitt's specimen. Neither had anything additional to say about marriage, each accepting the reality of Jane's situation.

"I am sorry for what I said about Mr. Bingley," Mary said as Jane was leaving. "I was angry at him for making you so unhappy. He is a good man, but he should have been strong enough to bear up under the pressure from his sisters."

"Nothing can be gained by speaking ill of Mr. Bingley, but I want you to know that I love you. If my actions with regard to Mr. Nesbitt have hurt you in any way, it was unintentional, and if we do marry, I shall do everything possible to make him a good wife. I promise you that. But there have already been so many turns in the road, who knows what lies ahead. I certainly do not."

⸻ ❈ ⸻

As soon as the Gardiners and Lizzy arrived at Longbourn, Jane told them everything she knew of the events in Brighton and updated them as to what had come to light since Jane's letter to Lizzy.

"Colonel Forster immediately dispatched an express rider as soon as it was discovered that Lydia had run away during the night. He came to Longbourn to meet Papa so they might go to London together. The poor man. He was very hard on himself, but when I had heard the whole of the story, short of posting a guard outside her door, I don't know what he could have done differently.

"It had been discovered that Lydia had been meeting someone in secret, and she was to have been sent home. Apparently, Wickham's identity was not immediately known, and by the time the colonel confirmed that it was he whom Lydia had been meeting, Wickham had gone into hiding. They have been traced as far as London, but in such a large city, they can remain hidden for however long they wish."

"Jane, I must disagree with you," Uncle Gardiner said. "A shortage of funds will force them out into the open. But I am hoping they may be discovered immediately, and to that end, I will join your father in London. In the meantime, we shall reunite with our children, and then Mrs. Gardiner and I shall visit with your mother to see if we can lift her spirits."

When the sisters were alone, Lizzy wanted to know how Jane was faring. She looked very tired and had circles under her eyes.

"I am well enough considering all that has gone on. Kitty and Mary have been very helpful with Mama. When she ventures downstairs, Kitty reads to her, and the sound of her voice seems to calm her. Mary plays soothing tunes and lullabies, as her nerves are in such a state that they will not support anything more vigorous."

"And how is Papa?"

"The only word that comes close to describing his present state is 'devastated.' Lizzy, do you think Wickham can be made to marry Lydia?"

"Why would he? She has no fortune and solves none of his problems. I don't know how such a man is to be worked on."

Mary, who had been listening from the foyer, came into the parlor. "I hope they do not marry. Everyone in Meryton already knows of her running away from Colonel Forster's house with Wickham, and if the news had escaped anyone's notice, the vicar preached a sermon about the fragility of a woman's reputation and the necessity of guarding one's virtue. Nothing can be done to restore her reputation whether she marries or not, so why are we encouraging our sixteen-year-old sister to marry her seducer? I think we should send a letter to Papa with our uncle urging that everything be done to prevent such a union and that Lydia be returned to Longbourn and her family. Hopefully, the news will not travel beyond Meryton and reach the ears of Mr. Nesbitt."

"Who?"

Jane, who had written nothing of her admirer to her sister, remained silent, but Mary said, "I shall leave you now. Jane has some good news to share."

"Are we speaking of Mr. Dalton Nesbitt, Aunt Susan's friend?"

Jane nodded.

"What has he to do with us?"

"I told you there were changes while you were gone, and one of them is that Mr. Nesbitt has been calling on me."

Lizzy laughed and then gave a sigh of relief. "For a second, you had me worried. Mr. Nesbitt! I can still picture him at Aunt Susan's house hopping up and down at his mother's every request."

"Lizzy, I am not in jest."

From her sister's tone, Lizzy understood that Jane truly was being courted by a very tall man of some thirty-odd years, who was still tied to his mother's apron strings.

"Lizzy, do not look at me like that. You know I had always hoped to marry for love, but since I now know that will not happen, I am doing the very best I can to secure my future as well as my family's."

"But, Jane, I have good news for you, and there has been precious little of it of late. While at Pemberley, I had an opportunity to speak briefly with Mr. Bingley, and I can say with certainty that he intends to renew his attentions to you as soon as he returns to Hertfordshire."

"You wrote that Mr. Bingley was well and in good spirits, and I was happy to hear it. But as for any courtship, I already have a suitor."

"I understand it will be a delicate matter to inform Mr. Nesbitt that you love another, but it must be done," Lizzy said emphatically. Jane shook her head, and Lizzy looked at her with growing alarm.

"I know what you are thinking, Lizzy. Mr. Nesbitt is not overly attractive, and as you say, he is excessively attentive to his mother. However, he visits with her permission, and so she is not an obstacle to the marriage."

"Marriage? To Mr. Nesbitt? Never! I know how hurt you were by what Mr. Bingley did, but the reasons you were separated no longer exist. He intends to proceed without his sisters' approval, and I know Mr. Darcy has withdrawn all objections to the match. But even if Mr. Darcy was still in opposition, Mr. Bingley no longer finds it necessary to obtain that gentleman's consent."

If Lizzy had imagined her sister would be jumping for joy over this piece of good news, she was disappointed. Jane sat in the window seat with her hands folded in her lap with a look of resolution. She had made her decision regarding Mr. Nesbitt, and she was holding firm.

"Jane, you cannot do this."

"We must be realistic. Mr. Bingley's change of heart happened before Lydia's misadventure. If his sisters were able to persuade him to go away from me before this unhappy event, imagine what they will do as soon as they find out about Lydia. And they will because Mrs. Morris writes her husband's business letters, and it is she who writes to Miss Bingley for instructions regarding the estate. You know her as well as I do, and she will be unable to resist sharing what she knows of Lydia's escapade. I am sure she has already shared with Caroline the sordid tale of Mr. Wickham successfully seducing Betsy Egger, who believed she was with child and told her brother. He has gone to Brighton to make Wickham marry her. Of course, he will be disappointed."

"Oh God! It's worse than I thought. Mary is right. We should be doing everything we can to prevent such a marriage."

"It is my opinion that Wickham can only be made to marry Lydia under the greatest inducements, and we are in no position to make them."

Lizzy was terribly upset by what Lydia had done. Whether they married or not, her young sister's future would be sown with unhappiness and regret, but at the moment, it was Jane's situation that demanded her attention.

"What happens to Lydia is beyond our control, but what is within our control is your future happiness with Mr. Bingley."

Jane stood up and told Lizzy she needed to see to their mother's dinner because she still preferred to take most of her meals in her room.

"Lizzy, Mr. Nesbitt may not be the ideal, but the one thing that you could never accuse him of is inconstancy. After Mr. Bingley left, I waited every day for the post to come. I was so sure there would be a letter for me explaining his absence. I even swallowed my pride and went into the village to Mr. Morris's office, so I might learn of any news regarding Netherfield. I have been hurt beyond what words can express, and I shall never put myself in a position to have that happen again." Jane, with tears in her eyes, continued. "And as for Mr. Bingley being independent of Mr. Darcy, I would more readily believe it if he had come directly to Longbourn. But he did not. Instead, he went to Pemberley. You must accept that that chapter on my life is closed, and there is nothing more to be said."

Chapter 42

THE SEARCH FOR LYDIA began as soon as Mercer hand-delivered Darcy's note to George Bingley at his London office. Methodically, Bingley's men went to work. They eliminated those sections of London where the arrival of a gentleman and a lady would bring too much notice. They then concentrated on the areas of town where someone who was short of funds, but who gave the impression of having money, might find a room. It was known that Wickham had left Brighton wearing his uniform, so that narrowed it further. A week later, one of Bingley's men was interviewing a certain Mrs. Epping who ran a boardinghouse with her husband, and for five pounds, she was willing to answer all questions asked of her.

"I knew someone would come looking for her," Mrs. Epping began. "And I'm glad you did. I am so sick of listening to those two argue. Him saying he wants what he wants, but her saying he ain't getting it until he give her her wedding clothes. I never heard no one talk about one thing as much as that girl talks about her wedding clothes. It got so I couldn't stand it no more, and I sent her across the way for two days to stay with my sister. But then she had enough and sent her back."

"Then it is your opinion that the couple did not consummate their relationship," Mr. Rhys asked Mrs. Epping.

"Well, I don't know about that. What I do know is that the two of them didn't have sex. That's what all them arguments was about."

"But they shared a room?"

"And I made up their room most nearly every day until they stopped paying for it. I can tell you the man was sleeping on a blanket on the floor, and the princess was sleeping in the bed. And if that ain't proof enough, Mrs. Royale, which is what she calls herself, spelled with an 'e' she says to me, come down one night 'cause Mr. Royale got drunk. He had got it in his head that he was going to have his way, and she run away from him after knocking him down. I can tell you that girl gives as good as she gets. That's when she told me they weren't married. No surprise there. And the reason why they was hiding out was because she was the daughter of a lord, whose name she couldn't mention, who wouldn't let them get married. She now wants to be known as Miss Augusta, like one of the royal princesses, even though I know her name is Lydia 'cause I heard it shouted often enough. That girl can tell some tall tales."

"How did they pay for the room?"

"With sovereigns to start, and then he give me a clasp from his cloak. I can get a nice price for it, so I told him that would take them to the end of the week. But I was almost hoping they couldn't pay so they would leave. I was getting complaints from the other lodgers."

"Have they had any visitors?"

"No, he ain't been out that door. He comes down every morning to read the newspaper after Mr. Epping finishes with it, but since he drinks wine all day long, he falls asleep right after their evening meal. While he's snoring away, Miss Augusta comes down and talks to me. She says he's got a friend who's bringing him the money to buy her wedding clothes. And I asks her why he don't go and get the money himself, and she says it's complicated. His father is an important man what lives in Derbyshire, and since the money has to come so far, that's what's taking so long."

Mr. Rhys gave Mrs. Epping another five pounds and an address and told her to send a messenger if there was any change in the routine of Mr. and Mrs. Royale.

※

While Mrs. Epping was talking to Mr. Rhys, Wickham was staring at a sleeping Lydia and counting the hours until he would be rid of her. Just another day or two, and it would be safe to leave the lodging house.

Before they even left Brighton, Lieutenant Fuller had followed through on his threat to go directly to Captain Wilcox because of Wickham's insistence on taking a sixteen-year-old girl with him. Fuller knew it would be Wilcox who would feel the brunt of Colonel Forster's wrath because it was he who had recommended Wickham for his wife's card parties. Wilcox would have his liver if he ever got his hands on him.

But a colonel in the militia has limited resources, and a search could not go on indefinitely. Colonel Forster would have to accept that the couple had disappeared into the recesses of the largest city in Christendom and could remain hidden indefinitely, and since the Bennets certainly didn't have the wherewithal to conduct a search, Wickham would be able to leave without fear of discovery. But in the meantime, he would have to endure the little brat's company. It was hard to believe it was little more than two weeks since they had left Brighton. It seemed like months.

By the time Wickham and Lydia had changed from the chaise to the hackney in Clapham, he was ready to roll his handkerchief into a ball and stuff it in her mouth. Her incessant chatter would have been annoying enough, but all she cared to talk about were her wedding clothes and where they would set up housekeeping. He knew her to be gullible, but it was turning out she was stupid as well. She believed everything he told her, and she took his lies and built castles in the air with them.

Once they arrived at the Epping lodging house, he was ready to claim his reward for all the frustrating clandestine meetings they had had under the pier. But when he pressed her, she turned on him, telling him he would not get her in bed until she knew for a fact that they were to be married. The only way he could prove that would happen was to buy her the goddamned wedding clothes, and so the standoff began.

He wrote a letter to every person he knew asking for money, explaining his bride was ill, and he needed help with the doctor bills. But he had heard from no one. All he had left was some jewelry he had taken from his paramour. He was trying to figure out what his next step would be when Mr. Rhys arrived at his door. A woman, who identified herself as Mrs. George Bingley, insisted Lydia come with her. Once a hysterical Lydia was reassured that the lady was acting on behalf of the Bennet family and that she and Wickham would be reunited, she agreed to go to the Bingley home in Cheapside. Wickham, who was sandwiched between two strong men, was told by Mr. Rhys to leave the lodging house as quietly as possible, and once out onto the street, he was thrown into a waiting hackney. Not knowing where he was going or what would happen to him, Wickham was terrified. But when he emerged from the carriage, he saw George Bingley's name painted above the door of a warehouse, and he was reassured. If the Bingleys were involved, it was likely Darcy was as well, and from his own personal experience, he knew that Darcy was willing to pay good money to get rid of a bad penny.

Chapter 43

At first light, Darcy went to the stables where his carriage was waiting. He realized he was leaving his sister to make the best of a bad situation, but with Anne and Richard there, he was confident she could deal with any problems that might arise. The three cousins agreed to meet before everyone came down to breakfast, and as they huddled in the study, they discussed how best to proceed.

"As the mistress of Pemberley, I feel I must apologize to Miss Bingley for the remarks Antony made last night," Georgiana began. "What he said was so offensive, I absolutely cringed. There's no excuse, not even for an earl."

"I agree," Richard said. "Only my brother could make Caroline Bingley a sympathetic character, but leave her to me. I shall do my best to divert her attention as well as the Hursts'."

"Even with that, Caroline remains our biggest problem," Anne said, "but one can hope that with Will gone for who knows how long, she will want to cut short her visit. As for Antony, I shall talk to him."

It was agreed that Georgiana would speak to Charles while they were out riding. "I suspect he already knows something is amiss. The atmosphere in the drawing room last night was hardly convivial, and with Will pacing the floor, it was obvious his thoughts were elsewhere."

At breakfast, Richard did not give Caroline any time to dwell on Darcy's absence. "Because of the rain, I understand you were denied a picnic, so I have arranged for one today. It will be in the gardens, so we need not even get into a carriage." Although the Hursts were included, the colonel had made it seem as if it was a personal invitation, and Caroline quickly forgot about Mr. Darcy's departure.

Georgiana was aware that Mr. Bingley knew nothing about her connection to George Wickham. In order for Charles to understand the gravity of the situation confronting Lydia and the Bennet family, she needed to acquaint him with what had happened in Ramsgate. Because of those events, Georgiana knew that Wickham's elopement with Lydia was no romance, and for reasons she could not fathom, he was willing to destroy the reputation of a sixteen-year-old girl.

"When Darcy and I encountered Wickham in Meryton," Charles said, "it was obvious they disliked each other, but for understandable reasons, your brother chose not to share the details of their history. You tell me that my brother, George, is presently looking for Lydia. Well, I can assure you that he will find her. He has what he calls his 'eyes' throughout London, and England for that matter.

"Under the circumstances, I feel my sisters and I should

leave Pemberley," Charles continued. "I only learned last night that Caroline and Louisa had received an invitation to go to Scarborough to visit friends, and it should be a simple matter to leave a few days earlier. As for me, before returning to London, I shall stop in Hertfordshire to offer my services to the Bennet family. However, I would be less than truthful if I did not tell you I have selfish reasons for calling at Longbourn. I am in love with Miss Jane Bennet, and it is my intention to make her an offer of marriage."

"My brother has told me of your interest in Miss Bennet, and I am very happy for you. I am sure it will be a source of joy to a family sorely lacking in it. May I be the first to offer my congratulations?"

"I would accept them gladly, but I am unsure of how my offer will be received. Miss Bennet has reason to be angry with me. But she is a kind person, and I have hope I shall be forgiven."

"Mr. Bingley, I have a picnic to arrange for this afternoon, and our cook, Mrs. Bradshaw, will want as much time to prepare as possible, so I must return to the house." Before turning her horse toward Pemberley, Georgiana added, "I am very glad you will not hold Lydia's behavior against Miss Bennet. She is innocent of all blame and should not suffer because of her sister's indiscretions." She only hoped her brother would agree with that statement.

Anne sent Jackson to talk to Lord Fitzwilliam's man, and after waiting thirty minutes, Gregg appeared, but only to say that Lord Fitzwilliam would not be dining at all today as he had a terrific headache.

"I did not ask him to dine. Gregg, tell your master he should be prepared to receive his cousin in one half hour."

When Anne went into Lord Fitzwilliam's apartment, she found him with a wet cloth over his eyes. She believed him when he said he had a pounding headache. Except for a glass or two of diluted port, he had little to drink since his arrival, and he was experiencing the unpleasant side effects of a quick withdrawal from alcohol.

Pointing to a letter on the table, he said, "I have already dictated a letter of apology to Miss Bingley. I find her incredibly irritating, but I was rude to a guest of my host. Fortunately, Darcy did not hear or he would have shown me the door."

"She is still here. Would you not want to tell her in person?"

"I can't, Anne. I truly can't. My nerves are stretched to the breaking point. I am greatly in need of a glass of wine, but I will not have it. Seeing Georgiana reminded me that I have two daughters who will come out into society in a few short years. I do not want to embarrass them. So I will remain at Pemberley until I am sober, and, hopefully, that will become a permanent condition."

"I want you to come to Rosings with me." Silence. "You haven't been to Rosings in years."

"There is a reason for that. Your mother lives there."

"You will not see as much of her as you think. She retires early. You get up late. If you took up riding again, you would be out of doors for most of the day. Besides, everyone is leaving, and you will not want to stay here by yourself."

"Everyone is leaving? Surely my behavior was not so objectionable that the guests are running for the nearest exit."

"Will had to return to London and left at dawn. Georgiana needs to prepare for her debut, and, frankly, I am tired and in need of a rest." Anne was in need of more than a rest. She was exhausted, and Mrs. Jenkinson was urging her to return to Rosings, especially since her mistress was taking drafts of laudanum to help her sleep.

"I actually would prefer to be in Kent," Antony said after thinking it over for a few moments. "My daughters are with my mother in Ashford, and I could go visit them."

Through all of this, Antony kept the cloth across his eyes, but Anne lifted it, so she might kiss his forehead, and her cousin took her hand and gently squeezed it. He loved this fragile woman more than he could say.

"You tell me Darcy is already gone? Damn! I had a message for him. An old friend of his from his time in France, the former Christina Caxton, is in London and wanted to visit with him."

"Where is she staying?"

"With Mrs. Conway. Apparently, the late Mr. Caxton was a supporter of Whig causes, and since Darcy is of a like mind, I am sure that is how they met."

"I do not know Mrs. Caxton, and at the moment, he has a lot to think about. But I shall break my journey in London, and I shall tell him. Visiting with an old friend might be exactly what he needs."

Chapter 44

THE PICNIC WENT MUCH better than expected largely due to the presence of Colonel Fitzwilliam and the absence of Lord Fitzwilliam. Richard was so successful in diverting Caroline's attention that Georgiana was beginning to wonder if there was more to it than just amusing a difficult guest. He had recently discussed with Will the possibility of selling his commission. But the only way he could leave the army was if he found a rich wife, and Caroline Bingley was very rich.

With Richard and Caroline engrossed in conversation, she turned her attention to the Hursts. But as soon as they had finished their lunch, Mr. Hurst found a comfortable spot under a tree and quickly fell asleep. As this was nothing out of the norm, Mrs. Hurst joined Caroline in conversing with the colonel. Compared to her calculating sister, Louisa was the most uncomplicated woman Georgiana had ever met.

Because Anne had decided to stay at the house to humor Antony, Charles and Georgiana found themselves looking to each other for company. With so much on their minds, neither had much to say.

Georgiana was thinking about how much her life had changed simply because she had reached her eighteenth birthday. Before leaving London, she had received a letter from Mrs. Reynolds with her recommendations as to which room each guest would use. Upon her arrival at Pemberley, she had to meet with Mrs. Bradshaw to go over the menus. A wise person never challenged Cook as she had been at Pemberley for more than twenty years and ran her own little fiefdom belowstairs. All these consultations were mere formalities because the servants were more capable than she in running the house, but they would not proceed without the master's or mistress's consent. But Georgiana did not want to discuss replacing linen with Mrs. Reynolds nor menus with Mrs. Bradshaw. She wanted to share with someone the excitement she was feeling about her upcoming debut and her dreams for the future as she had done with Elizabeth Bennet.

Following their ride to the Peak, Georgiana had shared with Elizabeth that she was penning a novel. Unlike her brother, Lizzy did not frown, but showed real interest in her story.

"The novel is about Pompeii at the time Mt. Vesuvius erupted. I have changed it a good deal since I started. Actually, I change it all the time. Thoughts keep popping into my head, and then I go in a new direction. Anyway, it is about two lovers who are kept apart because of their different places in society. Just when it seems as if they have surmounted all obstacles in their path, another woman enters the picture who is determined to keep them apart because she wants the man for herself, although he does not love her, which is evident to everyone *except* her. It is just at that time the volcano erupts, with its rivers of lava and suffocating gases, and ash and people running about willy-nilly.

Amidst this chaos, the lovers must find each other. At first, I thought I should have the woman who interferes in their romance overtaken by the lava flow, but that seemed a bit harsh, even though she is not likable at all."

Lizzy could hardly imagine who she was talking about. Although Georgiana was only three years younger than she, the difference in their ages seemed greater, probably because the daughters of society's elite tended to live sheltered existences until they married. If Georgiana was typical of her class, she would have been coddled by nurses before being turned over to governesses and tutors and piano and dance masters, all in preparation for that first season where, it was hoped, she would find a husband from among the aristocracy or landed gentry. But there was something different about Georgiana. She had a bit of the rebel in her.

"Has anyone read your writings?" Lizzy had asked.

"Oh, no! Will does not approve of women writing novels because he says it degrades them, but I see nothing degrading in it. Frances Burney was a lady-in-waiting to Queen Charlotte, and Maria Edgeworth's novels all have a moral to share. But I am not without hope as he is the first to admit that society is undergoing great changes. I just hope it undergoes them fast enough for them to benefit me." Elizabeth had encouraged her to keep writing and asked if she might read it when she had finished the first draft.

"I would be honored if you would read my humble manuscript."

Georgiana liked Elizabeth for many reasons, but she particularly admired how feisty she was. She had been greatly surprised when Elizabeth had talked back to Will at the stables. She had never seen anyone argue with her brother, and from their exchange, it was apparent that was not the first time they had engaged in an animated discussion. And from watching the two of them standing on the promontory, she was quite sure that his love was no longer unrequited. But now there was this horrible business with Lydia Bennet, and she was unsure what Will would do because it involved George Wickham. But there was no time to dwell on anything other than her obligations as mistress of Pemberley, and so she had to think about supper and that evening's entertainment and not about Caroline Bingley fleeing for her life in a burning Pompeii.

When Anne went into Lord Fitzwilliam's apartment, he was sitting in the same chair but without the cloth across his eyes, and he had color back in his cheeks.

"Gregg, why don't you go to the kitchen and have some lunch," Anne suggested. "I wish to speak to Lord Fitzwilliam."

"Whatever it is, I did not do it, Anne. I have not been out of the room. Have I, Gregg?"

"No, Milord. You have been here since Miss de Bourgh's last visit."

"I have even been nice to you, Gregg, haven't I?"

"Exceptionally so, Milord."

"No need for sarcasm, Gregg, but do go and have something to eat."

After his servant left, Anne said, "You do know that man is worth his weight in gold."

"Which is about what I owe him in wages. I have encouraged him to find another position, but he tells me he enjoys the excitement and unpredictability of serving me."

Looking around the room, Anne could see that she had interrupted Gregg's packing her cousin's clothes. "Antony, are you leaving Pemberley?"

"Yes. I am returning to town in the morning."

"But I thought it was not safe for you to be in London because Mr. Lynton had challenged you to a duel."

"Well, he is such a hothead that I am sure someone else has offended him in the interim. The reason I left town so abruptly was I feared he would actually come looking for me with a pistol and not wait for me to respond to his challenge. And if he calls me out again, I shall not fight. I do not mind being called a coward. Sticks and stones may break my bones, but I will not let Mr. Lynton shoot me."

"But you also said you were going to stay here until you had recovered."

"Until I was sober, which I am. I have not been this sober since… I cannot remember that far back. But I have received a letter from my mother telling me she has found a buyer for the manor house, so I must return to London."

"You are going to sell Briarwood, and your mother approves?" Anne asked in disbelief. Briarwood had been in the Fitzwilliam family for two hundred years. Its first incarnation was as a modest summerhouse built to escape the heat of London, but it had been expanded to its present size of one hundred plus rooms. No family, other than the Fizwilliams, had ever lived there.

"It was my mother who suggested it. We cannot live together, as she is an unrepentant scold. But we do like each other, and she knows of all I have done to maintain the estate. It is older, but not as beautiful as Rosings, and I cannot afford it."

"But your father left you so much money."

"He also left me with crumbling cottages, drains that do not drain, and a leaking roof. I have sold all our properties in Ireland and three hundred acres of parkland, and as I am sure you have heard, many of the paintings and antiquities. I was even forced to sell Grandmother Fitzwilliam's portrait, but because it is a Reynolds, I was advanced a good price. I am sure Darcy will buy it back, as he always does the right thing, which is why I mentioned it to him."

"Without explanation, I might add, which made you look very bad."

"Why should I bother to explain? I will never win Fitzwilliam Darcy's approval. I have wasted a good deal of money, and our cousin will not forgive me. Besides, the last time I was at Briarwood was nearly a year ago when Eleanor threatened to set *my* dogs on me if I came back. Now, that wasn't right. She should get her own dogs."

"Do you know who the purchaser is?"

"It would have to be someone like the Bingleys, who are drowning in money, as they are the only ones with the financial resources to make the necessary repairs."

"But Richard knows nothing of this."

"I know. But I did not want to give him the mistaken impression that he would have enough money to marry a woman who does not have a fortune of her own, such as Miss Pennington, the daughter of our solicitor." Looking out the window, he could see his brother walking arm-in-arm with Caroline Bingley in the gardens. If Richard married her, he would be paying a high price for financial independence, but it could very well happen.

"This is all beside the point, Anne. I am returning to London, and you are going with me. You have circles under your eyes, and you are pale. You are the smartest person, male or female, in our family, and whatever you have got up to here at Pemberley, I am sure you have succeeded. Now, it is time for you to go back to Rosings."

"It is out of the question as I cannot leave Georgiana. When she returns to London, that is when I shall return."

"I am sorry, my dear, but I must insist, as Mrs. Jenkinson came to me last night to tell me you are taking laudanum, which you do not do at Rosings."

"On occasion, I do take it at Rosings to suppress my coughing. I have taken it here because I do not want to cough in front of the Bingleys, as it can go on and on."

"All the more reason to return to Rosings. Richard told me last night that he must return to his regiment, so, if necessary, I will leave Gregg here to see Georgiana back to town. I suspect the Bingleys will want to leave because Darcy is gone. Even if all remained, you need not stay as Jackson manages the servants as well as any colonel commanding a regiment. So you see, my dear cousin, you need not worry. We leave our young cousin and friends in good hands."

Anne returned to her room to find Mrs. Jenkinson busy packing, so busy that she would not make eye contact with her mistress. Anne could never be angry with her companion, but she did not like it when others made decisions for her, which happened all too often with her mother at Rosings, and which Antony had just done. But there was something else that was bothering her, and when she realized what it was, she quickly returned to her cousin's room.

"Antony, how do you know that Mrs. Caxton is staying with Mrs. Conway? Mrs. Conway is an important person in the Whig opposition, and you are a Tory. I would think your paths would rarely cross, if at all."

"You are correct. I have never met Mrs. Conway. It was Mrs. Caxton herself who told me. Apparently, she knew our cousin from his time in France and remembered that his cousin was an earl. She sent a note asking if she could visit as she was trying to communicate with Darcy."

"And you received a stranger without a letter of introduction?"

"Yes, and very glad that I did. She is an enchanting creature—quite beautiful with a lovely neck, and I imagine very long legs, my greatest weakness. She declared herself to be an old friend of Darcy's, and I treated her as such. I did not speculate on their friendship, but if I had engaged in such an activity, I could easily have imagined them as being very, very close friends while in France, which makes her staying with Mrs. Conway quite interesting."

"Antony, Will knows that you shared personal information about him with *The Insider*, and he was very angry. Please promise me you will never do that again." The thought of two of Will's romantic interests living together under the same roof would sell out the magazine as he was considered to be one of London's most eligible bachelors.

"I can promise that quite easily, as it was more trouble than it was worth. But I was being pressed by my tailor, pun intended, and in need of ready cash. And I would like to correct the record. It is true I am guilty of telling the man from *The Insider* that Darcy was shortly to become engaged to Miss Montford, but my source was her brother, who assured me that the only thing left to do was to sign the marriage contract. However, I was not the source for the item about Darcy leaving Mrs. Conway's house in the early hours of the morning. I am sure he was seen by the man from *The Insider*. You know he does hang about in the shadows hoping for a story. On more than one occasion, he has hailed a cab for me."

"Maybe it would be best if we did not tell Will about Mrs. Caxton at the present time," Anne suggested. "He does have an awful lot on his mind."

"My lips are sealed, but since Mrs. Caxton knows so few people in London, I thought I might befriend her." Anne frowned. "Do not concern yourself, my dear cousin, I am not at the moment inclined to take a mistress, especially one with no money. But I must admit, if money was not a consideration, I would be sending her flowers upon my arrival in London."

Chapter 45

ALTHOUGH NOTHING NEW WAS known about Lydia, Mr. Gardiner convinced Mr. Bennet to return to Longbourn, where he could be of some comfort to his family and draw comfort from them as well. But before leaving for London, Mr. Bennet had promised that changes would be made, and he was as good as his word. When he saw Jane taking a tray up to her mother's room, he ordered it back to the kitchen.

"Unless someone is ill, we take our meals in the dining room, and I will deliver that news to your mother myself. However, I would like you to tell her I will be visiting shortly."

When Jane attempted to explain the fragile condition of their mother's nerves, Mr. Bennet responded, "Your mother's nerves have been my constant companion for more than twenty years, but we are about to part company."

When Mr. Bennet came into the room, Mrs. Bennet pretended to be asleep, but her husband was not in the mood for games.

"I am not leaving, Fanny, so please sit up." After a reluctant Mrs. Bennet appeared from under the covers, her husband continued. "My dear wife, I have done you a disservice all these years. You were very young when I married you, and I should have taken more care. But because I believed we would have a son to negate the entail and to see you through your old age, I went happily about my business and neglected my responsibilities as husband and father. As I am five years older than you, it is highly likely I shall die before you, and because of our financial condition, you will have to live within your means. Since you have little practice at it, as of today, we will economize, so that we might put aside as much money as possible. You will better manage the house, which means that Kitty must wear her frocks longer, and baubles are banned forthwith. There is more, but we shall discuss it in detail at another time. I look forward to dining with you this evening."

Mrs. Bennet did come down to supper, but her presence only served to shine a light on the tension in the family. No one seemed to want to make the effort to begin a conversation, so brief statements were followed by prolonged silences. Afterwards, everyone gathered in the front parlor, where Mary and Kitty were occupied by their newfound interest in needlework, and Mrs. Bennet was knitting a shawl, something she had not done in years. After Mr. Bennet retired to his study, Jane and Lizzy went to their bedroom so that they might talk.

"How has Kitty been bearing up under the weight of all of this bad news?" Lizzy asked her sister.

"Well enough. She was fortunate in that Papa went away so quickly, as he was furious with her when he learned she knew of Lydia's intended elopement. I do believe she regrets that she had not acted differently when she received Lydia's letter, but I doubt it would have made any difference anyway. But no more about Kitty or Mama or Mary. We have not spoken about you and what happened at Pemberley."

Lizzy closed her eyes and smiled at the memory. "Mr. Darcy could not have been more gracious, and we easily fell into conversation as people do who have known each other for a long time. I was deeply touched by his affection for Miss de Bourgh and the care he takes with his sister, and Pemberley quite transforms him. When we walked in the gardens, I felt as if he had shed the hard shell he puts on when he is uncomfortable with his company, as he most definitely was at the assembly *and* at Aunt Philips's card parties *and* at Lucas Lodge," Lizzy said, laughing. "But the Mr. Darcy I knew so well in Hertfordshire was also present. He is used to getting his own way, and he did not like it when I would not give in to him.

"I often found him looking at me, but not with that quizzical expression I had seen at Netherfield and Rosings. It was a softer look," and Lizzy remembered their time together in the stables when he had placed his hands on her waist and had run his fingers along her cheek. She had wanted to do the same to him. Would she ever have another such opportunity?

"The night before we departed Lambton, he asked if he could come to the inn to say good-bye to me. Not having read your letter, I agreed. When he arrived, I was quite upset, and he insisted on knowing the cause. I shall never forget his response when I mentioned Wickham's name. He stood up and stepped away from me, and the look on his face, I shall never forget. He left as quickly as civility would allow."

"But do you think it was his intention to make another offer?"

"I am quite sure of it because of several comments he made,

but I can't imagine he would ask for my hand now, especially if Lydia marries Wickham."

"But why should the actions of another prevent him from proposing to you? First his pride gets in the way and now this. To my mind, all obstacles to the union are self-imposed."

"That is unfair, Jane. You forget Wickham's designs on Miss Darcy, which would have bound his sister to a man we now know to be a seducer and debaucher."

"No, Lizzy. I have not forgotten. But Wickham's plan to elope with Mr. Darcy's sister failed, and she suffered nothing greater than embarrassment. So the fact is, Mr. Wickham is a scoundrel who has successfully deceived two impressionable young ladies. One has been restored to her family, none the worse for the experience, while Lydia will be branded for years to come even if she marries. Considering how unequally people from the different classes are treated, it is best we are kept apart."

"You are speaking like this because you are still hurting as a result of Mr. Bingley's actions."

"No, Lizzy. It is that I am wiser because of Mr. Bingley's actions. Now I better understand how the world works, and I have changed because of it."

Each day, the post was eagerly anticipated in hopes of news from London, and when Lizzy saw Mrs. Hill paying the postman, she asked her if there was a letter from Mr. Gardiner.

"No, miss. The only letter is for Miss Jane from Mr. Nesbitt. He writes so often that he left me money to pay the postman."

Lizzy delivered the letter to Jane, who sat reading it on the edge of the bed with a puzzled expression. When she finished, she threw herself backward and let out a cry and then began to rock back and forth with her arms across her chest. Lizzy immediately sought to comfort her sister over what was obviously very bad news, only to find that she was not crying, but laughing hysterically.

When Jane could finally speak, she sat up and said, "Apparently, word of Lydia's elopement has reached Watford, and Mr. Nesbitt writes his practice is not so well established that he can afford to be associated with scandal. As a result, he must withdraw his attentions. Oh, Lizzy, we are in dire straits indeed if I cannot even secure Mr. Nesbitt," and she began to laugh until tears rolled down her face.

"Then you are relieved by this news?" Lizzy asked hopefully.

"Oh, yes," she said, taking her sister's offered handkerchief. "He is a very nice man, but he can be quite odd," and she pulled a box out from underneath their bed and showed Lizzy the gifts he had given her.

"He sent you a lock of his mother's hair? I have never heard of such a thing." Lizzy wasn't sure if she found it to be funny or repulsive.

"I think it was his attempt to let me know his mother approved of me."

"There are other ways less tangible. For example, 'Jane, my mother likes you very much.'"

"I know. That's what I thought, but then he sent a bee trapped in tree resin. Mary believes the B was meant to represent Bennet."

"Or Beloved."

"Oh, I would never have guessed that. It would have been much too cryptic for me." And the two sisters started to laugh again, something they had not done in the long days since Lizzy's return. "There is another reason why I am glad it is over. Mary is in love with Mr. Nesbitt. Whenever he called, it was Mary who stayed with us and Mary who walked him to the gate, and, honestly, they do have a lot in common. It was she who identified the amber specimen. She would have been perfect for him, but now it doesn't matter. Neither of us is to have him."

"Well, Jane, I would not have thought it possible, but something good has come out of Lydia's elopement. You will not have to marry Mr. Nesbitt."

They again erupted into laughter, and it was a sound that drifted into their father's library and gave him hope that his lack of foresight had not destroyed the soul of his family.

Chapter 46

THE DAY AFTER DARCY'S arrival in London, he immediately went to see George Bingley, who was feeling confident that Lydia would quickly be found.

"It is merely a process of elimination. Since I received your letter, my associates have narrowed our area of search considerably. We have also spoken to his fellow officers, and in interviewing these men, we have learned something I am sure will distress you. Wickham has been spreading the lie that he is the natural son of Mr. David Darcy of Pemberley. I took the liberty of contacting your solicitor, Mr. Stone, who will be here within the hour with the file regarding the financial and personal information concerning Wickham's adoption by your estate manager."

George had anticipated Darcy's reaction, and he had a glass of wine at the ready. But no amount of wine could settle a man who had just heard the most malicious lie made against his beloved father.

"Once we have Wickham, we will put an end to this slander.

Wickham will not wish to spend any time in prison but, if he repeats this lie, he will be prosecuted to the fullest extent of the law."

By the time Mr. Stone arrived, Darcy could still feel the heat in his face generated by his hatred of Wickham, but he kept his mind clear. Since all the major players were now dead, his solicitor was free to reveal the full contents of the file.

"George Wickham was born to Martha Ferris, the personal maid of actress Elaine Trench and actor Adam Spendel. Your uncle, George Ashton, was an acquaintance of Miss Trench, and she knew that he had fathered a number of children, whom he had placed with families in the country. Because Miss Trench was fond of her maid, she asked Mr. Ashton to assist her in this regard."

Darcy looked puzzled. His parents were generous to a fault, but they were disgusted by George Ashton's affairs. Taking someone's illegitimate child might give the impression to the elder Darcy's brother-in-law that they condoned such actions.

"I have been the family solicitor for nearly thirty-five years, Mr. Darcy, and I can understand your confusion. However, your parents were very fond of the elder Mr. Wickham and his wife. They were childless, and with your parents' consent, they offered to raise the young George Wickham. As you know, your father was also fond of the boy, and he agreed to provide the funds necessary for his education and for a living in the church, the law, or the army. This was an act of generosity, and in no way obligates you or your heirs to provide any additional monetary assistance to Wickham. All of these facts are supported by the proper documentation. I might add that both of Wickham's natural parents are dead. That is all there is to it, sir."

That was all there was to it, except that it wasn't, and Lydia Bennet was proof of that.

That meeting had taken place three days earlier, and in that time, nothing new had come to light. Darcy's frustration was only equaled by his sense of guilt. Knowing Wickham's history of unpaid debts, gambling, and seduction, he had chosen to remain silent when he had seen Wickham in Meryton. It would have taken so little effort on his part to warn others about him. Mercer could have gone into the village and discreetly mentioned to one or two merchants that he knew Wickham left unpaid debts wherever he went. A private word with the vicar might have been sufficient to alert the young ladies of the village that Wickham was a man bent on relieving them of their maidenhood with no consequences to him. But he didn't do either of those things, as he was a Darcy and Darcys didn't involve themselves in such unsavory situations.

And what had his pride cost Elizabeth? He could hardly bear to think of her with tears streaming down her face and his inability to comfort her. To his mind the only way he could make amends was to recover her sister, and all of his hopes in that regard rested with George Bingley.

Mercer could see how heavily the business with Lydia and Wickham weighed on his master, and he encouraged him to go to his club or ride in the park—something—anything to keep his mind from dwelling on the missing couple. He took Mercer's advice and felt better for it, but today he intended to remain at the house and answer business letters, which is what he was doing when Mercer announced that Mrs. Aumont had presented her card and was waiting in a hackney for his reply.

"I do not know Mrs. Aumont."

"The lady said you would remember her as Christina Caxton."

Darcy was out of his chair like a bullet and immediately went to the window. Of course, he knew he would be unable to see her as she was in the cab, but he needed to be convinced she was actually there. And then the absurdity of his situation brought a smile to his face and then all-out laughter because if he did not laugh he might very well cry. Earlier in the day, he had been pining for Elizabeth with her luminous eyes and curly hair that refused to stay in place, and he had begged the Fates for some sort of diversion. Well, his plea had been answered.

"Sir, will you receive the lady?"

"Yes, Mercer. She is an old friend."

When Christina walked into the drawing room, six years of time melted away. Was it possible for someone not to age? Her blond hair and green eyes and flawless complexion—everything the same, including the most delicious lips he had ever tasted.

"Mrs. Aumont, welcome back to England."

"Mr. Darcy, it is very good to see you again," she said with a slight curtsey.

"Mercer, please arrange for some tea."

"No, thank you, Mr. Darcy. I am feeling guilty enough about coming here unannounced, so I shall keep my visit brief." Mrs. Aumont removed her pelisse to reveal a décolletage that stirred very pleasant memories.

Darcy instructed Mercer to pour two glasses of wine. "Have you returned to London permanently, Mrs. Aumont?"

"I shall answer your question only if you call me Christina." After Darcy nodded, she continued, "My husband died last year after a lengthy illness. Up until that time, my being English had never been a problem, but with Wellington fighting Joseph

Bonaparte in Spain, I was feeling less welcome. Without my husband's protection, I felt quite vulnerable. Mr. Aumont had secured a pass for me to leave France, and I thought it best to use it while I was still sure that I could."

Christina accepted the wine and took a tiny sip, which is something he remembered her doing. She explained that a woman could gain weight very quickly if she overindulged in food and drink, and she didn't want to lose her figure. She had obviously succeeded.

"Where are you staying?"

"With Mrs. Conway. She lives in…"

As soon as he heard Mrs. Conway's name, Darcy started coughing, nearly spitting out the wine. "Mrs. Conway of Bedford Square—the Whig hostess?" he croaked.

"Yes. She mentioned that you were acquaintances and of similar views politically, which I found quite gratifying because Mr. Caxton was a champion of Whig causes. I was surprised as I would have guessed that the Darcys would be Tories."

"I do lean more towards the Whig point of view. These wars will end eventually, and grain prices will go down rapidly. In addition to my own interests, we must be in a position to protect the small farmer and our tenants, who will suffer greatly if something is not done."

"That is all very admirable and interesting, William. But after six years, do you really want to talk about grain prices?"

"Sorry. I never was good at small talk."

"No, you weren't, but we didn't talk all that much, did we?"

"Not about politics. I am sure of that," Darcy said, feeling his neckcloth tighten.

"Do you remember our last time together?"

"It was Bordeaux, I believe. The home of the Comte de somebody. The name eludes me at the moment."

"I wasn't asking for a geographical reference. I meant where we stayed together."

How could he not remember? When you made love on and off all night, it tended to stay with you.

"Were you allowed to bring your personal possessions with you when you left France?" he said, changing the subject as delicately as a coach and six making a U-turn in the road.

"I was told my chests were to follow, but I am beginning to wonder if it will ever happen."

"You are short of funds then?"

"William, I do not wish it to appear that I have come with hat in hand."

"I will gladly provide you with assistance."

"That is very generous of you, but I must tell you there is an excellent chance I shall be unable to repay you."

"Please do not think of it as a loan but as an arrangement between friends. Shall I send the cheque around to Mrs. Conway's residence?"

"If you don't mind, may I come by tomorrow for a visit? We have not spoken at all about what you have been doing all these years, and Mrs. Conway tells me you remain a bachelor and a much sought after one."

Darcy assisted Mrs. Aumont with her pelisse, and she turned around and ran her fingers along his chin and tapped his lips lightly with her finger. "Until tomorrow. Shall we say 3:00?"

After Christina left, he collapsed into a chair. "Mercer, the gods are toying with me. I have always prided myself on keeping my life as uncomplicated as possible. So why, at this moment when it is in such turmoil, does my former lover appear at my door?" As he looked out the window, he watched as her hackney made its way through London's crowded streets. "Do you know that old adage, Mercer, 'Be careful what you wish for because you might get it?' Just this morning, I was in need of a diversion, and I got it—in spades."

"Perhaps, we will have good news shortly of Miss Lydia, and you will then be able to turn your full attention to Miss Elizabeth."

"That is my greatest hope, but in the meantime, please arrange for tea with Mrs. Aumont for tomorrow. And, Mercer, you may have all my breeches. In the future, I shall wear only trousers. Life is entirely too unpredictable."

Chapter 47

WHILE DARCY WAS DRESSING, he gave Mercer very specific instructions for that afternoon's engagement with Christina Caxton.

"I want a light meal served—not something that is going to take all afternoon. After we have finished eating, if Mrs. Aumont does not leave immediately, we shall go into the drawing room. But I do not want to be in there for more than fifteen minutes. I shall tell her I am expecting an important letter, which is the truth, and if she has not left by that time, I want you to come in and tell me the letter has arrived. I do not like deception. But she is an old friend, and I do not want to hurt her feelings. I just want her to leave."

It was a simple plan that went awry immediately as Mrs. Aumont sent word that she would not be able to join Darcy at the agreed-upon time, but would visit around 5:00, making it more difficult to show her the door after fifteen minutes. Darcy, who knew he was miserable at small talk, would be at a loss as to how to fill the time. There was nothing in the rules of deportment taught to him by his mother and governess that covered former lovers.

He was already on edge because earlier in the day he had gone to George Bingley's office in hopes of hearing some good news. But George dealt only in facts, and there was nothing new to report about Lydia and Wickham. Darcy wanted so much to write to Elizabeth, but what was there to say? "I am part of the reason your sister is with Wickham, and I haven't a clue where she is."

When Mercer showed Mrs. Aumont into the room, he took a deep breath. She was so beautiful. Who could resist her charms? He knew the answer: A man desperately in love with another could, and he gestured for her to sit on the sofa, while he sat on the chair opposite to her. But Christina patted the sofa and asked Darcy to join her. As soon as he sat down, he explained he was expecting a letter from a friend, and once he received it, he would need to leave immediately and hoped she would understand.

"I promise to be brief, and, therefore, let me begin immediately. Yesterday, your discomfort was so apparent that I thought I should not come back at all because I was embarrassed. But I wanted to explain my behavior," and she looked to him for a sign that she should proceed, and he nodded.

"My husband and I were living happily in a small villa in the south of France when he became ill, and he never regained his health. When he died, I found it necessary to sell almost everything we owned in order to pay the bills. Even with that, I was never able to fully settle the accounts, which made no one happy, including myself.

"Although I am half French, I was known as *La Femme Anglaise*, and because of the fighting between the French and English, I found a very cool welcome where there had once been a warm one. I was so uncomfortable that I decided to leave France. The farther north I traveled the more hostility I met. I finally called on an old friend who escorted me to the frontier, and I sailed from Ostend. I was so happy to be on English soil, but then it dawned on me. I had not given any thought as to what I would do once I reached England.

"Please remember I have not been in England for ten years, and the first person I thought about was Mrs. Conway because her husband and Mr. Caxton had been political allies and had corresponded for years. She was so kind and offered to provide me with a room. When she asked if I had any friends, I mentioned that I knew you. She said that was fortunate as you and she were good friends, but she knew you to be in the country. Then I remembered your cousin was an earl. So I wrote to him, and he sent a hackney for me."

"You met Lord Fitzwilliam? Good grief!"

"We spent a lovely afternoon together. I found him to be very amusing."

"Oh, he keeps his family in stitches."

"I can easily imagine him to be a thorn in the side of his relations, but he was quite gracious to me. He was very forward in the questions, and I confided in him that I had arrived in England with little more than my clothes and a promise of a draft from my bank, which I have not received. He said that he would help me in any way, except financially, as he was broke. I told him it was my intention to support myself as a dressmaker. My father was a tailor and my mother a seamstress, and basically, I served an apprenticeship under them. As a result, I can sew anything.

"It was then that he made the most incredible offer. He told me that all of his wife's dresses were upstairs. He explained they were estranged, and he had written to her to come get them. Her answer was that she would not wear anything she had ever worn when she was with him. In an example of supreme understatement, he said, 'She does not like me very much.'" Christina then stood up and took off her pelisse. "This is one of Lady Fitzwilliam's gowns, which I have remade with some additional fabric from another. Her dresses were out of style, but the material is beautiful. Is it not?" And she turned around, so he could admire all of the dress.

"It is lovely. You could easily become a dressmaker to a duchess."

"A *couturier*, William. A *couturier* can charge more than a dressmaker, and I already have a commission. Mrs. Conway gave my name to Lady Edgemont, which is why I was late."

"My sincere congratulations to you, Christina, and now that I have seen your handiwork, I shall certainly recommend you to others. But until you are established, I hope you will accept my cheque as my contribution to the support of an emerging *artiste*."

"Thank you, William. I wish I were in a position to refuse your offer, but I am not. As for yesterday, I must explain. Because I left everything familiar behind me, I was looking for a life raft to cling to until I could make my own way, and that is why I came here. But it was so obvious you were uncomfortable, possibly for many reasons, but I am quite sure of one. You are a man in love, but I do not think all is well there. I shall not pry. I will only say I hope that whatever keeps you apart will be quickly resolved. What we had in France remains a lovely memory for me, but it rightfully should stay a memory and I shall speak no more of it."

At that point, Mercer came into the room to tell his master

that the letter he was expecting had arrived, and he went so far as to place a letter on a tray.

"It is all right, Mercer. I can see to it later."

"Excuse me, sir, but this *is* the one you have been waiting for," and he held it up as proof that it really was a letter from George Bingley. Darcy was on his feet and gave a sigh of relief when he recognized Bingley's handwriting.

"I shall detain you no longer as you have urgent business to see to," Christina said. "I am just happy you really do need to leave, and it was not because you were trying to get rid of me." Darcy smiled weakly. "Go on. Read your letter. Mercer can hail a cab for me," and she held out her pelisse, so that Darcy might help her put it on. "I hope to see you about town," and she allowed him to kiss her hand, and then she went downstairs with Mercer.

Darcy tore through Bingley's seal, and there were the words he had been waiting for since he had arrived in London.

Mr. Darcy,

Wickham and Lydia Bennet have been found. They are not married. Despite their having shared a lodging room, it is my belief, based on testimony from the landlady, that she is as she was when she left Longbourn. Mr. and Mrs. Gardiner have taken their niece home with them, and a post rider has been sent to Longbourn to advise them of our success. However, Mr. Wickham remains in my custody. I would ask that you come to my offices at your earliest convenience so that we might proceed in making arrangements that will benefit the young Miss Bennet.
  Sincerely, George Bingley

By that time, Mercer had returned and poured Darcy a wine. "Lydia Bennet has been recovered and is in the care of her aunt and uncle. Her family will shortly have news that their daughter is safe. Hopefully, no matter what happens from this point on, the worst is behind us."

"May I suggest a letter to Miss Elizabeth might be in order, sir?"

"Not yet. Not until I have all the information. But at least now the picture of her with tear-stained cheeks at the inn in Derbyshire will be replaced by that of her dancing circles in the gardens of Pemberley," he said, smiling. "Mercer, please have a hackney out front in ten minutes. Too much time has already been lost," and he took the stairs two at a time.

Lizzy lay quietly in the dark with her sister beside her in a deep sleep. They had talked well into the night, and she smiled at the memory of how they had laughed about Mr. Nesbitt and his inept courtship. It was a welcome respite from the tension that had descended upon the Bennet household. Surely, it was a sign of healing when one could laugh again. Now, with Mr. Nesbitt out of the picture, maybe it would be possible to remind Jane of Mr. Bingley's many attributes. She would make no dramatic statements about true love and forgiveness, but rather talk about the times Jane and Mr. Bingley were together and their compatibility and shared memories.

Lizzy did not consider herself to be a romantic, certainly not like the ladies in a novel or a Shakespearean play, as she was much too practical for that. However, she did believe that two souls could come together, so that the one would know if something had happened to the other despite distance or war.

With all of her being, she believed she had touched Mr. Darcy's heart, and if he had stopped loving her, surely she would be able to sense that. But she had no such feeling.

The more she thought about their last time together at the inn at Lambton, the more convinced she was that he had not stepped away from her in disgust. Instead, he had already formed a plan to help find Lydia, thus explaining his hasty departure.

Again, she returned to the time they were together in the stables at Pemberley. If it had not been for Colonel Fitzwilliam's untimely arrival, he would have kissed her, and she would have looked into his beautiful gray-green eyes and told him that she loved him.

Wherever Mr. Darcy was, she believed he was still thinking of her as she could almost feel his presence. That would not be possible if he had put her out of his mind. No, she had reason to hope, and she would cling to that until proved wrong.

Chapter 48

Even though Hannah Bingley had seven children, and was raising two of her grandchildren, she had never met anyone like Lydia Bennet. Without embarrassment, the girl had explained that she had done nothing more serious than to give her parents a fright, and nothing Hannah had said had changed her mind. Before turning her over to the care of her aunt and uncle, Mrs. Bingley thought it would be helpful if Mr. Bingley talked with her.

When Mrs. Bingley brought her to her husband's study, Lydia wanted to chat about how much he looked like his younger brother, Charles, but without the spectacles, and, of course, Charles was too young to have so much gray hair. While Lydia chattered on and on, George said nothing. In the past, he found that silence tended to disconcert the other party, and once Lydia finally stopped talking, he could see she was growing uncomfortable.

When Mrs. Bingley returned with a tray with tea and biscuits, her husband had sent her away. "Thank you, my dear, but this is not a social call. Serious business is being conducted here." That scene had been worked out in advance, and Hannah had not even bothered to put tea in the teapot.

"Where is Mr. Wickham and when will I see him?" Lydia asked. She did not like this at all. He reminded her too much of her finger-wagging Aunt Susan, who was unhappy with everything Lydia had ever done.

"Wickham left his regiment without the permission of his senior officer, and there are matters in that regard that needed to be sorted. Additionally, he left Brighton with a young lady, who was not his wife, but who was a guest in the home of his colonel. It was a gross violation of the military code of ethics as well as common decency."

"But that was only because Wickham is so in love with me. Surely, Colonel Forster will understand that as he also is in love with a young woman."

"I can assure you Colonel Forster *does not* understand how one of his officers, whom he trusted to come into his home, could initiate secret meetings with a young lady under his protection, which has resulted in great damage to her reputation."

"But I have done nothing wrong. I know what people might think, but once I explain that Wickham and I never did anything, they will understand."

"If you believe that to be the case, Miss Lydia, then you have a higher opinion of mankind than I do. My experience is that most people are quite willing to believe the very worst about others. You will have a hard time convincing your acquaintances and relations that although you were gone for more than two weeks and had lived in a boardinghouse with a man without being married, you remain a maiden."

"But I am," Lydia said, shifting uncomfortably in her chair. "It was because we were waiting for Wickham to get the money to buy my wedding clothes. That was what was taking so long."

"My wife tells me you have placed a great deal of importance on your wedding clothes. For the sake of argument, let us say you are accoutered from head to toe to your satisfaction. You go to the church and are married, and when you walk down the church steps and get into a hackney, where do you tell the driver to take you?"

Lydia was practically squirming. She had not thought about anything past the wedding ceremony. Where *would* they go?

"First, we should go to my Aunt and Uncle Gardiner's. They are excessively fond of me."

"Still?"

"Of course, Uncle Gardiner is my mother's brother."

"As you say, Mr. Gardiner is your mother's brother, and as such, you have caused his sister great anxiety. In addition to that, he has neglected his family and business in his efforts to find you. I cannot imagine him welcoming with open arms the man who was responsible for wreaking havoc with the emotions of the Bennet and Gardiner families."

"Well, it will only be for a few days before we go to Longbourn."

"If you imagine a warm welcome there, I think you will be disappointed. Your father spent many days in London looking for you. He returned home in despair, fearing he would never see his youngest daughter again and that he had lost you to a man who violated every law of decency."

"But I will explain it was only because we are so in love that we did these things. In time, all will be forgiven."

"One can hope. However, you cannot expect your father to

allow such a man to stay in his home for any length of time as he would be a constant reminder of the disruption he has caused his family. And you have another problem. Since Wickham, at Colonel Forster's insistence, must leave the militia, I am curious as to what you will live on."

"We have more resources than you think, Mr. Bingley," Lydia said, smiling weakly. "Mr. Wickham is the natural son of a very wealthy man, and it is his intention to claim his share of the inheritance."

"Really? And who told him that natural sons are entitled to a share of an inheritance? There is nothing in the law that requires it."

"But his son is such a man that he will do what is right."

"May I ask who this gentleman is?"

"If you promise it will not leave this room, as Wickham would be very unhappy with me if he knew I had told anyone." Bingley gave her no assurances, but she decided to tell him anyway. "It is Mr. Darcy of Pemberley."

George Bingley leaned forward in his chair, so that he might get closer to a young woman whose ignorance of how the world worked was staggering. "My dear, do you know what the term 'slander' means?"

"It is when someone tells a lie."

"Yes, it is a lie, but one told to others to the point where it damages another's reputation. You have just repeated a slander against Mr. Darcy. We know who Wickham's father was, and he was not Mr. Darcy. So if you or Wickham should repeat this, you will be sued by the Darcy family, and when you are found guilty, you will go to prison."

For the first time since she came into the room, Lydia truly looked frightened. Wickham had assured her that the elder Mr. Darcy was his father, and that the younger Mr. Darcy would see them right. What would they do now?

"In light of all of this, I would suggest you return to your parents and hope for a new beginning. Wickham is a man completely without principle, and he will cause you great heartache if you should marry."

"But you don't know the real George Wickham. He is very kind and attentive, and he loves me so much that he was willing to risk everything to be with me."

Mr. Bingley laughed, which sent a chill down Lydia's spine. "He risked very little, my dear. It was you who risked everything. I shall say no more as your uncle will be here shortly to bring you to their home. I hope they can talk sense into you as the man you call 'my dear Wickham' is a seducer, a gamester, a liar, and a profligate, among other things. A leopard cannot change its spots, Miss Lydia, not even for you."

❦

When Darcy went to George Bingley's office, he expected to discuss his old enemy's demands, but Bingley made it clear that Wickham was not in a position to demand anything.

"If for no other reason, Wickham must cooperate with us, or he will be before a magistrate with regards to his outstanding debts quicker than he can say 'Jack Frost.' Marshalsea Prison is an unpleasant place on the best of days, and there are very few of those."

"Have you received instructions from Mr. Bennet?" Darcy asked. "Is he insisting that Lydia marry?"

"It is my understanding that it is her father's hope that she will return to her family unmarried. However, Mr. Bennet has signed a power of attorney giving Mr. Gardiner complete discretion in this matter."

"Please advise Mr. Gardiner that I shall do whatever is necessary to assist Miss Lydia if she foregoes marriage. I own a small estate in Hampshire where she might live until the storm passes. Money is not an issue; all her needs will be met."

"That is very generous of you, Mr. Darcy, but from the conversation I had with the young lady, I believe a marriage will take place."

"Where is Wickham?"

"In Brighton, where he had unfinished business. As discussed, Wickham will go into the regular army. A commission has been purchased in a regiment quartered in the north of England, and the colonel is a childhood friend of mine and is known for his discipline. Wickham will find life in the army to be very different from the militia. We are in a time of war, so if he thinks he can up and leave his regiment as he did in the militia, he will quickly come to realize his error. Deserters are hunted down and punished. All of this will be made clear to Wickham."

Darcy was then shown a document drafted by George Bingley and the Darcy family solicitor in which a trust was to be established for Lydia Bennet with funds provided by Mr. Darcy. The conditions for any withdrawal in excess of a designated monthly allowance were stringent, and anything out of the norm required the approval of Mr. Stone, the executor of the trust.

"We have left Wickham with no wiggle room, Mr. Darcy. These funds are to be made available only at certain banks, all of which I have a financial interest in. Every line of this document has been written with Miss Lydia's interests in mind, and emergency funds are available if she needs to return to Longbourn. If they are frugal, the funds are sufficient to meet their needs.

"In addition, Mr. Stone has drafted a second document, which Wickham must sign, in which he acknowledges the facts of his birth, and if he should make additional statements that can be construed in any way that he is the natural son of David Darcy of Pemberley, he will be prosecuted. After the document is signed, you will leave, so that Wickham will think the only reason you were in attendance was to protect the interests of the Darcy family."

Darcy stood up and thanked Mr. Bingley for all of his efforts and asked for an invoice to be sent to him at his earliest opportunity.

"There will be no charge, Mr. Darcy, not only because you are a friend and a business associate, but because I am the father of four daughters. Wickham's actions are a violation of everything I hold sacred."

"When will Wickham be coming to London?"

"In the next few days. By that time, Captain Wilcox and Lieutenant Fuller will have had sufficient time to deal with Wickham, and I understand a Mr. Egger of Meryton was also interested in meeting with him. When he left Meryton and Brighton, he burned his bridges and is friendless, which I imagine will become a permanent condition."

After leaving Bingley's office, Darcy recalled the time he had seen Lydia at Lucas Lodge. She had brazenly declared it was her intention to meet every officer in the regiment, and shortly thereafter, she had proceeded to chase after a young lieutenant. Jane and Elizabeth were aghast, but her parents ignored what he considered to be grossly inappropriate behavior. What you sow, so shall you reap. Harvest time had come.

As expected, Lydia refused to even consider not marrying her dear Wickham. With their voices added to those of Hannah and George Bingley, the Gardiners tried to convince their niece that such a man would make a terrible husband. But if Lydia had been able to withstand the odious Mr. George Bingley's withering looks and biting comments, the Gardiners presented no challenge to her at all. Even after it was explained that she would be received by her family with charity, she stood firm in her insistence that she marry. Mr. Bennet had anticipated her response. As a result, he had not even bothered to come to town.

There was only one person at Longbourn who was happy about the news from London—Mrs. Bennet. She was elated that her daughter was to be married, but not for the reason that everyone would have imagined. She had been in a state of high anxiety because she believed Lydia's elopement would damage the prospects of her other four daughters. If Lydia returned to Longbourn unmarried, many a gentleman would avoid a family who had received a fallen woman back into the fold.

When her husband read Mr. Gardiner's letter to her, she could hardly contain her joy. It was unfortunate Wickham's regiment was in the North, which would make visiting difficult, but if he distinguished himself in the army, then everyone would look at his wife quite differently when she returned to Meryton. But in the meantime, she hoped they would be allowed to stay at Longbourn for at least a month.

"Listen to me, Fanny," Mr. Bennet said before retiring. "I

shall receive Lydia and her husband here at Longbourn for no more than ten days. Although I shall be forced to sit at the dining table with Wickham, I shall not utter one word that can in any way be construed as conversation. You are not to give them one penny out of your household funds because Lydia will need to live on a budget for the rest of her life. As for taking Lydia and Wickham about the village to introduce the happy couple to our neighbors, I would not do it. You may take a lump of coal and wrap it up in fine paper and tie it with ribbons and bows, but it remains a lump of coal and no one will be fooled."

When Mr. Bennet called her "Fanny," she understood that anything he said was not subject to debate. But there were things her husband simply did not understand. It was absolutely critical that Lydia be reintroduced into society as quickly and as often as possible because, with each meeting, there would be a little less gossip among the tongue-waggers. Eventually, they would tire of the topic and would move on to dissecting others who had fallen from grace. The gossip surrounding Betsy Egger's false pregnancy had already been replaced with the announcement that sixty-year-old Mr. Long was to marry Mrs. Gantner of Sheffield, a woman half his age. And so it would go. Some other juicy morsel would replace the news of Lydia's unconventional marriage. It was just too bad Mr. Long hadn't waited until after Lydia's departure to the North to make his announcement. That news would have been a nice distraction from Lydia's marriage, but there would be others who would fall short. There always were.

Chapter 49

OF ALL THE GUESTS at Pemberley, Charles was the first to leave. After arranging for Belling to accompany his sisters and Mr. Hurst to Scarborough, he had asked Miss Darcy if he might depart as he had important business in Hertfordshire.

It was Kitty who first recognized the man on horseback as Mr. Bingley, and she immediately ran to the garden house where Jane and Lizzy were drying sprigs of rosemary. Lizzy was looking at her sister when Kitty told her the news, but her face remained unchanged. Jane had put on a protective shield, and Lizzy was no longer sure of the reception Mr. Bingley would receive.

By the time the sisters went into the parlor, their mother had already shared the news with Mr. Bingley that Lydia was shortly to be married, explaining it was only a matter of the time needed to publish the banns that was delaying the nuptials.

"I was aware Miss Lydia was soon to be married, and I offer my sincere wishes for the couple's health and happiness."

Mrs. Bennet rambled on for several more minutes before leaving with Kitty. The conversation that followed was stilted and awkward. Jane was polite but said little, and by the time they had finished their tea, Bingley was beginning to fear the worst. Miss Bennet no longer loved him. It was then that Mrs. Hill announced that Jane had a visitor.

"Who is it, Mrs. Hill?"

"An old friend, Miss Jane, who is waiting in the sitting room."

"But who is it?"

With everyone staring at her, Mrs. Hill finally said, "It is Mr. Nesbitt, miss."

Jane looked confused, but Lizzy's mouth fell open. Surely, he was not here to renew his attentions. Not now. Not at this critical moment.

After Jane left the room, Mr. Bingley's face showed that he was on the verge of despair. "Miss Elizabeth, it seems I am too late as Miss Bennet has a suitor."

"No, he is not a suitor as such. There was some interest, but not recently." But the statement was made with such a lack of conviction, it failed to reassure Mr. Bingley.

Lizzy was at a loss as to what to do. Should she go to Jane to make sure she did not accept an offer from Mr. Nesbitt or stay with Mr. Bingley to make sure he did not become even more discouraged and leave? She decided to remain where she was; Mr. Bingley was greatly in need of reassurance.

"Mr. Bingley, you said you knew of my sister Lydia's upcoming marriage. May I ask how you came by that information?"

"Mr. Darcy told me."

"Mr. Darcy? How would Mr. Darcy know?"

"The day after you left Pemberley, Darcy went to London to help find... I mean to offer his assistance in..."

"Sir, you may speak frankly. If you were unaware of the

circumstances regarding Lydia's elopement, you would be one of the few."

"I am not sure what you know, Miss Elizabeth, but Darcy has a history with Wickham. He felt that if he had made known the defects in his character, your sister would never have left Brighton with him. He recruited my brother, George, in the search, and it is my understanding that it was George's men who found the couple. But knowing Darcy, I am sure he has been working behind the scenes to do what he could to help your sister."

So she had guessed correctly. Darcy had left the inn at Lambton with the intention of finding Lydia, and now that he had succeeded, what would be his next step? Would he return to her or close the book on their relationship, especially since Lydia's marriage would make George Wickham his brother-in-law? For the present, she must put those thoughts aside and concentrate on Jane. What on earth was taking her so long?

When Jane went into the parlor, she found Mr. Nesbitt happily conversing with Mary about all the headaches involved in probating wills, with her sister hanging on every word as if each was a pearl of wisdom. But upon seeing Jane, Mary immediately left the room.

"Miss Bennet, it is a pleasure to see you again," Mr. Nesbitt said, rising.

"I must confess, sir, that in light of your last letter, I am surprised to find you at Longbourn."

"That is why I am here. My mother urged me to write the letter, and now I have come to tell you that I regard it as a cowardly act. Even though no plans were formalized, and thus no promises made, I should have come in person to tell you of the change in circumstances that prompted such an action. But before you think ill of my mother, please allow me to explain that she has raised me from the time of my father's death when I was five years old. I have been her life's work, and when she heard the news about your sister, she believed my career would be jeopardized if we married. But I have studied the law for most of my adult life. Although I believe your sister has made a grievous error in judgment, you cannot, by association, be held accountable for her actions. You are completely innocent of all wrongdoing, and as such, should not be punished. The law is very clear on this."

Jane wondered what constituted punishment: Mr. Nesbitt's ending the relationship or his attempt to begin anew? If it was the latter, then Jane had some sad news for the gentleman sitting across from her. As soon as Charles began speaking, stumbling through his sentences, every feeling she had for him had returned. His halting speech was one of the things she loved best about him, but instead of being with him, she was listening to Mr. Nesbitt instruct her as to her legal rights. At times, life could be very unfair.

"In the days since I wrote that letter," Mr. Nesbitt continued, "I have spent hours thinking about our time together. In hindsight, I could see that although you are pleasant company, Miss Bennet, I noted our conversations were strained. I had no such difficulty when talking to your sister Mary."

Jane, who had been avoiding making eye contact with Mr. Nesbitt, fearing he might find encouragement there, now looked at him right in his eyes.

"Mary? Are you saying that you are interested in Mary?"

"I have no wish to hurt you, Miss Bennet, but the purpose of my visit is to ask permission to call on Miss Mary. As I have discussed with you on previous visits, it is my intention to study for the bar. As a result, the length of any courtship may be considerable and…"

Jane jumped out of her chair and made no attempt to pretend his news had upset her. Instead, she asked if she might go tell Mary the good news.

Mr. Nesbitt, who had been prepared for the possibility of Jane shedding a tear or two, was relieved to find her quite pleased with his decision to court her younger sister. Jane did not have far to go to find her as she was standing outside the door. Despite her proximity, she had been unable to hear what the two soft-spoken parties had been saying to each other. When Jane told her the purpose of Mr. Nesbitt's visit, she stepped back from her sister.

"Of all people, Jane, I never thought that you would be so cruel. How can you say these things when you know how I feel about Mr. Nesbitt?"

"Mary, I am not in jest. Mr. Nesbitt is not here for me. He is here for you!"

It was another few minutes before Mary was convinced, but Jane finally pushed her toward the door. "I have business in the parlor, and you have business in the sitting room. Now, let us go to it."

⁂

When Jane returned to the parlor, she was positively glowing.

"It seems we are to have a wedding here at Longbourn."

"Oh, Jane," Lizzy whispered. She felt as if she was going to be ill, and from Mr. Bingley's expression, she was sure he was in a similar state.

"Mr. Nesbitt has come to Longbourn to ask for permission to court... Mary."

"Oh, heavens!" Lizzy said, collapsing into the sofa. "What wonderful news! Mary, you say?" Lizzy's eyes filled with tears of relief. "I must go to her immediately," but did so only after giving Mr. Bingley a big smile.

"Miss Bennet, may I offer my congratulations. There is nothing like an impending marriage to bring joy to a house. Well, possibly the birth of a child. However, you must have the wedding first. Although that is not always the case, but usually it is."

"I am in complete agreement, Mr. Bingley. There is nothing sweeter than finding the right person to love and cherish and to share your hopes and dreams with."

"Even if that person is a dunderhead?"

"Especially if that person is a dunderhead as he is most in need of affection," Jane said, smiling broadly.

Charles immediately crossed the room, and on bended knee, asked, "Miss Bennet, may I..."

"Yes."

"Yes what?"

"Never mind. Go ahead."

"Miss Bennet, may I ask for your hand in..."

"Yes."

"...marriage."

And Jane leaned over and firmly kissed her future husband on his lips, and the quiet Mr. Bingley let out a whoop that brought everyone in the house to the parlor.

Mr. Bennet had been in the study listening to Mr. Nesbitt's reasons for his choosing Mary over Jane. He had obviously given the subject a lot of thought as he had a litany of Mary's attributes at the ready. Because of his detailed presentation, Mr. Bennet was seeing his middle daughter in a different light. After calling Mary into the study and seeing how her love for this man had transformed her, he readily gave his consent. It was during Nesbitt's recitation regarding his legal aspirations that they had heard Mr. Bingley's shout.

When Mrs. Bennet realized that not only was Jane to be married, but Mary was to wed Mr. Nesbitt, she nearly collapsed, and Kitty had to pour her a glass of wine to calm her nerves.

"Oh, Mr. Bingley! Oh, Mr. Nesbitt! What happy news! You are perfectly suited for each other. Well, I don't mean each other. I mean for Jane and Mary. What I am trying to say is I wish to add my blessing to your unions," and she started to cry profusely with tears of joy. "Mary is to be married! Who would have ever thought?" And looking at Kitty, she remarked, "Now it is just you and Lizzy who must find husbands, but perhaps Mr. Bingley and Mr. Nesbitt have friends who are in need of a wife," a comment Kitty did not appreciate, but one that Lizzy had expected. Her mother would not be happy until all five of her daughters were married, and Lizzy's thoughts turned to Mr. Darcy in London.

Chapter 50

ANNE WAS NEAR TO exhaustion, but during the carriage ride to London, while Mrs. Jenkinson and Lord Fitzwilliam were sleeping, she continued to plan her next step to bring Elizabeth and Will together. She had come too far to concede defeat because of the actions of an irresponsible sixteen-year-old girl and a thirty-year-old degenerate. If it had not been for the change in circumstances brought about as a result of Lydia and Wickham's escapade, she might have accepted Antony's offer to visit with him for a month or so. She knew she could do some good there. With his daughters constantly in his thoughts, it seemed as if he really did want to begin a program of reform. It was one thing to embarrass one's spouse, especially Antony's mean-spirited wife, who put her in mind of Caroline Bingley, and quite another to humiliate two impressionable young girls, whom he loved dearly.

Upon arrival in London, Anne had written to her mother to inform her that she would rest for a few days at the townhouse before returning to Kent. It was while she had been picturing a typical evening meal with Mama dominating the conversation that the idea had come to her. During supper at Rosings, Anne would speak of the likely engagement of Mr. Charles Bingley to Miss Jane Bennet. She would work the conversation around to Jane's sister, Elizabeth, and would mention that Will and she had been together at Pemberley. That would prompt a cascade of questions, which she would answer truthfully. "Yes, Mama, I do believe Will is quite taken with Miss Elizabeth, so much so that I suspect he is in love with her." As soon as she learned of a possible alliance between Fitzwilliam Darcy and a farmer's daughter, she anticipated that her mother would order the carriage to be made ready to leave for London the next day, and it had happened exactly as she had predicted, except for one thing: Her mother had set out for Hertfordshire, not London.

And while her mother was busily interfering in Will's affairs, Anne had ample time to review the papers her solicitor had given to her while she was in town. In two weeks' time, she would reach her twenty-fifth birthday, and at that time, she would come into an inheritance left to her by her de Bourgh grandparents that had, up to that time, been controlled by her mother acting as trustee on her behalf. The papers contained many surprises, all of them pleasant. Not only was she now an heiress with a generous yearly allowance, but she also owned the lease on the house in town and rental properties in Tunbridge Wells and Weymouth. Although not a surprise, the *crème de la crème* was that she was now the mistress of Rosings Park.

As she had been instructed by her father in the last days of his life, Anne had met with the family solicitor, Mr. Markling, on her eighteenth birthday. According to the provisions of the will of the first Lord de Bourgh, only a de Bourgh, by blood, could inherit the estate.

"Apparently, when the original Lord de Bourgh purchased a barony from Charles II," Mr. Markling explained, "he was coolly received by the English elite, and his response was that no one but a de Bourgh would ever inherit Rosings. If you should die without issue, Miss de Bourgh, the estate will pass to your father's nephew, Martin Hargrove, who will then adopt the de Bourgh name."

He further explained that the will provided a life interest for her mother. However, once she had reached her twenty-fifth year, Anne would have the final say in all matters affecting the estate. She had no intention of taking on such responsibilities, but her new situation would provide an opportunity for negotiation between mother and daughter.

Looking at the numbers once again, Anne was amazed by the size of her fortune. Apparently, smuggling generated handsome profits, which had enabled generations of de Bourghs to vastly increase their wealth and to build and expand Rosings Park. But she immediately thought of all the things she could do with that much money. Firstly, she would attempt to recover everything Antony had sold from the Fitzwilliam estate to pay his bills. Secondly, improvements of the cottages would be accelerated. Thirdly, the parsonage would be expanded because Anne believed Charlotte would shortly have some good news to share.

A few days after she returned, she would visit Mr. Rampling, the sexton, who had taken care of the church for decades, and his forty-year-old bachelor son. Albert Rampling had been born with misshapen legs. Because it was so difficult for him to get about, he had been unable to find employment. Instead, he had dedicated his life to recording the traditions and customs of those who lived in southeast England, and one of her greatest pleasures was when he shared his latest historical nuggets with her. Now, she would be able to provide an annuity for the Ramplings. That would allow them to move out of their small, damp house into a larger cottage with a library where Albert could record his stories, and she might possibly assist him with organizing his notes. In any event, she would see to it that his writings were published.

As important as those things were, she was even more excited because now she would be able to provide her cousin, Colonel Fitzwilliam, with an allowance sufficient for him to follow his heart and to marry for love, and she believed the trail would take him right to the home of Miss Pennington, the daughter of the Fitzwilliam solicitor. The money would allow him to sell his commission in the army and to pursue his desire to study the law. There was so much to look forward to, not the least of which was a change in her relationship with her mother. In two years' time, Mama would be sixty years old, and the infirmities of age were already noticeable. She suffered from arthritis and gout, her hearing and eyesight had diminished, and she could no longer get around without her cane. The new arrangement might possibly bring the two women closer together, as Lady Catherine would look to Anne to provide the necessary care she had once provided to her daughter.

But discussions about their changed circumstances would have to wait until her mother had returned from her crusade to prevent a marriage between Will and Elizabeth. But like the Crusades, she would fail, and sometime in the near future, Lady

Catherine de Bourgh would have to acknowledge the marriage of her favorite nephew to a farmer's daughter from Hertfordshire. And that put a smile on her face.

Chapter 51

Georgiana loved all the hustle and bustle of London. She had been sitting on the window seat in her bedroom watching nannies pushing prams and servants walking their masters' dogs in the park when she saw Lady Catherine's carriage stop in front of the townhouse. Georgiana, who enjoyed gothic mysteries because they got her heart racing, found that there was nothing in her novels quite as frightening as Lady Catherine de Bourgh.

"Fitzwilliam Darcy! I demand you come here immediately," Aunt Catherine shouted from the foyer below.

Georgiana was unsure if her brother was even in the house. She had only just returned from a final fitting for her dress for the Warrens' ball where she would make her debut in one week's time. Will might possibly be at his solicitor's office in connection with the papers to be signed by Lydia Bennet and Wickham or in a business meeting with George Bingley. Unfortunately, she must assume he was not in the house, and with great reluctance, she went downstairs to meet her aunt.

"Where is your brother, Georgiana? I shall speak with him this very moment."

"Aunt Catherine, I don't know where…"

"Georgiana, it's all right," Will said, appearing miraculously from behind her. "You may return to your room. It seems as if our aunt has business with me." Georgiana hurried up the stairs, but as soon as Will and her aunt had gone into the sitting room, she put her ear to the door.

"I have just come from Hertfordshire and a most unpleasant interview with Miss Elizabeth Bennet with regard to a malicious rumor being circulated by either herself or her allies that you intend to make her an offer of marriage. When I insisted the report of your engagement be universally contradicted, she refused to do so," she said, shaking her cane at the window and the faraway Elizabeth Bennet, who was out there somewhere defying her. "When I asked for a promise that she would never enter into such an engagement, she said, 'I will make no promise of the kind.' She is an unfeeling and selfish girl, unworthy of my attention, and no one in my family will have any further association with her."

Darcy maintained the stoic exterior he adopted whenever he was around his aunt, but inside he was smiling. He could easily imagine Elizabeth standing opposite the august personage of Lady Catherine de Bourgh and stubbornly refusing to give ground.

"Aunt Catherine, Miss Elizabeth could not refute the rumors that I intend to make her an offer of marriage because they are true. As soon as Georgiana makes her debut, I shall be on the road to Longbourn Manor for just such a purpose."

"I forbid it! Your alliance will be a disgrace. If you persist,

I shall not receive you. Your name will never be mentioned by me again."

"That would be unfortunate, Aunt Catherine, but it will not deter me. I am in love with Elizabeth Bennet, and if she will have me, I intend to make her my wife."

"If she will have *you*! If that woman truly has any regard for you, she will refuse any such offer as you will be censured, slighted, and despised by all your acquaintances."

"I appreciate your concern, but you need not worry about matters that fall exclusively to me."

"Will you deny your mother her most cherished wish that you marry your cousin and my daughter?"

"My mother and father were deeply in love, and Mama wished the same for me. I love Anne as dearly as I do Georgiana, but as a sister, and her love for me is as a brother. Despite your hopes, it has never been otherwise. There is nothing you can say that will change my mind as to my choice of wife. I do not wish to be estranged from you, as you are dear to me and my mother was devoted to you. However, that is your choice. If you do not wish to see me again, I shall accept your decision. Likewise, you must accept mine."

Georgiana continued to listen to what had become a one-sided argument with her aunt's shrill voice reaching new heights. Confident that her brother could not be dissuaded from making an offer to Elizabeth Bennet, she returned to her room, but she knew when her aunt was leaving because she could hear the impact of her cane hitting each step. As soon as she saw her carriage pull away, she ran downstairs to her brother.

"Will, Aunt Catherine is very angry."

"That is an understatement," he said, laughing. "She objects to my having fallen in love with a woman who has no rank or position in society. Frankly, I am beginning to see that as an asset."

"Anne must have told her. How else would she know?"

"Oh, beyond a doubt, Anne is behind this. She knew exactly what her mother would do upon receiving such information."

"Will, since Miss Elizabeth has endured a good deal of abuse on your account, it seems only fair that you should go to Hertfordshire to apologize for the behavior of our aunt."

"You are right, Georgiana. It is my responsibility to go to Longbourn to make sure Elizabeth has suffered no permanent damage from Aunt Catherine's attack."

Georgiana ran to her brother and hugged and kissed him. "But, Will, you must go as soon as possible. I do not want you to wait for my debut. It is still six days off, and that is sufficient time for you to go to Longbourn to make Elizabeth an offer and to return in time to escort me to the Warrens' ball. Will you do this for me?"

Smiling and nodding, Darcy shouted for his valet. "Mercer! Mercer! Where are you?"

"Sir, I am here," Mercer answered from his perch.

"Tomorrow I am to go to Hertfordshire on important business, possibly the most important of my life. Please prepare for our departure."

"Trousers or breeches, sir?"

"Trousers."

Chapter 52

MRS. HILL HAD A view of the road from the kitchen window, and when she saw the carriage pull into the lane, she thought it must be Lady Catherine again. Who else could afford such a fine conveyance? After her visit, Miss Lizzy had told everyone that Her Ladyship was merely paying a courtesy call. Well, if that's what she called courtesy, Mrs. Hill would take a pass on civility. She could not hear what was being said, but she knew an angry voice when she heard it. And although it took her longer to figure out what the strange thumping noise was, when Lady Catherine came out of the parlor leading with her cane, that mystery was solved.

Instead of the grouchy grand lady Mrs. Hill was expecting, she opened the door to find Mr. Darcy holding a letter and asking that it be delivered to Miss Elizabeth and that he would wait for her answer in the garden. Mrs. Hill was reluctant to deliver the letter. What if the nephew was as angry as the aunt? She hated to see her sweet Miss Lizzy upset, especially since everyone in the house was in such a good mood. Miss Jane was engaged, Miss Mary had a suitor, and Miss Lydia was still in London not causing anyone any trouble at the moment.

"Mr. Darcy is here at Longbourn? Where?" Lizzy asked as Mrs. Hill handed her the letter. When she read its two sentences, she smiled. No wasted words here, but it was enough.

Dearest Elizabeth,

Although I come unannounced, I hope you will be able to spare a few minutes of your time for me. I shall wait for you in the garden.

Yours, Fitzwilliam Darcy

Quickly grabbing a bonnet and cloak, she was out the door. As soon as she saw Mr. Darcy sitting on a bench in the garden, her spirits soared. He was wearing a very fine coat and her favorite dark green waistcoat. He had come dressed to the nines to pay a call on her.

"Mr. Darcy, what a pleasant surprise."

"Miss Elizabeth," he said, bowing, "I am happy to hear you find my visit a pleasure considering my aunt's behavior in coming here. Her manners and speech were abominable, and I ask your forgiveness."

"You have nothing to be sorry for. Only your aunt should be held accountable for her speech, but she certainly does speak her mind."

"From what I heard from my aunt, you do likewise."

"Which should come as no surprise to you, Mr. Darcy."

"As long as it is not I who is on the receiving end of expressions of your displeasure, I shall always encourage you to speak your mind," and with that hint of a future together, he stepped forward and took her hand.

"Before you say anything else," Lizzy said, holding tightly to his hand, "I must thank you for what you did on Lydia's behalf."

"Please, I did very little, and I have no wish to speak of it."

"But, surely, you will allow me to…" but before she could complete the sentence, he took her in his arms and kissed her. It was not one kiss, but many, and with each kiss, she could feel his passion rising until she felt it necessary to gently push him away. "Sir, please, I have never been kissed before."

"Good," he said, and after untying her bonnet and tossing it on the bench, he pulled her close, and she felt his warm lips once again. As pleasant an experience as it was, propriety demanded she step away from him.

"Mr. Darcy, you are quite overwhelming me," she said while retrieving her bonnet and fixing her hair. "If you would, please come and sit beside me."

Darcy was about to get to the purpose of his visit, when Elizabeth said, "Before you begin, Mr. Darcy, I should caution you…"

"Caution me! Are you saying you will refuse my proposal?" he said, standing up. "What is it you want from me, Elizabeth? Shall I tear my heart from my chest and lay it before you? What must I do to secure your love?"

"Sir, you have my love, and I am not refusing you. I am merely suggesting that we move at a measured pace. We must have a courtship."

"Why on earth do we need a courtship? A courtship serves the purpose of exposing one's faults before vows are exchanged. Have you not seen me at my very worst?"

"I don't know, have I?"

"Oh, I can see you are enjoying yourself. You have my heart, and now you will toy with it," he said, laughing, but his laugh hid a growing impatience. He had been prepared to purchase a special license, so that they might marry immediately. But, now, she was talking about a courtship. "All right, then, three weeks of banns, and then we shall marry in the village church."

"Three weeks? That is not very long. Have you forgotten that until very recently we were adversaries?"

Darcy could not deny that. During their time together at Netherfield Park during Jane's illness, at the home of Sir William Lucas, and at the Netherfield ball, they had sparred on each occasion, and their adversarial postures had traveled with them to Kent, culminating in the scene at the parsonage. Only when they had met at Pemberley did their discourse take on a friendly tone, and their one private conversation in the gazebo had lasted no more than fifteen minutes.

"Agreed. You will have a courtship. What shall I bring when I come calling? Flowers? Jewels? Or should I order a fine carriage?"

"Flowers fade and jewels are locked up in boxes, and the last thing a Darcy needs is another carriage. What I want is for you to write me love letters or poetry."

"I have no gift for writing," he said, dismissing her request.

"I remember a conversation we had at Rosings regarding the importance of practice if one is ever to acquire a skill, whether it be playing the pianoforte or engaging strangers in conversation. Determination, effort, and practice are rewarded with success."

"Have my determination and effort to win your hand met with success?"

"Indeed they have."

"In that case, shall I get down on one knee?" Darcy asked.

"Only if you want dirty trousers, as it rained last night."

Darcy pulled her gently to him, and he asked, "Miss Elizabeth Bennet, will you accept my offer of marriage and agree to become my wife?" and with her head upon his chest and feeling the beating of his heart, she whispered, "Yes."

On the night of Georgiana's debut, Darcy had an inkling of what he would feel on such an occasion if Elizabeth and he had a daughter. He was flooded with memories of his little sister climbing on her first pony, walking through the maze with their mother, sitting next to her father on the phaeton holding the reins together, or running around a maypole with the village children. In the last five years, their lives had been so entwined that he could hardly believe he might have to part with her in a very short while. But it would happen, as the young men at the ball flew to her as moths to a flame.

He had hoped that it would have been possible for Elizabeth to return with him to London and to stay with the Gardiners, so that they might be together on this special evening. But her family's reaction to the announcement that they were to be married had been coolly received. He understood it was his own doing as his behavior at the assembly was still discussed in the neighborhood, and, subsequently, his role in Bingley's departure from Netherfield had been revealed. But because he had asked Elizabeth not to share with her parents his role in Lydia's fiasco, neither knew how indebted they were to him.

Mrs. Bennet's reaction to the news was one of shock. Now that Lydia and Jane were shortly to be married and Mary would eventually marry after Mr. Nesbitt had been called to the bar, she was feeling quite secure and mentioned to Lizzy that, unlike Mr. Bingley, Mr. Darcy was a disagreeable man and one who thought that he was above his company. Nevertheless, she should consent to become his wife.

"Think of the pin money and the dresses, the jewels, and the carriages. Nothing will be denied you, and then you can find a husband for Kitty by throwing her into the path of other rich gentlemen."

Mr. Bennet's reservations regarding the marriage were such that Darcy was concerned that he would withhold his blessing, which would have deeply hurt Elizabeth. It was obvious that she was her father's favorite child, and it was only after her father had talked to his daughter behind closed doors and had been reassured that her intended had no improper pride, that he was perfectly amiable, and that she loved him dearly, that he had given his consent. But he did so reluctantly.

Darcy left his future bride with her family for the purpose of rehabilitating his reputation, but he again cautioned her about revealing his role in Lydia and Wickham's upcoming marriage. After returning to London, he had called on the Gardiners in hopes of hearing that Lydia had reconsidered, but he was informed that she would not yield. Tired of listening to her aunt and uncle's pleas, she had finally put an end to their efforts when she had made a confession: She had lied to them when she told them that she was still a maiden. Mrs. Gardiner did not believe her, but the desired result was achieved.

But thoughts such as these should be reflected upon only in the darkest hours of the night and not at his sister's coming-out party. As he danced with Georgiana's friends and watched as they huddled in the corners between dances, giggling as girls always do, he delighted in the thought that his lovely sister had formed a deep attachment for Elizabeth. It was as he had always hoped.

At a time when Darcy had the pleasure of escorting his sister to a series of breakfasts and balls, there was an unpleasant piece of unfinished business to deal with. On this day, Lydia Bennet was to marry George Wickham.

Darcy was standing on the church steps when Lydia came bounding out of the hackney with her aunt and uncle. She had taken forever to mount the steps of St. Clement's as she wanted all of the people out and about to admire her wedding dress and bonnet. Passersby called out their good wishes, which was a good thing, because they were the only ones who did. When she entered the church, she looked around for her family. Why were they not here to share in the joy of her marriage? But the beaming bride shrugged off their absence as soon as she saw Wickham, who had arrived at the church in the uniform of his new regiment. If Darcy had cared one whit about him, he might have asked what accounted for the bruises on his face and the bandage on his hand, but he was confident he knew the answer. Wickham had had a rough reception in Brighton.

Darcy was surprised, but he should not have been, when he saw George and Hannah Bingley in the church. George always dotted his i's and crossed his t's, but once Lydia was married, his role would come to an end. The only humor in the situation was Lydia's face when she saw George Bingley. She had nearly walked into a pew in her effort to give him a wide berth. After the ceremony, George approached Darcy to reassure him that Lydia would be looked after.

"I have written to Wickham's colonel asking that he alert Mr. Stone if he thinks Lydia is being mistreated in any way. Even with that, she will face challenges once she reaches Newcastle. I grew up in the North, and its people are shaped by its harsh climate. We are coarser than our southern brethren, but more honest to my mind, and we have no tolerance for artifice and lies.

"In that same letter, I again warned Colonel Davenport of Wickham's proclivity for walking away from unpleasant situations. The colonel assured me that no such thing would happen, as his soldiers were going to be put through a rigorous regimen as he was anticipating that the regiment would shortly be receiving orders to go to the Peninsula to fight Napoleon's forces in Spain."

"The Peninsula? I had not thought. Were you aware of this when you helped secure Wickham's commission?"

"Wickham signed the requisite papers for a commission as an officer in an infantry regiment. His days of parading about the village in his well-tailored uniform so that the ladies might admire him are over. His shoulder will be put to the wheel. As for Wickham's possible deployment to Spain, he is an officer in His Majesty's Army, and as such, he will go where he is sent." After watching the young Lydia enter the carriage with Wickham, he added, "I am a man of faith, Mr. Darcy. As such, I believe good deeds are rewarded, and bad deeds are punished," and he said no more.

With the newlyweds traveling to Longbourn in three days' time, it would be impossible for Darcy to go to Hertfordshire to see Elizabeth. However, Elizabeth had written to say that Jane and she were coming to London so that her sister might purchase material for her wedding dress. This was the silver lining to the marriage he had just witnessed, and so there was something to celebrate after all.

Chapter 53

KITTY WAS A FAITHFUL reader of *The Insider,* and since her sisters were now engaged to men who occasionally appeared in the magazine, she began to read past issues looking for any instance when the names of Bingley, Darcy, or Fitzwilliam appeared.

"Jane, Mr. Bingley's name was once mentioned in connection with Miss Alice Winthorp, who married Sir Arthur Kentwell. It says here that he made his money in herring. Does that mean he fished for herring or sold herring?"

"If you are asking if Sir Arthur made his money as a fisherman or fishmonger, I am confident in saying 'no,'" Lizzy answered. "It is more likely he owned the ships or bought the entire catch."

"Lizzy, in this issue, it says Mr. Darcy was seen to be coming out of Mrs. Conway's house in Bedford Square near dawn. I wonder what he was doing there at such an hour?"

"Mrs. Conway is a prominent Whig hostess, and there is nothing suspect in a person with similar interests visiting her salon. And you must remember that half of those things are made up. It may very well be that Mr. Darcy was there, but left at 1:00 in the morning and the reporter decided that was close enough to dawn for him."

"Well, if what you say is true and half of it is made up, I wonder how much of what is written about Lord Fitzwilliam is the truth as he is in every issue. But the ladies he calls on must be from elite families because their names are hinted at, but not mentioned. In a recent issue, the earl's name does appear one time with Mr. Darcy's. It said there is a new *courtier* in town, a Madame Aumont. The two men provided her with the financial support she needed to open her own shop after she had fled France, and now she has a clientele that includes Lady Edgemont and a Polish countess."

"She must be the lady who made all of Miss Darcy's dresses for her debut," Lizzy said. "I remember she had a French name."

"Lizzy, since I must choose a dressmaker," Jane said, "why should she not be a friend of Mr. Darcy's, especially since she was approved by his sister and he has chosen to support her efforts to start a business?"

"Yes, I agree. I think it will make a nice surprise for Mr. Darcy," Lizzy added.

On Lizzy's first night in London, Mr. Bingley, Mr. Darcy, and his sister dined at the Gardiners' home. Darcy was pleased to see how happy Bingley and Miss Bennet were together. Another pleasure was to witness the friendship that was developing between Georgiana and Elizabeth. When he had heard Elizabeth ask his sister about the progress of her story, he knew Georgie would have an ally supporting her desire to write novels, and he felt the first crack in his resolve that his sister should do no such thing.

All of this was well and good, but it was nothing compared to his enjoyment at seeing Elizabeth. She need not say or do anything as her presence was enough to make him happy, and although he wanted to take her in his arms and kiss her, he understood they probably would not have a moment alone until they were married. Lizzy gave him a slight smile, and he wondered if she was thinking the same thing, too.

The next day the two couples went for a ride in an open carriage in St. James's Park, and a number of his friends and acquaintances had asked for an introduction to his beautiful companion. And so it had begun. Everyone would want to know about Elizabeth and who her parents were and what her accomplishments were and whether she was related to Viscount Louis Bennet. Let them pry and comment and criticize. He no longer cared about any of it.

The following afternoon, after returning from a breakfast he had attended with his sister, Darcy went straight to the Gardiners' home, where Jane happily showed Mr. Darcy the fabric she had chosen that morning for her wedding dress. He smiled at Elizabeth, and she knew he was thinking that shortly she would be doing the same thing.

"Mr. Darcy, I have employed your sister's dressmaker, Madame Aumont, and she has proved to be indispensable in picking out the material for my wedding dress. I was quite overwhelmed by all of the choices, and she is to make Lizzy's dress for the ball at Clermont House."

"Miss Bennet, who told you that Madame Aumont was my sister's dressmaker?" he asked in a serious tone of voice.

Jane looked to her sister, and Lizzy answered. "Mr. Darcy, we read that you and Lord Fitzwilliam had provided financial support for the start of Madame Aumont's business as she was an émigré who had left everything behind her in France. From that we assumed she was Miss Darcy's dressmaker."

Mr. Darcy made no reply. Instead, he went to the window and stared out at the street scene below. The sisters looked at each other. Obviously, they had erred in their assumption as Mr. Darcy was clearly unhappy. Because no formal announcement of their engagement had been made, Lizzy thought it improper to mention the family's name. Therefore, she did not tell Madame of her relationship with Mr. Darcy.

"Miss Bennet, my sister's dressmaker is Madame Delaine, and it is true I have provided Madame Aumont with limited financial support because promised funds from her bank in France were never transferred to her bank here in London. As to what support Lord Fitzwilliam offered Madame, I have no way of knowing that. I have never been in any business arrangement with my cousin as he has the financial intellect of a goat."

Lizzy bit her lower lip, knowing that she had made a serious mistake. How stupid of her! Mr. Darcy would never allow his name to be associated with someone who led a life that was the antithesis of his own. But she suspected Lord Fitzwilliam was not the main cause of his apparent unhappiness. His mood had altered at the mention of Madame's name, and that was before she had uttered one word about Lord Fitzwilliam.

That morning, the sisters had remarked on how beautiful Madame was. Lizzy had never seen eyes so green nor hair so golden, and Jane and Lizzy had guessed she was in her late twenties, five years short of the mark. Not only was Madame Aumont beautiful, but she was a most agreeable lady. While showing Jane the different patterns, she had shared that she had not been in England in ten years. Although she was English by birth, her heart was French, as that was where her mother was born and where she had spent her early childhood. From that conversation, Lizzy could deduce that Mr. Darcy must have met her during his tour of the Continent when he had been a young man without a care in the world. It was a time when he had attended masked balls in Venice and grand galas in Paris, and unless her instincts were completely wrong, the beautiful lady and the young Fitzwilliam Darcy had been intimate.

Mr. Darcy returned to the window and continued to say nothing.

"This is all my fault," Jane mouthed to her sister. "I assumed and now Mr. Darcy is unhappy."

But Lizzy knew that Mr. Darcy wasn't unhappy with anything Jane had done. He was unhappy because Lizzy knew what *he* had done.

⁂

Darcy had withdrawn to the far end of the room because he could hardly take in what had just happened. Christina Caxton was going to make Elizabeth's ball gown for the Clermont ball—the very ball where he intended to introduce his future wife into London society? This was Antony's doing, and he would have his hide the next time he saw him. But, in the meantime, had Elizabeth guessed from his reaction that Christina and he had a history? She was smart and intuitive, and she missed very little. Yes, she definitely knew. He finally asked Jane if he could be alone with her sister.

"It seems my past has caught up with me. Elizabeth, I am a man of twenty-eight years and have lived in the world, and I am no innocent. But because of the profound love I have for you,

I tried to erase the past. I wanted to think of no other woman as being a part of my life. I wanted to be your knight in shining armor—perfect and unblemished. But now that is not possible as I have been exposed."

Once again, she had guessed correctly, but the reason she had come to that conclusion so quickly was because she had already given his past some thought. While Kitty was reading aloud the different items in *The Insider* to her sisters, Lizzy had been thinking about Darcy's romantic interests. Surely, there had been other women in his life, as he was nearly thirty years old, and although she lived in a country town, it was impossible to be ignorant of what went on in London among the social elite. There wasn't anything odd about Mr. Darcy's name being mentioned in *The Insider*. What *was* unique was how infrequently it appeared in the gossip magazines considering the prominence of his family, his eligibility, and his large fortune. And had anything really changed because she now knew that Mr. Darcy was, as he put it, "no innocent?" No, Madame Aumont belonged to his distant past when he was bound to no one. It would have been worse to have it remain a secret. Secrets created barriers, and she wanted nothing like that in her marriage.

Darcy came and sat next to her, and she accepted his handkerchief and dabbed at her eyes. After composing herself after such a confession, she finally said, "You worried unnecessarily about my opinion of you. I have never thought of you as being perfect."

It wasn't until she smiled that he realized she was in jest, and he burst out laughing. "I know I am forgiven, my love, as you only tease your friends," and he kissed her gently on the lips. "But may I ask where you read the story about Christina?"

"I'm embarrassed to admit it, but I read it in *The Insider*."

"You read *The Insider*?" he asked with concern in his voice. He would not have thought of someone as sensible as Elizabeth reading what he considered to be a rag filled with half-truths and, in some cases, stories made up out of whole cloth.

"Everyone in the provinces reads *The Insider*, Mr. Darcy. We must have some amusement."

"Do you read every issue?" he asked with growing concern. Had she read about Miss Montford and Mrs. Conway? It would give her the impression he was inconstant in his affections.

"No, not every issue. But then I don't have to as Kitty tells us all about the most interesting items. She has even gone back and read past issues looking for your name." Lizzy could see that Darcy was growing increasingly uncomfortable, and she wanted to put his mind at ease. "Sir, I have no interest in your past alliances. Every relationship must have a starting point so that past errors may remain in the past. I do not wish to be reminded how wrong I was about Wickham's character, or how I failed to recognize your goodness. So, for me, our beginning must be at Pemberley when you said that its beauty must be shared."

Darcy smiled and nodded in agreement and then took a folded piece of paper out of his pocket. "You asked for love letters or poetry, and this is my first effort."

> *"Come live with me and be my love,*
> *And we will all the pleasures prove*
> *That valleys, groves, hills, and fields,*
> *Woods or steepy mountain yields.*

"And we will sit upon the rocks,
Seeing the shepherds feed their flocks,
By shallow rivers to whose falls
Melodious birds sing madrigals…

"And if these pleasures may thee move,
Come live with me and be my love.

"The shepherds' swains shall dance and sing
For thy delight each May morning:
If these delights thy mind may move,
Then live with me and be my love."

"It is a beautiful piece of poetry. In my opinion, it is Christopher Marlowe's finest work."

"Your request was that I write love letters or verse. You did not say they had to be original."

"Well, I shall credit you with making a start, but no matter how poorly you write, I would prefer your own composition."

"I promise I shall try to compose my own verses. However, I am sure the task would be made easier if I had my source of inspiration before me. So can we not set a date for our wedding?"

Lizzy stood up and walked away from him because, with his arms around her, she felt her resolution to have a courtship ebbing.

"Mr. Darcy, we are very different."

"One would hope," he said, smiling.

"We will face many challenges, including those you mentioned at Hunsford Lodge."

"Every marriage has difficulties, but there is nothing that cannot be overcome, got 'round, or blown away, if necessary."

Lizzy smiled but persisted. "Because we are from such disparate backgrounds, I do have concerns."

"Can you give me one example of any obstacle so great that it could possibly prevent our marriage?" he said with growing impatience.

"Well," Lizzy said, pretending to think long and hard, "what if I discovered you do not know how to ice-skate? It is a sport I greatly enjoy, probably as much as you enjoy riding."

"So this is what I have signed on for? Very well. Then I shall tell you I have concerns of my own. I wonder if you will ever learn how to sit on a horse properly," and he said this as he moved toward her.

"And I might inquire if you will scowl at me whenever I say something you do not like?" she asked as she stepped behind a chair.

And kneeling on the chair with his face inches from hers, he answered, "And do I need to be concerned that you will turn into a scold and point out all of my defects?"

Lizzy ran her fingers across his cheek and looked into his eyes, and in them, she saw their future. There really wasn't any reason to delay their marriage. She knew that two people who were so different in personality, but so alike in their stubbornness, would have struggles, but she also believed that love was transformative. She thought of how much they had changed in the months since they had first been introduced at the assembly.

"Yes, Mr. Darcy, we may set a date. May I suggest that we allow Georgiana to finish the season, especially since she is to be presented to Her Majesty? By that time, Jane and Mr. Bingley will be married, and they may come to our wedding breakfast.

We will all celebrate our new lives together with Anne and Colonel Fitzwilliam, and possibly Lady Catherine."

"So you are suggesting that in eight weeks' time we shall marry? Well, eight weeks is not overly long, so I agree," and then Lizzy kissed Mr. Darcy with a fervor that surprised him, and all of a sudden eight weeks seemed like a very long time indeed.

When Darcy returned home, he immediately informed Georgiana that Elizabeth had agreed to a wedding date two months hence. His sister was beside herself with joy. There was no one dearer in her life than her brother, and her greatest wish for him was that he would find someone who recognized his merits, that behind the money, family name, and rank was a solid man of character and understanding.

"Oh, Will, we will be very busy these next few weeks. Mr. Bingley and Miss Bennet are to be married, I am to be presented to the queen, and you are to take a wife. There is so much joy in our lives. We are truly blessed."

"Yes, I agree. Such events might possibly provide the plot for a gifted novelist, but I would think such a subject must be penned by a woman for the expression of such sentiments fall easily within the female sphere. And while you are writing your first draft, my dear sister, I shall put pen to paper and write to Anne to thank her for all she has done. For without her involvement, this affair could have ended very differently."

Darcy wrote to his dear cousin, sharing with Anne the good news of his engagement to Elizabeth Bennet and commenting upon the important role she had played in their romance. *The future Mr. and Mrs. Darcy will be forever grateful to the person who, by encouraging Elizabeth to travel into Derbyshire, has been the means of uniting them.*

About the Author

Mary Lydon Simonsen, the author of *Searching for Pemberley*, published by Sourcebooks, has combined her love of history and the novels of Jane Austen in her second novel, *The Perfect Bride for Mr. Darcy*. A third *Pride and Prejudice*-inspired novel, *A Wife for Mr. Darcy*, will be released by Sourcebooks in July 2011. She is also the author of two self-published novels: *The Second Date, Love Italian-American Style* and *Anne Elliot, A New Beginning*. The author lives in Arizona.

WICKHAM'S DIARY

AMANDA GRANGE

Jane Austen's quintessential bad boy has his say…

Enter the clandestine world of the cold-hearted Wickham…

…in the pages of his private diary. Always aware of the inferiority of his social status compared to his friend Fitzwilliam Darcy, Wickham chases wealth and women in an attempt to attain the power he lusts for. But as Wickham gambles and cavorts his way through his funds, Darcy still comes out on top.

But now Wickham has found his chance to seduce the young Georgiana Darcy, which will finally secure the fortune—and the revenge—he's always dreamed of…

Praise for Amanda Grange:

"Amanda Grange has taken on the challenge of reworking a much loved romance and succeeds brilliantly." —Historical Novels Review

"Amanda Grange is a writer who tells an engaging, thoroughly enjoyable story!" —Romance Reader at Heart

Available April 2011
978-1-4022-5186-3
$12.99 US

A Darcy Christmas

Amanda Grange, Sharon Lathan, & Carolyn Eberhart

A Holiday Tribute to Jane Austen

Mr. and Mrs. Darcy wish you a very Merry Christmas and a Happy New Year!

Share in the magic of the season in these three warm and wonderful holiday novellas from bestselling authors.

Christmas Present
By Amanda Grange

A Darcy Christmas
By Sharon Lathan

Mr. Darcy's Christmas Carol
By Carolyn Eberhart

978-1-4022-4339-4
$14.99 US/$17.99 CAN/£9.99 UK

Praise for Amanda Grange:

"Amanda Grange is a writer who tells an engaging, thoroughly enjoyable story!"
—Romance Reader at Heart

"Amanda Grange seems to have really got under Darcy's skin and retells the story with great feeling and sensitivity."
—Historical Novel Society

Praise for Sharon Lathan:

"I defy anyone not to fall further in love with Darcy after reading this book."
—Once Upon a Romance

"The everlasting love between Darcy and Lizzy will leave more than one reader swooning." —A Bibliophile's Bookshelf

In the Arms of Mr. Darcy
SHARON LATHAN

If only everyone could be as happy as they are...

Darcy and Elizabeth are as much in love as ever—even more so as their relationship matures. Their passion inspires everyone around them, and as winter turns to spring, romance blossoms around them.

Confirmed bachelor Richard Fitzwilliam sets his sights on a seemingly unattainable, beautiful widow; Georgiana Darcy learns to flirt outrageously; the very flighty Kitty Bennet develops her first crush, and Caroline Bingley meets her match.

But the path of true love never does run smooth, and Elizabeth and Darcy are kept busy navigating their friends and loved ones through the inevitable separations, misunderstandings, misgivings, and lovers' quarrels to reach their own happily ever afters...

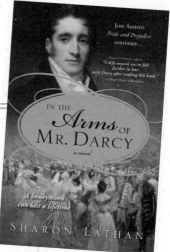

"If you love *Pride and Prejudice* sequels then this series should be on the top of your list!" —Royal Reviews

"Sharon really knows how to make Regency come alive." —Love Romance Passion

978-1-4022-3699-0
$14.99 US/$17.99 CAN/£9.99 UK

MY DEAREST MR. DARCY

SHARON LATHAN

Darcy is more deeply in love with his wife than ever

As the golden summer draws to a close and the Darcys look ahead to the end of their first year of marriage, Mr. Darcy could never have imagined his love could grow even deeper with the passage of time. Elizabeth is unpredictable and lively, pulling Darcy out of his stern and serious demeanor with her teasing and temptation.

But surprising events force the Darcys to weather absence and illness, and to discover whether they can find a way to build a bond of everlasting love and desire…

Praise for *Loving Mr. Darcy*:

"An intimately romantic sequel to Jane Austen's *Pride and Prejudice*…wonderfully colorful and fun." —Wendy's Book Corner

"If you want to fall in love with Mr. Darcy all over again…order yourself a copy."
—Royal Reviews

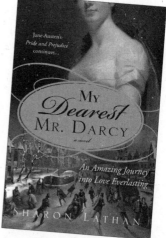

978-1-4022-1742-5
$14.99 US/$18.99 CAN/£7.99 UK

Darcy and Anne

Pride and Prejudice continues…

Judith Brocklehurst

"A beautiful tale." —A Bibliophile's Bookshelf

Without his help, she'll never be free...

Anne de Bourgh has never had a chance to figure out what she wants for herself, until a fortuitous accident on the way to Pemberley separates Anne from her formidable mother. With her stalwart cousin Fitzwilliam Darcy and his lively wife Elizabeth on her side, she begins to feel she might be able to spread her wings. But Lady Catherine's pride and determination to find Anne a suitable husband threaten to overwhelm Anne's newfound freedom and budding sense of self. And without Darcy's help, Anne will never have a chance to find true love...

"Brocklehurst transports you to another place and time." —A Journey of Books

"A charming book… It is lovely to see Anne's character blossom and fall in love." —Once Upon a Romance

"The twists and turns, as Anne tries to weave a path of happiness for herself, are subtle and enjoyable, and the much-loved characters of Pemberley remain true to form."
—A Bibliophile's Bookshelf

"A fun, truly fresh take on many of Austen's beloved characters."
—Write Meg

978-1-4022-2438-6
$12.99 US/$15.99 CAN/£6.99 UK

WILLOUGHBY'S RETURN

JANE AUSTEN'S *SENSE AND SENSIBILITY* CONTINUES

JANE ODIWE

"A tale of almost irresistible temptation."

A lost love returns, rekindling forgotten passions…

When Marianne Dashwood marries Colonel Brandon, she puts her heartbreak over dashing scoundrel John Willoughby behind her. Three years later, Willoughby's return throws Marianne into a tizzy of painful memories and exquisite feelings of uncertainty. Willoughby is as charming, as roguish, and as much in love with her as ever. And the timing couldn't be worse—with Colonel Brandon away and Willoughby determined to win her back…

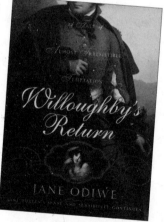

Praise for *Lydia Bennet's Story*:

"A breathtaking Regency romp!" —Diana Birchall, author of *Mrs. Darcy's Dilemma*

"An absolute delight." —Historical Novels Review

"Odiwe emulates Austen's famous wit, and manages to give Lydia a happily-ever-after ending worthy of any Regency romance heroine." —*Booklist*

"Odiwe pays nice homage to Austen's stylings and endears the reader to the formerly secondary character, spoiled and impulsive Lydia Bennet." —*Publishers Weekly*

978-1-4022-2267-2
$14.99 US/$18.99 CAN/£7.99 UK

THE OTHER MR. DARCY

PRIDE AND PREJUDICE CONTINUES...

MONICA FAIRVIEW

"A lovely story... a joy to read."
—Bookishly Attentive

Unpredictable courtships appear to run in the Darcy family...

When Caroline Bingley collapses to the floor and sobs at Mr. Darcy's wedding, imagine her humiliation when she discovers that a stranger has witnessed her emotional display. Miss Bingley, understandably, resents this gentleman very much, even if he is Mr. Darcy's American cousin. Mr. Robert Darcy is as charming as Mr. Fitzwilliam Darcy is proud, and he is stunned to find a beautiful young woman weeping broken-heartedly at his cousin's wedding. Such depth of love, he thinks, is rare and precious. For him, it's love at first sight...

"An intriguing concept... a delightful ride in the park."
—Austenprose

978-1-4022-2513-0
$14.99 US/$18.99 CAN/£7.99 UK

The Plight of the Darcy Brothers

A TALE OF SIBLINGS & SURPRISES

MARSHA ALTMAN

*"A charming tale of family and intrigue,
along with a deft bit of comedy."* —Publishers Weekly

Once again, it falls to Mr. Darcy to prevent a dreadful scandal...

Darcy and Elizabeth set off posthaste for the Continent to clear one of the Bennet sisters' reputations (this time it's Mary). But their madcap journey leads them to discover that the Darcy family has even deeper, darker secrets to hide. Meanwhile, back at Pemberley, the hapless Bingleys try to manage two unruly toddlers, and the ever-dastardly George Wickham arrives, determined to seize the Darcy fortune once and for all. Full of surprises, this lively *Pride and Prejudice* sequel plunges the Darcys and the Bingleys into a most delightful adventure.

"Ms. Altman takes Austen's beloved characters and makes them her own with lovely results."
—Once Upon A Romance

"Humorous, dramatic, romantic, and touching—all things I love in a Jane Austen sequel." —Grace's Book Blog

"Another rollicking fine adventure with the Darcys and Bingleys...ridiculously fun reading." —Bookfoolery & Babble

978-1-4022-2429-4
$14.99 US/$18.99 CAN/£7.99 UK

Mr. Fitzwilliam Darcy:
THE LAST MAN IN THE WORLD
A *Pride and Prejudice* Variation
ABIGAIL REYNOLDS

What if Elizabeth had accepted Mr. Darcy the first time he asked?

In Jane Austen's *Pride and Prejudice*, Elizabeth Bennet tells the proud Mr. Fitzwilliam Darcy that she wouldn't marry him if he were the last man in the world. But what if circumstances conspired to make her accept Darcy the first time he proposes? In this installment of Abigail Reynolds' acclaimed *Pride and Prejudice* Variations, Elizabeth agrees to marry Darcy against her better judgment, setting off a chain of events that nearly brings disaster to them both. Ultimately, Darcy and Elizabeth will have to work together on their tumultuous and passionate journey to make a success of their ill-timed marriage.

What readers are saying:

"A highly original story, immensely satisfying."

"Anyone who loves the story of Darcy and Elizabeth will love this variation."

"I was hooked from page one."

"A refreshing new look at what might have happened if..."

"Another good book to curl up with... I never wanted to put it down..."

978-1-4022-2947-3
$14.99 US/$18.99 CAN/£7.99 UK

Mr. Darcy Takes a Wife

LINDA BERDOLL

The #1 best-selling Pride and Prejudice sequel

"Wild, bawdy, and utterly enjoyable." —*Booklist*

Hold on to your bonnets!

Every woman wants to be Elizabeth Bennet Darcy—beautiful, gracious, universally admired, strong, daring, and outspoken—a thoroughly modern woman in crinolines. And every woman will fall madly in love with Mr. Darcy—tall, dark, and handsome, a nobleman and a heartthrob whose virility is matched only by his utter devotion to his wife. Their passion is consuming and idyllic—essentially, they can't keep their hands off each other—through a sweeping tale of adventure and misadventure, human folly and numerous mysteries of parentage. This sexy, epic, hilarious, poignant, and romantic sequel to *Pride and Prejudice* goes far beyond Jane Austen.

What readers are saying:

"I couldn't put it down."

"I didn't want it to end!"

"Berdoll does Jane Austen proud! ...A thoroughly delightful and engaging book."

"Delicious fun...I thoroughly enjoyed this book."

"My favorite *Pride and Prejudice* sequel so far."

978-1-4022-0273-5 • $16.95 US/ $19.99 CAN/ £9.99 UK

Eliza's Daughter

A Sequel to Jane Austen's Sense and Sensibility

JOAN AIKEN

"Others may try, but nobody comes close to Aiken in writing sequels to Jane Austen." —*Publishers Weekly*

A young woman longing for adventure and an artistic life...

Because she's an illegitimate child, Eliza is raised in the rural backwater with very little supervision. An intelligent, creative, and free-spirited heroine, unfettered by the strictures of her time, she makes friends with poets William Wordsworth and Samuel Coleridge, finds her way to London, and eventually travels the world, all the while seeking to solve the mystery of her parentage. With fierce determination and irrepressible spirits, Eliza carves out a life full of adventure and artistic endeavor.

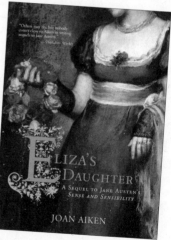

"Aiken's story is rich with humor, and her language is compelling. Readers captivated with Elinor and Marianne Dashwood in *Sense and Sensibility* will thoroughly enjoy Aiken's crystal gazing, but so will those unacquainted with Austen." —*Booklist*

"...innovative storyteller Aiken again pays tribute to Jane Austen in a cheerful spinoff of *Sense and Sensibility*." —*Kirkus Reviews*

978-1-4022-1288-8 • $14.95 US/ $15.99 CAN

The Pemberley Chronicles

A Companion Volume to Jane Austen's Pride and Prejudice

The Pemberley Chronicles: Book 1

REBECCA ANN COLLINS

"A lovely complementary novel to Jane Austen's *Pride and Prejudice*. Austen would surely give her smile of approval."
—BEVERLY WONG, AUTHOR OF *Pride & Prejudice Prudence*

The weddings are over, the saga begins

The guests (including millions of readers and viewers) wish the two happy couples health and happiness. As the music swells and the credits roll, two things are certain: Jane and Bingley will want for nothing, while Elizabeth and Darcy are to be the happiest couple in the world!

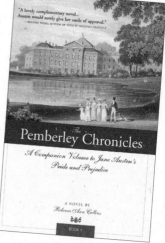

Elizabeth and Darcy's personal stories of love, marriage, money, and children are woven together with the threads of social and political history of England in the nineteenth century. As changes in industry and agriculture affect the people of Pemberley and the surrounding countryside, the Darcys strive to be progressive and forward-looking while upholding beloved traditions.

"Those with a taste for the balance and humour of Austen will find a worthy companion volume."
—*Book News*

978-1-4022-1153-9 • $14.95 US/ $17.95 CAN/ £7.99 UK

The Ladies of Longbourn

The acclaimed Pride and Prejudice sequel series
The Pemberley Chronicles: Book 4

REBECCA ANN COLLINS

"Interesting stories, enduring themes, gentle humour, and lively dialogue." —*Book News*

A complex and charming young woman of the Victorian age, tested to the limits of her endurance

The bestselling *Pemberley Chronicles* series continues the saga of the Darcys and Bingleys from Jane Austen's *Pride and Prejudice* and introduces imaginative new characters.

Anne-Marie Bradshaw is the granddaughter of Charles and Jane Bingley. Her father now owns Longbourn, the Bennet's estate in Hertfordshire. A young widow after a loveless marriage, Anne-Marie and her stepmother Anna, together with Charlotte Collins, widow of the unctuous Mr. Collins, are the Ladies of Longbourn. These smart, independent women challenge the conventional roles of women in the Victorian era, while they search for ways to build their own lasting legacies in an ever-changing world.

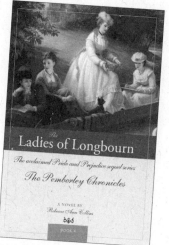

Jane Austen's original characters—Darcy, Elizabeth, Bingley, and Jane—anchor a dramatic story full of wit and compassion.

"A masterpiece that reaches the heart." —**BEVERLEY WONG,** **AUTHOR OF** *Pride & Prejudice Prudence*

978-1-4022-1219-2 • $14.95 US/ $15.99 CAN/ £7.99 UK

Mr. Darcy's Diary
AMANDA GRANGE

"A gift to a new generation of Darcy fans
and a treat for existing fans as well." —AUSTENBLOG

The only place Darcy could share his innermost feelings...

...was in the private pages of his diary. Torn between his sense of duty to his family name and his growing passion for Elizabeth Bennet, all he can do is struggle not to fall in love. A skillful and graceful imagining of the hero's point of view in one of the most beloved and enduring love stories of all time.

What readers are saying:

"A delicious treat for all Austen addicts."

"Amanda Grange knows her subject...I ended up reading the entire book in one sitting."

"Brilliant, you could almost hear Darcy's voice...I was so sad when it came to an end. I loved the visions she gave us of their married life."

"Amanda Grange has perfectly captured all of Jane Austen's clever wit and social observations to make *Mr. Darcy's Diary* a must read for any fan."

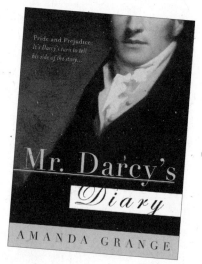

978-1-4022-0876-8 • $14.95 US/ $19.95 CAN/ £7.99 UK